Loner

Martin Forey

For myself

Acknowledgements:

I have nobody to thank.

Foreword

Have you ever wanted to kill somebody? No? You've certainly wished somebody dead at some point - that's a given. Quite possibly the one person in this godforsaken world you'd actually least like to have to live without - in the frustrated aftermath of a heated argument with a family member or loved one? You've probably *thought* about killing somebody at least, thought about how you'd do it, what method you'd choose – a gun, a knife (I always imagined this would be the most difficult – actually sticking it to somebody up close and personal, watching as the whites of their eyes bulged suddenly like hard-boiled eggs – or perhaps the most satisfying, depending on your own proclivity and personal motivation); a simulated motor vehicle 'accident' – how best you might get away with it, cover your tracks, destroy the evidence; how you might feel afterwards, whether you could live with the guilt or end up taking to drink and ultimately your own life. If you told me no to all of these then I'd call you a liar, though not to your face. And not because I'm scared of you – oh no, quite the opposite. If anything, I'm scared only of what *I* might be capable. Like you, I've thought about it. Felt that I could do it - that I wanted to even. It's just that with me, the feeling never went away.

A.

Late at night, the middle of the week and I'm sitting here alone with my thoughts as usual. They're not much company tonight, rather more like the unexpected caller who outstayed their welcome, obstinately refusing to pick up on the deliberately less-than-subtle yawning and lack of refills. The whole evening has been spent in front of the television again, half-heartedly staring at a succession of mundane offerings, flicking to and fro with such desperately optimistic frequency that I often forget what I'm watching by the time it returns from a commercial break. I'm also in the middle of a really good book at the moment but don't seem to have gotten very far with it tonight, what with the constant distraction of having to glance up at the set every five seconds or so in the worry that I might miss something interesting – which, of course, I won't. I like to read as much as possible. They do say that reading is to the mind what exercise is to the body and I really do think there's a lot in that. I read a lot and had I been on the quiz show that I watched tonight I'd have walked away with far more money than any of the contestants on the programme did.

I'm restless so decide to take a walk and get some air. This isn't something I do often, particularly after dark, but tonight I feel as though I'm trapped in my own skin and getting down on the lounge floor and trying to wear myself out with press-ups hasn't worked. I'm a regular at the local gym, like to keep in shape. On my dating site profile, I describe my build as *athletic*. One of my many first (and last) dates had the audacity to accuse me of false representation – to my face! I put her straight though. Shot-putters are athletes, I explained. Yeah, I put her straight alright. She won't be making *that* mistake again. I'm not particularly tall – about five seven – average. I'm stocky though. I may not be as big as some of the other guys I see down at Fit Farm but I'm stronger than any of them for my size and half of the muscle-bound gorillas are on steroids anyway. All show and no go. They probably couldn't pull up their own socks if their lives depended on it. I may not look it – I naturally carry a bit of extra timber - but I'm fitter than most of them too. Got more stamina. I see them look across when they get on the treadmill next to mine so I always speed things up to at least a bit more than whatever they're doing and make sure I carry on for a minute or two after they've finished. So, because of my fitness, I think all the press-ups have done is give me a bit of a pump and set the pulse racing. I feel charged. The veins are up in my darkly haired forearms and I have to take off my watch because it's getting too tight around my wrist.

I put on a fleece and some trainers, head off out the front door and take a left down the road. It's deathly quiet everywhere. The moon is bright in the sky, bathing everything in monochromatic blue. It's an antisceptically crisp, clear night with a real chill in the air. There'll be frost on the ground and people scraping the ice off their cars with credit cards tomorrow morning. I walk for a while past rows of sleeping houses, watching plumes of my own breath in front of me as I exhale with the exaggeration of a cigarette smoker. I'm getting colder now as the original warmth of my brief energetic outburst back home wears off, the sweat cool and clammy on my skin, and I fold my arms. Out of habit I take a look at my watch and panic briefly that I've lost it before almost immediately remembering that I took it off before leaving the flat. I do this a lot, particularly since it was a relatively expensive gift to myself.

Up ahead of me, going in the same direction on the other side of the road, there's a man walking his dog. It's a small, effeminate thing, possibly a Pekingese, stopping at every opportunity to cock its leg and mark its territory at the same spot where a hundred other dogs that evening have done the same thing. I wonder why any self-respecting heterosexual would choose this particular dog from the extensive range of breeds on offer. I watch him as he ambles along paying little or no attention to it, sniffing out stories about fifty yards behind him, and assume that he must be married. I comfort myself with this conclusion and by deciding that he probably hated it at first but grew to love it for the small window of peace and quiet it now offered him.

I'm walking slightly more quickly than the man in front of me so start to gain on him slowly. He turns around a couple of times to make sure the dog is still following and I see him register me behind him too. He looks about late forties, thinning hair, slightly overweight. An office worker, I imagine – he just has that puffy look. I cross the road to his pavement and when he turns around next I sense a slight unease from him at my presence there. I speed up a bit and deliberately scuff my heels so he knows I'm closing without turning his head. The street is morgue silent. I pass his dog and get near enough for him to think that I'm about to pass him too but then I slow down to his pace, staying a few yards behind him. He's definitely nervous now. There's no-one around – just the two of us. His unease is palpable. I have complete control over the situation and can hear my heart pumping in my chest with the excitement. I imagine his pulse has picked up a bit by now too. I know he must be making a decision to either speed up and risk revealing his fear, potentially eliciting a reaction from me, or stop to let me pass under the pretence that he's waiting for his dog to catch up. I'm close enough that he can't be in any doubt that my actions are deliberate. I bet he's wishing he had a bigger dog now, one that he'd chosen himself. I wait curiously, expectantly, holding my breath as I walk, for his decision. He slows suddenly and turns into the driveway of the only mid-sized terraced house in the row with a light on at the curtained upstairs window. I can almost smell his relief as, fumbling with his keys, he hurries up the front steps, manages his key into the lock and lets himself into the hallway, stopping to turn and wait for his scurrying mongrel and, without moving his head in my direction, eye me suspiciously as I cross over the road and walk back home in the opposite direction.

a.

Sheena O'Callaghan looked at the flashing red zeros on the bedside alarm-clock radio and realised immediately that there must have been a power cut in the night. *Shit, shit, shit!* she said to herself, already knowing without checking her watch, from the general quality of light streaming in through the blinds and the sounds of a busy world outside, that she'd overslept again. Throwing back the covers, she splashed her face with water at the bathroom sink, grabbed some underwear from the pine-effect chest of drawers at the end of the bed and dressed hurriedly, pulling on her *Little Soldiers* polo-shirt without even bothering to wash. She'd soon be covered in baby-food, vomit, powder-paints and crayon anyway so what did it matter? Foregoing breakfast too – she'd grab some cereal from the work kitchen, adding stealing from minors to her morning crime tally - she was soon on the road in her tired Ford Fiesta, impatiently sitting on the bumpers of the many Miss Daisy chauffeurs seemingly out in force early today and catching every cursed red light along the way, her cheeks increasingly rivalling their angry hue with each new enforced stoppage.

Linda was standing on the gravel forecourt as she arrived, arms folded across her ample bosom, checking her watch, not in pantomime exaggerated gesture for the late arrival's benefit but discretely, for her own, so that she had an accurate record of concrete facts to support the final formal written warning for which the young childcare assistant was almost certainly headed unless she bucked her ideas up – and fast. She didn't want to do it. She liked the girl. She had a certain Irish charm that was irresistible, but she couldn't be seen to court favour with any of her girls. They were a hard enough lot to motivate and manage at the best of times. She'd been in the business long enough to know that many of them wouldn't last, had chosen their early vocational path based solely on a few mildly successful babysitting jobs, usually for friends and family, often siblings, and generally only one or two sittees at a time. Spending six hours a day, five days a week, entertaining and looking after anything up to thirty screaming kids – complete strangers' kids – was a very different story; a very different story altogether. If she gave one of them an inch, the rest would take a mile.

Sheena bumped the car up the dropped kerb, adding further insult to the vehicle's already badly injured tracking, deliberately stamping on the brake pedal to bring the hatchback to a skidding halt, leaving two dark parallel grooves of displaced gravel behind her in an attempt to convey her appreciation of the need for a sense of urgency but almost immediately regretting it, realising that it could be perceived instead merely as further evidence of her recklessness – dangerous driving on the driveway of a children's nursery perhaps not the best demonstration of an individual's burgeoning suitability as a responsible adult role model.

'I'm so sorry Linda' she began, as she rushed across the space between them, leaving the car unlocked in all the rush - not that it was ever likely to be a prime target for thieves.

'Don't tell me. It's not your fault.'

'It's really *not* this time. Power-cut. Alarm didn't go off.'

'Well at least you're starting to show a little more imagination I suppose. That's a new one to add to the list.'

'See? Told you I have potential' said Sheena, grinning her best *you can't be mad at me for too long, now can you* smile, eliciting one in response.

'I may be smiling but it's really not funny' said the nursery proprietor, serious all of a sudden, her tone usurping any otherwise physical semblance of humour. 'I have to treat you all the same Sheena. Don't back me into a corner. I'll do what I have to do without ever looking back and I won't feel bad about it – not for a second. Consider this your ninth life.'

Sheena considered responding with a collusive *miaow* before thinking better than to push her luck, which was almost surely already at its limit.

'Understood', she said.

'I hope so Sheena. I really do. Now, the breakfasts and rooms are already prepped. There's not much left to do inside. They'll all be starting to arrive soon and we have a newbie starting today. Since you're already out here, I'd like you to handle the meet and greet and the whole induction process yourself. A Mrs Chambers will be bringing little Glenn along to join us shortly. This is your chance to undo some damage, to prove that my

7

perseverance with you is justified. I'll be milling around, observing from afar. Just keep that in mind.'

'No pressure then' replied Sheena.

'Childcare is a pressurised job Miss O'Callaghan. It's how you handle that pressure that determines whether it's the right one for you. Now, off you go and use some of that famous Irish charm on our customers and stop wasting it on me, trying to wrap me round your little finger and get yourself off the hook.'

'Yes Boss' said Sheena, saluting and clicking her heels together, unable to maintain seriousness for too long, before marching off to effuse with Mrs Oakley and her son Connor, the first of the morning's arrivals.

What am I going to do with her? Linda asked herself, watching and shaking her head, knowing that it was this very same scatterbrained, frivolously childlike mentality that would eventually make the young girl such a fabulous nursery worker, already a big hit with pretty much every one of their toddlers in a relatively short space of time. She knew that the girl's own repeated, tongue-in-cheek assurances of potential were actually well founded. It was *her* job to tap into it and eek it out, however much it might need dragging kicking and screaming sometimes.

Sheena ushered Connor over to Linda who took his hand and walked him inside. Like a giant turtle, the Spiderman rucksack on his back almost as big as himself, his smile in proportion, he didn't even bother to turn and wave to his mother, who likewise left the nursery forecourt looking considerably happier than she had when she'd arrived, comfortable in the knowledge that her son was in safe hands.

The next quarter of an hour or so saw children deposited and parents despatched with similarly effortless efficiency. She was a natural. Having kept a mental tally and periodically checked her watch, she was just about to head back inside to join the usual manic morning mayhem when the last of the stragglers drifted in from the pavement, two faces she'd never seen before – Master and Mrs Chambers, she presumed.

'Morning. Can I help you at all?' she beamed.

'Yes, hi. Sorry, we're not late are we? Wouldn't want to start off making a bad impression.'

'No, you're absolutely fine' said the Irish pot, hardly in a position to be darkly labelling any kettles this morning.

'I'm Mrs Chambers. This is Glenn. He starts today. I spoke to Linda on the phone?'

'Oh yes, of course. We've been expecting you. Come this way.'

Sheena spent the next half hour showing the two of them around the building, explaining how the different year groups worked and running through a few preliminary forms. They'd already been given a brief tour by Linda a few weeks back but it had been at the end of a day when they'd turned up unannounced and all the kids had already gone home. The Manageress advised Sheena that it might be nice to walk them both around again, in order to get a better feel for the atmosphere, the real day-to-day working environment that little Glenn would soon become a part of. As they made their way from room to room, he hung on to his guardian's coat-tails, hiding behind her legs as much as possible from the many intrigued gazes that he passed at his own eye level. It was nothing personal. Any new face in their heavily routine-driven midst was always an object of abject fascination - for a few seconds at least, until the next fleeting distraction took their fickle fancy. Having made a textbook faux-pas that Linda had quietly predicted, consciously failed to prevent, observed, even smiled at, Sheena was surprised to discover – through completion of the *legal guardian* section of the induction paperwork - that Mrs Chambers was actually Glenn's mother, not his Grandmother. She looked much older than the other mums that usually passed through their doors. Just one in a long list of experience-based lessons that she would come to learn, Sheena wouldn't be jumping to conclusions and making *that* mistake again. *None taken* said Mrs Chambers in response to the profuse, heartfelt apologies received, even softening the young girl's embarrassment still further by adding that it was perfectly understandable, that she heard the same mistaken assumption on a regular basis.

As Mrs Chambers filled out one of the forms herself, with the help of a little initial verbal guidance and red vinyl covered clipboard and biro, Sheena took in her son, looking forlorn, head down, feet dangling in the air from his grey plastic chair. His mother's comparatively advanced years had created a further generation gap that showed in his general appearance. His unruly hair was quite clearly cut at home, detracting attention from the hair-lip below, which was no fault of anyone's. His wear-worn, faded clothes looked older than himself – possibly charity shop or familial hand-me-downs – certainly more likely chosen on the basis of cost - or lack of - rather than any carefully

10

considered style statement. Looking at his Gra…. Mother, and the same theme applied. She seemed a nice enough lady - polite, friendly, even kind to Sheena when she could instead quite easily have indulged herself in the gloriously self-righteous gift of unfair treatment. It was just such a shame that she didn't seem to realise – or care - that, whether rightly or otherwise, people *did* judge books by their covers. A general mustiness permeated the air around the two of them, causing Sheena to think of the young lad in the Snoopy cartoons with the constant swarm of flies circling about his head. What *was* his name?

'All done. I think' said Mrs Chambers finally, handing over the clipboard to the young Montessori worker, who took the pen from her too, placing it in her mouth absent-mindedly – causing the new parent present to flinch in unnoticed, suppressed horror - as she ran her eye down the various boxes to ensure that all sections were completed and seemingly in order.

'You've left this one blank' said Sheena, referring to the empty space beneath the question *Does your child have any psychological / emotional / behavioural difficulties that you are aware of?* 'Was that intentional or did you just miss it?'

Linda's ears pricked up, her focus no longer on the administration that she was, to all outward intents and appearances, attending to at the other desk in the room.

Mrs Chambers leaned in to look at the form again, as if needing reminding of the exact wording of her only omission. She looked at it intently for some seconds.

'Mrs Chambers?' prompted Sheena, glancing over at her boss.

'Well, I left it blank because I wasn't sure if it was anything worth mentioning.'

'Sheena, why don't you ask Maria if she'll take Glenn and start getting him settled in to the group?' interjected Linda, casting a reassuring smile in his direction like an angler, hoping to hook him and start ever so slowly reeling him in as he raised his head at the mention of his own name, breaking the surface of the murky depths of his own nervous introspection.

Right on cue, at the mention of her name, the door burst open and a young girl, about Sheena's age, strode in, already a little out of breath from the morning's activities.

'Oh, sorry to interrupt' she said, eyeing the newcomers sitting looking up at her to her right. 'It's just that I seem to be missing one? I have a new name on my list. Not sure if that's a typo?'

'Maria' said Sheena, turning to face her guests with her usual veneer-chipping smile.

'Meet Typo. Or Glenn, as he prefers to be known. And this is his mother, Mrs Chambers.'

'Oh. Of course. I saw you being shown around earlier. Should've put two and two together. Sorry.'

'Maria, would you please take Glenn and integrate him with the other Tigers?' asked Linda, referring to the zoo-animal themed name of the specific group that the youngster would be joining.

'Come on then young man. Let's get you started shall we?' said Maria reaching for his hand.

The toddler looked first to his mother and then to Sheena – suddenly no longer the newest strange face in his life – for reassurance. 'Well, very nice to meet you Glenn' she said to him. 'I'll be spending some time with you later today, just as soon as we've sorted out a few boring grown-up bits with your mummy. Don't worry. They're not real Tigers. They don't bite' she added, thinking as soon as she'd said it that this wasn't always strictly true, that she had the scars to prove it.

Glenn jumped down from his seat and took Maria's hand without looking at her, his silent stare still trained on the girl with the strange accent.

'So, Glenn is it?' began Maria as she opened the door to lead him through.

'No' replied the youngster, turning to look at Sheena one last time. 'Typo.'

'He'll be fine' said Sheena, in response to Mrs Chambers' furrowed brow. 'I'll make sure that he settles in ok, don't you worry. Now, where were we? Oh yes. Was there something you needed to tell us?'

'Well, like I said, I'm not sure that it's anything important. Nothing diagnosed or official or anything like that. It's just that, it says 'emotional', so I wasn't sure…'

'Just tell us in your own words Mrs Chambers and we can decide if it's important. It's always worth mentioning anything that might help us better understand your son and enable us to work with him more effectively anyway, however small or trivial it might seem at the time.'

'It's just that he can be quite…..' she looked up to the ceiling, as if picturing episodes of scenes previously played out, thinking how best to describe them '…sensitive.'

'In what way exactly? Can you give us an example?'

'Oh, it's nothing specific. Nothing you can put your finger on. He's just very quiet. Doesn't speak much. In fact, I'm amazed he did just then. Something of a minor miracle if you know Glenn like I do. Doesn't smile much either. Very serious. Much more so than any of my others. He's a bright lad though. Can already read pretty well. Loves to draw. He's good too, particularly for his age. Takes after me. I was always artistic as a girl. Gave it all up when I had kids though of course. Just never seemed to find the time.'

'So that's all?' clarified Sheena, looking across to Linda again for a confirmatory expression that this was all fine, nothing particularly unusual or cause for concern. 'He's never been statemented or anything? No anger management issues, violent outbursts, anything like that?

'What, Glenn?' laughed Mrs Chambers, as if the idea of any such thing were preposterous, unthinkable. 'Oh no. Quite the opposite. He keeps it all bottled up inside, whatever *it* is.'

'Ok. Well, I don't think there's any real need for alarm there then' replied Sheena, scribbling a couple of key words down in the box provided before vocalising them. 'Lots of youngsters can be quite introverted at his age. These are very formative years Mrs Chambers. Hopefully spending time around children his own age will help to socialise and bring him out of his shell a little more. He'll have plenty of opportunity to express his creative side too. Lots of art resources for him to get stuck into so he should be very happy here.'

'I hope so' said Mrs Chambers, thinking *very happy* perhaps a rather optimistic goal where her youngest was concerned.

B.

I'm not currently working. *Between jobs* is, I believe, the phrase used by those who don't want to be labelled as merely unemployed, don't want the stigma, the judgemental, pitying looks. Oh, I've had jobs. Quite a few in fact. Jack of all trades me, though apparently master of none as yet identified. Lost every one of them though. Well, that's not actually strictly true. Lost implies negligence, a certain wanton carelessness on my part - that I didn't take adequate care of them, covet them sufficiently, forgot where I'd left them last. It's not my fault though, honestly it's not. Had every one of them taken away, unjustly stolen from me is more accurate. I'm conscientious, reliable, one hundred per-cent committed to whatever I do. Stalwart. It's people that are the problem. I've worked in a library, been a post-man, security guard, even a janitor at the local school and they don't let you work in an educational establishment with minors without first carrying out some pretty thorough vetting.

I liked that job at the library - surrounded by all those great, inspirational works of literature. The advertisement for the vacancy had specified that *experience working in a library* was *useful though not essential* but that the *successful applicant must have a genuine love of books.* Well, I ticked that box with a red indelible marker,

15

metaphorically speaking. I considered the working environment, how it would be nice and quiet, brim-full of academics, heads bowed, studiously working on their world changing PHDs; little old ladies reading Mills & Boon romances for free, saving their pittance government pensions for an afternoon cream tea. It seemed absolutely ideal - tailor-made for me. I went down that day and spoke to somebody on reception, filled out an application form there and then and was delighted when they contacted me a few days later to arrange an interview. I knew I'd got the job right away. You just know when you're being politely fobbed off and when *we have a few other applicants to see first before making a decision* really means, *it's going to be one of them, and if it isn't, we're going to carry on looking, forever if that's what it takes - have a nice life, not that I care if you do or don't.* I think it was my passion for reading which came through strongly and sealed the deal. There wasn't a book mentioned that I hadn't read, no matter how hard the interviewer tried to find one. Ironically, it was partly this very same love of books that ultimately led to my untimely demise. *Must have a love of books* they claim, then penalise you for reading them and losing track of time when you're surrounded by them all day. As it turned out, the environment wasn't all that I'd expected it to be anyway. Standards there left a lot to be desired and somebody had to say something. Armies of excitable college kids assembling in the communal study areas, abusing the place, using it as a meeting point, a glorified youth club, somewhere to congregate when it was cold and wet outside. So it was fine to address it with *them* when they were getting excessively animated and

16

boisterous, distracting the more deserving patrons who were using the facility for its intended purpose, but it was a problem when you did the same with colleagues. Usual story. Double standards. Or *no* standards. Make the rules up as you go along. One for staff and one for customers. Whatever happened to leading by example?

So I sought out jobs where I could work autonomously. I like that word. Autonomously. I have it down on my personal profile on my CV – *able to work autonomously or as part of a team.* Perhaps I should amend that last part, particularly since I also declare a claim to be *honest and reliable* – unless of course I left the former in and took the latter out. But no, I'm no liar. It's one of the things I pride myself on most. For if you don't have truth then what are you?

Either way, whether it was the not I suspect wholly unique revelation, there in irrefutable lower case black and white, that I'm able to work autonomously that set me apart from the crowd and guaranteed my seamless entry into the luke-warm embrace of the British postal service or otherwise (possibly a near desperate need for Christmas cover laxing usually more stringent entry criteria for example?), there I found myself. My wistful fantasies of strolling nonchalantly up and down empty cobbled streets, the rising sun warm against my contentment-flushed cheeks, clicking my heels together as I whistled a merry tune, doffing my cap to dust-men and white-aproned bakers unloading red plastic delivery crates as they joined in, a real-life morning musical set against a stage-set back-drop of gold and salmon pink sky were, as it turned out, just that – fantasies. As were my ideas of finishing work at ten am,

17

enjoying the rest of the day, replete in the glow of a hard day's work already well done. Firstly, the sun was rarely even up, let alone on my back. I rose and worked mostly in joyless darkness whilst out on rounds, particularly since I was recruited during the festive season and barely made it through 'til Spring. And even if I had lasted longer, seen every season come and go, there is simply *no* good weather in which to be a postman. At the height of winter you're negotiating slippery frost and ice–covered foot-paths with a dead weight slung over your shoulder, rendering you constantly off balance. Letters may be light, but paper is heavy - hold a single ream in your hand for a few minutes and you start to get the idea. Rain is rain so should be perfectly self explanatory – if there's a single thing on God's green earth made better, more pleasant to do by it then I haven't found it yet, no matter how much Mr Kelly might create a song and dance about it. And those warm summer mornings? What's welcomely received as a relatively rare British treat when ambling to the corner shop to bring back a paper becomes a veritable curse when you're lugging round a large vinyl bag full of the stuff for several hours, the stinging sweat rolling into your sun-blinded eyes. And the reason for my departure from Her Majesty's mail service? My only heinous crime? That I was among those last in and hence those first out when came the inevitable post-festive cull, following first a brief tail-off period during which on-line credit points were recouped and thoughtful yet ultimately undesirable surprise gift ideas were unspiritably returned and exchanged.

My brief stint as rather grandiosely titled 'security guard' merely served to add yet another unfulfilling disappointment to the pile. You may now, with the benefit of hindsight, find it…what…amusing (?) to discover that I once toyed with the idea of joining the police force. An extremely proactive national advertising campaign and widespread recruitment drive touched my moral sensibilities and awakened in me dreams of yet another potential new and improved version of myself – that of celebrated local crime-fighter, scourge of the criminal underworld, my pursuit of justice slowed only by the weight of my heavily decorated lapels – but that all turned to Sand-man's dust, falling quickly by the wayside when it transpired that I was able to unearth neither a twig of recent descendancy from a 'minority' (ha!) ethnic group nor any suppressed hankerings after same gender romantic encounters. So I became a security guard – or rather, as it transpired, a uniformed receptionist. The barely visited office block that I 'secured' was on the main route home from a local secondary modern. Since comings and goings through the revolving doors were scarce, I found myself increasingly enjoying the fresh – save for the belching exhausts at least - air out front, focusing on the comings and goings there instead, watching the world go by - an activity for which I would surely take a convincingly solid twenty- four carat gold should it ever become an Olympic event. Unfortunately this meant that I became a focus of unwanted attention myself. The passing teenage lads started chatting to me kindly at first but it seemed that the more effort I made to fit in and talk to them on their own level in return, the larger the drifting gulf of commonality between us and subsequently the further their communications descended into flagrant derision,

19

particularly when young girls were in their midst. Affectionately delivered nicknames of *Rambo*, *Robo-Cop* and even *Super Ted* were soon replaced by words not fit for print. These I could tolerate – names will never hurt me and all that – but when the sticks and stones were launched from the upper-deck window of a blazer-packed double-decker in the form of raw eggs – presumably sourced with their pre-considered target in mind – I knew that the time had come to move on. *Why didn't you just go inside?* I hear you ask, *remain at reception, where you were meant to be in the first place?* What? And give them the satisfaction? Let them laugh at me through the plate-glass, hiding behind my desk from a bunch of pimple-faced kids? No, I don't think so. And it's not that I was scared. Oh no, let me be quite clear on this point. Like I said before, my only fear is of what I might be capable. The reception area is all on CCTV – and I should know, I spent enough time looking at it. I doubt there's a judge or jury in the land that would look very favourably upon footage of a grown man beating a bunch of fifteen year olds to within an inch of their adolescent lives, there for all to see in pixelated black and white, however substandard the grainy quality of the image. No, probably best for all concerned that I walked away when I did.

And the janitor role? I'm sure over-zealous psychiatrists would have a field day with that one, jumping to all sorts of nonsensical conclusions about why I chose to place myself smack into the middle of a barracks from whose soldiers I'd already suffered such a cruel and unprovoked attack. If they were kind, they might interpret it as my facing my demons head on – *flooding* I believe it's called – the word just popped into my head from some distant, long since forgotten publication stashed deeply away in the bulging files of my memory marked *Rarely Used* - though I may have just imagined it of course. The theory – and it is just that, a theory, and one that I myself have absolutely no wish to test – running something along the lines that, should you suffer from arachnophobia (and yes, I chose this example deliberately so that I might use the correct, widely known terminology without alienating my reader), an effective remedy might be to lay you out in a bath and cover you with a tub-full of spiders; the idea being that, after this ordeal, if you didn't end up suffering from Post-Traumatic Stress Disorder to boot, encountering a single web-spinner should pale into silky insignificance in comparison. Personally, I can't think of anything more likely to exacerbate my own fear of the things. That and my expansive trivia banks furnishing me with the knowledge that *all* spiders have venomous fangs with which they kill their prey – even money spiders, whose aphid victims no doubt don't perceive a liaison with them to be quite as fortunate as we do. Those who knew then what they know now might have interpreted my motive as one of revenge, an opportunity to track down my physical and verbal assailants and find some way to pour the precisely measured quantity of caustic soda onto the scales of justice and restore my own poor wounded emotional equilibrium. But they'd be wrong – on both counts. The fact is that I've been a little creative, embellished the truth a little in the interests of artistic license. Just as the security guard role was in reality nothing more than that of glorified receptionist, so my janitorial duties were restricted to those of cleaning and….well….just cleaning mostly. Wiping down desks, emptying bins and mopping corridors. So, if we're being picky - and I already told you how much I covet the truth - I guess you could say I was a cleaner and not be too far from it. I tell you this not merely to purge my aching conscience but because it's relevant. The working hours were after lesson time, when – or so I assumed – the kids had all gone home. What I hadn't bargained on, somewhat naively perhaps, despite having attended schools (several in fact) myself as a younger lad, were the any number of reasons why there might still be pupils loitering around the building after three thirty – namely the various sports and extra-curricular clubs and, of course (it seems obvious now), those serving detentions - and hence inevitably, those most likely to include the less savoury characters among their lot; those who might be the types to abuse virtual strangers in the street and launch missiles at them from the safe anonymity of passing public transport for example. Needless to say, my position there too became prematurely untenable.

So no, I'm not working at the moment. Claiming JSA. Job Seekers Allowance. I hated having to visit the Job Centre at first, justifying myself to some complete stranger when I didn't even belong there in the first place. I'm not like the others, turning up year in year out, clearly spending more time hanging around there than they do in the shower, holding out their grubby, unwashed bowls, not so politely begging sir for another meagre spoonful of gruel. I'm a *very* well read, intelligent man. Ask any one of the many educational psychologists I saw as a child and they'll tell you the same thing. So why is it that I can't even hold

22

down a menial job that's twenty thousand leagues beneath me? Surely it's obvious? Mismatch. I shouldn't be being put forward for them in the first place, that's why. But it's a CV that gets you in front of an employer and unfortunately you can't just squeeze in *incredibly intelligent, well read, excellent literacy skills* between *able to work autonomously or as part of a team* and *honest and reliable* and expect the executive offers to come rolling in. No, you have to have formal qualifications and to get those, you needed to have attended school regularly and stayed there until the end so that they'd let you sit exams - which for me wasn't an option. Again, not my fault. It's people that were the problem.

But for now at least, I don't mind going to sign on quite so much. I've got used to it and actually even look forward to having a fortnightly chat with a familiar, friendly face, even if it *is* paid to be there.

b.

Sheena rose to a dawn chorus, warbled by a smattering of electronic devices, all set to sing at the same on-screen time but unfortunately not quite perfectly synched with each other so that the first, her digital watch, was still halfway through a shrill round of gimmicky beeping tone before next her bedside alarm, followed closely by wind-up clock all chimed in like some contemporary gadget version of London's Burning. She couldn't afford to be late again this morning. After yesterday's initial shaky start, Linda had steeped praise on her for her performance throughout the remainder of the day and, due to her obvious people skills, had assigned her the task of unofficial morning 'hostess' for the rest of the week. It wasn't a promotion or anything but it was an enviable role, one that meant she didn't have to carry out the mundane and messy preparatory tasks inside and could focus instead on what she did best – socialising. Her mind wandered to the little new lad with the hair lip. The two words he'd said in the office yesterday had been the last he'd uttered all day. *Such soulful little eyes. What was going on behind them?* she wondered. She decided to make him her own little project. A case study of sorts. Hopefully she could learn as much from him as he from her.

Linda, standing out front with a mug of steaming coffee, checked her watch, this time with a raised eyebrow of pleasant surprise as she watched the little blue Fiesta pull slowly and calmly onto the Little Soldiers driveway. The flashing orange indicator bulb, despite the complete absence of any other traffic close by, made her smile inwardly. She was trying, bless her. She was really trying.

'Am I first?' asked Sheena, stepping out of the car excitedly, looking around and seeing no other vehicles, only Linda's Vauxhall Cavalier, on the forecourt.

'Not quite' said Linda, genuinely wishing she could have answered differently. 'Abi's already inside setting up. Boyfriend dropped her off' she added, reading the Irish girl's thoughts.

'Oh, right' said Sheena, clearly deflated at her superhuman – for her, anyway – effort not having quite achieved its intended goal.

'Still' said Linda. 'Silver's not bad. At least you're on the podium. Go inside and get yourself a cuppa before the hoards start arriving. I imagine you'll need some help waking up fully after losing an hour's sleep this morning.'

'It's not....' began Sheena indignantly, turning to correct her superior that it wasn't as much as all that before seeing the sardonic look on her face, smiling and heading inside.

Sheena on a two or three was a joy to behold. The mums and kids all seemed to love her. She could do no wrong - and even if she did, this somehow served merely to add to her disarming, ditzy charm, rather than detract from it. Sheena after a caffeine hit on a seven or eight was something else. Other worldly. She twirled and swirled from person to person, group to group, like a honey-bee amidst a flower-bed, busily pollinating happy reassurance upon whomsoever she touched, leaving them blooming gloriously in a smitten, satisfied wake behind her. All the while she looked out for Mrs Chambers. Perhaps she'd arrive slightly later than the other mums like she had yesterday. She mentioned having other children. Perhaps she had other school run commitments. Having held court and systematically seduced every last parent, Sheena watched the last of them drifting off, nattering amongst themselves. As they rounded the low brick wall at the entrance to the driveway, she watched in consternation as a mop of unruly blonde hair made its way toward them in the opposite direction, negotiating past them to reveal the lone figure of little Linus – yes, that was it! Now where did that come from all of a sudden? - Chambers and his giant rucksack.

'Well good morning Typo!' said Sheena, wanting to ingratiate herself as quickly as possible and remembering the favourable response – the only response – that this had received yesterday. 'Are you on your own? Where's your mummy?'

'In the car. She couldn't park. She had to take my brother to school. She dropped me off right outside' said Glenn.

Notwithstanding yesterday's monosyllabic coupling, she hadn't yet heard him speak before so couldn't yet be sure if the robotic delivery was normal but something about his enunciation made her think that this was a script - words that had been drummed into him, instructed not to forget, to

26

recite at the opportune moment; namely now. Either way, he was only pre-school. She shouldn't be leaving him alone out on the pavement like that, even if it was right outside the door. Not that Sheena had seen or heard a car pass by that would've fit with the right timing and his story. No, Mum should've at least made sure that he was safely ensconsed with a staff member before pulling away. She'd mention it to Linda. Maybe it was a one-off. She'd keep an eye on it throughout the week. No point making a big deal out of it right now and alarming the boy unnecessarily – he seemed fragile enough as it was.

'Well let's get you inside shall we? You're doing drawing this morning' she said, having remembered what his mother had said about his artistic skills and hoping to force out of him a grudging smile which never came.

Sheena handed the late arrival over to her co-worker, Maria, who welcomed him into her room, a barely detectable edge of frostiness betraying the thin line of her smile, Sheena unable to determine for certain if she'd imagined it or, if she hadn't, whether it was targeted at Glenn for being late again and messing up the opening of her session or at herself, Sheena, perhaps resentment at her acquiring her new, more favourable additional responsibilities out front.

'Tea-room catch-up at break-time?' offered Sheena, dipping a toe in the cool water, adding a little warm.

'If you've got time' said Maria with another eye-missing smile, confirming her colleague's suspicions. So she *did* have a problem. Smiles all around on the surface though, as was always the rule in front of the children, even at the height of the most serious of inter-staff bust-ups (and

27

amongst a team of predominantly teenage and early twenties young girls, there were many), neither noticed little Glenn who stood looking from one to the other, expressionless, not yet having gravitated towards those of his own age in the room.

'Great' said Sheena brightly, pretending not to have noticed the chilly undercurrent. 'First there gets the kettle on. See you later' and she skipped away, off to spread sunshine elsewhere in the building where it might be more gratefully received.

'Ok, children. Now, as I was saying before we were interrupted' said Maria to the sea of faces looking up in earnest from their positions sitting cross-legged on the interlocking sections of pink and green rubber-matted flooring in front of her, a new addition now among their number, on the end of the back row, arms hugging the knees which were raised up before him, 'This morning we're going to do some drawing. Now today's theme is *My Family*. I want you all to try to produce a picture that tells me something about your own family. It might tell me what your daddy does for a living. If he was a fireman for example, you might want to try putting a fire engine or a ladder in the picture. If you've got any pets, a cat or a dog for instance, you might want to include those. Try anything that makes your picture different, that makes it stand out from everybody else's – anything that means something, that's important to you - or they'll probably all end up looking pretty much the same. So, everyone clear on what we're doing? Any questions? No? Ok then, I'll take that as a yes. Everyone happy? Yes? I said everyone happy?'

she finished, a little louder this time, to a chorus of *Yes Miss Winters.* Barely turned eighteen herself, she was the only member of the team who asked the children to address her in this way; the others, even Linda, preferring more informal Christian names. *They need to learn respect from an early age* reasoned Maria, *they won't be on first name terms with their school teachers.*

There was a general scurry of activity as the youngsters busied themselves, collecting handed-out over-size sheets of paper, pots of pens and pencils from shelving units and moved to their various positions around the room, some perching on low, brightly coloured plastic one-piece moulded chairs at grey plastic tables and some preferring to spread out on the floor where they could express themselves more exuberantly without fear of encroaching on the creative boundaries of their fellow artists. Maria watched them work, moving around the room to assist where required and offer guidance and support, focusing on her favourites, something that she shouldn't have, those that were more willing and able and hence those that needed her help and attention the least. *Art Therapy* as the session was timetabled; once merely happy to be called simply *drawing* or *painting,* the new age title had been bestowed upon the traditional nursery activity in light of a commonly accepted recognition among the scientific and healthcare community that art could provide an insight into the deepest inner workings of the, as yet undeveloped, infant mind. Indeed, beyond this, it had been widely accepted, indeed even supposedly proven, as an effective safeguarding tool in the identification of issues of domestic abuse and neglect; case-studies presenting occasions where children had been able to express with charcoal and crayon what they had been unable or too afraid to vocalise.

Walking around the room, peering over the shoulders of her workforce of variously pigmented Oompa-Loompas, tongues protruding from between lips in hunched concentration, Maria observed the fruits of their labours. As predicted, by the end of the morning session, just as would equally be expected of any adult evening class, there were finished products of distinctly varying ability, the vast majority revealing Lowryesque figures stood beside square, four-windowed houses, happily smiling beneath the yellow beams radiating outward from a yellow corner sun. Some had been more ambitious in their efforts to add a little extra content, though her instructions had perhaps been somewhat misinterpreted – either that or a surprisingly high percentage of her pre-school group happened to be in possession of a single cat and dog and fire-fighters for parents.

Whilst one piece stood out for its creator's obvious innate general ability and clear understanding of the mandate – one of Maria's forbidden favourites, Toby Miller's two-hour colourful felt-pen creation showed a typically competently executed image of a man in a striped suit and tie, stood with his wife and two children, beside a rather crude but clearly recognisable red convertible sports car; Maria had seen the investment banker dropping Toby off in the mornings in it on a couple of occasions on his way to the train station en route to one of his rare late starts – there was only one which really stood out as *different*. The image depicted a line-up of nine figures, four smaller, of equal size, holding hands on either side, with another significantly larger figure in the centre, standing alone, un-linked to those around it. *It*. That was the strange thing about it. *One* of the strange things about it. Every one of the nine figures, whilst demonstrating a remarkably mature deftness of hand for one so young, was somehow incredibly detailed and yet revealed absolutely nothing, completely anonymous and androgynous all at the same time. The way that the image had been crafted was unusual too – the colours used, or rather, the lack of. Every other child in the room, as was usual, had automatically reached for the most brightly coloured materials at their disposal with which to maximise the visual impact of their picture. Glenn Chambers had done the exact opposite, choosing blacks and browns and dark greens and navy blues, resulting in an altogether more sombre affair yet still packing an undeniably powerful punch.

'Is that your Daddy in the middle?' asked Maria, focusing on what she perceived to be a relative triviality, failing to offer any praise whatever in recognition of the quite unbelievable quality of his artistry – whether not wishing to be seen to heap excessively preferential praise on an individual's work in front of his peers or prevented by some other, less admirable force it was hard to tell.

Avoiding her gaze, Glenn sat silently looking at his own work and shook his head.

'No? It's *not* your Daddy?' she repeated.

Another shake of the head.

'Well who *is* it then?' she pushed.

'Me.'

31

C.

I like Thai. Yep, I'd say that that was definitely my favourite. And then, what next? Well I like Asian mostly; Taiwanese, Cantonese, Vietnamese. Chinese and Japanese – how anybody can mix these two up is beyond me – they're chalk and cheese, and you won't get two more different dishes than that. Nobody ever ordered the chalk-board at the end of a meal did they? I'm not particularly bothered about the rest but if I *had* to go European, I'd probably prefer Greek, Italian or Spanish, even French, over English every time. Oh, I almost forgot about Afro-Caribbean. Perhaps slot that in somewhere between Asian and European. Anything a little more exotic than plain old home-grown is fine by me - apart from Indian maybe. Just a personal preference. Not for me. Not sure why really. Perhaps a little *too* exotic. American? Forget it. What? Oh, ha ha. I see the confusion. Perfectly understandable. My fault. No, I'm talking about women. Although, come to think of it, I'd say that coincidentally my culinary inclinations pretty much mirror those for the fairer sex almost exactly - which is handy if and when I ever meet one again and take her out for a meal – unless of course, like me, she's sick of her own culture's offerings and prefers to venture further afield to sate her appetite. No, Asian for me every time.   They're just so polite,

32

respectful....appreciative. They let you talk, show interest, don't talk over you. Some people say that that's because they don't even speak the lingo, can't understand a word you're saying, as if the language barrier must be this big issue when they've not even been in the country five minutes - but personally I've never found that. It's not like any of the English women I've met have had much worth hearing anyway. Inane, Marlboro-Light and Pinot-fuelled drivel about shopping and who was just evicted from the latest moronic reality show is something that I can quite happily live without thank you very much. What is it with those programmes that people find so appealing anyway? Glorified, Victorian freak-shows, wheeling out the talentless, the delusional, the bewildered - often quite clearly genuinely mentally disaffected - in a laser-lit spectacle of dry-ice and tears for the mindless masses to laugh and poke fun at in their millions. No, I'll stick with the Orientals. I've heard them spoken of critically on occasion for being overly subservient, obsequious even (another word I like – might start compiling a list) but that's just another ill-informed misapprehension. It's because they have integrity, show gratitude, respect for their elders; it's deeply ingrained in their culture. You only have to look at them and observe how immaculately turned out they are, how sleek and shiny their glossy straight black hair to see that they take pride in themselves, their appearance. Show me an Asian woman wandering about in public in a pair of pink velour jogging bottoms tucked into her crumpled Ugg boots and I'll happily stand corrected. No, Thai women don't spend the whole time you're out on a first date with them distractedly checking their phones

33

every five minutes or so as if waiting on an urgent hospital update regarding some critically ill, imminently departing parent. If they do, then they at least have the decency to be a little more discrete about it and wait until they visit the ladies'. And while we're on the subject of phones, they don't use LOL in place of a full-stop at the end of *every* text message either, regardless of whether the preceding grammatically inaccurate sentence is of any comedic value or otherwise – which usually it isn't. You could argue that that's because many of them don't know what it means but I'd counter that that's the whole point, that neither it seems do English women either. Perhaps that's why I like their food too – the same savoury ingredients of character that flavour the rest of their culture also shine through on the palate. In fact, all this talk has whipped up quite an appetite. I'm positively salivating. Now, where's that card I picked up from that phone-box recently? It's been some time since I last treated myself to a home delivery.

c.

'So, what do you make of this then?' asked Maria, throwing the sheet of paper down on the table in the staff tea-room, covering the pile of outdated, well-thumbed gossip magazines long since fit for the waste-paper basket. Her tone was almost defiant, as if she were arguing her case, defending a corner that nobody had as yet attacked.

Sheena paused from squashing a tea-bag against the side of a mug with a spoon to see what the *this* was that she was to make something of. What she saw caused her to momentarily lose concentration in the rote task, dropping the bag into the hot drink with a muttered curse, fishing it quickly back out again with the tips of her fingers.

'Wow!' she said, the art-critic in her not yet fully awakened, unsure of exactly what she was looking at. 'One of the kids did that?' she added, the question rhetorical yet still somehow necessary.

'Yep.'

'Wow' she repeated again, a little more subdued this time, the shock factor subsiding, 'That's amazing!'

'Amazing?' sneered Maria 'It's downright *weird* is what it is.'

'Who did it?' asked Sheena, already well aware of what the answer would be. She'd wondered what was going on behind those intense, mournful little eyes of his, sure that

35

the vacant stare was anything but – now she knew she was right.

'Who do you think?' replied Maria 'Heir Lipp of the Gestapo of course.'

'The Chambers boy?' clarified Sheena, feigning ignorance, that she hadn't known all along, from the moment she'd turned to look at the new home-made temporary table cloth, exactly to whom they were referring. 'Why are you calling him that? He's only been here a couple of days.'

'Long enough' replied Maria.

'For what?'

'To know that he's clearly a future serial killer in the making.'

'Why do you say that though? What's he done wrong?'

'Nothing. Yet. He just gives me the creeps, that's all.'

'Well I think he seems quite sweet. Just a little... troubled, that's all. We don't know much about him yet' added the Irish girl, about to mention the fact that he'd appeared to arrive alone that morning before checking herself, not wishing to fan the flames that she saw to be already licking at the base of little Glenn Chamber's stake. To her mind, people were innocent until proven guilty, not the other way around. She knew all too well that Maria would rather dunk the stool and ask questions later.

'Hardly a glowing accolade' scoffed Maria. 'You think *everyone's* sweet. You think I should show it to Linda?'

'Well you can show it to her, I guess. No harm in it. But I'm not sure what your issue with it is. Granted it's unusual but you can't deny that it's impressive. It's not like there are any severed heads on the floor with necks spewing blood or anything.'

'It's not just the drawings. It's what he said when I asked him about it. Who do you think the people in the picture are?'

'I don't know. Well his mum referred to her *others*. Not sure why but I got the impression that there were quite a few of them. So.... brothers and sisters maybe? I'd have said that that's dad in the middle but I'm guessing from your question that I'd be wrong. It's hard to tell what sex they all are. Is that mum in the middle then?'

'No' said Maria, blowing a raspberry by way of game-show wrong answer buzzer. 'Try again.'

'Big brother?'

'Nope. That's *him* apparently. Now tell me that a cee-psych wouldn't have something to say about that.'

'I don't think you need to be a child psychologist to make sense of that one. If he's the youngest of many then perhaps that's just his wanting to be bigger, more like his elder siblings. The fact that he's in the middle just says to me that he likes or wants to have his family all around him.'

'You don't think that the fact that they're all holding hands except him is weird? You don't think the fact that they're all virtually identical and he's double their size in the middle is weird.'

'Not particularly. Jesus, Maria, he's not even four yet. I think you're reading too much into it.'

'Exactly my point. He's not even four and he produces something like this. If this isn't evidence of a predisposed Messiah complex then I don't know what is.'

'Predisposed Messiah complex? Get you!' mocked Sheena, genuinely impressed by the terminology and her colleague's sudden expertise. 'Well show it to Linda then if it makes you feel better. She's bound to see it at some point anyway. You usually display their art-work on the walls don't you?'

'Yeah, but I wasn't going to with this one.'

'Why not?'

'It's just that it's so much better than all the rest. I don't want the other kids getting downhearted, thinking that their work isn't good enough.'

'Well you can't put all the others up *except* his. If anything, he should be rewarded for producing good work, not punished. Kids have to learn that some people are better at certain things than others at some point. That's just life. You can't shield them from it forever.'

'It's not just that.'

'What then?'

'I'm afraid it might freak them out. I mean, it's pretty scary looking.'

'Funny' laughed Sheena, spooning sugar into her own mug, 'never had you down as the timid type.'

'It's not me I'm worried about. It's them.'

'Well you can't single him out Maria, it just isn't fair.'

'Fine. I won't put *any* of them up then.'

'Well I think that would probably be better than putting up all but one. But you don't have to take my word for it. See what Linda thinks when you show her.'

38

'Oh, I'm sure she'll agree with *you*' said Maria, the sarcasm in her tone unsuppressed as she turned to leave the room, only to find Glenn Chambers standing in the hallway, just outside the door. 'Oh!' she said, with a start 'What are you doing there?' The expressionless face looking up at her remained silent. 'Are you lost?'. A single shake of the head. 'How long have you been standing there?' she asked, finally, a sudden realisation just beginning to dawn brightly over the horizon. The youngster held her gaze, returning her quizzical expression with one that said *long enough,* then walked quietly away.

D.

I'm in my flat, watching the lunchtime news. There was an article today about a guy who blew himself up in a cinema - or was it a shopping centre? I forget already - somewhere out in the Middle East – I forget that too. He was a British National who converted to Islam, using some ridiculously twisted interpretation of a religious doctrine as an excuse to carry out atrocities against hundreds, maybe thousands of innocent people. It's not even like he'd been conditioned to hold his fundamentalist extremist ideals as gospel from an early age; been raised in a sand-blown, shell-damaged wasteland with nothing to live for but hate and petrol bombs. No, he'd been put through red-brick University by middle-class suburbanite parents whose most radical decision to date had once been to have red with fish. I couldn't help wondering what the real reason was, what made him so angry with the world that he wanted to leave it and take as many people as possible out with him. It would seem logical, from the evidence, that its people that were his problem. I wonder if he even knew himself.

Next up was an item about the latest in a long list of celebrities who'd been arrested in connection with a number of sexual assaults against minors some decades back. He'd been accused of using his position of power to touch them inappropriately, abusing the trust they'd placed in him to satisfy his own sordid gratification. Firstly I wondered if he'd actually done it. Either he had, providing yet another example of the sorry state of the human condition, or he hadn't and they'd made the whole thing up, jumping on a careening, wobbly-wheeled bandwagon in some malicious pursuit of minor fame and fortune at the cost of another's publicly shattered life – thereby providing even further example. Assuming his guilt, that there's no smoke without fire, I wondered if he'd thought about it much over the years, what he'd done, and, if he'd changed greatly in that time, actually learnt something, whether he'd felt remorse, regret or if, for the very same reasons, that he hadn't at all, that he now looked upon that abuser as another man entirely – the wound either healed closed or wrenched further asunder with the passing of each new day.

And so it went on. Genocide in Africa, football hooliganism in Greece, Centenarian pensioner and decorated World War Two veteran beaten to death in his own home for the contents of his wallet – a single week's basic government pension. And on and on and on.

Why is it that we give so much air time to murderous dictators, serial killers, rapists, paedophiles - their names and faces entered into the history books, undeservingly immortalised forever in bold, upper case fonts of deepest, darkest black, whilst the countless doctors, nurses, soldiers, aide-workers, those nameless players who have contributed their selfless verse to the ever rolling powerful play, fail even to get a fleeting mention in the credits.

Why?

d.

At end of morning break the staff were out in full force, corralling the herds of youngsters that romped around the outdoor yard area like skittish sheep searching in vain for a hiding place from the nursery worker collies behind plastic mini-slides and climbing frames. Eventually rounded up and shepherded into their respective mural-decorated holding pens, a trail of sand from the play-pit outside tracing their route in, Glenn Chambers joined his group, joining the rest of the Tigers for *Cognitive Play Therapy* – play-time in old money. Primary coloured plastic boxes of toys and games were brought out from one of the many large resource cabinets that lined one whole end of the room, laid out before the children in a veritable smorgasbord of fun and interactive sensory stimulation - and they wasted no time in getting stuck in and playing God for a while, shaping the destiny of the imagination-fuelled micro-worlds that they instantly set about creating. Plastic animals marched indecisively in and out of a wooden ark in zoologically mismatched pairs, herbivores happily accompanying their natural carnivore predators, whilst die-cast vehicles collided with each other and went on their separate ways with scant regard for any exchange of insurance details. Unlikely romances blossomed between leggy catwalk model air hostesses and ursine

42

suitors, physically mismatched giants in comparison. Glenn Chambers waited until the rest of his group had looted the goods on offer and perused what remained. A wooden trolley filled with simple coloured wooden blocks caught his eye. Marked as *suitable for ages 2+* on the original, long since discarded packaging, the somewhat antiquated plaything was still popular with the younger children, reception and a year or so upward, but generally stood neglected among the pre-schools. He wheeled it away to a corner, carefully and considerately negotiating his peers and the many obstacles already strewn across the ground. Parking it up away from the other children on an area of parquet flooring around the room's perimeter - a polished mahogany frame to the coloured rubber matting - satisfied that this would suit his purpose well, he pulled the sleeve of his sweatshirt down over his palm, gripping it with his fingers, and cleaned a small area on the ground, making sure to first clear it of any dust and grit. Maria watched in fascination as he then proceeded to take a first block from the trolley and place it there on the pre-prepared surface. He reached into the trolley to take another and then another, placing them one atop another with all the care and precision of a brain surgeon reaching into the cranial cavity, matching their edges flush and crisp to maximise the potential for attaining as great a stature as possible. He'd reached the dizzy heights of seven when his actions caught the eye of another in the room. Action Man had had enough. Toby Miller pulled The Incredible Hulk off of him, separating the two of them, a temporary reprieve for the khaki-clad military man until he was inevitably beaten to a pulp again at a later date. Suddenly

Ultimate Smack Down didn't seem nearly so appealing as playing with some coloured wooden cubes. Leaving the two combatants to sort it out amongst themselves, he stood up and made a bee-line for the smaller boy playing quietly over in the corner. Glenn Chambers was stood before his rainbow tower, preparing to carefully set down block number eight, when the other boy in his peripheral vision broke his concentration. He watched as Toby Miller grabbed the push-handle and began to drive the trolley away.

'I'm using it' said Glenn, politely, grabbing the frame of the handle with a clenched fist.

'It's for everyone' answered Toby, pulling at it, as if to shake him free.

'You had your chance. You didn't want it. I need the blocks for my tower' replied Glenn, holding fast.

'Well let me help then' compromised Toby, sensing that he wasn't going to get his own way this time. He took a green block from the trolley and began to walk towards the tentative structure.

'No. I want to do it myself. I want to see how high I can get it on my own. Green is wrong anyway.'

'What do you mean? Why is green wrong?'

'They have to be in order.'

'So what colour's next then?'

'Red.'

Toby Miller reached for a red block and moved forward again, only to have his path to the cuboid totem pole blocked by its creator.

'No. I need to do it myself or it won't count' reiterated Glenn, turning to return to the delicate task in hand. As he did so, Toby Miller shoved him hard in the back, sending him sprawling across the floor, on top of his toppled high-rise.

Maria, who had been looking on the whole time, rushed over to intervene. As she helped Glenn up from his position face-down on top of the bed of uncomfortable wooden blocks, expecting the usual histrionics that always accompanied such an episode, she was surprised to discover a completely impassive expression.

Not a single tear blotted his cheek.

'What's going on here?' she asked, her question investigative yet her tone more accusatory, if anything somehow targeted more at the victim than his assailant.

'He wouldn't share' said Toby petulantly.

'I needed them for my tower' said Glenn, as if to himself rather than justifying his actions to those around him.

'Well there are about fifty blocks in the trolley' said Maria, more than doubling the actual number and presumably, to her mind at least, her point. 'Certainly plenty to go around.'

'Twenty-four' said Glenn.

'I'm sorry?'

'Blocks in the trolley. Four wide and six long. Twenty-four.'

Rather than acknowledge the positive, what appeared amazingly to be an accurate demonstration of an awareness of his four – or possibly even six – times table, Maria instead took umbrage at being corrected, undermined by a toddler.

'Well, either way, still plenty to go around. You were never going to use them all.'

'I might have' said Glenn.

'Well you didn't, did you?' said the nursery worker, openly irritated now. 'You didn't even get to double figures.' She'd been counting, intrigued at the spectacle, even finding herself holding her breath at moments.

'And whose fault is that?' Glenn looked at Toby, no hint of malice or resentment evident, merely self assured in his knowledge of the answer to her question.

'Yours for not sharing, that's whose. Let that be a lesson to you. You'll know what to do next time now, won't you?'

'Yes' said Glenn, matter-of-factly, though Maria was not at all sure that they were on the same page. Not even the same book.

E.

Friday night and I have a date. A first date. We've never met before but it's not exactly a blind date. I've seen her picture and we've been chatting online for quite a while now. I hope she isn't too disappointed. I'm really funny on email or text-speak – charismatic even. I have a chance to think about what I want to say, compose a message and edit it before hitting send rather than letting my nerves get the better of me, causing me to blurt out the wrong thing like I frequently do in person. I always mean well but somehow what comes out all too often gets taken the wrong way and then I usually end up making things ten times worse, digging myself ever deeper into an early grave in my flustered, excessive attempts to justify my actions or explain myself. But I'm adamant that that's not going to happen tonight. No, tonight is going to be a good night.

Her name's Kim. I'm assuming that that's her real name but who knows? You can never be too sure who you're speaking to on the Internet. You have to be really careful. One minute you could be quite innocently chatting to an attractive thirty-seven year old divorcee from Brighton and the next minute the police are smashing your front door in with one of those red hand-held metal battering rams like they use on the cop reality shows on

47

TV, confiscating your computer as evidence to support their child grooming accusations – or is it allegations? That's one of the reasons I don't use my own name when I'm on there. Online I'm Danny – after John Travolta's character in Grease. I figured that if I was going to use a pseudonym, then I may as well choose a cool one and they don't come much cooler than Danny Zuko do they? Obviously I don't use the surname - I'd tell you that too but I don't want you looking me up, sending me stupid, childish messages in light of what you now know about me, using my honesty and openness against me. Anyway, I originally thought she might be an Oriental – they often use the name Kim as an Anglicised abbreviation of their real name, presumably on the no doubt accurate assumption that most English men are too ignorant or just too plain stupid to make the effort to pronounce a name that isn't in the *Bumper Book of British Baby Names.* That's why I originally posted her a message – that and the fact that her profile professed a *love of animals.* So on paper – screen - we already had at least one thing in common. She turned out to be English but by then she'd replied and quite favourably too so I decided to go against my usual rule and stick with it, see where it went. And where it's now headed is to The Red Lion at eight o'clock this evening. Apparently that's her local. I wasn't sure if I should see that as a good or bad sign; good in that she obviously has enough faith from our conversations that she's happy enough, not too embarrassed, to be seen out with me, meet me in a bar where she no doubt knows lots of the regulars; bad in that she has a *local* in the first place. I don't mind a woman who likes the odd tipple but I don't want one of

48

those chain-smoking, desiccated husks of a creature with a pickled liver, a face like chamois leather and a voice two octaves deeper than my own. Or maybe there are actually no goods. Maybe she wants to meet me in a bar full of people she knows in case I turn out to be a head-case. Which of course I'm not.

I wish I hadn't just thought that. Now I feel nervous, on the back foot, like I'm going for an interview, entering the unknown, her terrain, her colleagues looking on all around us, judging. I'm not even sure why I'm going now. I should've just kept our relationship in the virtual world where I belong, where I'm comfortable, where I can be anyone, anything I want. I consider messaging her to cancel but it's already after seven thirty and chances are that even if she hasn't yet left home, she'll still have spent time getting ready. And she's unlikely to be looking at her computer now anyway. I can't let her down like that. No, I've made my bed – time to lie in it. God, what I wouldn't give right now to go back in time, to have not made these plans, to instead be going to bed, pulling the covers up over my head and escaping into my dreams until morning.

I splash on some cologne. Cologne. Funny. The word relaxes me. So old fashioned now. Does anybody still use it anymore? The word I mean. I don't think so. Unless perhaps being ironic. I guess Germany's fourth largest city just isn't chic enough for contemporary tastes. It's all *aftershave*s this and *scents* and pretentious French accents that now isn't it? You know when you hear one of those on the advert that you're going to be paying three times what you really ought to – and all to douse yourself in some cloying artificial aroma, smothering the pheromones which

49

nature kindly evolved over millions of years to send out the appropriate signals, to attract the opposite sex, let them know you're interested. No wonder everyone's so confused. But I splash some on anyway. It's just what you do on a date. Shows you've made an effort I guess – not that tipping a little Aramis into your palm and smacking it against your cheeks represents a particularly superhuman effort, I'm sure.

I'm jabbering. Stalling. I need to get moving or I'll be late. It's poor etiquette, unchivalrous, to keep a lady waiting. I grab my jacket from the banister and leave the flat.

Arriving at the pub, which with better care could've been a characterful, traditional looking old tavern, and first impressions are not good. A group of grubby regulars stands outside, cackling together like a primeval coven, gravel laughter scratching the air amidst a cloud of pungent cigarette smoke. At their centre, a heavily pregnant woman holds court, lank hair scraped back, still wearing the remnants of last night's make-up and clothes; a large vodka in her roll-up-free hand oiling the wheels of the stand-up routine already now well underway. Wading quickly through the hazy Old Holborn smog, and inside is not much better. A few vacant faces look in my direction as I enter, making me feel as though I've just stepped in off of the moors, and I half expect somebody somewhere to miss a dartboard and blame it on me. But they soon go back to whatever they were doing, which seems to consist mainly of staring at the drink on the table in front of them. A swarm of bar flies buzzes around one end of the tacky wooden bar, laughing and joking with the gum-chewing barmaid who fails to acknowledge me - deliberately or otherwise I can't be sure - as I lean forward to attract her attention, my elbows sticking to the dark, ring-stained wood as I do so. She isn't exactly rushed off her feet – most of the revellers seem to be outside smoking - but still the bar and tables are littered with grimy empties sitting atop flattened crisp packet beer mats. An oversize pull-down screen shows a big match which nobody is really watching, despite a good number of the patrons presumably keen sports fans, judging from their football shirts and tattoos. Occasionally one of them glances up at it over his companion's shoulder and makes a half-interested comment, almost dutifully, an ongoing right of passage. I wonder what Kim sees in this place. Perhaps it's her love of animals that brings her here. The place is like a boarding kennels for Jack Russells and Staffordshire Bull-Terriers, which lie looking bored at the feet of their owners, lifting their heads every now and then in hope of a high point to their evening - a pork scratching or two passed down under the table. I fully expect to find a group of their visor-wearing, cigar-chomping canine counterparts playing poker in a smoky ante-room out back.

'Excuse me' I call to the barmaid, feeling that I've held my twenty out-stretched across the divide and into her domain now for long enough. She shoots me an acid glare which lets me know that she clearly thinks me the rudest person in the world for having had the audacity to interrupt her conversation, which she immediately returns to - if only to let me know that she'll come when she's good and ready and not a moment sooner. She says something to them and they laugh, looking in my direction. Perhaps I should've

51

just waited patiently in silence. Perhaps I expect too much. She finally drags herself away from her no doubt existential discussion and comes over to serve me.

'Yes please?' she says, the effort all too much, her jaw presumably exhausted from all that gum chewing, the results of which I get a good look at. I'm surprised to get a please.

'Hi. What beers do you have please?' I say, returning one of my own.

Arms folded, leaning back at the hips, she looks from left to right at the dull, unpolished brass taps, as if that should tell me all I needed to know.

'Do you have any guest ales?' I enquire.

'They're all guests darlin'' she snorts, looking across to her goonies. 'None of them lives here permanently.' I should mention at this point that I have a pet hate – one of my many - for being called *darling* – usually delivered with a dropped *g* - by anyone noticeably younger than myself.

'Comedy gold' I mutter under my breath and she shoots me another of her Medusa stares, even though she can't possibly have heard exactly what I said. Focusing on the back of her head in the back-bar mirror behind her – because isn't that what Perseus did? - or was it Jason? - I sigh visibly, return a patient smile and try again. 'Do you have any bitters on special that you can recommend?'

'I'd *recommend*' she says, quoting me sarcastically 'the Middle Finger, but it's off right now.

Better, I think. She's wasted in here. She should be out on the comedy circuit with the other gargoyles outside.

'Just one of these then please' I say politely, tapping the handle of a house beer.

She uses what appears to be the last of her remaining energy to pour me a pint of murky froth and for that I'm grateful, counting out the exact money from the change in my wallet to save her the effort of working it out for herself. I sit myself down at a table in the corner where I can see the door. I stack empties and half empties one inside the other to make room for my own glass, moving some of the stacks to the adjoining table, taking care to hold them by the base so as to avoid coming into contact with any areas which might have been in the foul mouths of who knew what undesirables.

I try to sup my drink slowly but it's difficult when you're on your own and don't have the distraction of conversation to delay things. I lift the glass to my lips again and again, as much out of boredom and something to do as any real desire to quench my thirst. There's a rack of newspapers on the wall close by but despite my wish to have something to focus on, other than the faces periodically glancing over at me, wondering what I'm doing there, a new face, alone in a strange venue on a Friday night – or am I just imagining it? - I don't reach for one, figuring that to do so will mean I'm only a whippet and flat cap away from being one of those lonesome old men that I used to look at and feel a pang of sadness for when I was younger. Not exactly the suave, sophisticated look I'm aiming for when trying to make a good first impression – although I'm increasingly wondering if suave and sophisticated aren't exactly the particular qualities my date looks for in a suitor.

As I stand at the bar again, waiting patiently – and in silence – for another drink, a waft of cool air at my back informs me that the pub door has just opened and I look again to the back-bar mirror for assistance. The dark tinted glass lends a sepia quality to the images within so I can't be certain of its accuracy but what seems to be a *very* attractive young woman walks in – alone. I turn excitedly for clarification and am delighted to find the starker overhead lighting revealing her to be even more beautiful in the flesh. They say the camera never lies. Well whatever one took that photo that she used for her profile picture was not exactly being completely honest. It didn't do her justice at all. In fact, that picture is a *travesty* of justice. Long, blonde, full-bodied Farrah-Fawcett style flicks bounce in the light from a naked bulb as she walks, glowing like a golden halo in a Michelangelo. In a movie her entrance would've been shot in slow-motion and accompanied by a soundtrack of religious chorus call, the stuff of revelation. Her short – though not excessively so – skirt pays perfect compliment to a pair of long, slim, gazelle-like legs, shod in six-inch heels, transporting her across the bar with an easy confidence and grace. She doesn't seem to notice the Mexican wave of heads – even the dogs - turning to stare at her open-mouthed as she passes; or more likely she's used to it, has learnt to focus forward like the catwalk model that she could easily be.

I almost wish she wasn't quite *so* good looking. Now I'm *really* nervous. I'm just glad I got here before her and had time for a quick pre-date drink to relax me – although with hindsight, I'd have gone for something stronger. Her looks are sobering. I bet that's a compliment she's never been paid before – and she must've heard them all. Feeling exposed, that she can read my thoughts, I self-consciously touch my hand to my face, feigning tucking some hair behind an ear in a vain attempt to stop my brain-waves escaping. Perhaps now, for the first time, I understand the whole after-shave thing. If she could pick up on what my pheromones were saying right now, she'd probably turn right back around and flee. I said this was going to be a good night. Just don't mess it up. Danny Zuko, Danny Zuko, Danny Zuko.

As she heads towards me, I smile - something that admittedly I rarely do these days but really ought by now to have got properly sorted. My mouth just doesn't seem to know what to do with itself all of a sudden. My lips quiver with a mind of their own as I'm caught deliberating between gentle, pursed, play it cool or broad, clearly overjoyed to see you, bared teeth - the net result, combined with eyes which I've neglected to consider, being that of mildly deranged grimace. Even so, she smiles back at me - a smile that even the brown tinted mirror behind me couldn't fail to agree was the fairest of them all.

I venture to speak, holding out my hand to shake hers as she approaches but at the last moment she changes course and veers off to the right, looking down with a confused frown at my hand which is already falling slowly back to my side, equally confused, unsure whether it's needed or not. When she looks at me again, it's defensively, as if I'm clearly some sort of creep, rather than the kind, angelic smile she gave me just a couple of seconds earlier. How quickly we can change from friend to foe at the slightest turn, others' perception of us on a permanent knife edge, able to slip one side or the other with the next good or bad decision – or fall straight down, onto the blade. I want to explain, let her know that her initial judgement was right, that it was a misunderstanding, but I've been there before. I'll only end up making things worse as she tries to shun me and my desperation to put things right grows out of my control.

Unbelievably, she heads over to the two guys wearing local football team away kit shirts, kissing one of them on the mouth as he puts his arm round the small of her back, placing his hand on her backside in a clear territorial display of ownership to any other potential rival alpha males looking to challenge his position for mating rights. Perhaps he feels threatened by my presence here, saw the spark of connection between us when she first walked in. She looks over a couple of times, glancing round, and I'm sure he clocks it. He doesn't deserve her. How do I know? I can just tell. Beyond claiming his trophy on arrival, he barely acknowledges her, continues speaking with his matching set mate and pretending to be interested in the game. I see her say something then point to the friend, clearly asking them if they want another drink. *She* asks *them!* He doesn't even have the decency to offer her a drink when she turns up. But then I begin to wonder if she has an ulterior motive. Perhaps there's another reason that she wants to come to the bar. I tuck my hair behind my ears again and stare ahead, checking my copper-tinted reflection in the mirror. For once, I like what I see. My skin looks darker, giving me a more swarthy edge and even though I know it's only the effect of the tinted glass, still it gives me a little more confidence, on top of the second pint that I've now almost finished.

'Same again?' asks Chuckles behind the bar, clearly even bored of the bar-fly conversation now. I just now noticed her actually clearing some of the tables and collecting glasses, presumably having finally run out of them behind the bar, and am guessing that it's given her a little momentum – for after all, who can honestly say that they don't resent having to do something when they haven't been busy for a period?

'No, please' I say, gesturing to the goddess along the bar from me.

'Oh no' she says, to the barmaid, not to me, clearly shy, 'He was here before me.'

I feel my heart melt a little. Breeding as well as beauty. I just knew I was right about her.

'No, *please'*, I insist. 'Ladies first' I say, feeling pretty smooth, attempting my best Danny Zuko smoulder. If I was wearing a leather biker jacket I'd have thrown up the collar right then.

'Thank you' she says, making fluttery eye contact briefly before ordering two lagers and a glass of house white.

Head still facing forward, my eyes alternate between surreptitious flickers to her on my right and straight ahead, at my reflection, urging myself to stop being such a pussy and say something else. You could cut the sexual tension between us with a knife. There again with the knife analogies. 'Sorry about earlier' I offer eventually, my two pint self saying it quickly before she returns to her life forever or the regular me steps in and stops him.

57

'Sorry?' she says.

'I was just apologising for earlier. When you came in. It's just that...' and then suddenly I'm lost for words. It dawns on me halfway through the sentence that my explanation for what she probably perceived as my coming onto her is that I mistook her for a blind date of sorts. I don't want her to know that I'm meant to be meeting another woman; that I go on dates with virtual strangers. No, what I *want* is for her to know that, right now, at this very instant, she is the only one in the world for me. Don't want to spoil the special moment with mention of other women who would mean absolutely nothing to me if she would only look at me again the way she did when she first walked in.

'It's fine' she says dismissively, sparing my feelings, and God bless her dear sweet heart for that.

'No, it really isn't. It's unforgivable. I'm meant to be meeting someone. An old school friend I haven't seen for a long time. You look a lot like her, that's all' I say. I'm pleased with this story pulled from out of the bag on two levels. Firstly, it explains, quite plausibly, why I might not have recognised my date even though I'd met them before, had known them previously, and secondly – and perhaps even more importantly – because it tells her that I know women who look like her already and that they're quite happy to meet with me for a drink on a Friday night. It tells her that I'm in her league. And I could've just left it there, quit while I'm ahead, but oh no, two pint Danny has to bowl in and push his luck. 'You're a lot prettier than she is though.'

'Well...erm…thanks' she laughs, nervously. 'But you don't know that. She might've blossomed since you saw her last.'

Modest too.

'No. She won't have' I say, knowing that she won't have because *she* doesn't exist, clutching at straws, sensing that she's about to leave me to return to the clutches of that undeserving Neanderthal who won't appreciate her, treat her like a Princess like I would.

'Well…like I say…you don't know that' she repeats, looking a little uncomfortable now, and turns to go.

'No. I do know' I say, thinking that I've already been dishonest enough and what future can there possibly be for us, founded on a bed of lies? – that I *do* still covet the truth above all else, that it wasn't me, it was two-pint Danny that told a little white one, that all's fair in love and war - before blurting out to her receding back 'I know because I made her up!'

I've done it again. Said the wrong thing whilst trying to do right. I check my reflection again, shake my head at it in disappointment, watching it drink and order another pint. And not until I've handed over the correct money again and taken a sip of the cooler new beverage do I remember why I'm even here in the first place. I'm meant to be on a date. I check my watch. Nearly nine and she isn't here. Looks like another disappointing let down, although I have to say I'm partly relieved. I'll finish this drink and make tracks, get an early night like I'd wanted all along. I remain at the bar, because it barely seems worth getting too comfortable when I'm not planning on sticking around. And also, because I like the view – my Latin alter-ego in front of me and Angel-Delight over to my right. She's having a conversation with the two guys but she's on the periphery, not *in* it. I see her checking me out and her fella sees it too. He glances around and follows the arrow of her eyes, weighing up the competition. He turns back and, placing a proprietorial hand on her hip, says something to her, probably jealous, scolding words and she says something back, presumably justifying her actions, refuting his accusations. I know it shouldn't, but the obvious tension between them makes me happy. Just a few covert glimpses and already the cracks are starting to appear. Perhaps they'll have a full-on bust-up and he'll leave without her, go on to a club or something. Perhaps I'll stick around a little longer after all, see what happens.

And I don't have to wait too long before something *does* happen. As I return my focus back to my drink, facing forward, leaving the rot to set in for a bit, Football-Shirt appears; double-trouble in the mirror and my periphery. He invades my personal space, standing confrontationally square on, so close that I can smell the strong lager, the cigarettes, the residue of last night's curry on his breath.

'You see something you like?' he says. I think a fleck of saliva lands on my cheek.

I say nothing, looking at my reflection, telling it to stay calm. What would Danny Zuko do? Bad example. He'd probably just deck him right there and then like he did when he was trying out for sports. I take a calm, steady sip of my drink, deliberately slowly, looking bored.

'Nothing to say? Well you had plenty to say to my bird a minute ago apparently.'

Is it a question? Hard to tell. The intonation started out that way but seemed to finish up more a statement of fact – one of which obviously I'm already well aware, although I'd say that *plenty* was perhaps stretching it somewhat. I decide on the latter so continue to coolly sip my drink. 'I asked you a question' he clarifies eventually, bristling, clearly reading my thoughts.

'Firstly' I say, not bothering to turn to face him – I can see him in the reflection straight ahead after all and that version is softer, not nearly so ugly – 'she isn't *yours*. And secondly, she isn't a bird. I'd say there's only one strutting peacock around here and it isn't her. They're all male for a start. Not that I'd expect *you* to know that.'

His aimed-for intimidation hasn't worked and he's clearly unnerved by it. He starts to shift his weight from foot to foot, as if getting ready to come out of his corner flailing the moment I call seconds out. 'What the fuck are you talking about?' he says, spitting the words, his face contorted in a hateful sneer. Why is it that nasty pieces of work invariably look like the nasty pieces of work that they are? Their actual physical appearance, their facial features I mean. Is it that they have a genetic predisposition to nastiness, their anatomical, intellectual and emotional DNA inextricably linked or have the lines of hate and bitterness, lines in indelible permanent marker sketched in later by a caricaturist of darkness, morphed their features? You never see a photo-fit image on Crimewatch or in the newspaper and think *aah, he looks like a nice guy.* No, they always look like exactly what they are. Scum.

His dark, closely cropped hair reveals a number of head-scars, evidence of previous bar battles. I wonder why scars

61

make people look tougher when all they really prove is a wound received and not one doled out. 'At least you'll be used to it' I think to myself, although his response tells me that I inadvertently did so out loud.

'Used to what?' he says, confused. I can tell that only seconds remain before things get physical. He clearly isn't my intellectual match, isn't going to vanquish me in verbal combat, and he knows it. This realisation usually means only one thing. 'What the fuck are you talking about?' he says again, his repertoire clearly limited.

'I don't like swearing' I say. 'And besides, you already used that one.'

'What are you? Some sort of fucking retard?' he says, when didn't I quite clearly just say that I *don't* like swearing? It's indicative of a lack of vocabulary, the expletive the pea-shooter of the verbal arsenal. I obviously need to reiterate.

'Left or right?' I say, sighing dramatically, wearily. He looks at me confused - like he didn't hear me properly. So I say it again. 'Left or right? You can choose.' Again, the perplexed look follows. 'No? Indecisive? Very well, then I'll choose for you. Now, let's see. My left so that would be your right, yes?' I say.

'What the fu....'

I grab a half finished bottle from the many on the bar to my left, twist at the waist and smash it across his right temple, just above the ear. He goes down like a sack of spuds. There is a *lot* of blood - always is with head wounds, but then he must already know that. 'Yes, I know' I say evenly, regulating my breathing - I hate losing my temper, it shows a distinct lack of control. I don't condone

62

violence either but sometimes needs must, 'What the eff am I talking about? I quite clearly explained that I do *not* like swearing. Particularly not when there are ladies present' I add, for extra gallant effect, and because I mean it.

His friend just stands there like a lemon - his face has even assumed a pale yellowy tinge - as I gesture to the barmaid with the jagged remains. 'You' I say, 'pass me a bottle of vodka. Please. That's if you're not too busy of course.' A litre bottle is taken from a shelf beneath the bar and pushed across it towards me almost instantaneously. It's amazing how much better the customer service when you have a broken bottle in your hand. Football shirt is in the throes of attempting to sit up, staring in a daze at the blood on his clothes and hands, but I put my foot on his chest, push him back down and, pinning him there, unscrew the cap of the spirit and pour a good slug of it over his head, aiming for the deep, haemorrhaging gash.

'That should sterilize the wound for now' I say, looking directly at his friend with the warm smile of a Good Samaritan. 'But I'd suggest that you take him to the accident and emergency ward as soon as possible where he'll be able to receive the appropriate medical care. Head wounds invariably look much worse than they are. They'll soon stem the bleeding and then it should clean up quite nicely. I kept within the hair line so he can always grow it out if he wants to cover it up later, although from what I can gather, that doesn't seem to have bothered him too much so far'

Lemon just looks at me again, as if unable to quite take in what he's just witnessed.

'Quickly' I press, snapping him from his catatonia 'He's losing a lot of blood' and he rushes over to help his friend, putting one of his bloodied arms around his own neck and hoisting him up from the threadbare, beer-marinated carpet, one eye never leaving the broken bottle still in my hand. He manages to haul-walk him outside, the cold night air bringing colour back to his cheeks but the citrus hue soon returns to his complexion when he turns to see me follow him out, though instantly relaxing a little again as his eyes dart instinctively down and see the improvised weapon no longer there in my hands, one of which I raise to hail a passing taxi-cab which almost pulls an emergency brake in its effort to pull up in time in the road outside and secure the fare. Stepping from the curb, I walk out to the vehicle, open the front passenger door, lean in and say 'hospital please', holding the rear door open for football shirts one and two to slide warily in, which they do, the slap of my palm on the car's roof signalling to the driver to be on his way as I slam the door shut. .

I step back inside and this time my entrance commands a little more authority, a little more respect. Miraculously, nobody appears to have called the police, although from my observations of the evening thus far, I'd wager that most of the faces here would sooner avoid any contact with the law enforcement authorities wherever possible. I walk up to the bar to a background tune of Human League's 'Don't You Want Me' squawking timidly over the tinny sound system, and, along with everyone else, the barmaid eyes me nervously as I take my wallet from my pocket, reach into a side compartment, pull out a crisp new twenty and place it down on the bar, putting an empty on top of it to hold it

64

down. 'For the vodka' I say. 'I'm sorry you had to see that' I then say, turning to Angel Hair, who, throughout this whole scene, hasn't uttered a single sound, and I make to leave once more. As I reach the door, a chap sitting drinking alone at a corner table next to it shuffles across the bench seating, as if trying to get to me from behind the table.

'Hey' he says.

I stop at the door, one hand holding the handle, and turn to face him.

'Nice one' he says, nodding appreciatively, holding out a clenched fist, which I guess he's expecting me to bump with my own. 'He's had that coming for time.'

I look down at his hand and, appalled by his poor grammar, leave him hanging and walk out the door.

I'm twenty or thirty yards down the road when I hear the clippety-clop of spiked hooves cantering after me.

'Hey!' a voice calls out 'Hold up! Wait a second!'

I know who it is without turning, was expecting it before it happened, knew my instincts were right all along. But still I take a few extra paces, savouring the moment, before drawing up. Once again, if I'd been wearing that biker jacket, I'd have pulled up the collars against the biting cold and sparked up a hand-rolled which would have hung tenuously from my lips, defying gravity, the flame from my stainless Zippo lighting my rugged features in an atmospheric amber glow as I turn slowly to see Angel Hair chasing after me.

'It's me who should apologise' she says, a little out of breath on catching up with me. 'It was my fault. I shouldn't have said anything. He's not usually the jealous

65

type but for some reason he saw you and flipped. Guess, he didn't know who he was dealing with eh?'

'Guess not' I say, because how can I argue after that?

'Come on' she says, smiling and linking my arm, 'The night's still young. Let's go get a drink somewhere.'

F.

The truth, the whole truth and nothing but the truth. Well, to tell you the truth, it's always been that last part that I struggle with sometimes.

'Nothing to say? Well you had plenty to say to my bird a minute ago apparently'

'Sorry about that. It was a misunderstanding' I say. 'I did try to apologise to your lady already.'

'Yeah, so she tells me. You often go around making up stories about old school friends as a ploy to pick up other people's birds do you?'

'That came out all wrong' I say. 'I was just embarrassed. The truth is, I'm meant to be on a kind of blind date and I thought that she might be her. Seems I was mistaken.'

'Seems you were. Big time' says Football Shirt, the physical challenge ebbing from his body language, beginning to believe me before suddenly thinking of something, the doubt rising again in his re-puffing chest. 'So where is she then, this hot date of yours?'

'I don't know' I answer, and then, to add a little more sympathetic weight to my cause, I decide to tell him the whole truth. 'Looks like I've been blown out.'

'Well I'd say that's the least of your worries. You're lucky you never got yourself *knocked* spark out.'

'Leave him alone Mick, you big bully. Why don't you pick on someone your own size?' comes a guttural voice from behind me. Miraculously, it's Joan Rivers, the smutty comedienne from the outside smoking ring who comes to my rescue, stinking of cigarettes and all red faced from the outdoor heat-lamp that she's been slowly toasting herself under like a human kebab for the past hour. Up closer I'm not so sure that she *is* actually pregnant. She looks like she might've been not that long ago and hasn't yet shed the baby weight. I make a mental note not to even refer to it. I've made that mistake before and it didn't turn out at all well.

'Whoa, sorry' says who I now know to be Mick, laughing, holding his hands up in mock surrender, 'didn't realise he was here with his mum' and he walks back to recomplete his threesome.

'Arsehole' says Joan Rivers.
I turn to face my defender. 'Thanks' I say, before adding 'I had it covered, but thanks anyway.'

'Oh yeah, you really had it covered' says Joan, smiling a nicotine-stained smile. 'How about you cover me a drink?'

She's rough around the edges – and not even just around the edges – but her eyes tell me that she wasn't always like that, that life, perhaps a succession of unfortunate arbitrary choices, made her that way, as I suppose it shapes us all to be who and what we are eventually. Something about her feels strangely familiar, like we've met in a former life or something. Not déjà vu exactly, but something like it.

'Sure' I say, and the bar-maid is already at the optics, pouring a double vodka and orange, not too heavy on the orange. I get the impression that I'm not the first person this evening, or any other for that matter, to be collared by this woman at the bar for a free drink. At least she's sort of earned it I suppose. The bar-maid slides it across the bar and I just about manage to scrape together the correct change for a final time. I don't want to break a note if I don't have to and I'm not planning on sticking around any longer after I finish the now lukewarm drink I have already.

'Got you buying her drinks already, has she?' calls out Football Shirt – sorry but calling him Mick, even though I now know that to be his name, just seems too familiar - from across the bar. 'Watch out Kim, you don't want his imaginary girlfriend turning up and catching you cracking onto him!' he cackles at the hilarity of his own material.

And that's when it dawns on me why she seems so familiar, like we've met before. Because we have. Kind of. Over the Internet. Seems that I was right about that photo after all – a *definite* travesty of justice. I don't mean to seem unkind but she should be arrested under a breach of Trading Standards regulations or something. That profile picture must be at least twenty years old – assuming that is that it's even of her in the first place. Fortunately mine isn't much more accurate a representation of the present subject before her and I don't think she's twigged. An afternoon of large vodkas has probably helped my case too.

'Just ignore him' she says, thanking me for the drink, taking a healthy swig and wiping her mouth with the back of her hand. 'So, I didn't see you sneak in. Not seen you in here before. What's your name?'

I look at her looking at me, see the sadness behind the glassiness of her eyes that no amount of alcohol can drown.

69

I think how much I value honesty, that I've lied enough tonight already, that it didn't help me any. Honesty is the best policy right? This time certainly.

'Chambers' I say, surname first, like James Bond. 'Glenn Chambers.'

e.

Smoke wafted into Sheena's face from her co-worker's cigarette.

'You want to swap rooms after lunch?' asked Maria, flicking ash to the ground, her words brought to life by the wispy grey clouds that drifted from her lips between them. It wasn't uncommon for the staff to mix up their groups. Linda felt that it helped with the children's social interaction to be exposed to as many different adult faces as possible, that it wasn't necessarily healthy to have them forge bonds that were too strong, could cause them to become emotionally dependant upon any one individual, particularly when their time here was, by definition, so transient.

'I don't mind. Any reason?'

'Just thought you might like to spend some time with your precious little Typo' said Maria, her wry smile intended to convey a tongue in her cheek whilst actually revealing one notably more forked.

'Ok then. I could probably do with a change anyway' said Sheena, faux-nonchalantly. The fact remained that she *had* been itching to spend a little more time with the Chambers boy, to see if she could connect with him, get to the bottom of what made him tick. There was something about his quiet self assurance that unnerved others but which she herself found intriguing. The family portrait shown to her so derogatorily by Maria had only strengthened her resolve to fathom the mystery still further. 'And don't worry' she added, 'I'll look after your precious little Toby-Woby.'

'Touché' said Maria.

After the way that Maria had described his lack of involvement in the group, Sheena was surprised to discover Glenn Chambers at the front of the queue in the corridor outside the room after lunch, seemingly eager to enter and get started. Admittedly he wasn't speaking or participating in the general hubbub of activity behind him but he was at least keen to be there. Sheena opened the door and watched them pile in, aiming to tip the newbie a collusive wink, knowing that she shouldn't target it but wanting him to feel that she understood, even though in truth she really didn't, that she was on his side, just as she was with all of them. But he never looked in her direction, so focused was he on getting himself inside. The kids off-loaded their ruck-sacks at the back of the room and prepared to sit down at the various chairs dotted around, awaiting guidance from their leader. Alphabet. But not the usual unimaginative chanting of the same old tired, repetitive song, over and over, pile-driving it into their minds, there to remain until buried with them in their graves. No, Sheena made everything, even the most mundane of activities, that bit more fun.

Having given them their instructions, she made her way around the room, setting them up with the necessary materials and squatting down beside them to offer support, instinctively grouping them together at different tables which she'd come in during her lunch-break to lay out differently in advance. Each group had an approximately even mix of gregarious and introverted, advanced and less able, the aim being that the quieter ones would temper the more bumptious, the latter engage the reserved and the more able help to shimmy along their more struggling neighbours in an early form of peer mentoring. All seemed to be going smoothly to plan when she suddenly looked up from helping a pig-tailed, cherub-cheeked blonde girl to discover that she was missing a body. She didn't need to do a head count to realise that she was right, that Glenn Chambers was nowhere to be seen. Experienced enough to know not to panic, that it was unlikely that he could've gone far, Sheena took a breath and scanned the room. She hadn't seen him disappear. She was near the door so would surely have noticed him leave the room. He had to still be here. She crouched down low to check under the tables, looking through the kelp-bed of chubby legs for a mop of unruly blonde hair. No sign. The Wendy house. He had to be in there. He surely hadn't shut himself in the storage cupboards. Reassuring the little girl that she'd come back to her in a moment, Sheena walked over to the tent-like structure in the corner of the room and peered through the glassless window in one orange material wall, relieved to find him sitting there, cross legged on the floor, hunched over a wad of paper, quietly drawing, clearly focused on the task in hand.

'You not joining us Typo?' she asked, again hopeful that the nickname might help give her a little leverage.

A shake of the head.

'Why not?' asked Sheena. 'Don't you want to learn your ABC's like everyone else?'

Another shake of the head.

'Do you mind telling me why?' she asked, the kindliness of her tone clear that she genuinely wanted to know, without any hint of reprimand.

Glenn continued with his art-work, the only sound between them that of pencil against page. Unsure after a time if he was still considering his reply, Sheena was just about to prompt him again when, without his looking up, she got her answer.

'Z y x w v u t, s r q p o n m l k, j i h g f e d, c b a'

'Wow! Impressive' said Sheena, meaning every word – both of them. 'So you already know it backwards then?'

A nod.

'Where did you learn that?'

A shrug.

'Did you teach yourself?'

A nod.

'Ok mister. Fair enough. Since I know you like to draw and I guess we should nurture young talent where we find it, I'm going to let you carry on with what you're doing for now. I guess you're not causing anybody any trouble. But I can't be seen to let people get away with doing what they want or everyone will want to do the same and then all hell will break loose. So, just this once, as you're still settling in, I'll let you finish what you're doing. But on one condition. That starting tomorrow, you make an effort to get a little more involved with the rest of the group, ok?'

A nod.

'Deal?' clarified Sheena.

Another nod. And a smile.

The afternoon progressed on in much the same way – the majority of Sheena's group making perhaps not exactly huge leaps but at least pigeon steps forward in their slow but steady acquisition of alphabetic prowess, whilst Glenn Chambers remained hidden away in his makeshift studio, quietly beavering away with an extended focus quite uncharacteristic of children his own age. Sheena stuck her head in through the window every now and then to offer a smile, to let him know that though out of sight he may be, out of mind he wasn't. But he seemed oblivious, head bowed, intent on his doodling and she found herself watching him work with much the same oblivion to the world around her until she became self-aware and consciously snapped herself out of it to return to the others. She was looking forward to afternoon break when she'd get a chance to take a look at his latest Rorschachian masterpiece.

Having moved on from the letters round to the numbers game, the children took up where they'd previously left off learning to count, working through picture books with images of rows of apples, pigs and other sundry items, before moving on to more tangible three dimensional objects, including the coloured blocks salvaged from the ruins of The Chambers Tower. Sheena considered speaking again with Glenn, seeing if she might be able to negotiate his return to the outside world with this new learning tangent but thought better of it, worried that he might perceive it as her reneging on their agreement and setting back her hopes of ever gaining his confidence - that and her prediction that he'd probably only fire her away again with a rocket-launch style countdown anyway. No, a deal was a deal.

The sound of bustling movement and chatter trickled in mini-waterfalls from adjoining rooms out into the river of the main corridor, building to a white-water rapid as it roared past Sheena's room in a torrent of tiny-tots, spilling out into the whirl-pool of the yard area, announcing the fact that it was two o'clock already. Her group, herself included, had all been so engaged in what they were doing that they'd completely lost track of time, some seeming almost disappointed to have to stop where usually they'd be out of the door at the click of the vertical minute hand like greyhounds from a trap.

Sheena escorted them out of the room, checking that her colleagues were on hand to supervise, as per the afternoon rota. 'Come on Typo', she called out to the silent Wendy House. 'Even great artists have to take a break some time.' There was a sound of movement from inside and a mop of hair appeared through the unzipped doorway, stepping out with his huge sheets of paper like a moth from its chrysalis stage, about to unfold its wings for the first time. Glenn Chambers walked over to the centre table, placed them down slowly, smoothing them out flat, taking as much care as possible not to crease or damage them, before heading out under Sheena's outstretched arm, still holding the door ajar for him to leave through. 'Go and have fun' she said to his back as she went back inside and over to the table to appraise his work.

A pair of frown lines set deeply between her eyebrows as soon as she looked at the first picture - lines of confusion at first, unsure quite just what to make of what *exactly* she was looking at. She turned the page back to look at the one beneath it, and then the next and then the next and then the next. Same thing every time. And this time, the first three words that sprang to mind were not *Wow* and *That's amazing!* but *Oh... My... God!* They weren't new drawings at all but those that the children had spent hours enthusiastically slaving over that morning – except this time with a marked difference. The faces of each and every person, every family member in the pictures, had been blacked out, their smiling, happy features erased forever. Macabre enough in itself maybe, but to Sheena, that wasn't the strangest thing about it. If it was malicious, she'd have expected it to be carried out in more of a rage; angry scribblings engraved into the page, criss-crossing in a random flurry of fist-clenched curves and slashing straight lines – but no, great time and care had clearly been taken here to make a good and thorough job of it, colouring in perfectly neatly, not going over the edges. In a funny sort of way, it had to be admired. It was a *very* precisely executed piece of sabotage. Sheena thought about what to do. She knew that if Maria saw this then that would be Glenn Chambers' card marked for good. Maybe she should simply *lose* them all. It might not be so difficult. Maria had said that she wasn't going to display them so maybe she wouldn't even notice them missing. But no, she knew deep down that perhaps her more cynical colleague wasn't so completely off the mark after all. This latest handiwork had provided the fertiliser to accelerate the growth of the tiny seed Maria had planted into a sapling. She couldn't just ignore this, brush it under the carpet, cover for him.

77

God, the very fact that she was even thinking in these phrases should be telling her enough. She needed to show them to Linda. But she wanted to speak with Glenn first, give him a chance to explain.

Sheena went outside, her eyes scouring the throng of hyperactivity - running, jumping, jostling bodies bouncing around the enclosed yard like ball-bearings in a pin-ball machine. Unsurprisingly, Glenn Chambers was stood alone, looking up at the sky. Sheena followed his gaze, wondering what had caught his attention – a bird? a plane? Superman? – but she saw nothing, only an empty sky.

'Hey Typo' she said, approaching him. 'Whatcha looking at?'

Without averting his gaze, Glenn merely pointed.

'Am I missing something?' she asked, squinting her eyes as if to gain some level of telescopic advantage. 'There's nothing there is there?'

'I know. That's what I'm looking at.'

'Oh. That's pretty deep. So, a philosopher as well as an artist are we?' she joked, to which the boy merely shrugged. 'Look, can you look at me for a minute please Glenn?' she said, the use of his real name revealing that she was about to be serious. He lowered his head slowly and levelled her, on her haunches in front of him, with his eyes. 'I need to ask you about the pictures. Do you know that what you did was wrong?'

A nod. A simple, non-verbal, affirmative answer to a simple closed question. An accompanying look that said *yes of course, is there a problem?*

'Then can I ask why you did it?'

A nod. A pause.

78

'Erm…ok then…so, erm, why did you do it?'

'Because Toby was mean to me.'

'Toby? A boy in your class?' asked Sheena, knowing *exactly* to whom he was referring. If anyone in this building was a budding Machiavellian in the making it was him.

A nod.

'Just Toby?'

Another nod.

'Nobody else?'

A shake of the head.

'So why did you ruin *everybody's* pictures?' Sheena asked, a barely detectable flicker of his eyes at the mention of the word *ruin* causing her to wonder if he perhaps genuinely believed that he'd improved them in some way - before furnishing her with his explanation.

'I didn't know which one was his.'

G.

The lunchtime news is on again. It's not all rape and pillage today like it was the last time I watched. I'm not sure how conscious a decision this was, whether the producer wanted a change, chose the content specifically with one in mind, but there appears to be a definitive theme throughout. Today in the world - lies, deceit, corruption. In fact, I don't think there's a news bulletin that *doesn't* cover most, if not all, of the Seven Deadly Sins or show breakage of most of the Ten Commandments. Might start keeping a tally. Guess I'll need to refresh my memory on what they are first – if a job's worth doing. Pretty high up on this afternoon's agenda though is greed. There's an article about a footballer being paid an inordinate sum of money, over a quarter of a million pounds a week – a week mind! – to kick a leather sphere around a field. All that money to play football. To *play* football. And I wouldn't mind but it's not even as if they play fair. Supposedly sportsmen at the highest level, they repeatedly prove themselves to be as unsporting a people – because they are surely that, a breed all their own - as you could ever hope not to meet, the vast majority from what I've seen taking every possible opportunity to dive on the ground, particularly when the penalty box looms, feigning injury, rolling around on the floor holding their faces in near death throes when the slow-motion replay clearly shows either contact made elsewhere or worse, no contact at all. The hands of both teams will invariably plunge into the air every time the ball goes out of play and then meet together in supplication, gathering around the referee, pleading with him to change his mind whenever a decision doesn't meet with their approval, as if this may work and such a thing has *ever* happened before. Why are these elements of the game not addressed, covered with such fastidiously detailed emphasis as their salary negotiations? What sort of example are we setting our young people? If they were in any other form of employ, such consistent and flagrant breaches of the pre-agreed code of conduct, the terms and conditions of employment – on national television for millions to witness, no less – would surely result in disciplinary action aplenty and ultimately, permanent dismissal.

There are articles about politicians, those senior figures of authority funded by us and meant to be working on our behalf, taking time out from slinging mud at each other, squabbling amongst themselves like children – sorry children – to spend our hard-earned taxes on themselves, financing such unnecessary luxury items as second homes, fancy cars, exotic holidays and, more ridiculously though gaining significantly greater coverage, a duck-house for a garden pond. Personally I resent the duck-house a lot less than I do all the rest. The poor things get a pretty raw deal floating around all exposed out there in the middle of winter, and a little extra shelter wouldn't go amiss.

And so it goes on; multi-millionaire singers in rehab, overdosing on drugs, not sufficiently satisfied with the adulation of hundreds of thousands of adoring, screaming fans and global recording recognition as stimulant enough; Hollywood movie stars coveting not just their neighbours' wives but the nannies, the maids and anyone else they can get their perfectly manicured hands on whilst their glamorous model wives' backs are turned - no doubt off somewhere doing the same. Fame and fortune are wheeled out hand in hand, the Bonnie and Clyde of the modern world, taking down victim after victim, the gluttonous masses gorging on the fruits of their success until they choke.

And these are our disciples, our blind leaders, the figures that society looks to for hope, for aspiration, for entertainment, fulfilment; a benchmark of superficial wealth and illusory happiness that, when it crumbles publicly around their ears, provides us with still further column inches for dissection and titillation as we pass judgement and point our fingers at those very monsters that we ourselves created.

f.

'Still looking out for Freak Boy?' said Maria, venturing out onto the forecourt to check on her colleague who was still stood on the pavement, keeping an eye out up and down the road for any sign of a vehicle or, more significantly, any lack of one.

'He's been late the last couple of days' explained Sheena, ignoring the derogatory reference, not having mentioned his suspected solitary arrival of the previous day. 'He'll probably be here in a minute. I just want to make sure he gets in ok.'

'On his own again, you mean?' said Maria, revealing that Linda must have already told her. Sheena and the nursery proprietor had had a discussion yesterday afternoon and agreed a compromise – that should Glenn Chambers appear to arrive unaccompanied again the following morning, they'd arrange a safeguarding meeting with his guardian to express their concerns and advise them of the possibility of notification to Social Services should the same thing ever happen again. Thankfully, Linda had reluctantly agreed not to mention the desecrated art work to Maria, to hide it away on top of the tall metal storage cupboard in her office, aware that her staff member was already prone to favouritism and, by the same token therefore, quite possibly persecution too. But she'd assured

83

the young Irish worker that she wouldn't shelve any further potential irregularities, should they rear an ugly head – that these would be addressed at a meeting with the parents and quite possibly any other appropriate specialist external agencies too. She'd put the concerns raised thus far down to teething problems – any more would need full on dental treatment, possibly even extraction.

'Yeah. I know he makes you uneasy but I'm worried about him' said Sheena.

'You always were a sucker for a sympathy case' said Maria, her tone derisory, suggesting that they'd been here a thousand times before.

'I just think that we need to be there for the ones that need us most more than ever. Not hold it against them and single them out.'

'Like I do, you mean?' snapped Maria, defensive.

'It's not about you' said Sheena, tired now of trying to appease her colleague, no longer caring what she thought, aware from experience that there was no changing her mindset – any more than there was her own. 'Come on, we have other kids to deal with.'

Inside, Maria rejoined her room where a flustered Childcare apprentice was temporarily holding the fort. Sheena, timetabled to float between rooms during the first session to enable her time to come in from her meet and greet duties, went straight to Linda's office to deliver the news that she'd hoped not to have to give.

'Well?' asked Linda. 'Alone again?'

'No. Worse. No sign.'

'Well that's that decided then' said Linda, the receiver already in her hand 'We'll have to phone home either way.

I just pray that my giving this situation the benefit of the doubt isn't going to come back to haunt me. I'll never forgive myself if he's been sent off out on his own and never made it here.'

Linda had the contacts book open on the desk in front of her and was dialling the number when Sheena interrupted her. 'Wait!' she said excitedly, 'Look!' and pointed at the portable TV on the neighbouring desk. Wired up to a handful of security cameras around the building, the screen was divided into four squares, the bottom right quarter, trained on the main entrance, revealing a fuzzy monochrome image of a large rucksack and snorkel parker, stood on tip-toe, reaching for the door-bell. 'He's here!' she said, almost yelling in her relief and rushing off to let him in.

'We were getting worried about you' began Sheena 'Where's your mummy?'

Glenn looked at her silently - remembering his lines? Either he forgot them or chose instead to say nothing, perhaps even then not wishing to perpetuate a lie.

'Did your mummy drop you off?' asked Sheena, looking past him, over him, for a sign of departing activity.

'She's gone away' he said.

'Away? From here you mean? Just now?'

Silence.

'You can tell me the truth. You won't get into trouble. Did you travel here alone?' she asked, trying a new angle.

Again, nothing.

'Ok. Well let's get you in with the others then, shall we?' she said finally, thinking that whatever he said would make little difference anyway, not without hard evidence of an accompanying adult anywhere to be seen. That phone call home would still need to be made. And after the scare that she'd just had, Sheena suddenly wasn't quite so willing to cut corners or make exceptions to the rules. She'd no longer look at Linda as quite such an inflexible automaton in these matters. From now on, just like her, she'd play everything exactly by the book. You couldn't afford to gamble when the stakes were the lives of infants. She knew that she'd learn from Glenn Chambers and here was a stark lesson well and truly drummed home.

'Well?' said Linda.

'Looks like we need to make that call' said Sheena. 'Might be an idea to try the land-line now. If she picks up then we pretty much know that she didn't drop him off herself.'

Linda looked down at the number still on the pad in front of her and dialled.

'Voicemail' she half mouthed, half whispered, when it kicked in after a few seconds, as if the machine were already listening in – to which Sheena raised her eyebrows and shrugged her mouth in an inverted U, as if to say *well that's a good sign at least.* 'Hi, this is a message for Mr or Mrs Chambers. It's Linda Barrington from Little Soldiers. Could you please give me a call as soon as you get a chance? No need to panic, Glenn's absolutely fine, but we do have some possible concerns that we'd like to discuss with you. Thank you. Well, that's that' she said, placing the receiver back down in its cradle. 'Let's just hope that she calls back before the end of the day.'

Gone away. The phrase niggled at the back of Sheena's mind, burrowing deeper like a maggot throughout the morning where it would eventually become a fat bluebottle, buzzing around her head until she swatted it. *If in doubt, there is no doubt*, her mother had always said to her, although she'd been referring to the edibility of food past its official sell-by date at the time. Sheena had since embraced the philosophy more widely and it had served her well. With the wisdom of her recent lesson still fresh in her mind, she knew that she had to do something. She might not need to wait too long. If Mrs Chambers called back and turned up for a meeting later then hopefully they'd get all the answers that they needed, agreeable or otherwise, soon enough. But, in the meantime, Sheena instinctively felt that there was more to this, a story to be unearthed. She didn't want to be one of those frustrating characters in the films that caused her to scream at the TV set, yelling at them to for God's sake do something, to act on their suspicions, reveal what was staring them right in the face. In the movies, the wife, friend, whoever, would invariably end up getting the idea eventually, looking right under their noses, often nearly too late, frequently visiting the local library to scroll through reels of microfiche, tracking down an old newspaper article containing some dastardly revelation.

So that's what she did.

On her way home that afternoon, she stopped off in town, taking advantage of the relatively early nursery finish time to make the most of the remaining couple of hours that the library was still open. She worked quickly, her young eyes scan-reading screen after screen, unsure exactly what she was expecting to find, looking out for mention of the word

Chambers, pausing and scrolling back occasionally when she saw anything which caught her eye – several mentions of her old school for example. She'd been politely asked to start wrapping things up, the cleaner already worrying around her, eager to get at the desk that she was still using with their polish and cloth, when she stumbled upon what she firmly believed to be just what she'd been looking for all along. The dastardly two year old newspaper article read:

'YOUNG WOMAN TAKES LAW INTO OWN HANDS

A young woman was yesterday convicted of life imprisonment for murdering her husband. Lorraine Chambers (22), was charged in the early hours of yesterday afternoon with poisoning Gordon Chambers (25) using rat poison, with intent to kill, after it is claimed that she suffered years of domestic violence at his hand. The full week that the jury took to arrive at a majority verdict was presumably due in part to the various unorthodox changes to the defence plea, including involuntary manslaughter on the grounds of diminished responsibility (the defendant was diagnosed with severe Post Natal Depression at the time, following the birth of their only son) and self defence – both of which were rejected by the resident judge presiding due to the extended and premeditated nature of the killing, stating in his summing up that 'though it seems clear that the accused appears to have been suffering for some time under a sustained and brutal regime, we cannot as a society be seen to condone members of the public taking the law into their own hands or we risk a culture of vigilantism in which murder and justice cannot be separated.'

So *that* was what was going on behind those sad eyes of his. Poor little thing. How much did he know? What had he seen? This explained why he'd come to the nursery so late on. Mrs Chambers – if that was her name – had said that they'd only recently moved to the area, but it seemed likely that it was only Glenn that had really, to come and live with his grandparents. And that explained why she was *so* agreeable about the 'misunderstanding' over her parentage. But none of this excused or explained his not being brought in to nursery by an adult each morning. There was still that loose end to be tied up.

She took a print-out of the article, apologising to staff for holding them up, thanked them for their patience, then left.

g.

'The little shit!' exclaimed Maria, bursting into the room.

'I'm sorry?' replied Sheena, standing at the kitchen units, staring at the kettle, waiting for it to boil, clearly unfamiliar with the proverb.

'Blotto' or whatever you call him.

'Typo?' corrected Sheena.

'Yeah, Type O – for odd. Jesus Sheena, why didn't you tell me?'

'Tell you what?' asked Sheena, thinking that perhaps Linda had gone back on her promise and mentioned the discussion that the two of them had had following her findings of a day earlier.

'About the pictures of course. The little shit has ruined them all.'

'Don't keep calling him that' said Sheena, more protective of him than ever, particularly in light of what she thought she now knew.

'Well he is. A right little shit. You're not seriously telling me you still don't think so now after what he's done? He's just plain evil.'

'How do you know anyway?'

'What, you didn't think I'd find them? I knew as soon as I realised they were missing that you'd hidden them for a reason. And I knew that reason would be an obnoxious little shit with a hair-lip. You could've picked a better hiding place – or, better still, destroyed the evidence. Not that they weren't destroyed enough already.'

'Look, I don't blame you for being angry. I don't expect you to understand…'

'Oh, I understand alright. It's you that doesn't get it. He doesn't belong here. I'm going to tell Linda' she said and Sheena was about to react, to inform her that their superior already knew about the pictures, quite possibly knew a great deal more in fact, but didn't want to incriminate her, implicate her in a deception that she herself had instigated.

'So that's where you'd got to. Come on you' said a female voice behind Maria suddenly as Anna, the young Childcare apprentice, took Glenn Chambers by the hand and led him away.

'Jesus Christ!' said Maria.

h.

In the afternoon, Maria welcomed the children into her room. Glenn Chambers hung back and let the others enter.

'Come on' said Maria to the loitering figure 'I haven't got all day.'

'Miss Winters, can I speak to you please?' he said.

'Yes, of course' she replied, impatient but simultaneously softened by his use of her preferred polite, formal address and intrigued – he hadn't previously initiated *any* conversation with her until now. 'What's up?'

'I just wanted to say sorry about the pictures' he offered, looking remorsefully down at his feet which tap-kicked gently at each other.

'That's ok. It's done now' said Maria dismissively, thinking that his dutiful apology was only brought on by his having heard her talking about it in the kitchen.

'No, it's not ok. I shouldn't have done it. I was cross with Toby for ruining my tower but it was all my fault. I should've let him share.'

'Well' said Maria, somewhat taken aback 'It's very nice of you to admit it and say sorry. Very grown-up. Perhaps you'd like to apologise to Toby too?'

Glenn looked up from his feet which had now stopped fidgeting. He looked the nursery worker in the eye and she smiled at him, a smile that told him that she'd won, that she was the boss in this room, not him.

'Well?' she said. 'I think that would be a nice gesture, don't you?'

He continued to hold her gaze, his eyes narrowing momentarily, before returning a conceding smile. What was he apologising *for* exactly? From what he'd heard, nobody knew about the defaced drawings. 'Ok' he said.

'Good boy' said Maria, hardly believing her own words. 'Stay there. I'll just go and get him.'

A few moments later and Maria returned with her little pet.

'Well, here he is. Toby, Glenn has something he'd like to say to you.'

Toby looked confused, the episode of the previous day all but erased from his mind, a whole bunch of similar scenarios and outcomes having since played out already that morning with other more forgiving victims.

'I just wanted to say sorry' said Glenn.

'What for?' asked Toby.

'For yesterday. For not sharing the bricks.'

'What bricks?'

'The building blocks. The ones I was making a tower with before I fell on it and knocked it over.'

'Oh, erm, that's ok' said Toby, still looking confused, not seeming to have any recollection of the incident referred to. 'Can I go back in now please Maria?' he said, these two alone on first name terms.

'Yes, of course. Off you go. Well' said Maria, turning back to Glenn 'that wasn't so bad now was it?'

'No' he answered. 'And Maria…'

'Yes?'

'From now on, I promise to share *everything.*'

Pleased with the outcome of her mini restorative practice session, Maria's next period went from strength to strength. Glenn Chambers played *Ultimate Smack-down* with Toby Miller, though not literally of course, despite the latter's propensity for physical contact. Naturally Toby was Hulk and Glenn Action Man, a soldier under fire from the countless smashing blows which rained down repeatedly upon him. Much to Toby's delight, he lay there and took his punishment like a man. Glenn had his hand up in response to *every* question asked, his enthusiasm and surprisingly broad wealth of general knowledge bordering on the irritating – particularly to his previous sparring partner who suddenly found himself no longer the smartest kid in the room. Even Maria found herself beginning to lower her guard as he produced a drawing for her – of her – a remarkable likeness, not necessarily from a facial features perspective but from his use of hair-style, colour and clothing.

'It's brilliant' said Maria, holding it up to take a good look at it. 'You even got the clothes under my tabard right. I like the brown gloves.'

Glenn merely looked at her admiring the picture and smiled at her appreciation as she considered what a monumental corner they'd obviously turned.

So at break time, Sheena was surprised to discover an almost complete turnaround in Maria's appraisal of the new lad in their midst.

'Maybe I was a bit hasty' she admitted. 'Perhaps he's not so bad after all. I think he's definitely got potential. He just needed a bit of discipline. Maybe it's not such a bad thing that he heard me talking about him. At least now he knows I'm not a soft touch and that I tell it like it is. Probably respects me more for it in the long run, rather than letting them all think they can do no wrong like some people.'

'Me, you mean?' said Sheena, smiling, the round table of veiled accusations having rotated full circle.

'Well, you must admit, you do pussy-foot around them sometimes. They need to learn to take responsibility for their own actions or they'll think they can do whatever they want. You're not doing them any favours in the long run.'

'Oh, hi Glenn' said Sheena, glancing over her colleague's shoulder, causing her to spin around in shock.

'You bitch!' said Maria, smiling at the empty corridor and the prankster laughing her head off in front of her.

'Did I miss something?' asked Linda, sticking her head around the door.

'No, just Sheena's twisted Irish sense of humour' said Maria.

'Racist' said Sheena.

'Meeting at three' said Linda to Sheena, the answer-phone message evidently having been returned. 'I'd like you to join us.'

'Ok' said Sheena as Linda rushed off to answer the ever-ringing telephone.

'What's that about?' asked Maria, curious.

'Oh, just a meeting with a parent' said Sheena, trying her hardest though failing to appear casual, not wishing to put the brakes on her colleague's positive momentum.

'Hmm' said Maria, not in the least bit fooled, a very good idea of which parent – even though technically she very likely wasn't one at all.

Final session of the afternoon was going as well as the last, Maria even covering for Glenn at one point when one youngster asked if their family drawings were going to be displayed and she answered that there wouldn't be room once they'd pinned up their pieces from today, which, to enforce her point, she then proceeded to do, squashing the blu-tacked corners against the wall with her thumb whilst Anna supervised a few rounds of singing and clapping, even taking the usual amateur performance up a notch with a competent demonstration of keyboard skills on the hand-held Casio organ – a couple of AA batteries kidnapped from the back of a talking dolly. Despite her father's grumbles, apparently two years of childhood piano lessons hadn't been a complete waste of time and money after all.

The wheels on the bus had gone round and round what was starting to feel like literally all day long and there'd been multiple sneezing victims of the bubonic plague risen from the dead when an unpleasant odour began to cloy the air, a smell with which any nursery worker was only too familiar – though usually more common to the reception children than the pre-schools. Maria's nostrils twitched as she stood on a chair, securing the final corner of Glenn's portrait of her. She turned to see the artist, no longer a link in the latest ring of roses, looking embarrassed and

96

uncomfortable, Anna oblivious, lost in leading her circle of song.

Maria stepped down from the plastic chair and went to him, squatting down in front of him.

'You had an accident?'

A nod.

'Shall we go and get you cleaned up? I've got a change of clothes that would fit you perfectly. Really trendy stuff too.'

Another nod.

Maria signalled discretely to Anna what she was doing, then took Glenn by the hand and out to a toileting area that was used for just such eventualities, though usually in a much more contained disposable nappy. By the time she'd got him to the room, excrement had run down his legs like gravy, even as far as his socks, so that almost his entire outfit would need to be replaced. He'd even attempted to clean it from his legs with his hands then wiped his soiled palms across his sweatshirt, the T-shirt beneath the only garment that managed to escape looking like he'd spread Marmite over it.

Using every ounce of practised restraint within her means not to visibly gag in front of him, Maria removed his clothing, placing it all into a plastic bag, carefully pulling the sweatshirt over his head. She removed his underwear in a precision operation, attempting to contain the main stinking squashed cigar that still lay inside them like a hammock, but he moved his legs awkwardly and they twisted, the contents falling onto the tiled floor for her to pick up between her fingers with tissue and mop down with disinfectant later.

She heard a sniff and felt his body rack with the effort of stifling a sob as she wiped him down with antisceptic baby wipes.

'It's ok' she said. 'You're not the first and you certainly won't be the last.'

'His whole body trembled and she realised that, on top of the upset, he was probably cold too.

'Don't worry' she said 'We'll soon have you in some nice warm clothes. Superman ones too if I'm not mistaken.'

As she finished cleaning him up, helping him step into a pair of crisp, white cotton underpants and pull on a new, clean woollen sock, she looked up at him, ready to give him her best *don't worry, this will be our little secret* look - and saw the real reason for his shaking. He wasn't trying to stifle racking sobs at all.

He was trying not to laugh.

i.

Little Soldiers

Day Nursery, Pre-School & After School Club

<u>Minutes of Safeguarding Meeting – 3pm Wednesday April 1st 1975</u>

Present:

Linda Barrington (LB) – Nursery Proprietor / Manager

Sheena O'Callaghan (SOC) – Childcare Assistant / Minutes

Maureen Chambers (MC) – Guardian / Glenn Chambers (GC)

Purpose of meeting:

To raise / identify potential Child Protection concerns over safe travel arrangements re Glenn Chambers and ascertain a satisfactory outcome moving forward.

Mrs Chambers arrived punctually and was escorted into the office whilst GC was supervised elsewhere by a qualified Childcare Assistant. LB opened by explaining the purpose of the meeting as per above, with specific reference to the apparent lack of an accompanying adult for the past two consecutive mornings, as highlighted by SOC on each occasion. LB also informed MC that, since contacting her earlier that day, certain additional information had come to light which may shed some doubt as to MC's true parental status and that she would appreciate MC providing clarification herself in order to prevent further unnecessary external investigation being carried out. MC was presented with a print-out of a newspaper article (copy attached) which suggested that Glenn's real mother and father may be absent from the family home due to long-term incarceration and death. MC confessed immediately to being Glenn's grandmother, not his mother. When asked by LB why she

100

had lied, explaining that it was not so unusual to have a grandparent assuming legal guardianship, MC explained that, whilst this may well be so, the exact circumstances surrounding the arrangement were not usually so extreme as in this case. She further elaborated that she felt it easier not to mention the truth for fear that it would lead to further awkward questions which might affect her grandson's being offered a nursery place and which, even if he were, could ultimately impact on others preconceptions of him, stating that she didn't want him 'tarred with the same brush'. LB informed MC that she understood.

LB then moved on to the issue of transportation, asking MC for the specific details of how GC had travelled to nursery today and yesterday. MC confirmed that she herself had brought him in both times but that she had let him make his own way for the last hundred yards whilst she watched from the corner of a side-turning further down the road to make sure that he got in safely. LB asked why she didn't just bring him all the way, explaining that a hundred yards was still potential distance enough for him to wander into the road and have an accident. MC explained that she believed GC to be extremely intelligent, remarkably independent for his age and highly unlikely to do so, confirming that the only reason she didn't come all the way to the door was due to the heavy bruising around her eye and cheekbone and a cut lip. She claimed that she didn't want people seeing her looking the way she did and making rash judgements as to how it might have happened. LB asked her how in fact it did happen to which MC replied that she knew it sounded cliché but that she walked into a door, expanding that she was embarrassed, that it was a clear glass patio door which she'd thought was open but wasn't. LB reminded MC that she had a duty of care towards all of the children under her wing and was obligated to pass on any suspicions she might have pertaining to their domestic situation where they may be at risk of or even exposed to third party violence. She closed by asking MC if there was anything else she felt might be worthy of mention, particularly with this in mind. MC appeared to think about the question for some time before confirming that she had nothing further to add.

Details of Further Action:

1) MC to escort GC to door each morning and check in with a member of staff. SOC / LB to monitor.

2) LB to contact LADO (Local Authority Designated Child Protection Officer) / Social Services with immediate

effect to notify them of findings and
seek further advice and guidance.

H.

Today is sign-on day. I like an early appointment, requested they change my slot even, so I can get it over with first thing and get on with my day without the weight of it hanging over me like a dark cloud just waiting for the first signs of spitting - which funnily enough is something you see a lot of whilst waiting outside the Job Centre for the doors to open. I'm there with the others though, unlike like most of them, not because I'm desperate for the cash. I live frugally, don't want for much, inherited a little money – well quite a bit actually – enough to pay outright for the one bedroom flat I now live in anyway. I even have a few savings put by for a rainy day – although if that's a metaphor for a dark period in your life then I'd best get spending. No, to tell the truth, I could probably live quite comfortably without the extra financial help but I want my stamp paid, my National Insurance contributions, if I'm to rely on a basic state pension when I'm older – assuming of course that the government isn't funding my cost of living, a roof over my head and porridge in my belly, in some other way.

So, as I say, I stand with the other reprobates, the serial dossers, those who've paid in the least but withdraw the most. Predictably, a young lad puffs on his cigarette with all the vigour of an asthma sufferer on an inhaler, letting the smoke drift into my face as he gobs a yellow nicotine-pool onto the pavement. His girlfriend – presumably, but who can say with this lot? – accepts the cigarette that he kindly offers to share with her, taking a similarly long drag, letting the inch-long dog-end break off and flutter down like ashen snow-fall on to her distended, with-child stomach – this one is heavily, unquestionably pregnant – and the head of the infant slumbering softly in the buggy in front of her. Poor little sod. What chance does he have? Or his embryonic sibling? - assuming of course that the passive, pre-natal damage there, hasn't already been done. Doesn't he care about his unborn child? Obviously not. It's probably not his.

He catches me looking down, turning my nose up at his puddle of bodily residue and clearly finds my disapproval equally abhorrent. Taking the final dying remains of the pale orange stogie from his partner, he takes a long, exaggerated toke, blows the exhalant mixture of carbon and carbon dioxide in my direction, hocks loudly like a choleric Arab and spits a flourescent green globule onto the floor again, missing my feet by inches - either a very good shot or intended not to miss. I look around. Nobody else bats an eyelid. What the hell is wrong with these people? I feel the rage building up inside me like floodwaters at a dam, the pressure too much for it to take, the integrity of the structure compromised in places as fine hairline cracks begin to ripple through it, small jets appearing sporadically across its surface, spouting outward in highly pressurised jettisons as the cracks come to an end in first tiny holes, growing ever more gaping as chunks of masonry tumble crashing into the previously still, calm waters below. I'm

105

not taking it anymore. I'm going to say something. Somebody has to. I feel the blood drain from my face, the fight-or-flight response sending it instead to my limbs where it will be of greater use. I don't care if he *has* got his woman and kid with him. I choose fight.

But I.... *he's* saved by a sudden call to arms from a click behind us as the security guard opens the door and lets everybody in. He's lucky - will never know just how close he came.

As we file in, I make a point of going out of my way to smile knowingly at the security guard, a look that says *I understand, I've been there before myself, got the blood (egg) stained T-shirt.* Security guard at the dole office? I imagine he gets a lot of grief. Bet he doesn't get paid nearly as much as he should either, putting himself on the front line in potential harm's way every day like that. Perhaps he thrives on it, the buzz of unpredictable, ever-present danger, bubbling beneath the surface, about to kick off at any time – but his face says otherwise.

So I sit down and am disappointed to be told that Jenny, my usual Personal Adviser, is off sick today. I express my concerns, my hope that it's nothing serious. I ask if there's any chance I could maybe get her address to send her a get-well-soon card. This new face looks at me as if I'm some sort of stalker then explains robotically, as if stating the perfectly obvious to an imbecile, that to do so would be a breach of their confidentiality regulations. She suggests instead that perhaps I leave one with reception if I really *must,* that someone will make sure she gets it. The way she says it though – anyone would think I'd just asked if she knew a good recipe for slow-cooked rabbit, rather than

106

offer a kind sentiment. I have no faith that a card would ever get to her in this way - I've dealt with reception before – so that's the end of that.

And that sets the tone for the remainder of what *was* my looked forward to fortnightly meeting. She asks me the same routine questions as normal, though not in the warm, supportive way that Jenny usually does - letting me know that she's on my side, that we're in this, working on finding me a job together, that that's *her* job. No, she interrogates me. I feel as though I'm talking to a faceless voice behind a bright, blinding spot-light, trying to think on my feet with lightning speed to evade the accusatorily delivered questions she fires at me, trying to catch me out. I don't know why I should be made to feel so nervous, shifting uncomfortably in my seat from buttock to buttock, sitting on the backs of my hands to prevent over-gesticulation. I have nothing to hide. I always tell the truth. I may add a bit extra sometimes but I never leave stuff out.

Twenty minutes later and we – she – has 'agreed' to put me forward for a number of low-level, poorly-paid jobs that I already know won't last, assuming of course that I even get one of them in the first place. She tells me not to worry, that a couple of them don't involve a face-to-face interview, that it's all done over the phone or even in one case that you all but get the job based solely on her referral. I *wasn't* worried, but now I am. What does she mean by that? Her saying it merely makes me think that perhaps I should have cause to worry in the first place. Is she saying that she doesn't think I'd come across well at interview? Again, I don't know why I should let it bother me. It's not

107

like I want any of the jobs she suggested anyway. But it does.

I of course explained that I believed the positions she identified to be beneath me, my general level of intellect and ability, but this seemed merely to irritate her, as if I were being obnoxious, had delusions of grandeur above my station, was saying it solely to make her life difficult and delay her rigidly scheduled next appointment. It's not like I was expecting to take over the Virgin empire or anything - I just felt I had a little more to offer than minimum wage grunt work. She pulled out a printed copy of my updated CV from my brown card file, browsed down it as though my entire being were embodied within those two sheets of dog-eared A4, then arbitrarily dismissed my misguided self-appraisal, my future vocational success in her excessively moisturised, ostentatiously cheap-gold-ringed hands.

'That may well be the case' she patronised, as though she didn't believe it to be anything of the sort, 'but unfortunately you have no formal qualifications to speak of and an employment history that can only be described as .... checkered. Not exactly what most of our clients are seeking for their more prestigious roles I'm afraid'.

But she isn't *afraid* at all. Anything but. Her words contain not the slightest hint of regret. If anything, she's pleased - smug even - a tiny victorious battle in a war which she can never win.

But I know when to quit so I thank her for her time, ask her to pass on my well wishes to Jenny - which she agrees to do but I know she won't – and then I get up and leave, smiling again at my security guard brother on the way out.

108

Next stop the Post Office. Oh I get to visit all the local high spots. I get in line and shuffle up and down the chrome-poled, red-roped aisle, in no hurry, glad of the time being killed outside the solitary confines of my flat. I wait, watching whilst the counter staff attempt to establish conversations, required transactions, with half (three quarters, more like) deaf little old ladies through thickened security glass; ten minutes of which might result in a second-class stamp being affixed to a regular letter which could've just been put through the slot of the post-box on the pavement outside. I wonder at what stage in their life they, the elderly, decide to give in and get themselves one of those tartan shopping trolleys. The place is always heavily congested with them. I wonder where you even buy them. I don't recall ever having seen them in the shops – but then I suppose I haven't been looking. Probably the same place that the old boys buy those beige, zip-up, weather-proof jackets and soft, grey, Velcro-fastening shoes. Argos maybe? They have everything in there. I might find out soon enough – their warehouse is one of the places I could end up if Jenny's stand-in has her way.

Eventually I get to the counter and withdraw a hundred pounds. I like dealing in cash, don't trust cards – you never know who's getting hold of your details – but I also like the feeling I get when I ask for it. A hundred pounds. It still sounds like such a lot of money to me – just like it always did when I was a kid. A hundred pounds. *How would you like it?* They always ask. *Fifties please* I say, as if there will be a stack of them. I always say it quite loudly too, kidding myself that I need to speak up for the same reason that the pensioners can't be heard - because of the transparent sound barrier between the teller and myself - but deep down I know that it's because I want the other customers to hear. It's one of the few times when I feel like a success – well, not such a failure at least. I march out of there, chest puffed and head held high, like Rockefeller.

Finally, wallet metaphorically bulging, I head for the supermarket to do my weekly shop. I have a fairly standard list of items that I always purchase, assuming of course that I don't go in there with an empty stomach and end up treating myself to all sorts of indulgent extras. Fortunately it's not been too long since I had breakfast so I pretty much stick to the list. Unfortunately, this means that, because I probably know where everything is better than most of the staff, the visit doesn't take me long, meaning more time to use up back at home. I slow myself down and loiter around the home-wares section, picking up scented candles and sniffing them, squishing goose-down-effect pillows and generally stopping to pick up and handle anything on a shelf with a red discount sticker in front of it; the original price almost irrelevant, a non-consideration in my simplistically marketed perception of this unnecessary, must-have bargain. I place a set of kitchen knives in my trolley. Seventy per-cent off. Seventy! I can't believe my luck – that there are still any left. Perhaps they've only just reduced them. I spend so long wandering up and down the aisles that I eventually attract the attention of the security guard, who eyes me suspiciously. *Another* security guard. I think what a measure of ourselves it is that we need so many of them to protect us from *us* in the first place. At first I'm a little offended by his nonchalant ambles back and forth which are fooling nobody, least of all a former industry insider like me, but then I change my mind, thinking that I don't blame him, that I *have* been there for some time with an ulterior motive, albeit stealing no more than a little time. At least he's conscientious, trying to do the job he's paid for. It's a shame a few more people don't take a leaf out of his book, a little more professional pride in their work.

I smile at him, one ex-security guard to a current - in the same way that fellow VW Beetle drivers acknowledge each other with a flash of headlights as they pass on the road - then head for the tills, intermittently held up by dawdling shoppers who seem to have absolutely no spatial awareness, no concept that other customers use this facility too and are waiting at their shoulder to pass, hoping not to have to resort to a cough or *excuse me* which, no matter how politely delivered, invariably receives an affronted glare.

I've been keeping an approximate mental tally as I worked my way around the store and am pleased when the figure announced by the till-worker matches exactly with what I had in mind. It comes to just under fifty pounds – a little more than normal but that'll be the knives – which is good news. It means that I'll get two opportunities to pay with a fifty, to see the look of admiration on an assistant's face as I hand it over, apologising for not having anything smaller. I bag up the items, savour the moment of payment then head home.

By one-thirty, I've already unpacked, made and eaten lunch and done all my housework chores. Based on an approximate bed-time of eleven-thirty, that means I still

111

have about ten hours to fill. I empty my wallet of its bulge of receipts, collected over a couple of weeks, and place them in the flip-bin in the cupboard under the kitchen counter, taking care not to inadvertently discard the unspent fifty which I take out and look at, holding it up to the light to check the watermark and the silver strip like they do in the shops. I've never really studied one before. I look at the picture of Elizabeth and wonder if, amongst all her many regal dignitary engagements, she ever gets time to pause and reflect, think about by what pure random chance it was that she was born into the position that she was – if she ever thinks about how she managed to end up there, against all the odds; how, amongst all those many millions of frantic, wriggling sperm, hers was the one that got through, won the epic channel swim to the ova, head-butted its way through and then, not satisfied with this monumental accomplishment, went on to become arguably the most senior ranking figure in the social hierarchy of our planet, amongst the many billions of other lives she could've otherwise inherited – mine for example. And I take a strange comfort in this thought – that the Queen of England is no better than me – only luckier – that I'm already a winner - that we all are, by the sheer nature of our very existence. Perhaps she'd even kill to switch places, to trade a day surrounded by fawning, curtseying, awe-struck subjects, shaking hands and white-gloved waving, for twenty-four hours of glorious anonymity, of a normality that she will never know. Perhaps the grass always appears greener, even when you're standing in the Garden of Eden. Perhaps. Perhaps not.

I'm not sure how old she was when the image on the pink banknote was first created but it strikes me that she hasn't changed that much over the years – perhaps it's the perennial royal hairstyle. She looks pretty. Pretty in pink. And that's when I decide what to do to fill the next couple of hours.

By the time the movie ends, what with the various pauses for tea and bathroom breaks, it's getting on for late afternoon. I eject the old VHS cassette from the video player, thinking how much I enjoyed it, that I should really think about replacing it on DVD. I don't yet have a Blu-Ray player but it's definitely something I'm considering. I love movies almost as much as I love books – and for the same reason too; the temporary immersion, the escape that they provide from the real world. Sometimes, of course, the one they transport you to can be traumatic, harrowing even, but that only makes you appreciate what you've already got a little more, so it's win win really. I liked Duckie the best – could really relate to him. Putting the video-tape away in its designated slot on the shelf in my wardrobe, I return to the lounge and sit down on the sofa, switching off the video with the remote controller. The blank, granulated screen is replaced by mainstream TV- a commercial break predictably. There's an advert for a dog-food boasting ingredients of prime quality beef fillet. It looks genuinely appetising, the sort of thing you wouldn't necessarily send back at a posh restaurant if it was served up in meagre portions with a sprig of decorative parsley atop, ridiculously over-priced, labelled bourgeois beef bourguignon and washed down with a glass of fine, velvety Merlot. I wonder if aliens landed on our planet, whether

113

they'd think it strange that we kill one animal, one sentient being of a different species from ourselves, to feed another. Running with the idea still further, I wonder if they'd think it the most terrible waste that we bury our deceased in expensive, varnished mahogany boxes in the ground, delaying the process of re-assimilation back to the earth they came from, when they could instead provide such an expansive source of readily available food to our already over-populated and under-resourced floating spheroid. These aren't my own ideas you understand. I'm not suggesting that we should do this. I'm just saying that I wonder if that's what *they* would think, whether their frames of reference, their boundaries of normality, of acceptability, would be markedly different from our own. Perhaps that's exactly what we need, a fresh pair of completely objective eyes – and who knows, they might have ten a-piece. These meandering thoughts are what fill my empty spaces, the time spent alone without other voices with which to exchange pleasantries, only those in my own head.

I think I mentioned before, perhaps indirectly, that I'm an animal lover. I'm not a vegetarian – I'm discussing the possibility of cannibalism as a sustainable human (and pet?) food source for God's sake - but I'd like to be. I'm a firm believer in Karma, that what goes around comes around. By that token, a life spent eating other living things doesn't bode too well for the after-life. Perhaps I was a carnivore in my previous incarnation – might explain a few things. But no, I justify my dietary choices, get my conscience off on a technicality; that I'm anatomically omnivorous, my dental structure, digestive system evolutionarily designed to eat meat. But by the same token, I guess you could argue that the very fact that I've evolved a conscience in the first place should negate that argument.

I consider going to the gym, to work off some of the surplus energy that I feel building up inside me. If nothing else, it will get me out of the house too. But then I remember that, among the household chores completed when I got back earlier, I put on a fresh wash-load and my kit is in the machine, doing a spin-class without me.

I think about getting some dinner on the go. I like opening the fridge when I've just been food shopping, seeing it all crammed with groceries like that, its purpose in life being fully realised. I look at the various packets on the middle shelf, the one where I always put the meat items. There's diced pork, chicken breasts (free-range of course – I'm not a monster), meatballs. I was planning on using the chicken to make a nice stir-fry but as I pick them up and hold them in their hermetically sealed final resting place (notwithstanding my stomach, the toilet bowl, the local sewage system and whatever else comes next) suddenly I'm not so hungry anymore. The word 'breast' on the packaging makes me feel nauseous, the anatomical reference somehow anthropomorphising the contents. Anthropomorphising. There's another great word for my list (I never did start that). I'm not showing off. It means…well, I don't wish to patronise you - you probably already know what it means. If you don't then maybe just look it up. So anyway, I finally decide on a stir-fry regardless, just without the protein. I top and tail mange-tout, snap the bases off some asparagus spears, crush lemongrass, split and de-seed a couple of red chillies and toss it all in a pan of hot oil with some pak-choi and tender-stem broccoli.

It's delicious. I can't even say that I really missed the chicken. Maybe vegetarianism isn't such an idealistic pipe-dream after all. Perhaps there's still time to get my Karmic balance back on track and have better luck next time, though I don't want to wish my life away. Or maybe I do - maybe that's *just* what I want.

I watch The Simpsons and a number of quiz shows, impressing no-one with my encyclopaedic general knowledge. I'm still in front of the box by the time the early evening news comes on announcing yet more atrocities and self-annihilation and that's my cue to get up off my behind. I potter around the house, keeping one eye and ear on the TV, waiting for the familiar exit theme-music which lets me know that I'm just a commercial break away from the mid-week evening movie. I've been looking forward to it all week. It's *Oldie but Goodie* month. They've been showing classics from the eighties, most of which I've already seen but are well worth watching again, particularly given how long it's been since my first viewing.

I get the washing and drying-up done so that conditions are perfect, so that I can sit down and properly relax when the film starts. I use the loo even though I don't really need it yet, because I don't have Sky and can't pause live TV - though there's the ad breaks, *always* the ad-breaks – and make a cup of tea, taking it to join a handful of custard creams and myself on the sofa, just in time to catch the snare-drum-roll, to watch the search-lights shine their beautiful sweeping beams.

116

Names come up onto the screen, announcing the Hollywood thespians whose make believe lives I am due to share this evening:

Patrick Bergin

Julia Roberts

Great. I love Julia Roberts. Pretty Woman is probably one of my favourite movies of all time. Certainly very accurately named. She's absolutely beautiful – reminds me of a swan. The part I like best is when Richard Gere catches that slimy little weasel partner of his mistreating her character Vivienne and lays him out flat. He really lets him have it. I love that bit.

The film is called Sleeping with the Enemy. I know the name - rings a bell - but don't think I've seen this one before. Excellent. Even better.

Only it isn't. I'm not sure why but I find it hard to watch and only manage to make it through about half an hour before I turn it off. And I don't even mean that I just turn over, switch to another channel. No, I mean that I switch it off *completely*, getting up to unplug it at the wall even, and find myself ten minutes later still staring at the blank, lifeless screen. Except that somehow, even though it's fully off, the power completely disconnected, it isn't entirely lifeless. Dark shadows move in the reflection of the glass, as though the film were still running, eventually

117

replaced by my own face in the screen as I realise that I've been daydreaming, gone to another place. But now I'm back.

I don't switch the TV back on again. I don't listen to the radio. I don't pick up my book. I don't do *anything*. I just sit there – in the darkness, because I always turn all the lights off when I watch a movie, for full cinematic effect – for a *long* time. A couple of hours maybe. I couldn't honestly say what I was doing there for all that time. I don't remember having any of my weird 'alone time' thoughts; ideas that could serve mankind for the greater good. I don't even remember having any inane ones, trivial nonsense of no use to anyone. Nothing. It's as if my brain, like the TV set, had been temporarily unplugged.

Perhaps it's a result of all that immobility but I now have that trapped inside my own skin feeling again that I get from time to time. It's as though my insides are a glass jar, my energy levels flowing to the surface but having got there, rather than break and be allowed to overflow, the meniscus keeps stretching, blowing up like a liquid bubble inside me that I can't get a pin at to burst, pushing everything else outward, impossible to ignore. I know the press-ups won't help – they never do. I know that getting some air and taking a walk just might.

So I pull on my shoes and jacket and take a right out the front door. I know it's late by now but it's very quiet out all the same, Wednesday clearly not high on the list for most people's choice of a night out. I walk. I walk past fried chicken shops, late-night supermarket locals with youngsters, certainly a lot younger than they should be, sitting cross-legged on the floor outside, hoping for some

118

small shower of change to rain down on them, passed on by their donors from the black plastic till-trays of the serving staff inside. The garish tube lighting inside is softened by the toughened plate glass, washing over me as I pass, the occasional swoosh of a sweeping vehicle's headlights catching me too in their periphery. And I walk. And I walk some more. I walk for so long that before I know it I find I've unknowingly ventured into an area with which I'm unfamiliar. High-rises loom out of the ground, their monolithic dark silhouettes against the inky blue horizon sparking some equally dark, distant memory which blackens my mood. All those grey lives crammed into those precarious, tall, grey towers. I wonder what qualifications you need to get an entry level job in demolition. I make a mental note to ask Jenny when she's back in. At least, I hope she'll be back. The thought that she might not be darkens my mood even further.

A late night convenience store represents a last island of humanity before I sail on into a dark abyss of empty tenement blocks and run-down residential properties, their flaking, chip-boarded windows unlit from within. The human silence and crisp, still air give a feeling of calm, but it's that before a storm rather than a Zen oneness with everything. It's cold, the dragon-breath in front of my face serving as a constant reminder that I'm still alive, that I haven't unwittingly ventured over to some supernatural dark side, some Twilight Zone of non-existence, discovering when I turn to find my way back that I'm unable, that it no longer exists. And who would miss me after all? Jenny at the Job Centre? She might not even be back. Who does that leave? Now that I own my own flat

119

outright, I don't even have a landlord. Not even a mortgage company to chase payment arrears. So who then? Some faceless worker at a call-centre when I don't pay my gas? Would they even send anyone round? Perhaps a couple of polite reminder letters, followed by a more angry red, are all that stand between me and oblivion, my time on this earth cut off forever, along with my utility services. Aren't walks meant to be good for clearing your head? Perhaps I should've just stayed in and put on another film, something jolly. But I needed the exercise, couldn't stand to sit there looking at that screen a moment longer. I look up at the street lamps, positioned too far apart so that their weak amber glows don't join hands, leaving dark patches between them, as if they've had a blazing row and can't leave but don't wish to communicate with each other either. The night is so cold that the air immediately beneath their weak bulbs seems to breathe, the stifled breath of a child playing dead.

And suddenly I'm not alone on the street. I hear the distant clack of heels echoing in the nothingness before I see the young woman walking up ahead of me. She's dawdling, apparently in no hurry to be anywhere quickly, despite being dressed for much warmer weather, and so I soon start to gain on her. Except this time, I don't like it, don't get a buzz out of the fact that she may be unnerved by my presence, just the two of us, alone together out on these empty streets, no witnesses. Not that she seems in the least bit bothered by my presence. I'm not sure how I know this. Just something in her posture, her general demeanour perhaps, tells me that she couldn't care less, is more comfortable in this environment than me even. In a reversal of my previous move, I cross the road to the opposing pavement, the one that she isn't walking on, in an attempt to show her that she needn't worry, that I mean no harm. As I start to come alongside her, keeping my head facing forward to suggest that I have no wish to ogle her, despite the brevity of her skirt and contrasting longevity of leg, I'm surprised to catch her in the corner of my eye, crossing the street towards *me*. I turn to look at her and she's most definitely aiming *for* me. I smile a half-smile, barely even that really, one which could be quickly turned into something else, an innocent biting of the lower lip perhaps, if it appears that I'm mistaken.

'Hey' she says, leaving me in no doubt.

'Hey' I echo.

'You got a light?' she says.

'No, sorry. Afraid I don't smoke' I apologise, wishing for the first time in my life that I did, that I had something in common with this woman that meant I could drag the moment out a little longer – if you'll pardon the pun. She isn't exactly what you'd call beautiful but, with a little more luck, she could've been. She reminds me of Angel Hair, only a budget version – same long blond hair, but the roots are showing;   same gazelle-like legs, but they're shod in cheap vinyl stilettos a size too big, meaning that they slip off her heels as she walks – no doubt the reason for the bloody, bunched–up sticking plaster which is falling away there, due for imminent replacement. She sports a bomber jacket with fake fur collars – at least I hope they're fake – with what looks like very little underneath; certainly not appropriate winter wear anyway. Perhaps she's on her way back from a club. Her teeth are all there but, like the

121

lamp-posts, appear to have fallen out with each other. A childhood brace would've worked wonders for her, transforming the overall effect of what is clearly a very pretty face under all that poorly applied make-up. The thick foundation and exaggerated lipstick make me think of a clown – the only thing missing, though notable by its absence, the tear beneath one of her iridescent blue-shadowed eyes. 'What are you doing out so late on your own?' I say suddenly, almost too quickly, a Tourette's tick of a question before I change my mind. It's not often that a person – a woman no less – initiates conversation with me, however insignificant their motive. My own question surprises me but I'm glad now that it's out there, that I've at least tried.

'I could ask you the same thing' she says, smiling 'I've not seen you around here before.'

'Do you know everyone round here then?' I ask, thinking that it's a funny thing for her to have said.

'Pretty much' she says.

'So, what *are* you doing?' I repeat, realising that she didn't answer.

'What are you, my dad?' she asks. 'Ere, you're not Old Bill are you?'

'Old...? No I was just worried for you, that's all. The streets aren't safe at night for a young girl to be walking around places like this on your own.'

'Places like this?'

'You know, deserted, no one around. You never know who might be out, prowling the streets, looking for someone vulnerable.'

'It's not so bad' she says, convincing no one, least of all herself.

'So, what *are* you doing?' I press, keen to keep the communication going. 'On your way back from a disco or something?' I say, immediately regretting the choice of word.

'Ha ha. Disco. Classic. You're funny' she says, in a way that suggests she means in a good way. 'No, I work around here.'

'Oh. On your way home? You've been working late. What do you do, if you don't mind me asking?'

'I'm in customer service' she says 'Actually, I'm still working. The late shift. Just came out for a cigarette break but realised I'd used my last one. That's when I saw you.'

I look around, the buildings around us all dark, wondering which one her office is in. 'Oh, nice. Well I was going to offer to walk you home but so long as you're ok…' I say, making to leave, though whether continuing on or back the way I came I haven't quite decided. Perhaps she senses my indecision.

'Hey' she says 'I've got an idea. You seem like a nice guy. How do you fancy doing something?'

'Something?' I say, hardly able to believe my ears 'Together you mean?'

'Yes' she says, the *of course* silent though implied. 'You and me. A few drinks. Have some fun. My place isn't far from here. What do you say? You can walk me home, make sure I get there in one piece. Not chopped up into lots of little ones by one of those evil night-prowlers you warned me about.'

'Are you sure?' I say, and then, like an idiot 'Aren't you meant to be working? Won't you get into trouble?' 'Oh yeah' she says, regretfully 'Good point.' She looks at her watch, as if weighing up possible options. 'Look. I get paid by the hour. I've only got another couple left. I can't expect you to wait for me but....'

'But what?' I say, thinking that I'd be quite happy to wait, to catch hypothermia, in exchange for a little womanly warmth and affection.

'No, it's really cheeky' she says.

'Just say it. I'm not easily offended' I push, thinking that if that's the case then why *have* I been so often?'

'Well, if you were happy to cover my lost earnings, I could punch out now, just only get paid for the time I've worked. My boss would be fine with it.'

'How much would you lose?' I ask, thinking that I still have the unspent fifty in my wallet.

'A score should about do it?' she suggests, the tone bartering. It seems a positive bargain. I'd have forsaken the fifty.

'Twenty pounds?' I say, just to be sure.

'Yes handsome. Twenty pounds. Sterling. I'll make sure you get your money's worth. I promise you'll have a good time. What do you say?'

What I *want* to say is that I've already had my money's worth - that I'd have paid that just to hear her call me handsome. 'Ok. That sounds nice.' I say.

'You're funny' she says again, though this time I'm not sure why. I like it though.

'So, where's your place then?' I ask, waiting for her to lead the way.

124

'Money first' she says 'No offence but, like you said, there are some dodgy characters around.'

'Oh, yes, of course' I say, fumbling for my wallet. 'Sorry, afraid I only have this' I say, holding out the pink note, half-expecting her to ask me if I have anything smaller.

'Tycoon, eh?' she laughs 'Proper landed on my feet here. Like that Julia Roberts in Pretty Woman' she says, and I think that it's a sign, Cupid's arrow shot across my bow. 'Don't worry Dickie. I've got a friend lives just along from here. Will nip in and get some change.'

It's not until she says it that I realise I haven't even asked her name yet, that she hasn't asked mine – and her in customer service and all. I go to correct her before realising that she's assigned me a pseudonym based on Richard Gere. I've had worse nicknames. *A lot worse.* I decide to keep shtum.

We walk along the street and she links my arm. As we stroll she jabbers away, so much so that I barely need to speak myself - which is good; at least I can't say the wrong thing and mess it all up like I usually do. I think I detect a faint whiff of alcohol on her which surprises me as she's just come straight from work, but then I realise that she might have had a drink at lunchtime – probably entertaining clients - or maybe even that the smell is coming from the streets themselves. I'm in heaven – I just never expected it to be quite so dark.

A block along and she slows up at a doorway, a black rectangular shadow in the grey brick wall to our left. 'This is the place' she says 'Just wait here. Won't be long.'

And she's gone, a white rabbit down a warren, the black hole in the wall swallowing her up like a beautiful shooting star, leaving its trail of glittering dust floating down onto the pavement next to me.

I wait, allowing myself a gormless, self-satisfied smile now that she's not around to see it. I don't want to scare her off by looking too keen. I've made that mistake before. I'm only glad that she's a talker. The silence now feels even more so, now that she's gone, more so than it was before I bumped into her.

I'm still waiting, the cold reclaiming its grip, when I hear the sound of movement from inside and footsteps coming down a staircase. They sound different; perhaps she's changed out of those ridiculously uncomfortable looking heels she was wearing. I'm amazed she wears them all day for work but figure that she's probably on the phone seated at a desk most of the time. But then I remember that this isn't her place. Unless of course she's borrowed a pair from her friend.

The metal door scrapes open and out steps a figure with whom she certainly wouldn't share shoes. He looks at me and, without saying anything, lights up a cigarette, the plastic disposable lighter revealing sunken cheekbones set in a pock-marked face. He isn't particularly big built – taller though probably weighs less than me – but he has that look, the look that I talked about previously, the look that says that he's not a very nice person.

I go to say something, to ask if the young woman whose name I still don't know is coming out soon when he speaks first.

'Sorry. Change of plan' he says.

126

'I'm sorry?'

'Skye won't be entertaining you this evening after all.'

Well at least now I know her name.

'Are you sure?' I say, thinking that maybe he's mixed my new friend up with her friend who lives here, as it dawns on me suddenly that this *is* the friend, that she hadn't referred to their gender.

'I'm sure' he says, not looking at me, focusing on the smoke rings that he's perfected as they float on up, dissolving into the darkness.

'But why?'

'I don't consider it in the best interests of her career' he says. For a thug, he's articulate, I'll give him that.

'And who are you?' I ask.

'Her agent.'

'Agent?' I repeat. 'For what? She told me she was in customer service.'

'Yeah, ok' he says, a mild smirk of amusement crossing his lips, falling short of his eyes as he puffs out another perfect wobbling circle.

'I'm serious' I say.

'Look mate' he says, 'She's a…performer. If you want to label it customer service, relationship manager, whatever, then that's fine by me. Either way, your booking has now been cancelled.'

'Sorry' I say, becoming exasperated 'But I think there's been some misunderstanding…'

'Look mate' he says, his tone taking a more sinister turn as he steps forward into the streetlight, 'It's *you* that doesn't understand. Now piss off before I call security.'

'Security?' I say, looking around me, thinking that he's bluffing.

'Yeah' he says, opening his denim jacket with the sheepskin collar to reveal the handle of a lock-knife sticking out from an inside pocket. 'Security.'

'What about my money?' I say, already stepping back off the kerb and into the road.

'Deposit' he says 'Non-refundable. Bookings may be subject to cancellation or change at any time. Should've read the small print.'

I never signed anything I think. *I never signed up for any of this.*

j.

Glenn Chambers lay there listening to the shrill calls from downstairs announcing time to get up for school. Anne, his fifth foster mother in as many years, seemed different from the others; he had a good feeling about her – that this one might actually work out long-term, last the distance, at least until he was deemed a young adult and able to make his own way in the world. He actually referred to her as his foster *mum*, rather than his foster *carer*, which was hopefully a good sign. Her thick Irish brogue was always going to identify her as an unlikely birth mother, an immediately obvious separation between them, but ironically this was one of the things that he'd liked about her most, that drew him closer to her on first meeting. He wasn't sure why but something about the way she spoke felt comfortable, familiar, like he'd known her all his life; an oversees relative that had stepped into the breach to take up her Fairy God-motherly duties. Unfortunately the same couldn't be said for his latest school, the most recent of many new starts, each of which had come as a package deal complete with complimentary guardian. He hugged his bunched up quilt, holding on for dear life, spooning it with the desperate embrace of a long-lost lover. He *really* didn't want to go in but he'd pulled his quota of credible sickies already this term. One more and there'd be letters sent home, asking Anne to come up to the school to discuss his attendance record and he didn't want to put her out, not when she'd been so very good to him. Short of serious, irrefutable personal injury, a broken limb or the like, it looked like he'd be going in on a regular basis now for the foreseeable future. The idea of self harming crossed his mind but he just didn't have it in him; that and the fact that he liked to think he'd put the Ed Psych visits behind him now. He didn't want to rake up that whole unpleasant business all over again - patronising, bespectacled strangers droning on in affected empathetic monotone, rummaging around in his past like salivating pensioners at a jumble sale, delving ever deeper into the moth-eaten cast-offs of his childhood, keen to be the first to unearth some precious, valuable little find for themselves that no one else had spotted, more in pursuit of professional recognition than anything else. Paradoxically, his choosing not to engineer personal injury and go in was probably the decision most likely to result in his sustaining one. It was never going to be easy for a hormonal teenager to come in late in the day and attempt to ingratiate himself with an already established dynamic of strongly forged groups and individual friendships, but even more so when that newcomer had a quirky appearance and arguably even more quirky personality. It wasn't just the hair-lip either, which all attempts to cover with the first downy dusting of adolescent moustache had only exacerbated still further. Unusual physical features could make or break a pupil yes, but it wasn't the anatomical feature itself that dictated which way the pendulum of judgement swung. For some, an atypical physical 'defect' or even social trait could mark them out as special, the difference a blessing, the young person's character either built around and upon it or dictated by it. It didn't matter whether it was a lazy eye, freakish height (up or down) or something as innocuous as ginger hair; it was how you carried it, embraced it, presented it to your peers that confirmed it to them as gift or curse. It was all in the packaging. Unfortunately Glenn Chambers' was a plain, brown, cardboard box.

He thought of what the day ahead held for him, thinking that he should be used to it by now, the jeers and taunts or worse, the ostracism – of all the many moves, the countless upheavals in his life, it was Coventry where he'd found the greatest stability. The thought made him feel physically sick. He could quite feasibly argue the case for an upset stomach and his conscience would be clear. But no, if anything that would only off-set one of those occasions when he'd been creative with the truth. He was going in.

There were some pluses though. St Michael's Roman Catholic School for Boys – his non-faith entry gained by right of present legal guardianship - was only a ten minute walk away from his current residence, meaning no need for difficult bus journeys from which there was no escaping the usual torrent of missiles, the flicked ears, the lit matches extinguished on the back of the neck, the contents of his bag spilled out and thrown around, makeshift balls for impromptu games of piggy-in-the-middle, only to be discarded – on the floor, requiring him to crawl around frantically collecting them from under seats before his stop came, between legs which kicked out at him, if he were lucky; out the window if he wasn't – when they became bored and hungry for the next torment-based event in the persecution pentathlon. Also, as the name suggests, there were no girls, meaning no embarrassing awkwardness or further mass-mocking when he misread the signs, mistaking sympathy or sarcasm for genuine affection, his unrequited love made public and turned against him into hatred.

A faith school, morning assembly was always pretty full on. The Head-teacher stood in his raised pulpit, next to a large organ, the huge brass pipes covering the whole of the main hall's front wall to his left, looking down on his congregation, arms outstretched beseechingly like Jesus himself reading excerpts from the Bible, extolling life lessons which presumably he expected his students to carry with them throughout their time roaming the hallowed corridors of his school. That morning he read from Revelation:

'…But the fearful, and unbelieving, and the abominable, and murderers, and whoremongers, and sorcerers, and idolaters, and all liars, shall have their part in the lake which burneth with fire and brimstone: which is the second death.'

Of the nearly one thousand bodies in the hall, including the teachers – possibly even the speaker himself - there was only one that was really sitting up and truly listening, taking note of the words being spoken. Pretty heavy stuff. But what did they mean? So, were the fearful judged to be no better than murderers? Wasn't the fear punishment enough in itself? And who decided what constituted *abominable*? Where was the line? And what about justifiable cause? He'd heard that you should turn the other cheek but what about an eye for an eye? It was confusing.

132

He made a note to look into it further, pay more attention in Religious Studies, raise his hand and ask a few questions, at the risk of singling himself out, providing the inevitable added material for his peers to use against him – no longer a mere freak, now a Bible-bashing, religious one to boot – alienating himself still further. Whatever – nothing he did would make any difference for the better anyway. He'd learned that much at least. His attempts to be different, more like his peers, make friends, had only ever backfired horribly. Might as well just be himself and suffer the consequences. Better to be disliked for someone you were than liked for someone you weren't. He'd read that somewhere – although wasn't at all convinced it were true. No, if he could choose, he'd take the latter right now every time – although thus far hadn't even managed to get people to like him for who he wasn't.

The morning panned out much as expected. Boys fought laughingly, jostling for position, rushing to their seats at the beginning of each lesson, not because they were good students, eager to get the learning started, but because none of them wanted to get left with the only seat remaining - the *electric chair* as it became known - the one next to Chambers, the weirdo new lad. He ignored them, pretending not to notice, which of course only further perpetuated their perception of him as an anti-social odd-ball. The value of the adjoining seat would change later in the term as its obvious merits became apparent: that Glenn Chambers was easily the brightest kid in the class and therefore a useful untapped resource ripe for plagiarism. At least in this single sex school he wouldn't misinterpret their leaning across and surreptitious glances as interest in *him*,

133

in connecting with him on some human, non-academic level. Even so, he made no attempt to shield his answers, showed no indignation at the infringement, reluctant to stand in the way of anything which might bring him closer to others, however tenuously.

First break was spent alone as usual, eating his prawn cocktail crisps, pouring the crumbs into his mouth because the packet had been taken from the bag under his desk during last period and squashed, a muffled explosion that had raised a mildly interested eyebrow from their history teacher, Mr Noakes. It should've been a warning sign; that he'd strayed into a mine field, to be wary of other IED's, but he wasn't thinking. Or rather, he *was* thinking, but still about the morning's assembly sermon, which gnawed away at him, an unscratchable itch in the inner ear. As he pulled back the ring-pull on his can of Coke, it exploded, carbonated foam shrapnel peppering his face and clothes as he jumped backward, holding it out at arm's length in an ungraceful attempt to save some of the contents without having to wear them. The leading man as per usual, the scene was played out before a lively audience, whose cheers and laughter rippled around the playground like a Mexican wave, attracting the interest of those who hadn't been in on the prank but could now still share in the moment, jeering and pointing. Oh to be the centre of an appreciative crowd's attention in some other form – Captain of the football team, just having scored the winning goal of the tournament final in the closing seconds of extra time - to be hoisted atop their shoulders and carried aloft, the all conquering hero, paraded around the grounds for all to admire. At least they'd remember him – even if for all the wrong reasons.

Second break, lunch-time, saw a potential breakthrough. Glenn had just finished eating his squashed, black banana-mush sandwiches and drinking his carton of Ribena when a voice called out to him.

'Hey, Glenda!' came the shout from just across the school field. It wasn't exactly what his daydreams had in mind but it was better than being invisible.

'Me?' he said, pointing at his own chest for clarification.

'Yeah, you. Get yourself over here. We're a man short.'

Was it a trick? Should he go? Did he have a choice? It didn't exactly sound like a question. And besides, it was a chance to interact, to show them that he was just like them. Only he wasn't.

With no small degree of trepidation, Glenn walked over to where the group of eleven lads were stood, taking off their blazers and throwing them down on the ground on top of the clusters of sports bags there to create makeshift goal posts.

'We need you to make up the numbers' said the big lad who'd called him over.

Glenn looked at him, unsure what to say. Again, he hadn't been asked a question.

'You have played football before?

'Yeah. Sort of' said Glenn, hoping that Nintendo counted.

'Sort of?'

'I mean yes. Yes, I've played. Of course. Lots of times' he said, still referring to Nintendo.

'Great' said Big Lad, looking dubious.

The other lads were silent, sniggering and casting each other looks that said *well this should be interesting.*

'Okay' said Big Lad, clearly running the show, 'Team Captains, me and Ferret. I'll pick first. Grandad' he said, as a lad with prematurely grey hair stepped forward to take his place by his leader's side.

'Badger' said Ferret, selecting a boy who'd strangely opted for gothic as his preferred style of choice; his efforts to home-dye his blonde hair black having resulted in a strange streaked pattern of light and dark sections. Glenn wondered if all their nicknames were to be based on hair colour alone. Taking into account the animal themes also prevalent, he figured that perhaps Mouse might've been a more fitting name for himself than Glenda or, to use the full title bestowed upon him, Glenda the Bender. At least their's were loosely founded in fact. Unless unknowingly, he'd never given them cause to question his sexual orientation; not that teenagers needed cause. He acknowledged too the appropriateness of the selection - that two members of the Mustelid order, the weasel family, should gravitate towards each other so. He considered voicing the observation but even *he* heard how this would sound before it came out and thankfully managed to stop himself before it were too late.

'Iron Man'- fixed braces on teeth and a metal plate in his leg, following a broken tibia in an illegal moped accident.

'Lemmy' – long hair.

136

'Rocky' – recently joined a local boxing club. Had visited once and not returned since; a fact he had failed to mention with quite so much bravado as his initial appointment.

'Spazmo' – nothing specific immediately obvious but somehow right nonetheless. Did he have a mild limp or was that an affectation?

'Bug's Life' – small.

'Hawkeye' – thick, black-rimmed glasses with bottle-base lenses. It didn't sit well with Glenn that he was on the opposing team to Iron-Man but he comforted himself with the fact that they were temporary enemies in the early stages of the Avengers comics, when Loki had used his magic Sceptre to secure his allegiance. Again, he stayed silent, keeping his thoughts to himself. If it didn't bother them….

'Donut' said Big Lad to the overweight figure stood beside Glenn Chambers, munching on an energy bar in preparation for the upcoming event.

'No way!' said Ferret. 'That's not fair! You worked it out. We're not having Glenda!'

'You have to' laughed Big Lad, not denying the accusation. 'It'll be unfair otherwise.'

'It's unfair anyway. *You* have him. Seven against five. We'll still beat you.'

'No, he's all yours.'

'You called him over' grumbled Ferret.

'There wasn't anyone else nearby that wasn't already doing something' said Big Lad, the two of them continuing to discuss Glenn Chambers as though he wasn't standing there, within immediate earshot. 'Look, he can go in goal.

137

If you're as good as you say then he won't even really need to do anything will he? It'll just be like he's a spectator.'

A spectator. Now that was something that Glenn Chambers *was* good at – and not in some virtual, games-console driven world either. He'd been one his whole life – most often at his own.

'Yeah' said Ferret, appeased, his friend's use of the most basic psychology imaginable clearly all that was needed to placate him. 'Ok then Glenda. Looks like you're in goal. Try not to fuck it up.'

Eleven names announced – he still didn't know Big Lad's name – and not one real one used; unless of course one or more of them had parents with a pretty cruel sense of humour. Even *he* had a nickname now. To anyone else, it would've been an insult - to him, it was progress. He'd been included, allowed in through a secret door to a magical world of fun and friendship. He'd been chosen - a member of a team. He was playing football with a group of lads his own age and it wasn't because a PE teacher had insisted. He'd been invited - by one of their own.

Game on.

A gesture of good will, Big Lad let Ferret's team kick off; the team captain and his number two, Badger, clearly the two best players on their team as they immediately stormed down the middle of the un-marked pitch, easily passing their lunging opponents with fancy step-overs and practised one-twos, the synchronicity between them a thing of beauty. They scored a goal in the first minute of play, Donut's sheer bulk not sufficient to block the trajectory of the ball as it was sky-rocketed past him, just sneaking in under the invisible cross-bar. They were legends. Glenn

138

Chambers cheered a whispered *yesss!* to himself at the other end of the pitch, punching the air. No longer just a member of a team. He was on the *winning* team.

But it didn't turn out to be quite the walkover that at first it looked like it would. Big Lad's team had been caught napping in the opening seconds of the game. They wouldn't make the same mistake again. They were actually pretty well matched, with Big Lad and Granddad providing the equivalent striking aces from their side though, fortunately for Glenn, his team had equal if not superior defensive talents in the shape of Hawkeye, who never seemed to take his own bespectacled eyes off the ball for a second, and Spazmo, who was anything but, his name almost ironic, any sign of a limp now long since vacated in favour of impeccable timing and fearless courage in the face of a more physically formidable challenge.

Five minutes from the end of the second fifteen minute half – half an hour being all they could manage to squeeze in during the remaining lunch break – and Big Lad skipped past Lemmy, whose hair was stuck to his sweaty face so badly that it was a wonder he could see at all. His last line of defence penetrated - Spazmo and Hawkeye having been involved in a pitch-length move which had left them up by the opposition's goal-mouth, unable to get back in time to prevent the break – and Glenn was faced with Big Lad in a one-on-one, a clash of the titans; brains versus brawn. Which way would he go? A feint to the left then a side-tap to the right or vice versa? He'd seen him do that a lot throughout the game. Perhaps a chip over his head where he'd instead come out to meet him, to cut off his angles, like he'd watched Donut do to good effect at the other end, favouring it over a more energetic and potentially uncomfortable dive. He closed him down further, to reduce the likelihood of this last option working, and that's when Big Lad made his move.

A toe-punt. Right. In. The. Face. All his trickery throughout the game and he chose to kick it straight at the keeper. What was the best he was hoping for? That it would be unleashed with such force that it would carry his opponent backwards and over the line, ball and all? Or perhaps he just realised that he wasn't going to score, that he'd been strategically outwitted and so decided to take his man down with him. And take him down he most certainly did. The ball, which had been pumped up - rather over zealously so just prior to the start of the game, following complaints that it was flat - hit him like a desk globe, square in the nose. He went down, holding his face like a theatrical professional, only this time with good reason. Water burst from his eyes with the impact and a mixture of blood and snot streamed down from his nostrils as he knelt on all fours, watching it drip onto the grass beneath him, running down the individual blades and into the cold, damp earth.

Rather than apologise, show any concern whatsoever, Big Lad collected the ball up at his feet as it rebounded back towards him, falling conveniently for him to knock it easily into the goal, bouncing in off a pile of jumpers and black school shoes swapped for trainers, to the hearty congratulations of his team-mates who gathered around him, the day saved.

Glenn Chambers ran the back of his hand and wrist across the underside of his nose, snorting out, pinching it

140

between his fingers to clear it and wiping the water from his cheeks.

'For fuck's sake Chambers!' said Ferret, the draw snatched from the jaws of victory his only concern, 'Get up you fucking cry-baby! The game's not over yet.'

And then the bell went. And it was.

I.

The following morning I wake to discover that, in the cold light of day, I'm still seething, stewing on the events of last night. Sleeping on it has done nothing to alleviate my mood. Rather, a restless, unsettled night of tossing and turning felt like I was lying on a bed of nails, a succession of not exactly nightmares but certainly dark, disturbing dreams, sucking me into their bowels and spewing me out into the morning feeling fraught and frayed around the edges. Night Sky, as I am now calling her, took advantage of me. I should've known it was too good to be true. What a fool. They do say there's none like an old one. Or perhaps it was *her* that was taken advantage of. Perhaps her broker, or whatever he calls himself, was actually a jealous ex-boyfriend who'd turned up unexpectedly at her place, still had a key, was waiting to surprise her when she came home from work. But no, hold on, my head's still a bit fuzzy, sleep-addled. It wasn't *her* place, it was her friend's. Well that's it then. That makes more sense. Stands to reason they'd have had mutual friends from their time together. He was obviously visiting her friend for the evening and was pleasantly surprised to see her when she turned up. Or perhaps not so pleasantly. Perhaps there was more to his visit with her friend than just friendship and Sky had walked in on the two of them, catching them out, an ugly scene ensuing. Perhaps that's why he'd needed to come outside for a cigarette. Perhaps *she* was the real victim in all this. Perhaps she was lying on *her* bed right now, staring up at the ceiling, bathed in sweat after a restless night of tossing and turning.

The thought makes me feel not better exactly but guilty for wallowing in indulgent self-pity when an innocent young woman could've been upset in all this too. The guilt counteracts my previous feelings, not erasing them but covering them like a child pulling a blanket over their head to protect them from the demon in the wardrobe, as if that would ever be enough.

Another day stretches out before me. I have no plans, nothing with which to break it up, no appointment with the Job Centre, no visit to the supermarket or the Post Office to give me purpose, a reason to rise. I lay in bed for longer than I should, staring up at the ceiling, thinking of her doing the same, watching the thin shard of sunlight from the gap in the curtains arc across the moonscape artex like a minute hand, a sweeping solar Rolex, marking the passage of time, the minutes ticking slowly into hours. I pull the quilt over my head - an equally vain attempt to block out the closet-monster of the outside world - but the effect is only that I trap a piece of it under there with me, filling the space around me, cloying the air like trapped flatulence which I breathe in, breathe out, breathe in.

The onset of midday spurs me into action. I will *not* allow myself to become one of those people who don't get out of bed until the afternoon. I'm better than that. I get up and walk out to the kitchen to make a cup of tea. I switch on the TV but the news is showing on the last channel I watched – more fat-cat bankers found guilty of insider trading - so I switch over. There's a show which, as far as I can make out, is solely designed to create arguments between people, airing their dirty laundry – and it really is quite filthy – in front of the nation. The host is deliberately antagonistic, provoking enraged responses from his guests with questions about their partners' (who by the way are sitting right next to them on stage) previous infidelities - usually involving their other halves' friends or siblings - even going so far as to deploy a polygraph (lie detector – sorry, I don't mean to condescend but saves you looking it up in case you weren't sure. You probably already knew – if only because you've already seen these programmes yourself) as an excuse to pose a series of graphically explicit questions, really getting down into the sordid nitty gritty, the disgusting, dirty detail. I wonder what's in it for these people. Do they get paid? Even so, is it really worth the money, which I can't imagine would be much anyway - perhaps their transport costs reimbursed and a free pre-pack sandwich in the broadcasting company's canteen? Would *any* amount be enough? Are people now really *that* desperate for their fifteen minutes of fleeting fame that they'd choose a chat-show of all places to take a paternity test? Do these people have no shame? Don't tell me – I already know. It was a rhetorical question – one that doesn't need wiring up to a machine to answer.

Having had more than my fill of dirty laundry, I go to check on my own, sipping my mug of tea as I walk into the bathroom and give my gym gear, which hangs on the concertina airer propped up in the bath, a squeeze, checking that it's now dry. It is. Well, maybe still a bit damp around the neckline but close enough. It's going to be soggy soon enough anyway. I fold it up and place it in my sports bag. I take my mug back to the kitchen and rinse it under the tap, placing it on the drainer. *Keeper for a Day* it says along the side, the yellow words overlaying an image of overlapping animals – a lion, tiger, rhino and giraffe. That was a great day - one of my best ever. I found out about it on the internet and decided to treat myself. A bit of an extravagance – over the hallowed hundred pound mark – but worth every penny. Well, it *was* my birthday. I got to go in the enclosures *with* the animals! There were various different package options. I chose mammals because I donate sponsorship to Save the Rhinos and wanted to see if I could get to see one up real close, maybe even touch one. None of the packages specified included the rhinos but I'd visited the zoo on numerous previous occasions and knew that the giraffes were located in the Africa enclosures, immediately next-door. I figured that if I showed enough enthusiasm, went on about them enough throughout the day, then they might take the hint and bend the rules. I'm happy to say that it worked. I got to hand-feed one. I got to stroke it. They look really hard and tough when you see them on TV - like giant walking boulders – but, in the thick grey flesh, the skin around their face is actually a lot softer than you think. Their eyes may be small – they have notoriously poor eyesight – but as he munched that straw, taking it ever so gently from my palm with his soft rubbery lips, there was a sadness in them, a mutual connection as they met mine. You'll probably say I'm crazy, but I really think he understood - knew that I cared.

I asked so many questions that day but I even answered a few too. I'm not being critical, far from it, the staff there were all amazing, so helpful and obliging, adding on extras when requested and at no extra charge too, but I actually had to correct one of the keepers on a couple of occasions when the information given wasn't quite factually accurate. I wouldn't necessarily have said anything, wasn't particularly bothered for myself as I already knew the truth, but I was worried for the other guests who'd paid their hard-earned money. Perhaps I shouldn't have said anything in front of everyone. I think he might've felt that I undermined him. That really wasn't my intention. I was just trying to help. Perhaps I should've just taken him to one side, then let him tell the others himself. Oh well. What's done is done. Despite his earlier scowls, he was pretty good about it in the end. When we got back to the main building to collect our certificates and goodie-bags – mug included - the head keeper asked if everyone had had a good day, if it had been informative. *Yeah* joked the guy who'd been showing us around *I learned loads.* At least, I think he was joking. Everybody laughed anyway, although it might've been one of those awkward, nervous ones I often hear. Yeah that was a great time. I got to spend my special day with all sorts of exotic animals and a whole bunch of like-minded people. It doesn't get much better than that. I even swapped contact details with a few of them. I haven't yet had a reply to my emails but you know what busy lives people lead. I hope they liked the photos of the day that I sent them. I took hundreds. Maybe I shouldn't have attached so many with each mail - the files might've been too big to go through. Perhaps they haven't ever received them. I'll break them down into smaller collections, resend them. That's something I can do this

146

afternoon when I get back from the gym, after lunch. Funny how the smallest thing can alter your mood, dictate the way your day turns out. And all because of a mug.

The gym is packed when I arrive. It's lunchtime I suppose, local workers on their breaks, cramming in a quick session before heading back to their booths for the afternoon. The changing rooms are busy, steam from the constantly running   showers drifting out into the main area, the air damp, making drying off difficult for those in a hurry. I change quickly, unable to bear the rough and ready conversations about *this bird* and *that bird* shouted by bloated ape-men across the room for the benefit of all around to hear. What is it about a changing room that turns men into macho barrow-boys? Not me. I'm out of there, before I breathe in any of their sweat, body-odour and testosterone, which hangs in the air like the steam from the showers.

For as long as I can remember I've always wanted muscles. I think it all started as a kid when I read my first comic. In fact, I think I was 'reading' comics before I could even read, the pictures telling the story without words even needed. I marvelled (no pun intended) at the costumed superheroes within their colourful pages, fighting injustice, taking on the criminal underworld single-handed, and wanted to be them – or, at the very least, to *look* like them. In later years it was Sylvester Stallone whose posters adorned my bedroom walls (when I was allowed – different homes, different rules) – a living, breathing embodiment of those previously only two dimensional idols. He showed me that the real world could be just like it was in those

147

graphic novels. Rocky came from nothing to become the Heavyweight Champion of the World, taking on guys much bigger and stronger than himself through raw grit, courage and determination. Rambo showed me that it was possible to fight back, that you could be pushed just so far before you snapped and then those who'd been pushing would suffer the consequences – and in spades. Only of course, as I realised as I got older, it *wasn't* the real world – it was just acting. But Sly *did* come from nothing, watching a Muhammad Ali fight through a TV-shop window in Hell's Kitchen before getting the idea for a script, even insisting that either he starred in the eponymous role – he, a complete unknown - or they didn't take it. They wanted to cast a more famous leading man. He could've just sold the rights to that script and walked away into obscurity but no, he had the conviction, the self-belief to stick to his guns and stand his ground. Man, forget Rocky, forget Rambo, I don't care if he's only an actor or not, that guy had courage. How many people could honestly say they wouldn't have been happy enough with selling the film rights? It's easy to say now, but I'll bet not many. Perhaps that's why he was so convincing in those roles – because there was a part of him in them.

So anyway, that's what I'm aiming for, although at the moment I'm more Blubber than Clubber. Too much time spent at home comfort eating. I plan to put that right. I get on the cross-trainer and zone out for half an hour, my legs pumping along independently of the rest of my body as I watch the screen in front of me. Yet another vacuous, unimaginative pop-music video; the shirtless, tattooed, gold-toothed, ostentatiously bejewelled lead singer surrounded by a writhing mass of tediously scantily clad backing dancers, before cutting to a scene with expensive cars, white Bentleys and the like, pulling up alongside convertible hot-rods, their Chicano hydraulic suspension bouncing them up and down with almost as much vigour as the dancers' boobs in front of them. Presumably the people responsible for churning out this carbon-copy tripe work in a supposedly creative industry. They should be shot for crimes against art. Mercifully the video ends but is instantly replaced by another. If it wasn't for the white writing at the bottom of the screen telling me what was playing, I'd have thought I was still watching the same one. Thankfully the sound isn't on - the screens are just there for the visuals – although the thumping bass being pumped out over the centre's main speakers isn't much better. There's another screen to the left of the one directly in front of me but it's showing the news – Sky news, on a constant rotation, the ticker-tape news-reel running along the bottom meaning that unless I close my eyes, I'll be reading the same misery on a loop, drumming it into me over and over, draining me of energy far more than the cardio machines ever could. And so I do just that – I close my eyes. It's not like I'm going to bump into anyone.

k.

They'd left him out there, lying on the grass. When he'd finally arrived at lesson, five minutes late after a trip to the toilets to clean himself up, his teacher had reprimanded him for his timekeeping then all but accused him of fighting. Glenn Chambers had never had a fight his whole life – unless of course you *counted* his whole life.

They weren't his friends. Never were. Not even for a moment. What part of *some people never learn* didn't he understand? They'd used him, needed him for their stupid game – or worse, they hadn't really needed him at all, had used the imbalance of player numbers as an excuse to bring him in, humiliate him, cause him deliberate physical harm, and all under the guise of an accident, one that carried no disciplinary repercussions, a perfect crime which no amount of witnesses could testify against without merely confirming the perpetrators' original intentions. But there was no such thing as perfect. There was always that one person who couldn't keep their mouth shut and had to brag to another about what they'd gotten away with or some witness turned vigilante who knew better than to rely on going through the long drawn-out official channels, only to end up getting a nil result at the end. In this case, that person was him.

Glenn spat the toothpaste into the sink, rinsed, dabbed his chin with a towel then went downstairs.

'Oh! What happened to your face?' said Anne, fussing, concerned. She hadn't noticed anything amiss last night. He'd been in the kitchen fixing himself a sandwich when she'd come in from work, avoiding eye contact, rushing off up to his room with it, shouting as he mounted the stairs three at a time that he had homework to do, that he wasn't really that hungry, would skip a proper dinner if that was ok with her. She'd been only too happy to acquiesce, impressed with his dedication. But the bruising had really come out overnight, leaving him with two impressive black eyes, purple smudges spreading outward from the bridge of his nose.

'Football injury' said Glenn, happy to be able to give it as the truth, no matter how unhappy he was about it.

'Football?' repeated Anne, doubtful.

'Yeah. Ball in the face' he specified.

'Oh right' she said, the words not really there, as though she were thinking others, considering whether or not she should voice them. 'How's everything going at school? You making friends?' she asked, when what she really meant was enemies.

'It's ok. Our team nearly won yesterday' he said, still grasping onto the one game of football he'd ever been included in like a cherished heirloom, despite the state of play at the whistle, the use of *our team* considered, an appeasement tool to reassure his Foster Mother that he wasn't being excluded as she knew from reading through his voluminous case file that he had been previously. 'Was a draw though. They got one in right at the end. I almost

151

stopped it. Managed to block the shot but he got a lucky rebound.' He hoped his terminology was adequate, made him sound like an aficionado.

'It was really a ball in the face?' she asked 'They were nice to you?'

'They were fighting over who had me on their team' he answered with a smile, managing still to look her in the eye.

'Well that's good then' she said. 'You know you're welcome to bring any of them back to the house if you want to.'

'Thanks Anne' he replied, knowing that he never would.

The assembly hall was bubbling with yet more fire and brimstone that morning as the aptly named Headteacher, Mr Savage, swooshed his cape with all the dramatic overemphasis of a matador whilst reading from Deuteronomy:

'Vengeance is Mine, and retribution, In due time their foot will slip; For the day of their calamity is near, And the impending things are hastening upon them.'

If it was meant to strike the fear of God into his pupils, for one at least it had the polar opposite effect, the vengeance spoken of belonging not to the Lord but to him, Glenn Chambers. Oh their foot would slip alright – and next time it wouldn't be a ball past him and into the goal. Or perhaps…..

'Hey, what's with the sunglasses, Chambers?' said Big Lad as Glenn walked into the carpentry and joinery workshop to take his place at a work-bench and learn about skirting boards for the next double session. He wasn't wearing any.

'Yeah, nice shades, Glenda' laughed Ferret.

'Auditioning for CHiPs, Poncerello?' chimed in another lad whose name Glenn couldn't remember.

'Oh I don't know. I reckon they fit pretty well' snickered another.

'Ok, ok' called out Mr Holland, their woodwork teacher, 'that's quite enough, settle down, we've lots to get through.'

The session went well, Glenn pleasantly surprised to discover that he was actually more practically minded than he'd ever imagined. He'd always considered himself to be an exclusively academic learner, a thinker, a man of words, but it turned out that he was actually pretty handy too. He liked working with his hands, the immediate, quantifiable results, the tangible satisfaction of a physical end product. He liked using the materials, the blocks of smooth wood to be shaped under the router, the smell of sawdust, the way the larger chippings curled as they fell, floating to the ground, joining the small pile already forming there, reminding him of the bedding he once got to change on a regular basis for the beautiful honey-coloured hamster that he'd adopted, fastidiously helping to look after it at one of his former foster placements. Unfortunately, the rodent's time there had outlasted his own.

But most of all, he liked handling the tools, the feel of the wooden handles in his palm, carved from age-old trees, a wonderful completeness - the tools themselves made with tools made with tools made with tools, the metal blades unsheathed from his grip. He felt powerful, a superhero – a one clawed Wolverine, able to inflict serious damage with a single slash, suddenly no longer quite so vulnerable. He held a chisel, turning it in his hand. He thought about the previous day, those stupid boys and their stupid game, a hand involuntarily moving to his face. The chisel slipped up inside his shirt sleeve, then slipped back down again, the tip of the blade sliding in under the leather strap of his watch where it remained, tucked neatly out of harm's way for the rest of the lesson.

Another break-time was passed pouring crisp crumbs into his mouth and emptying his bag of lunchbox and books by the waste bin in order to tip the remaining cheese and onion escapees from the bottom, where the packet had split. Sometimes the deliberately squashed opening was worse than others, meaning a need for the routine morning housekeeping task not always being necessary. Today wasn't one of those days.

The two sessions after lunch were spent in the company of one of the institution's more tyrannical teachers. For everyone else in the room, his lessons were looked forward to with a mixed sense of dread and fear. For Glenn Chambers, they were the exact opposite – precisely what they were meant to be there for in the first place - forty minute windows of persecution-free learning. The fact that he was the most conscientious, committed and able student in the room meant that he was also the dictator's favourite, a fact which was quite apparent, thereby tossing yet another dry log onto the hell-fires of his own damnation. As Mr Bellingham leaned over his shoulder, assisting him with the charting of thermo-graphic contour lines, Glenn revelled in the secret thrill of the chisel nestling just centimetres from his hand, right under the nose of his teacher.

154

The bell went for lunch, the reverberating aftermath of its chimes accompanied by the relieved sighs of all but one of the students in the room. No more double Bell-End for another week. Unusually today, Glenn was looking forward to lunchtime too. Rather than take his packed lunch to the food-hall where he had the benefit of staff supervision like normal, he ventured straight out onto the school field, a tiger in the tall grass, prowling, shoulders hunched, tracking his prey from afar, biding his time, waiting to see where it settled to graze. Big Lad, Ferret and a handful of the other boys from yesterday's game, as well as a few others, pitched their camp, throwing down bags and blazers and squatting cross-legged on the ground to eat their meagre paternal offerings. Glenn did a head count. One, two, three, four, five, six, seven, eight, nine......nine. Perfect. Five-a-side. With him at least.

He sat down himself and ate his egg and cress, the loud crunch of a Golden Delicious alerting his quarry to his presence there, a satellite orbiting their atmosphere. He followed up with a mint Club for dessert, ignoring the dental advice of finishing with the apple to clean the plaque from his teeth, and waited, his lips pursed together, sipping Um Bongo from a carton through a tiny, thin straw, making sure to hoover up every last drop from the corner in an uncouthly audible wet sucking sound.

He pretended not to pay attention as the lads finished their paltry lunches and played catch-up, performing an assessment of their numbers, the penny dropping. He heard the argument, the undisguised heated discussion, that followed, and then:

'Hey, Chambers' called out Big Lad.

It was all too easy.

'Yes?' said Glenn, looking up from his comic as if he'd only just noticed them there for the first time.

'Stop wanking over pictures of men in tights and get yourself over here. We need you in goal again.'

No discussion. No *would you like to help us out again old pal*? No *sorry about yesterday buddy, you up to another game?* Just barked orders. Well, dogs could be put down if they became a problem.

'Ok' said Glenn, sending the caped crusader back to his black vinyl Adidas Bat-Cave. 'Just coming.'

This time he was on Big Lad's side - presumably only right that he should get lumbered since he'd had it all his way yesterday. He was a fair, democratic leader if nothing else. The game kicked off and play was soon underway. Glenn's captain and Ferret were both on the same side today, their previous friendly rivalry a thing of the past as they ran rings around the opposition, showing off with unnecessary displays of ball control, undeniably impressive though not welcomed too warmly by their team-mates who shouted and cursed at their unwillingness to pass, to use the space they had created for themselves. Twice the two deadly marksmen missed easy goal opportunities through their unwillingness to relinquish the ball, involve others they deemed of lesser ability in their selfish two-man set pieces.

Five minutes in, still nil nil, and Ferret got himself in trouble, three on one against and backed up down the left wing, forced to dribble along the touchline and deep into his own half. This was his chance – and so early on in the game too.

156

'Keeper's ball' shouted Glenn, echoing the exclamations he'd heard from Lemmy at the other end when he'd wanted possession.

Ferret looked up from his frantic footwork, glanced about, realised that there really were no other options, then passed the ball back towards his own goal. Glenn watched it roll towards him, let it come, made as if to kick it clear on the bouncing volley, then missed it, kicking the air just beside it as it trundled past him, across the white line of the actual marked pitch that was being used at one end.

'Fuck me Glenda! What the fuck are you doing?' shouted Ferret, to the jubilant cheers and taunts from his opposing teammates, laughing at him, his own goal, rather than at the keeper's faux pas - a player from whom no more was expected.

Glenn walked back behind the line to where the ball had come to a gently wobbling halt and bent down to pick it up. As he did so, he let the chisel slide down through his watch strap, gripping the handle at its base and driving the blade into the scuffed white leather. There was no pop, no dramatic explosion, just a muffled *pffft*. He scooped the already rapidly flattening football up in his hands and kicked it back to the middle of the pitch for a fresh kick-off, before it went down completely.

Ferret, still muttering profanities, trapped the ball under his feet to take it to the makeshift centre spot, the softness beneath his trainer immediately letting him know that the game was over.

'The ball's fucked!' he said.

You're lucky it's just the ball thought Glenn, smiling to himself, happy to be on the losing team.

157

J.

Sign-on day comes round again before I know it, marking another fortnight of used-up life gone by. Fourteen days. Three hundred and thirty-six hours. Twenty thousand one hundred and sixty minutes. One million two hundred and nine thousand six hundred seconds – and every one of them felt. I'm optimistic that Jenny will be back today where I'll get the opportunity to slip in a light-hearted comment about her substitute, the inferior service provided compared with her own much lighter, more personal touch. We'll share a knowing look and a smile, one that says *you're a naughty boy, you'll get me in trouble* as she fails to comment, both of us understanding that she can't, isn't allowed, can't be seen to agree with me, but we both of us know it to be true. But when I arrive – at eight fifty-nine so I have to spend as little time as possible with the three S's - spitting, smoking and swearing – I'm disappointed to discover Miss Congeniality still seated in Jenny's chair.

'Any news on Jenny?' I ask as, having been called quite quickly, I take my place in front of her.

'Jenny?'

'Yes. You know, the lady that I usually deal with.'

'Oh. No' she says, laughing at the obviousness that had confused her. 'No, you still have to deal with me I'm afraid' she says, as if the negative inference isn't firmly founded in fact.

I sit and look at the top of her head as she stares down at the notes on the desk in front of her, periodically glancing up at the screen to cross-reference. Her roots need doing and she could use some T-Gel dermatological shampoo, the white strip of scalp dotted with flakes of dry skin.

'So I'm putting you forward for something next week' she says finally, the statement one of fact rather than of negotiated discussion. 'The council are looking to appoint a number of new Civil Enforcement Officers' she says 'There's an induction day next week. It's not guaranteed, they're booking in a whole bunch of people and then taking the ones they deem most suitable'.

'Civil...?' I begin

'Civil Enforcement Officers' she repeats, cutting me off, dressing it up like I don't know exactly what the fancy title really means.

Traffic wardens.

Like I haven't spent enough time in the stocks already as it is. Forget the rotten fruit – may as well just let the guillotine blade fall right now.

'Like I said, it's by no means a done deal but they obviously saw something in your CV that they liked' she says, like I should be grateful for their interest – me, a straight A student in every school I ever attended – and there were many. 'Perhaps it was the security guard background, the uniform and everything, you know' she explains, when no, I *don't* know. What the Hell has *that* got to do with anything? Like, because I've worn a uniform once before then that automatically qualifies me for any role that requires the sporting of one again – and an entirely different one at that. *By that token* I feel like

159

saying *are there perchance any Military Commander roles going spare?* Perhaps she thinks that any clients who come in wearing a wig should be put forward for roles as High Court Judges. I doubt they use the Job Centre for those though – I've certainly never seen one on their books. If they had then I'd have remembered. I think I'd make a pretty good judge. Possibly my dream role now I come to think of it – spending my days setting the balance of right and fairness straight, putting criminals away behind bars where they belong. But I'd probably only end up losing my job for being too conscientious, doing things right like usual. The prisons would be overcrowded and they'd look to me as the cause, using my heavy-handed approach as a scapegoat rather than focus on building more prisons like they really should. Prison Warden. Now there's a job that involves wearing of a uniform and disciplining criminals. A closer match to Security Guard than Traffic Warden – sorry, Civil Enforcement Officer – at any rate. But obviously I don't actually say any of this. I can tell she already thinks that I'm awkward, deluded as to my status in life, my lofty aspirations not to be despised by the general public even more than I already am. But she's right, they must've seen something in my CV that took their fancy or why would they have short-listed me? Perhaps it was that word *autonomous* again. Able to work *autonomously.* Perhaps that's the bit I should take out, rather than *as part of a team.* Why would I want to proactively pitch myself at roles that require spending even more time alone? I've had enough of those already and none of them were exactly what you'd call careers. I'll sort that out when I get home.

160

'I'm not sure it's really for me' is what I actually say. She looks at me like a parent whose child has just told them they don't want to eat their vegetables. And I don't, no matter how much cheese sauce she thinks she's poured over the cauliflower.

'What do you mean?' she says, when isn't it perfectly clear what I mean?

'I mean, I'm not sure that that's something I really want to do' I say, and she shoots me another scathing look that this time quite clearly says *well beggars can't be choosers.* But they can. They can always choose to keep begging.

'Well you need to do *something* she says. I've got targets to meet.'

Oh, well, why didn't you say something sooner? In that case, of course I'll be more than happy to sign over my life forthwith for you to do with as you wish.

'Yes, I'm aware that I need to do *something'* I echo, equally sarcastically 'I'm just not so sure that I want to do *anything.*' I mean anything as in *any old thing* but I think she misses the intonation and assumes that I'm just saying that I don't want to do anything as in *anything at all.* I wouldn't have had this problem with Jenny.

'I could've put you forward for the bins. They're recruiting there too' she says, like she's offering me diamonds over broken glass rather than merely the lesser of two evils. In fact, I'm not even sure that she's offered me that. At least as a refuse collector – or Environmental Waste Management Consultant as they no doubt call it nowadays – you get to enjoy a little camaraderie, working with a driver and another handler, no doubt whistling and singing your way through your round as you bring your

161

working day to a close before most people have even started theirs. I don't think I've ever seen a miserable looking bin-man – they always look as happy as pigs…. Well, you get the idea.

I'm not sure if it's a conscious thing, whether my expression speaks words as clearly as hers does; that she's just realised that her targets are not an acceptable reason to give a client for sending them on an inappropriate referral but, unknowingly or otherwise, she then plays her trump card.

'Hmm. Ok. Fair enough. Let's see if we can find you something that you *are* happy with' she says, implying that I won't be happy with whatever dream role she comes up with next. 'I need to get you booked onto something or Jenny's not going to be happy when she gets back.'

When, not *if*.

'What do you mean?' I ask. 'Why wouldn't she be happy?'

'Well, I'm covering her case-load while she's off. If I don't place her clients then it affects her targets. She's proud to have consistently been one of the top performing advisers here for the last couple of years. If her numbers drop then it's me she'll probably blame but they're still her numbers at the end of the day.'

'That's not very fair' I say.

'No, maybe not. But that's the way it is. Looks bad for her even though it's not really her fault.'

No, it's mine, I think.

'Ok. I guess it can't hurt to go along' I say.

So, with my appointment at the council's offices all booked in for Monday morning, I leave the Job Centre and

162

do my usual Wednesday rounds, heading to the Post Office to clear them out, withdrawing my usual hundred in fifties, breaking one at the supermarket shortly afterwards, the other remaining in my wallet, reminding me of the one I lost, scuffing the knee of happiness that having completed my dole visit for another fortnight had only just given me. At home I fix a sandwich and do my chores and then, unable to face even chancing the tripe that mainstream TV has to offer right now, I decide instead to put on another movie. I'm spoilt for choice, the VHS tapes and newer DVDs nestled alongside each other like variously statured schoolboys standing on the field at lunchtime, waiting to be picked by the day's appointed team captain, none of them wanting the humiliation of being the last man standing. I run my eye along their rows, a drill sergeant at inspection, trying to decide which one stands out, appeals to my present mood. Usually something happens, an unrelated thought, an overheard reference, that chooses a title for me (you'll recall the Pretty in Pink / Fifty Pound note example) but today this hasn't happened - hence the drawn out decision task. I end up going for Staying Alive, for no other reason than that I haven't seen it for a while – months rather than weeks - and I really love John Travolta. He's been in some great movies – some very underrated ones too (Phenomenon for example, which, just like Pretty Woman, really is very aptly named). He's very diverse too. The roles at the original peak of his fame in the Seventies could've easily typecast him as a one trick pony but oh no, he's played all sorts, and all to equally convincing effect.

I say for no other reason, but maybe the title was a subliminal choice – what I feel like I'm doing right now.

163

Anyway, the film was better than I remembered. JT plays this guy Tony who basically gets messed around – *played* I think they say nowadays - by this performer who clearly thinks she's better than him, something special, even though she went to bed with him after five minutes of meeting him. But he ends up coming through in the end with flying colours, bagging the lead role in a Broadway show and getting the girl – another one, a nice one. I like the bit when he struts at the end, just like he does in Saturday Night Fever. I'd like to do that but a) I don't really have a reason and b) everyone would think I'd lost my mind. Despite being horrible to him for most of the film, I think that the nasty girl looked at him with renewed interest at the end when he clearly wasn't bothered about her anymore. Perhaps that's what I should do – play a bit hard to get. Jeez, if I was any harder to get, I'd disappear off the face of the earth completely.

Have I ever been in love? Yes. About a hundred times a day and always unrequited. Every time I see a beautiful woman, or not even necessarily such a classical beauty but one who shows me the smallest kindness – a sweet smile as she hands over my change – and I know I can't, will never have her (which, on previous performance, will be always) a little bit of me falls in love, the tiniest scar left on my heart, never to be quite the same again. But love, like the hand of fate, is a fickle beast and I'm soon moving on and falling in love all over again.

As I press the stop button and rise from my reclining position on the sofa to collect the tape (another that will soon need replacing on a more modern format – especially given how often this particular one gets played) the TV sparks back into life, the trailer at the end of the home make-over programme that just finished announcing that the midweek movie is due to start after the break. It's still *Oldie but Goodie Season,* only now they're into Autumn, the eighties having made way for the falling leaves of the nineties. And guess what tonight's offering is? Isn't it annoying when someone says that? *Guess who I saw today, you'll never guess.* Then why ask? Obviously you won't guess. Well, you might, but given that there are hundreds, if not thousands, of movies released every decade, you'd be pretty damn lucky. Either that or I've grossly underestimated you and if I have, for that I'm truly sorry. You might have narrowed it down somewhat based on what you know about me so far, thought about why I'd be making a big deal about asking you to guess in the first place. But I'm still being precisely one of those people that I myself find so irritating. Ok, I'll just tell you. No, let me give you a clue. It's only another John Travolta movie! No? Another? He was the lead role, well, one of them anyway – joint, with another very well known name. Actually *joint* should give you another clue. Still no? Ok, well how about if I told you that this was the seminal comeback movie that plucked him from a wasteland of eighties obscurity and catapulted him back to Hollywood superstardom? Then you'd have it, right? Bingo! Of course Pulp Fiction! What else?

The cinematic equivalent of a book of short stories, what's really great about this movie is the dialogue, all the best lines of which are shared between JT's character Vincent Vega and Samuel L Jackson's (I wonder what the L stands for – must look that up later) Jules. For me though, the stand-out performance is Travolta's. His character may not appear particularly tough – he looks like what he is; a middle-aged, druggie hippy with an ill-fitting suit and a paunch – but when he squares up to the Heavyweight Champion of the World in a gloomily lit bar, you never question which of them would come off worse in the end. Even Butch himself is lost for words.

But, in spite of all this and much as it pains me to admit it, it's Vincent's partner Joules that has *the* single best line in the movie. Just before he shoots somebody – *pops a cap in their ass* – he quotes a passage from The Bible – Ezekiel 25:17 to be precise. Needless to say that, although my Headteacher may well have used this one too – it's certainly the kind of thing he went in for - it isn't as a result of my assembly inspired interest in religious studies that I know the quote by heart:

'The path of the righteous man is beset on all sides by the inequities of the selfish and the tyranny of evil men. Blessed is he, who in the name of charity and good will, shepherds the weak through the valley of darkness, for he is truly his brother's keeper and the finder of lost children. And I will strike down upon thee with great vengeance and furious anger those who would attempt to poison and destroy my brothers. And you will know my name is the Lord when I lay my vengeance upon thee.'

I wonder if God really exists. I hope so. If he does and I've read that right, then it's nice to know that at least *someone's* on my side.

I wonder if Tarantino – if anybody - had to pay someone copyright royalties for quoting from The Good Book.

1.

Glenn Chambers' journey home from school offered two on-foot options; one a round trip of approximately half an hour, the other a more simple, L-shaped route of around ten minutes. It would seem then, on the surface of it at least, that there was no real need for consideration - the latter the obvious and only choice - but this was not necessarily the case. The more brief route constituted a short-cut across the large rhombus of the original and involved turning into an unmade road; a darkly-shaded dirt-track - particularly during the winter months when it was almost pitch black some moonless, starless nights – leading through an area of tree-dense woodland popular with drinkers, glue-sniffers and other ne'er-do-wells. But it did shave the better part of an hour off of the round trip, meaning more intense but less pavement time out on the streets where something bad could happen. It was a trade off, a route less habituated by the majority of St Michael's students, one that Glenn was prepared to take.

That evening, he regretted taking it the moment his feet crunched against the gravel, negotiating the uneven, pot-holed surface, avoiding the murky puddles and rounded the sweep of the entrance curve to be faced with a group of lads, standing there smoking, their push-bikes lying on the floor beside them, the wheels still gently spinning. He

167

recognised them as boys from his year, some from his form group, some not. Ferret and Rocky were among them. It was too late to turn back. They'd seen him. He felt like a rabbit caught out suddenly, cut off from his warren by a salivating fox.

Trying his hardest not to make eye contact, to be invisible, which wasn't usually a problem for him except on the only occasions when he wanted to be, his progress slowed momentarily, the briefest of hesitations before he realised that he couldn't be seen to falter, had to plough on regardless and hope for the best – which of course was never the way things worked out for him, this looking like it was about to be no exception.

'Aah, look who it is – Peter Shitton' said Ferret, the laughter of his associates forced, out of proportion.

'Prat Jennings' said a blonde lad with a long fringe that hid dead-fish eyes and they laughed again, though this time not as much, Ferret looking pleased with the contribution.

The others said nothing, appearing but failing to think of other goal-keeper related puns.

'Gay Clemence' said a tall, skinny, dark lad with a mullet finally, far too late, the moment gone.

'You did that on purpose' said Ferret, ignoring the latest quip, the others now serious too, following his lead.

'Did what?' said Glenn, feigning ignorance.

'You know *what*. Today. On the field. You did it on purpose. Why? You only made yourself look stupid.'

But they both knew that that wasn't true and Glenn knew that Ferret knew that he knew.

'I don't know what you mean' said Glenn, but he couldn't help himself, sabotaged his own lie with a flicker

168

of the eyes that deep down wanted his adversary to gaze searchingly into them and know the truth.

'Well either you did it on purpose or you're even shitter at football than I thought you were.'

'I guess you overestimated me' said Glenn but rather than being self-deprecating as the words themselves suggested, the intonation said otherwise. He *spoke* over but he *said* under.

'I guess I did' said Ferret, disarmed momentarily, the verbal attack fizzling out since his opponent had, on paper at least, agreed with him, leaving him with nowhere to go with that particular line of approach. But Glenn Chambers wasn't getting off the hook *that* easily. 'Well, let's see if you're better at any other sports, shall we?' he said, moving onto phase two and looking to his accomplice with a nod. Rocky bent down and unzipped his canvas, navy Pan Am sports bag, moving a damp towel to one side and taking out a pair of bright, blood-red boxing gloves with *Lonsdale* embossed in bold black letters around the white unlaced cuffs. Bought recently by a delighted father when he'd expressed an interest in following in the pugilistic family footsteps, they looked virtually unused from their single outing at the local boys club a couple of weeks back. So much so that if he'd kept the original packaging, he could've probably returned them to the sports shop that he'd bought them from and gotten away with it. But instead he kept them with him, safely ensconced in his bag, a chalice of masculinity, evidence that his nickname was warranted. Rummaging under his games kit and books, he then took out a second pair – his older brother's – these much more of a dark maroon in colour, the leather cracked

169

and worn, tenderised over a period of years against countless skulls, jaws and ribs.

'Put them on' said Ferret, as Rocky handed them to him, Ferret taking the nice new looking pair, unaware or perhaps uninterested that these were more padded than the older ones, would give his challenger the advantage in a fair fight – which of course it was never going to be.

'Look, I don't want any trouble' said Glenn too late, the gauntlet already taken up, having unwittingly accepted the gloves that were thrust upon him.

'Well we don't always get what we want in life, do we?' said Ferret.

'I'm not putting them on' said Glenn defiantly, naively hoping that this would be an end to it, leave his tormentor with no place else to go.

'Look Bender' he said, 'Either you lace up or I'll assume that you'd rather go bare knuckle.' He had a manic glint in his eye, challenging, *wanting* Glenn to refuse again. And Glenn saw it, had seen that look too many times before to mistake it for anything else.

He said nothing, breathed a sigh of nervous resignation and began pulling on the gloves, his trembling hand sliding easily into the first with the help of his free-hand pulling it on, the second more of a struggle as he attempted to grip the wrist section with his oversized padded thumb and fingers. He managed to get them both fully on, his hands embedded deeply into the large, fat leather mittens to halfway up his forearms. When finally he raised his head to ask for help with the strings, he saw Ferret standing there facing him, a thin-lipped smile on his face, his gloves now back jutting out of the top of Rocky's still open sports-bag.

He barely had time to furrow a confused brow before Ferret hit him, punching him hard in the nose and mouth with an un-gloved fist, the knuckle bare save for the single large eight-carat-gold sovereign that decorated it.

Glenn sat down on the ground with a thud, the jolt jarring up his spine not even felt as he held his face in his hands, the taste of iron in his throat telling him that he was swallowing blood from a split lip, his tongue rolling over his already aching teeth, a cursory inspection that they were all still present and correct. More blood streamed from his nose for the second time in as many days, though if he'd thought the ball in the face was painful....

The lads stood around him, over him, laughing - ring-ropes of ridicule - pulled the gloves unceremoniously from his hands, threw their bags over their shoulders, picked up their bikes and rode away.

K.

The L stands for Leroy. I'm not ashamed to admit that with hindsight that didn't really come as any great surprise to me. Like, I looked at it there on the screen, on Wikipedia, and said to myself *oh yeah, of course.* Oh, I'm not racist or anything. We already established that I prefer ethnic minority cultures over my own and I believe I even went so far as to specify Afro-Caribbean as pretty high up on the list. But don't worry, I'm not going to claim that many of my best friends are black – because isn't that what people always do to defend some clearly racist comment just or about to be uttered? I think we both know that in my case that simply isn't true. You need friends to have best ones, for starters, whatever the colour. No, I'm definitely not racist. Why is it that just the act of denying being racist in itself makes you sound racist? The old adage *he doth protest too much?* But I'm not – I'm really not. No, if I'm guilty of negative prejudice against *any* one race on this earth it's the *human* race. I choose any other species over my own every time. In fact, I say *my own* but I really don't feel that they belong to me – or rather, I to them. I love animals. It astounds me that we have the sheer audacity to use the word to describe people who behave horribly when in truth we're the only creatures on the planet who ever act out of malice. Animals only ever behave logically, in the sole interests of their own survival and the perpetuation of their species; the only thing selfish about them the procreation gene – assuming of course that you buy what old Charlie told us and aren't relying on some celestial fairy tale to see you serenaded into the afterlife by cherub harps and trumpets on a fluffy cumulonimbus of everlasting happiness. They love unconditionally, never judging and without motive for personal gain – unless of course you count food and shelter which, as I've already explained, is a symptom of their instinctive drive to stay alive. And you know what really irks me, really twists the ironic knife? That we then have the cheek to use the word *humane* to describe a kindness, the method most without pain – *putting out of their misery* - the word a derivative of the most miserable, selfish, mindlessly violent and destructive species in the history of the known universe. And *who* exactly are the animals? Civilisation? Hah! The word would make me cry if it didn't make me laugh so.

m.

The next morning was a mission of avoidance, a mission that, impossibly, Glenn Chambers managed somehow to accomplish, despite Anne's knocking at his bedroom door every five minutes, asking if everything was ok, if he was sure he didn't want to have dinner with the rest of them, that couldn't his homework wait half an hour? She wasn't convinced, sensed that something was up. And with good reason – there was – his lip mainly. It was swollen up like a Lilo. The top was badly cut and the bottom looked like he was pulling a *Joey* face, which of course he would never do, didn't even agree with others when they did it, wondered if they ever stopped to think about what they were actually doing - that they were mocking a person, a living, breathing human being with a severe mental and physical disability.As if facing his fellow students wasn't enough of an ordeal at the best of times, today he had to go in looking like the Elephant Man.

As predicted, his arrival through the black wrought-iron gates yielded no small level of mirth and merriment. Walking with blinkers on, he managed to block out the pointing and staring as he crossed the school field but, inside, negotiating the comparatively narrow corridors was a different story altogether. The fascinated gazes, the unrestrained comments and overtly hostile, targeted taunts

174

were impossible to ignore; many of them based on his hair-lip scar - 'Split your lip again, Chambers?' / 'Thought he only split your lip the once?' - various takes on the same basic theme - but some more imaginative than others. He particularly liked a couple of the Rocky references popular at the time - 'Blubber Laing' and 'Apollo Weed' standing out among them. Names of certain obscure musical artists – *Chesney* one of the more common and looked like it was going to stick; well it was certainly better than *Glenda* anyway - left him temporarily bemused before he took the bait, asking what they meant, only to be told that they too had been one hit wonders. News of the incident, the cause of his unsightly appearance, had clearly already gotten around.

The gawping stares pursued him into the assembly hall, rippling around the murmuring throng like a domino world record attempt - but Glenn Chambers didn't even notice, so busy was he listening to that morning's sermon, the theme of which seemed to be continuing in a vein similar to that of the past few days. Taking from Matthew, 'Doc' Savage read aloud in his usual inimitable style:

'Then Jesus said unto him, Put up again thy sword into his place: for all they that take the sword shall perish with the sword.'

The sword. Glenn's feet subconsciously gripped the brown leather satchel that sat at his feet - the satchel that still housed the chisel taken from yesterday's carpentry workshop - and pushed it back under his seat. *Let them laugh* he said to himself. *Let them all have a good laugh.*

The exit from the hall mirrored his entrance, heads turning to look in his direction, each leaning across to that

175

next to them to whisper some indiscreet comment, as if he didn't have peripheral vision, couldn't see them staring. And that was just the teachers, lined up at the side of the hall, supervising the kids, ushering them along, cajoling the stragglers, shouting at them to settle down, take their bags from their shoulders, lose the gum.

And so it continued throughout the morning, his resolve strengthened with each new judgemental, mocking, taunting face he passed.

At midday he holed himself up in the canteen, sitting as near to the teachers as possible to capitalise on the security they represented but also to ensure that he was seen by them, sitting there, alone as usual, nibbling like a mouse at his peanut butter and jam sandwiches, eeking them out, making them last. He even made a point of going over to speak to one of them, sat at a table with the others, questioning Mr Northwood on a particular point of detail on his Physics homework, only to be told that though his conscientiousness was admirable, it was lunchtime and teachers liked to have theirs too. Overhearing the exchange, another of his colleagues commented that he wished he could get some of *his* students to muster as much enthusiasm, which raised a small laugh and nods of agreement from around the table. Glenn Chambers apologised for interrupting, confirming that he would ask him about it again later, happy that his work there was done, his alibi – and what better than a whole table-full of teachers? – established.

At the very end of lunchtime, the clank and clutter of plates being cleared and scraped coming through the serving hatch of the school's kitchens, Glenn slipped

176

quietly from the dinner hall. He needed to work fast. The five minute warning bell had already tolled a few minutes hence and he didn't want to get to lesson late and arouse suspicion later. Under normal circumstances, a student's tardiness would barely be acknowledged with any great significance and certainly not be recalled the following day, but Glenn Chambers wasn't normal. Always keen to avoid the corridor scuffles and get the learning underway, he was *never* late - except of course when he'd just received a ball in the face from point blank range.

He glanced around. The field was quiet, most of the kids having already filed in. Somebody could come around the corner of the red brick building and catch him in the act at any moment but Glenn Chambers was smarter than that. He'd be able to see someone coming in the gleaming reflections of the staff cars parked opposite. He thanked Heaven for small mercies, that some of the teachers took the trouble to clean and polish them at the weekends, buffing them up nicely to suit his purpose.

He looked along the row of wheels protruding from the open frontage of the rusty bike shed, sheltering beneath the corrugated-iron roof. There were some nice machines there. Expensive looking. Top of the range BMX's; Skyway, Mongoose, Diamondback, Kuwahara, Redline – they were all there, brightly coloured five spoke mags in red, yellow, blue, green – works of art; Grifters, Bombers, skinny, curly-barred Racers, long-handled Choppers perfect for backies – though not tonight.

Taking the chisel from his bag, he wasted no time, no pause for last minute reservations which might cast the smallest shadow of doubt into his mind. *Laugh* he said to

177

himself. *Laugh it up. Laugh as you walk home,* and he moved along the length of the shed – actually three adjacent sheds joined end to end – stabbing the chisel into each tyre as he went, slashing the padded saddles, the only hesitation coming when he arrived at a bicycle that was clearly a girl's bike – a visiting Sixth Former from St Agnes's, the neighbouring Catholic girls school - pink with tassels hanging from the handlebars for example - a few of which he left un-punctured, unable to quite bring himself to do it. A handful of the bikes he recognised. He'd seen them before – only yesterday – lying on the floor of the dirt-track as he was pulling on his gloves, preparing to fight. He carved the seats of these up extra nice, gouging them with the blade good and proper, though calmly, not in a rage, bits of sponge-foam sprinkling the floor beneath. He remembered one from when it had been ridden away – the blue Raleigh Burner with the distinctive plastic yellow wheels and bar pads. He left it untouched.

'Perish with the sword' he said softly, and went off to class, before he was late.

L.

I've been thinking about getting a dog. I'm home a lot nowadays, especially since losing my job. Not that I'm really interested in getting the job, but I wonder if there's any rule against traffic wardens – sorry, Civil Enforcement Officers (hey, just realised that I could tell people I was a CEO for a government organisation – if I was so inclined, which of course I'm not) – taking their dogs out to work with them. I wonder if anyone's ever even asked – God knows they could use the protection. I can think of no logical reason why not. Maybe I'll ask on Monday. Who knows, my suggestion may change the face of the profession forever. Lots of people love dogs – particularly fellow dog owners. Might make the officers themselves seem more warm and approachable and less prone to abuse – particularly if the dog in question happens to be a Rottweiler, Alsatian or the like. The dogs would certainly get a good walking – in fact, it seems the ideal profession for a dog-owner - and if they're good enough for the police….. Yep, I'll definitely bring it up on Monday.

So anyway, this afternoon I find myself standing in the lobby of The Woof Garden's reception, waiting for someone to see to me. A short, rotund lady with a voluminous bosom and frizzy grey hair that she appears to have long since given up either styling or even brushing comes out to greet me. I go to shake her hand but she tells me that she won't if that's ok as she wipes them both on the front of her bottle green *Woof Garden* sweatshirt by way of explanation - that her hands are clearly very dirty. We have a brief preliminary chat and she asks me a few basic questions, her frown deepening with the consecutive revelations that I a) live in a small one bedroom flat, b) am unemployed and c) have never owned a dog before, although have had some limited experience of an assortment of different breeds gained through my various placements within the care system. In as firm but kind a way possible, she stresses the huge commitment that comes with owning a dog, the time spent walking, playing, grooming, the financial burden, the substantial veterinary bills, vaccination injections, holiday boarding and so on and so forth. For somebody whose job it is to try to rehome the many waifs and strays in her possession, it's like she's trying her utmost to put me off. But I don't mind – I understand that she's doing it for all the right reasons, to ensure that the cycle of rejection doesn't continue on repeat, the poor animals' attachment issues becoming ever greater, more entrenched, each time they return to her. I know that feeling all too well and the very last thing in the world I want to do is be responsible for exacerbating it.

She suggests that I take a walk around on my own for a bit and get a feel for the animals, assuring me that there will be workers dotted around the rescue centre that should be able to answer any questions I might have along the way.

The first thing that hits me is the smell – a putrid stench of faeces and urine, ammonia filling the air like mustard gas, burning my lungs. And the foot soldiers are the dogs themselves, shell-shocked, trench-footed, stood on cold, damp concrete floors wet of their own doing or the constant pressure washers attempting to keep up. Oh, the staff are trying their best to stay on top of it all but it's a battle that can never be won, as more and more casualties are brought in by the day, the week, the year – five minute wonders, unwanted Christmas gifts, underestimated responsibilities. Beseeching doe-eyed faces look up at me, appealing to my compassionate nature, silently pleading to *please take me away from all this*, to a loving home where they'll be looked after, cared for properly like they should've been all along. And I know that feeling all too well too - have seen that exact same look in their eyes before, in the bathroom mirror. Now, more than ever, do I fully understand the phrase *hangdog expression.* I shuffle along, through the maze of cages, looking at the animals looking back at me like inmates on death row, awaiting sentence or perhaps, if they're lucky, some miraculous last minute reprieve. Enclosures pass me by, a procession of canine themed carnival floats, each one symbolising a different dog-related phrase or saying – and there are many. Sick as a dog; dog tired; beaten like a dog - there are as many incarcerated exhibits as there are expressions – every one having led a dog's life, been treated like a dog, had their day. If it's the size of the fight in the dog then looks like most of these have already thrown in the towel. Man's best friend? Pah! With friends like that... The soundtrack is a cacophony of whines and whimpers, a mongrel mental asylum, unconvincing ferocious barks and snarls, angry with the world though still more than a little afraid of it. A

181

brindle-coated Staff rises up at the wire mesh on its hind legs, attempting to stand out from the rest. It works and I stop to fuss him, crouching down to talk to him, give him a little attention, let him know that he has hope, *can* be noticed. I notice that he has tiny marks, dark circles, among the brindling of his back and I recognise them immediately. Cigarette burns. I've seen them before only it wasn't on a dog, no matter how many times he might've called her bitch. *Devil Pokes.* The words pop into my head from out of nowhere, some long-suppressed memory - a paramecium still swimming in circles in the stagnant pools of my mind.

Dressed in standard issue company green sweatshirt, combat trousers and wellingtons, a young girl hoses down a concrete gulley, attempting to dilute clear the rivers of yellow that run there, coaxing brown flotsam along the channels to the drain hole at the end where it can be flushed away. I stop and ask her about this particular animal and she confirms my suspicions, that he was a victim of severe maltreatment. I accompany her as she works, chatting to her about the animals we pass, getting the heads up on each, like a customer on a second-hand car lot, checking the mileage, the service record, finding out if any of these poor old battered jalopies are worth purchasing – only here, the worse the history, the more likely the sale. No *one careful owner* here. Their log books read like a specials board of the most extreme S&M restaurant imaginable; beaten with a tyre iron, set on fire, thrown from an upstairs window.

But eventually I just feel guilty for even being there in the first place, getting their hopes up when I have to face facts and accept that I won't be making any decisions today. I couldn't leave one at home alone in my small flat all day and who knows what the future holds in store for me with regards to my working arrangements? Even if I don't get the traffic warden role, I don't plan on being unemployed forever. When my contribution-based JSA comes to an end in a few months, I'll switch to means tested and then they'll take into account my savings and I won't qualify for a dime. Never mind that my family paid tax on every penny earned to pay for the property that was passed on to me fair and square, which I then couldn't even afford to move into, had to sell to cover the inheritance tax on it, paying into the system all over again. I don't want to start frittering away my safety net. I'll need that later. Certainly doesn't look like I'll have a wife or kids to take care of me if I make it to be elderly and infirm, and nursing homes cost money. *Nursing home.* Ah, the light at the end of the tunnel. For some people, the idea of ending up in a care home for the elderly is their worst fear, sheer hell. Not for me. No, for me it's something to look forward to – captive companions, friendly nurses (often oriental), my bed made, unending games of dominoes, Scrabble, cards, guest visits from local theatre groups, impromptu complimentary beauty treatments, group movie nights around the set, snatched snippets of conversation with other residents' relatives - my idea of heaven, assuming of course that I still have all my marbles – and if I haven't, well then I won't know any different will I?

'Sir? Are you ok? Do you need anything else?' says the young girl in front of me, water dripping from the nozzle of her hose where she's turned it off at the wall.

I thank her for her time, letting her know that she's been more than helpful and leave, explaining to the owner on my way out that it's been most informative, a real eye-opener, that I may return, once I've established a more stable home environment myself and can guarantee an animal the happiness it deserves - which seems to make her happy.

n.

When Glenn arrived at school the following morning, he knew immediately that he'd made an impression, though this time for a somewhat different reason. His puffy face was no longer the main focus of the teachers' attention as he passed them, huddled together in groups, discussions held in earnest, bringing them all together, hierarchical differences set aside for the time being, a united front. The atmosphere in the hall was audibly different too, held a distinctly different timbre, as though all nine-hundred and eighty – seventy-nine – kids were taking part in one huge but single conversation, the topic unchanging from row to row.

A door opened and Mr Savage entered his pulpit, his presence alone all that was needed to silence the masses. For once, they were keen to hear what he had to say.

'For he is the minister of God to thee for good. But if thou do that which is evil, be afraid; for he beareth not the sword in vain: for he is the minister of God, a revenger to execute wrath on him that doeth evil' he said, quoting from Romans and pausing, looking out across the sea of faces waiting expectantly for what was to follow. He let them wait, allowed them to stew, knowing that the guilty party was out there somewhere, sitting among them. He just needed to weedle them out. And he would. Oh, he would,

185

they could be sure of that. 'Who knows why I choose these words this morning?' he said, not expecting an answer, a raised hand. The passage had been selected as a warning to the perpetrator that he should be afraid, that wrath would be executed on the evil that *they'd* carried out - but Glenn Chambers didn't hear it that way. To him, it merely enforced his belief that he'd done the right thing – in the eyes of The Lord at least. To *his* mind, the wrath had already been executed for the evils committed against *him*. *He* was the minister of God. 'Now it has come to my attention that yesterday, an act of mindless vandalism on an unprecedented scale was committed against the pupils of St Michael's, quite possibly by one of your own' *Your own – clever move* thought Glenn Chambers *not saying 'our own' like he always does when referring to scholastic or sporting achievement.* The head knew exactly what he was doing, wanted the kids to turn on themselves, create dissention in their ranks, let them do the work, fish out the culprit for him. 'Now never let it be said that I'm not a fair man' he went on. 'I'm going to give you a number of options, let *you* decide how best we resolve this ugly matter moving forward. Now, of course, the first option, and the most honourable, would be for the guilty party to step forward, not now necessarily, I don't expect that, but come to see me in my office and own up, stand up and take responsibility for your actions like a young man, begin to redress the balance of this most cowardly of acts. Then and only then might we have some hope of salvaging the situation and with it your own place at this school. I'll understand if you'd rather not speak to me personally; you may prefer to confess to another member of staff and this will be equally

186

acceptable. So, make that four options. The next would be that if you know who did this, have information that may lead to their arrest' – he'd clearly seen one too many episodes of Crimewatch – 'you pass the information on, in the strictest confidence of course, safe in the knowledge that your loyalty to St Michael's will be recognised and rewarded at every available turn throughout the remainder of your time here. Now obviously, by the very nature of this unprovoked attack, there must be plenty of you out there with very good, justifiable reason for coming forward. The final option is that we try to see the positives here, acknowledge the message, the cry for help that you are clearly trying to send us. Since an hour seems an excessive period of time necessary to eat your lunch, the boredom perhaps a contributory factor here, we may have to seriously consider halving the length of your mid-day break and adding the time on to lessons where it may be spent more productively.' This last comment elicited a rumbling groan of objection around the hall. 'Settle down, settle down! I didn't say that this was definitely happening. I merely suggested that it may *become* necessary but only as a last resort, should we not manage to clear the matter up in some other, much more agreeable way. Now don't worry, I'm quite sure that with your help, with all of us working together, it won't be necessary' he said, smiling.

187

0.

Edward Savage shuffled papers around the green leather surface of his desk, took his pen out of the pewter ink-well and replaced it, swivelled on his chair and looked out the window, across the school field, over the tops of the white rugby H's to the soft watercolour of blue-grey industrial chimneys on the distant horizon. This really was a blasted nuisance. He'd had a number of parents on the blower already that morning, informing him of the criminal damage to their sons' property, threatening to call the police, go to the papers, like he didn't already know about it, hadn't had the same call a dozen times already, and what was he going to do about it, they thought this was meant to be a decent school, that standards were obviously slipping. *Have faith* he'd told them, this his trademark line, the one the kids used when they were doing their impressions of him – and admittedly pretty accurate ones too; he'd heard them. It was the unofficial school motto, would've been emblazoned in Latin on the crests of their blazer pockets if he could've had his way, many believing it to be what the words there meant anyway.

A knock at the door.

'Come!' announced Mr Savage, expecting it to be Mel, whom he'd instructed to come to his office straight after assembly in order that he might dictate a formal letter about the whole unsightly incident to send out to parents, reassure them how seriously the school took something like this, let them know that every step within its means was being taken to bring the matter to a satisfactory conclusion as soon as possible for all concerned.

But it was a student that entered.

'Good God lad! What happened to your face?' he barked, assuming that this was why the boy was there.

'I'm sorry Sir? Oh, what, this? No, it's nothing Sir. Sporting injury. I did it yesterday' he explained dismissively.

'Oh right. Fair enough' said Savage, taking the explanation literally at face value, the rugby H's still fresh in his mind's eye. 'Then what can I do for you young man?'

'Well, it's really what I can do for you. For the school I mean' said Glenn.

'Oh yes?' said the Head, his interest aroused suddenly.

'Yes. About yesterday Sir.'

'Yes?'

'Well it might be nothing. I wasn't really sure if I should even come here but you did say we should speak up if we thought it might help, and I don't think anyone really wants to lose their lunch hour' he said, giving his best look of concern, the implication that he was doing this for the good of them all when ironically he was probably the only person in the whole school who would've preferred the shorter break.

'Yes, yes!' said Savage, impatient, a shark that just detected a drop of blood land in the water, already

189

spreading. 'Just get to the point lad! What do you *think* you know?'

'Well, like I said sir, it might not be anything important but I thought I saw a lad from my class hanging around the bike-sheds at lunchtime yesterday, looking…. suspicious'

Edward Savage's shoulders slumped.

'Is that it? You came all the way up to my office to tell me *that*? People hang around bike-sheds, lad. That's what they're for, congregating at and smoking behind – that and storing bikes in obviously. I need something a bit more substantial than *looking suspicious,* I'm afraid.'

'Well it's not just that Sir' said Glenn, feigning reluctance, that his figurehead was teasing the information out of him. 'It's just that he seemed to have some kind of *weapon* in his hand at the time.'

'Weapon?' repeated Savage. Now *this* was more like it.

'Yes Sir. A tool I think. Like a screw-driver or something.'

'And you're quite sure about this?' said Savage.

'Yes Sir. I remember wondering what he was doing with it, thinking that he was probably fixing his bike, tightening a loose bolt or something. It wasn't until just now that I started to put two and two together and thought they might be linked.

'And do you happen to know the identity of this suspicious looking tool-wielder by any chance?'

'Yes Sir. Like I said, he's in my class, Sir.'

'Well would you mind sharing it with me then?' said Savage.

'Yes Sir. I mean, no Sir. I don't mind. It's Fretwell, Sir. Gary Fretwell.'

190

M.

Monday morning. Induction day. Within five minutes of arrival at the council offices and I already know that things aren't going to go well. The ID badge that I'm issued with reads *Gwen Chambers*. Gwen! I mean, seriously, do I look anything like a woman? I've got a beard for God's sake. But when I bring it to the receptionist's attention, politely asking if she minds changing it, she acts like I'm being unreasonable, informing me with condescending indifference that she'll get around to it just as soon as she's dealt with the rest of the queue which, from what I've observed during my brief time here so far, doesn't look like it's going to be cleared any time soon as more and more bodies roll through the revolving doors like gobstoppers from a gumball machine. And I'm absolutely right, the induction coordinator coming out to greet us all sitting there, instructing all those here for the parking attendant training (seems even *he* can't bring himself to use the pretentious current terminology) to please follow him, forcing me to abandon all hope of an exchange, resigned to the fact that I'm going to have to spend the rest of the morning with a group of people I've never met before, wearing a female name tag. It's not like I'm sexist or anything but Jeez, why does this kind of stuff never seem to

191

happen to anyone else? Oh well, on the bright side, maybe it'll prove an effective, interesting conversation starter.

But it doesn't. As is usually the case whenever I explore unfamiliar territory, go anywhere new, it seems that everyone else already knows each other. Except they don't of course – it just seems that way, people striking up easy, flowing rapport with those around them, sharing default comments about the unusually inclement weather, swapping stories about their journeys in, the horrendous traffic on the A this, the M that and blah blah blah. I just can't seem to do it, can't bring myself to force inane monologue for the sake of it - cliché sentences that I already hear myself uttering, boring myself silly before they're even out there on my lips. A compromise, I prepare myself to share a *what is the world coming to when they can't even get your name right* face, a roll of the eyes and a few well chosen words that let them know that I don't really belong here either, that I only came under mild Job Centre duress - but nobody even notices or, if they do, they certainly don't comment. So I sit in silence, sipping a complimentary cup of weak, grey, lukewarm tea – in a real cup and saucer no less; none of your Styrofoam nonsense here - as the coordinator (Senior something or other – an institutionalised clone - I forget his name already) opens with the introductions. Usually at these things they suggest an icebreaker, working around the room, getting those present to introduce themselves, say where they're from, why they're here, that sort of thing - and normally I hate that, dread it almost, but today, when for once I would welcome it - the opportunity to correct my badge, perhaps even make a pithy, light-hearted quip about having no plans to change my name just yet, at least not until the gender reassignment op has been successful - they don't do it. Obviously. Instead it's straight into the main body of the presentation which, unsurprisingly, is as dull as dishwater – assuming, that is, that you first removed the dishes and any small bits of floating food debris from the surface.

But people seem genuinely interested in this stuff, hands stretched eagerly into the air, attempting to reach higher than their neighbours like kindergarten kids, desperate to attract the speaker's attention and get their fascinating question out there first, surely more for the sake of appearance than any genuine interest in the actual subject matter.

The chief content of the first hour or so covers the intricacies of legal and illegal parking, that which constitutes a legitimately positioned vehicle and, more importantly, that which doesn't and therefore amounts to a ticketable offence. Slideshow images, photographs of variously positioned car wheels, kerbs and yellow line combinations, are flashed up large onto an interactive whiteboard, the group asked to proffer their verdicts of innocent or guilty - which they do, actually enjoying themselves, proud of themselves even, the grinning buffoon on the remote equally content, basking in the satisfying glow of yet another successful session as grown men and women chant out the patently obvious answers like primary school children reciting their ABC's.

Having congratulated us on how well we've done, I half expect to be given a bag of Jelly Tots and a gold star as we're told that we're to have a fifteen minute refreshment break, for people to use the bathroom and top up on teas and coffees – when what we all know it really means for most of the candidates present is a desperate rush to get outside and smoke themselves half to death for quarter of an hour, sucking on their cherished Lambert and Butlers like their lives depend on it – which in a way they do. Foolishly I go outside myself to get some air but there isn't any fresh, the panic-puffers creating an instant smog which spreads out upon the breeze, swirling around the front steps, trapped in a vortex created by the walls of the open-fronted courtyard. There isn't time to venture far so I stand just along from them, unsuccessfully attempting to find a spot upwind. I watch them from ten yards away - laughing and joking like old friends, sparking up each others' cigarettes, sharing their own where their new best friends have accidentally on purpose forgotten theirs - and it may as well be ten miles. Why can't I be more like them? It all seems so effortless. But then nothing worth having comes easily. Maybe it's not them excluding me. Maybe it's me excluding *them*. Perhaps it has been all along.

I wasn't expecting that – that a traffic warden recruitment day would turn into a self-help group meeting. But it *has* given me food for thought so I decide to return to the second half of the morning with a renewed optimism, a determination to get involved, although perhaps not excessively so – I might end up being offered a place and then I'll have to explain my reasons for not wanting to take it to Robocop at the Job Centre, assuming that Jenny's still not back.

But my good intentions are soon dampened on the arrival of a cardboard box of uniforms, the speaker pulling one out and showing us the exact outfit that we would be expected to wear, the black air-cushioned Doctor Martens, explaining how many miles the average officer walks in a day, that we'll need to cast all hope of stylish fashion statement aside in favour of ergonomic comfort and practicality. Next out of the box is a fluorescent yellow/green tabard, meant to be worn over the uniform – like we wouldn't be enough of a target already. When a raised hand asks *why the vest?*, it's explained that it's for the inevitable Health and Safety reasons, when surely keeping a low profile would be much safer – if anything, we should be wearing camouflage. Once the coordinator seems satisfied that he has everyone on side (he clearly hasn't been studying the whole room) he delves a little deeper into some of the tricks of the trade; how it's a good idea, for example, to arrive at a car-park just before six pm when people think they'll turn up late and get away with not buying a ticket; like flouting the five minute leniency rule, put in place to allow for minor discrepancies between discordant time-pieces. When I raise my hand and ask *isn't that a bit… you know…sneaky?,* expanding that surely our role is to be preventing inconsiderate, obstructive, potentially hazardous parking rather than just trying to generate revenue, I can tell by the way he glares at me and asks me my name again that he's already made up his mind, decided that I'm not the man for the job, that being a traffic warden clearly isn't in my blood. *If they break the rules, they pay the price* he says – which as it happens turns out to be twenty five pounds if settled immediately, rising to forty if not paid within fourteen days.

The last ten minutes of the morning are set aside for group Q and A, to recap on the information covered so far and address any queries or concerns that people might have before the more interactive tasks due to take place in the afternoon. I raise my hand, along with the others, happy to be able to contribute a potentially interesting question, one that he might never have been asked. He works around the room, systematically lowering hands, fielding their questions with a practised expertise. He's heard them all before. But not mine, possibly. Maybe this will help endear me to him a little more after the whole *sneaky* difference of opinion. I clock the moment that I catch his eye but he pretends I don't as he chooses someone, *anyone* else, other than me. Finally though, there are no other hands still raised – perhaps he was hoping the blood might drain from mine and I'd give up, lower it back down again before he got to me – and he turns to say 'Yes, please?' with forced politeness.

'Yes' I say, excited about the originality of my question, particularly in comparison with all the others, most of which seemed to be asked merely to catch his eye, to look good, the answers requiring only a modicum of common sense rather than any industry specialist knowledge. 'I wondered where the profession stood on dogs.'

The rest of the room turn in their seats to look at me, clearly interested to witness the source of this most intriguing of questions.

'Dogs?' repeats our illustrious leader.

'Yes. How do they feel about staff taking their dogs with them on their rounds?'

'Oh, I see' says Jobsworth. 'Erm, well to tell you the truth, that's a new one on me. In all the years that I've been running these sessions, I can honestly say that it's never come up.'

A couple of the other candidates – quite possibly dog owners - chatter animatedly among themselves, nodding in firm agreement that it's a good question, a valid point, that why shouldn't they be allowed, since the job is based outside and pretty much involves walking the streets all day. Jobsworth seems mildly irked, that his professional integrity has been compromised, his self-promoted image of all-knowing parking oracle shattered right before his subjects' eyes.

'I've never heard of it before' he admits, 'Certainly never seen it. But I'm not sure if there's any Government legislation on it that says you *can't* specifically. I'll look into it whilst you're all having lunch and hopefully let you know this afternoon.'

'Thank you' I say, thinking that thanks to me, hopefully even *he* will have learnt something today.

'What sort is it?' he asks.

'I'm sorry?' I reply.

'Your dog. What breed is it? Just out of interest.'

'Oh, I don't have a dog' I say, and he, along with everyone else in the room, those whom I felt were just warming to me, looks at me wide-eyed, a couple of mouths even dropping open – and I mean literally, like they would if you were exaggerating, miming pretending to be shocked.

Now he *really* thinks I've asked just to show him up, make his life difficult. I think it's probably now safe to say that I no longer need to worry about getting any excuses ready for Robocop. I'm about to explain, let them all know

197

why I asked, tell him about my recent visit to the rescue centre and my hopes of re-homing one of their long-suffering residents, when another hand goes up – of course it does – just in time for one final irrelevant question before he calls time out for lunch.

In the heavily subsidised cafeteria, I queue up with my brown veneer plastic tray, pushing it along the chrome runners with the others until I arrive at a heat-lamp-lit display case of rectangular silver trays, each containing a similar bubbling brown slop of indeterminate origin. I go down the middle, taking a chance, figuring that one is likely as good as another, garnishing it with a portion of chips, the last of the batch, small, dried fragments of salted, deep-fried starch spooned out from the corner like wood-chippings. Taking a carton of Just Juice – because surely *that* can't contain anything else – with which to wash it all down, I flash my badge at the cashier to secure concession prices and pay, hesitating at the edge of the room with my tray still balanced in my hands. A handful of the others from my group are seated at a round table across the way. There's an empty seat. I take a deep breath and head over.

'Is this seat taken?' I ask, when clearly it isn't, receiving a wary shake of the head as a response as they return to their conversation, discussing the events of the day so far. I decide not to speak unless spoken to, think about what I say before I say it, wait for an opportune moment to explain my dog comment. But the longer I listen, the further away from them I feel again, as if I'm physically a long way off - despite sitting right there among them - behind a soundproof glass divide and they wouldn't hear me even if I did speak, as though I'm watching them on some horrendous reality TV show. It's like there's a direct correlation between the number of people in my immediate vicinity and how alone in the world I feel. One of the younger men at the table seems under the seriously misguided apprehension that the standard issue Civil Enforcement Officer attire will help him pick up women because *ladies love a man in uniform, right?* Wrong. I'm pretty sure that not this time matey. Try asking for her number as she catches you slapping a ticket under her wiper and see how far you get. I say nothing – but incredibly, nobody else corrects him either, not even the females present, who laugh along just as heartily as the others. A larger, older chap, quite clearly an obnoxious fellow, even before opening his mouth to confirm it, starts talking about all the commission he's going to make, issuing tickets left, right and centre at the slightest infringement, and once again the others are with him every step of the way, no doubt already choosing the colour of leather interior they intend to spec at the Lamborghini dealership. They all seem quite oblivious to the fact that perhaps somewhat miraculously the subject of remuneration hasn't even been raised yet, that traffic wardens don't earn commission, aren't even financially rewarded with performance related bonuses from what I can make out, and I've done a bit of internet research myself already (couldn't find anything about dogs though, although I did read an interesting article that proposed traffic wardens being given the authority to hand out fines for non-clearance of dog-mess – which should make them even more popular).

I'm not sure I can take much more. The fierce look the induction guy gave me was absolutely right – I'm not cut out for this line of work. I've nothing against the profession in principle, believe that they provide a valuable public service even. I'm just not sure I'm small-minded enough to be any good at it, to rival the victim-hungry competition - and I'm not sure my fragile self–esteem could face being dismissed from yet another role that I never even wanted in the first place. I don't even know why I'm deliberating really - after this morning, it's not like I'm going to be offered a place now anyway. My name's on the course sign-in sheet at least- they'll know I attended.

Conversation still in full flow, nobody seems to notice as I take my tray from the table, walk over and place it in the tall rack-on-wheels and leave the building, not bothering to sign myself out at reception. Gwen Chambers was never there anyway.

p.

'Come in!' called Alan Cartwright to the top of the year eight lad's head, just visible through the wire-mesh classroom door window.

'I have a note from Mr Savage, Sir' said the lad, venturing timidly into the room, dodging a well-aimed paper-ball missile, trying his best to ignore the default derogatory comments issued by his seniors and handing over a folded piece of lined paper, torn neatly with the aid of a ruler from a wire-bound notepad.

Glenn Chambers sat quietly at his desk on one end of the front row. Today he was glad of his anonymity. Head down, nobody noticed his eyes narrow, a subconscious attempt not to reveal the smile now in them, his mouth set fast in a perfect hyphen.

The teacher, already irritated by the interruption when he'd only just managed to get his year eleven class to settle down, snatched the note from the young boy's hand, opened it up and read impatiently:

Alan,

Could you please bring Gary Fretwell to my office as a matter of urgency? Please make sure that he brings his coat, bag and any other possessions on his person with him, ensuring that you keep him in sight at all times.

Thanks

ES

As a matter of urgency. He assumed that that meant immediately, right now, in the middle of session. Great. Surely whatever it was could wait another half an hour, at least until…. And then it dawned on him exactly just what this might be about.

'Right, class. You've been set your work; you should all now know exactly what you need to do. Unfortunately I've been called away for a moment to deal with something that's come up at the last minute and can't be avoided. I'm going to ask Mr Bellingham to look in on you whilst I'm gone' he lied, well aware that the mere mention of old Bell-End's name (yes, even some of the other teachers used it, though not within earshot of course) struck terror into the hearts of all at St Michael's – including some of the more junior staff and teaching assistants. 'If there's any funny business, if I hear any complaints from other teachers about noise from this room, I will personally make sure that each and every one of you repeats this lesson again, under supervision, at the end of the day. Do I make myself clear?'

'Yes, sir' chanted thirty voices in unison, a sarcastic but sincerely delivered riposte.

'Fretwell' said Mr Cartwright 'Would you collect your things and come with me please?'

202

'Me, Sir?' said Ferret, pointing at himself.

'Your name is Fretwell, is it not?'

'Yes, Sir, but…'

'Then yes, you, Sir. Now, please' and, looking genuinely perplexed, Gary Fretwell gathered his stuff together and followed his teacher out of the room, to singsong catcalls of *Ooooh!* and *You're gonna get in trouble!*

The walk along the corridors was a long one, especially the last couple of turns, the final phase of the labyrinth leading him into the area set aside for the Senior Leadership Team and ultimately the Head himself feeling like the last few steps to the gallows. Rarely was anyone ever called up here to receive praise. This meant trouble.

'Could I quickly use the loo first please, Sir?' asked Ferret, immediately arousing his chaperone's suspicion.

'You should've gone before lesson' said his teacher. 'We're only ten minutes into the morning.'

'I didn't need to go then' said Fretwell, telling the truth, the nerves having got the better of him.

'Well, I'd prefer that you wait' said Mr Cartwright, not wishing to have to accompany him into the lavatories and watch whilst he urinated – or worse.

Alan Cartwright knocked on the door of his boss's office and waited for the standard 'Come!' which always followed. It came and he did, as instructed, pushing open the door and ushering the young lad in.

'Gary Fretwell, Mr Savage, as requested' he said.

'Aah, so *this* is Fretwell is it? Take a seat lad' said the Headteacher. Alan Cartwright made to leave, presuming his work here done and keen to get back to his classroom before all hell broke loose, assuming that it hadn't already.

'No, no, Mr Cartwright. I'd like you to stay too please. Please, pull up a pew,' said the Head, and the English teacher understood immediately – he needed a witness.

'Fretwell' said Mr Savage, looking at him – *into* him.

'Yes, Sir' said Ferret, his voice wavering, betraying his fear – a fear of the unknown. What was he doing here? Had someone reported him for thumping that freaky new kid? There wasn't anyone there at the time but his own crew and there's no way they wouldn't cover for him. Unless Chambers grassed him up himself. His face would certainly have provided some pretty compelling evidence. But it would be their word against his, five against one. It hadn't even happened on school property.

'Gary James Fretwell' said Savage, as much to himself as to anyone else in the room, continuing to appraise his exhibit, glancing down at an open file on his desk. 'I see you've had a rather....*interesting* disciplinary record. Far from exemplary but then not too horrendous either, I suppose. A couple of accusations of bullying in year eight – nothing proven - withdrawn. Innocent until proven guilty. Lean on them did you?' he asked.

'Lean...?'

'Consistent low-level disruptive behaviour' he went on 'back-chatting teachers, that sort of thing; couple of half day suspensions, no fixed exclusions. Not the best but certainly by no means the worst.'

'No, Sir' said Ferret, sensing a glimmer of hope, that maybe it wasn't going to be anything so bad after all.

'No history of criminal damage that I can make out - not your usual M.O.'

204

'No, Sir' said Fretwell, brightening, oblivious to where this was all headed.

'Would you mind turning out your pockets please, Mr Fretwell' asked Savage, no question-mark necessary 'and placing the contents on my desk.'

'Do you mind if I ask why, Sir?' ventured the school-boy, nervous again suddenly.

'Yes, Mr Fretwell, I *do* mind' said Savage, his tone adopting a distinctly less cordial edge all of a sudden. 'I'll be asking the questions here, thank you all the same. If you have nothing to hide then it won't really matter why I'm asking, now will it?'

'No, Sir' said Ferret, beginning to do as instructed, rummaging around among the crumb-lined pockets of his blazer and placing items down one at a time as he found them - a handful of Pannini football stickers, three of which were duplicates, a dog-eared school library card now seeing daylight for the first time since initially pocketed, a couple of clear Bic biros with missing lids, bits of fluffy fuzz stuck to their nibs, and a Nintendo Donkey Kong Game & Watch handheld.

'Your coat too, please' said Mr Savage, gesturing at the blue snorkel parker with the grey, fur-lined hood draped over the lad's sports bag on the floor by his chair.

Ferret emptied the outer pockets, containing only a couple of conkers brought in ready for drilling in carpentry lesson, then turned the coat inside out to reveal the bright orange quilted lining, pulling out the white cotton innards of the inside pocket to further establish its emptiness.

'And now your bag' said Savage, the subconscious lack of *please* suggesting that this was where his interest really

205

lay, where he expected to find what he was looking for, if anywhere.

Ferret took out a pile of exercise books, reddening as he placed them down, the cover of each one scrawled with doodles, crudely rendered caricatures of some of the more unmistakable teachers at St Michaels, though thankfully not Mr Savage himself, at least not on those that were visible. He then took out a pair of filthy football boots, the studs caked in dried mud and grass – he held them hovering over the desk with a questioning expression before the Head-teacher told him to put them down on the floor and then, as an afterthought, asked Mr Cartwright to check that there was nothing inside them. Ferret then took out a damp rolled up towel and the rest of his games kit – a muddied green football shirt with *Fretwell10* written on the back (he'd asked his mother to sew it on especially), shorts that were barely still white in places and a musky pair of long, floppy, green sports socks, heavy with half-dry mud and sweat.

'That's everything' said Ferret, holding the bag upside down and giving it a confirmatory shake, little bits of dried mud and crisps raining down on the freshly vacuumed carpet of Mr Savage's office, doing the boy no favours.

'Not quite' said Savage.
Ferret eyed his interrogator with a quizzical expression, half expecting him to begin pulling on a pair of white latex gloves.

'Would you mind unrolling the towel please?' said Savage, the intonation and dismissive hand gesture suggesting that he'd really rather not have to touch it himself if he could at all help it.

206

Still looking confused but wanting this all to be over, never imagining he'd have thought it but actually wishing to get back to lesson, Ferret slowly unravelled the mysterious towel which he'd already been a little surprised to find rolled up all neat and tight like that in his bag. Usually he just stuffed it in there.

He felt it before he even reached the final turn, knew something was wrong, that something was in there that hadn't been there before, that didn't belong. And as he lifted the towel up from the desk, a magician delivering the big reveal, he watched in fascination at his own trick as the wooden-handled chisel rolled out and across the desk, coming gently to rest against a pen drawing of a comically bulbous-nosed Mr Alves on the front cover of his history book.

N.

I'm glad I brought my kit with me. My gym is en-route, about halfway between the council offices and home. I'd planned on going at the end of the day, at one of my usual times, when the induction process had finished at five as the printed agenda had said it would, but now I'm early. I like to go during peak times – either early lunch or after office hours – when it's busier. It may surprise you but I prefer it when it's busy. I can plug in my iPod, get on the machines and be out in the world, alone in company without looking like a loser. There's always a lot of other people there on their own too – it's one of the few things nowadays that it seems perfectly acceptable to do by yourself. *Autonomously* – there it is again. Perhaps that's what I am – an automaton. When I go to the cinema, for example, and they ask *how many?* I always sense their pity when I reply *just one please.* But why? Why should going to watch a movie alone, one of the few things you can do when you specifically don't want anybody talking beside you, be seen as odd? Surely it's even more unusual to choose to go with someone and then spend the whole evening pretty much ignoring each other. But anyway, I like to go when it's busy. Not in a seedy way but I like it when there are attractive women there – something nice to look at and, playing a numbers game, I might even have a

208

slim chance of striking up a conversation with one of them. They look all lithe and shapely in their figure-accentuating Lycra and it's always nice to look. I don't think there's anything wrong with that either, just so long as I don't touch. I mean, no one objects to tweed-sporting academics standing in a hushed gallery staring at a Botticelli, spouting pretentious twaddle about appreciating the beauty of the female form, so why should looking at the real thing be any different? Women are beautiful creatures, all of them, and should be recognised as such. I've heard lads in there laughing unkindly at some of the more overweight forms struggling along on the exercise bikes, pounding the running machines, dripping crisp-salty sweat all over the laminate flooring - but at least they're trying, at least they're doing something about it. That's why I like the gym, because, meatheads aside, at least people are in there because they care about something, if only their own appearance.

I hope that came across in the spirit that it was intended and not in a pervy way. You probably already made some assumptions about me - *single guy, lives alone, no girlfriend, bet he's on that internet for hours every night.* But I'm not, I'm really not – at least, not in the way that you mean. Yes, I spend an inordinate amount of time surfing the web, but I'm looking up trivia, expanding my general knowledge, learning how the tight skin around a giraffe's legs works like surgical stockings or how, at a conservative estimate, the population of China would be bigger by the entire population of the United States if they hadn't introduced their birth control measures when they did – that sort of thing. I can't seem to key in a search

209

without a link to some dodgy site flashing up on the screen though. Oh don't get me wrong, I've looked. Curiosity killed the cat and all that - and I'm a man at the end of the day. A man with needs. But I don't need *that*. Image after image of women being degraded, defiled, de-whatever else you can think of, being called slut and bitch and whore like it's foreplay, misogyny packaged as eroticism. It turns my stomach. I can't believe it's allowed – legal even. I can't even open a door for a woman or offer up my seat on the bus without being called sexist and yet....

Anyway, I get to the gym early. It's like a club I'm not a member at. I realise, myself included, just how routine-driven peoples' lives are, that I don't recognise a single familiar face when usually it's a new face that I notice. It's much quieter than usual, most of the office workers now in the showers or already back at their desks, wolfing down a quick half-stale prawn mayo sandwich from the newsagents next door or a Greggs sausage roll. I don't like it nearly so much, can't hide, blend into the huffing, puffing crowds - in fact, quite the opposite. With no swathe of bodies to obstruct, the huge walls of mirrors seem to catch me from every angle, bouncing around the room, multiplying me, reflective clones filling the gym with a whole team of Glenns when one of me is surely more than enough – I can't even get *him* right.

There's a huge guy stalking the free-weights area, pacing up and down like a pumped up panther, well, more like a rhinoceros actually, checking himself in the mirrors with each new turn as if claiming his territory – which, from the size of him, this most certainly must be. He doesn't look like *he's* bothered about the fly's eye

210

reflections, looks like there aren't nearly enough for his liking in fact. I'm not sure that *huge* does him justice either. Enormous? Ginormous? Is that even a real word? (note to self - another thing for me to look up on the internet later). Humongous? Gargantuan? Colossal? I'm not sure where these all fit in relation to each other, what the sliding scale of sizes would be. So many things to know, so little time – but thank God for the internet or I'd have to rely on the local library and I'm not particularly welcome there now.

Mr Muscle alternates between sets – one of weights and one of checking himself out in the mirror to evaluate the full effect of the set just completed, flexing his arms into various positions, the serrations between his muscles looking like they were drawn on with a marker pen. He wears what appears to be the remains of a cloth T-shirt, a logo reading *MaxFlex* on the front, the collar area open to reveal his clavicle and the top of a pair of cartoon pectorals; the sleeves missing and the whole not quite long enough to cover his twitching torso, presumably to enable easier regular verification of his abdominal muscles which he crunches forward in a standing curl to flex and reassess - as if they might've changed considerably since two minutes ago when he last checked. His ridiculously small spandex shorts leave little to the imagination, and I guess that's the point, though from what I can tell he's nothing to write home about in that department – the steroids have clearly taken their toll. He acts like he's the only one in the area, not as if anyone else can see him, but then, when you're the size of half a house I guess you can afford not to really care what other people think.

211

But he *does* realise that other people can see him. I haven't realised it but whilst I've been mulling these things all over in my mind, I've been staring at him the whole time. And he's clocked it – oh, he's probably clocked it half a dozen times, from various angles. I say *staring* when what I mean is that my head and eyes were facing in his direction whilst my mind was elsewhere. He stares back at me, apparently angry with me for something... what?...looking? Surely he wants people to look or why has he gone to such extreme lengths to do that to himself, create such a figure of abject fascination. And that's what I am - fascinated. I can't deny it. It's like he's a real life superhero, just stepped out of the pages of one of my childhood comics, like in that A-Ha video. And he's not just any old comic-book character either – he's The Incredible Hulk. No, make that The Thing, you know, the big guy from The Fantastic Four. He has boulders for shoulders and a liberal application of fake-tan has rendered him orange, the colour of new bricks. He looks like he's been creosoted and God knows he's as big as a fence. At least he'll be well protected when he leaves – it's pouring outside.

And then I realise that I've just done it again – been daydreaming whilst the whole time facing in his direction. I really must learn to ask my brain and the rest of my body to start working together more closely, rather than so independently of each other like they have been lately. As they do just that. My eyes focusing outward rather than inward like they just were previously, I realise that he's still staring at me - and he doesn't look like he's cheered up any since the last time I noticed. I'm also pretty sure that *his*

212

eyes are working *with* his brain, that he's staring *at* me, not merely in my direction, that he wants me to be quite clear on this point. I realise that the issue isn't that I was looking at him; it's that I didn't look away when he looked back and then again not when he tried staring me down either, inadvertently taking things to the next stage. Because that's all it takes, as preposterous as it seems - the line between provoking a fight and just going about your daily business, perfectly innocently and unharmed. A look, a look back, a look held for just a fraction of a second too long, that then becomes an affront, a primeval challenge for dominancy, to head up a pride that no longer even exists. But the damage has been done and, try as I might, I can't seem to take it back. Everywhere I look, try to look away, I catch his eye in another mirror and I can't seem to help myself, can't stop looking back again to check whether or not he's still looking at me, whether it, whatever *it* is, is still in the air. But it most definitely is. And I realise that nothing I can say or do is probably going to change that now. This guy wants trouble. When you're as big as him then why wouldn't you? You certainly wouldn't back down from an accidental Chambers death stare.

I step up onto the rubber belt of one of the running machines, my back turned to him, facing the wall – but inevitably it's a wall of mirrors, somehow making our line of sight even more unavoidable and so, my behaviour seeming even more odd for getting on and then off again without doing anything there, I move to a shoulder press machine, sitting down on the padded cushion, busying myself making some adjustments, moving the metal pin that selects your chosen resistance and fine-tuning the

213

height setting of the seat, the angle of the hand-grips. When I turn to face forward again, Monster Man has somehow managed to come over without my hearing - no ripples forming on the surface of the water in my drink bottle like I'd have expected from such a Tyrannosaurus – and is now stood right in front of me.

'You see something you like mate?' he says, bearing down over me, seated before him. When he says *mate,* he means the opposite.

'No' I say, telling the truth 'Nothing I like.'

'Well stop staring at me then you little faggot' he says, and shoves my chest, pushing me against the padded back-support designed to bear excess pressure as though he half expected to put me through it. 'Unless you want to wake up staring at a hospital ceiling.'

Little faggot. Strangely, of the two, it's the word *little* that upsets me most. I'd say I was about average – five seven and a half, maybe even eight on a good day – but then I guess compared with him everybody's small.

His mobile phone rings loudly – the Rocky theme tune. I know it well, am horrified that such a classic, a favourite of my own, would be tarnished by this brute's appreciation, and he walks away to answer it, shouting into the handset for the benefit of anyone vaguely within earshot, talking about some big deal he's got all set up and how he's *gonna make a nice bit of bunce on this one.* And that's when it clicks, when I realise why I've been so fascinated by him all along. It wasn't just his Hulk-like bulk after all, though that would've been reason enough to stare. I know him. Knew him. Knew who he was at least. Can't believe I didn't spot it sooner. But he's considerably bigger than he

214

was the last time I saw him and he was big enough even then. In fact, he looks like he *ate* that person I once knew. It's Big Lad – or Wayne Jennings as I later discovered his real name to be.

His voice acts like a catalyst, re-firing in me all sorts of childhood emotions, unspent frustrations, the years of persecution or worse, the alienation – a form of long-term solitary confinement without the walls, letting me know the whole time what I was missing out on. I'm intent on staying calm though. I move the pin down the weight stack a few notches, think that maybe I'll vent my anger that way, but after a couple of sets, moving the pin further and further down until I'm pressing the whole stack, I realise that it isn't going to work, that I need to address the cause of my negative emotion at its source.

Jennings is lying on his back, bench-pressing an Olympic bar with an impressive array of metal plates on each end. I tot them up from where I sit, not needing to look at the numbers embossed into their middles, the different colours for each size already familiar to me. Two twenties, two tens and a five - that's kilos, not pounds, by the way – on each end. So, let's see, sixty five either side, that makes one thirty plus say another fifteen at least for the bar - so we're looking at a hundred and forty five all told. A substantial weight admittedly but, in my opinion, not great for his size, for the power to weight ratio. That's not much more than I do myself and he must be double my size. All show and no go. But he's struggling with it, making an almighty racket, shouting like he's in the final of World's Strongest Man, wanting people to look over and

215

see what he's doing, wasting valuable oxygen that he clearly badly needs re-routed to his over-stuffed muscles.

I walk calmly over.

'Need a spot?' I say, appearing behind his head, referring to the accepted gym-speak for assisting a training partner with a final few reps when needed, when the body is fading, reaching fatigue point. This time it's me bearing down on him, only he's significantly more prone than I was, laying flat on his back beneath me, upside down looking up, visibly confused as to why I, of all people, would be offering my services when clearly he earlier expected me to offer a very different service altogether.

He grunts, the effort of speaking clearly too much for the remainder of physical effort he has left in him. I take it as a yes. I hold the bar near its middle, in between his gorilla grip.

'My goodness, that *is* heavy' I say, holding the barbell away from the rack which he was clearly about to return it to, expecting me to help. A look of panic flashes across his eyes like a prison-tower searchlight, sweeping the courtyard for a way out, the escape route just taken and therefore still open, the warning sirens in his head still whining.

'What....' he manages, and I pray to God that he's not going to finish the sentence with *the fuck are you doing* but lucky for him he doesn't, doesn't have the breath, what with all the inconvenience of supporting a hundred and forty five kilograms of trembling metal over his head like that. Just imagine what would happen if he hadn't managed to lock his arms out, couldn't hold it any longer. It would've had nowhere to go but down. The weight

216

would've very likely broken his sternum – the weakest part of the skeleton I heard somewhere, though will need to look that up later - crushed his ribcage, possibly even resulting in a punctured lung. He might even have died. He still might.

'So I'm a faggot am I?' I say. 'Have you not seen yourself? You spend enough time looking in the mirror. You lie there with your blonde highlights, your fake-tan and your crop-top and hot pants and *I'm* the faggot, when I think we both know that there's only one meatball in here today and it certainly isn't me now is it? Now, from what I've read, and I read a lot, there's usually only one real reason for such deep-rooted homophobia. Stop trying to suppress it, trap it in among all that gristle. Let it out. It's nothing to be ashamed of' I say, my tone perfectly calm, polite, friendly even. The bar is shaking violently now, his face below purple with the exertion, knots of veins rippling the sides of his head and neck. 'Look, no harm done I suppose. Let's just kiss and make up shall we? Friends?' I say, offering my hand, still holding the bar firmly in place suspended above him with the other. 'No? Don't want to shake on it? That's not very friendly now is it? Ok, fair enough. Well then, let me give you a little piece of advice instead before I go. Next time you want to threaten somebody, perhaps don't then go and lie down in front of them with a huge lump of metal over your head. Understand?'

He lies there, almost crying with the exertion, near to breaking point. He's breathing heavily, short, sharp bursts, like a panic attack, desperately sucking in air to oxygenate

217

his blood which is screaming out for *a little help here please*.

'Do you not have muscles in your ears? I said *understand*?' I repeat.

'Understand!' he tries to shout but it comes out like a cough.

'Good. Ok then. Had enough?' I ask, milking the moment of one last drop.

'Yes' he manages – just, as if releasing the word will also set free his last remaining ounce of strength.

And then I remember all the times I was held in the mud, face down, knees in my back, one arm pushed up behind me at an obscene angle; for all their poor grasp of physics, my tormentors – him included - seeming somehow to know the exact load-bearing limit before my elbow would finally snap. I remember one of the few words that I ever spoke to my peers at break times, usually at their insistence:

'So what do you say when you've had enough?' I ask. I realise that I'm pushing my luck – his - now, that he is probably beyond *his* usual load-bearing limit. But I was good at geometry, at physics, at pretty much all of them. It's amazing how much better you learn when you have no friends to distract you from your studies. To think that I have no formal qualifications - that it's because of people like this. No, not even people *like* this – because of *him*, and others like him.

He looks at me wide-eyed, believing now what I'm truly capable of.

'S-s-s-s...' I say, prompting him. 'When we've had enough, we say s-s-s-s....'

'Sorry?' he puffs.

'Well, I'm sure you are now' I say 'But no, that's not what I meant. Not what I meant at all. No, what do you say when you've had enough, when you can't take any more and you want someone to release you, set you free? Now I *know* you went to school' I say, because obviously I do, though perhaps not so obviously to him.

'Submit!' he gasps, finally realising what I'm driving at, and then again, smaller, a confirmation, to make sure I got it. 'Submit.'

O.

'You see something you like mate?' he says to me.

'No' I say, and I think of adding *nothing I like,* because I don't, not if he's going to ask all hostile like that. He clearly doesn't see me as a mate in the making at all. In fact, it's the friendliest of his words that most confirms his question to be aggressive, a confrontation. Oh, I *think* of saying lots of things. I *think* of saying *I aint your friend Palooko,* like Vincent says to Butch in Pulp Fiction. I imagine him pretending that he hasn't heard me properly, can't quite believe his ears, of me saying *you heard me just fine Punchy.* But what I actually say is just *no,* and not even a very convincing one at that.

'Well, stop staring at me then, you little faggot' he says, shoving me back hard in my seat 'unless you wanna wake up staring at a hospital ceiling.'

'No…. I don't' I mumble, like it needed saying.

'And don't even think about showering here today' he says 'unless of course they let you use the ladies''

If he only knew just how happy that would make me. I think of telling him but true to form say nothing, aware that whatever I say will probably come out all wrong, like I'm being facetious, and only antagonise the situation. Better to stay quiet and let people think you're a weirdo than speak up and confirm it. It's what I should have on my family crest, if I had a family to warrant one: *In dubio, si taceam* – if in doubt, say nowt. That's not the literal translation of course, but the meaning is pretty much the same. Oh don't worry, I don't speak Latin – I'm not *that* much of a smart alec – I looked it up once, another time when I'd been in a similar situation at school and been thinking about it, what I'd have if I had to choose. We had a headmaster who used to always say *Have Faith,* like it was his catchphrase. People said it was what the words - *Forti nihi dificile* – on our school crest meant, but I wasn't so sure so I looked it up. You didn't have to speak the lingo to realise that three Latin words to explain two English ones didn't sound right. If anything it would've been the other way around. And as for *dificile* – *w*ell, you can probably work that one out for yourself. No, the school motto basically translated as *To the determined, nothing is difficult. Have faith* would've been *fidem habent,* just in case you were interested.

I realise I've drifted off, been staring into space – the space where Man Mountain is still stood, looking at me like I'm a spider in a jar.

'I thought I just told you to stop staring at me, you little bender' he says, and the word sparks a memory that jolts through me like an electric shock. I realise why I've been so fascinated by him all this time - why, subconsciously, I couldn't stop looking over. It's because I know him, knew him once upon a time. Thankfully he doesn't seem to remember me – I guess the beard is useful for something, and not just covering up the unsightly scar between my upper lip and septum. But now *Big Lad* just doesn't do him justice any more. Giant Man. The Orange Giant. Perhaps

221

he could get a job as the promotional front-man for tinned carrots. *Ho, ho, ho, Orange Giant!*

Wayne Jennings. I can't believe I didn't make the connection sooner. I wonder for the briefest of moments if I should mention it, if it might forge some kind of historic bond between us that wipes the slate clean, instantly negating all this nasty unpleasantness. But then I'm not so sure. Maybe the years since leaving school will have given him time to think about the past, for the idea that perhaps Glenn Chambers was responsible for his best friend Ferret leaving school that day never to return, to have found a way into that thick skull of his. Perhaps his friend had spoken with him about it after, described how he'd been escorted off the premises for his temporary suspension pending further investigation, how he'd been removing the padlock from his bike when the teacher accompanying had spotted that his was the only boy's one with an undamaged saddle, that this had pretty much sealed his fate, his continued vehement denials forcing the Headteacher's hand and his own permanent expulsion from St Michael's. Edward Savage's baying parents had wanted blood and no pussy-footed final written warning was going to suffice. Perhaps the two of them had carried out an amateur investigation into the facts together. It wouldn't have been hard to come up with a motive, a likely prime suspect. Perhaps Big Lad had known all along; perhaps they all had but hadn't acted on it for fear of further reprisals. I take comfort in this thought. It makes me smile.

'What the fuck are you grinning at?' says Jennings. God, is he still there?

'Sorry' I say 'I was miles away.'

222

'Well, you'd better be by the time I finish up here' he says, walking away, waist-thick thighs chafing, looking like he's messed his hot-pants when if anyone should have, it's me - and I decide that my workout is probably over.

'Sorry, mate, but the Fosters is off' said Skunk, handing his best friend a pint of crisp, effervescent lager, holding it up to the light to admire it as though it were some precious golden chalice. 'Went for the Stella instead.'

'Bloody hell, Skunk' replied Chip, placing the glass on top of the quiz machine 'some of us have to get up for work in the morning.'

'Well, it was that or Carling' he said.

'Fair enough' conceded Chip, frantically trying to recall who sang Video Killed the Radio Star.'

'The Buggles' said Skunk, leaning over his drinking buddy's shoulder to press at the appropriate, corresponding button, his friend fending him off, keen to remain in control. '*Definitely* The Buggles'. Chip pressed it, but not before first pausing briefly, to suggest that it was his own idea, that he would've got it anyway.

'Told ya' said Skunk, taking a self-congratulatory sip of his pint as reward. The next question came up on the screen. 'Shrew!' he shouted - an immediate response to being asked to name the world's smallest mammal. 'Gotta be shrew. Pygmy shrew specifically I think. Press it! Just trust me!' he said.

'How the hell did you know that? You spend too much time at home watching TV' said Chip with a smile.

'Animal Planet baby' said Skunk smiling back as his friend did as he was told and made the selection. A large red cross came up on the screen with a childish raspberry type sound telling them that it was game over. 'Bumble-bee bat! What the hell is that? I thought that was the joke option.'

'Your mate would've known that' said Chip, laughing.

'He's *your* mate. You're the one who brought him home that day' said Skunk, as if referring to a stray dog. 'Where is laughing boy anyway?'

'At home I think' said Chip, 'I told him I was going for dinner over at my folks'. He'd have wanted to come otherwise.'

'Think he's gonna realise that was a lie when you come home half-cut and stinking of booze' said Skunk.

'Nah. I'll just say I bumped into you on the way home and we stopped for a pint.'

'Again?' said Skunk.

'I know. Amazing coincidence, eh?' said Chip. 'Three times in one week. What are the chances?'

The two of them laughed as Chip rummaged around in his pockets for some more change for the machine. There was a top prize of five pounds for those who managed to go all the way - as a general rule of thumb, he usually spent an average of about ten trying to win it. Perhaps it was this gambler streak in him, the fondness for a game of online poker or an occasional drunken visit to the nearby local casino that had given him his nickname – or perhaps it was something a little less Monte Carlo and a little more

225

McDonalds, the frequency of staggering trips to the roulette table on the way home from the pub rivalled only by the call of the local chippie or kebab shop, his dish-du-nuit always accompanied by a namesake side order, dressed in burger sauce, curry sauce or gravy, depending on whichever beverage had first primed his discerning palate that evening. Or perhaps, less likely, it was simply because of the startling resemblance he bore to his father.

The origin of his flat-mate's nickname was presumably similarly multi-sourced, the obvious primary conclusion being that it was based on a penchant for smoking weed, large quantities of the stuff, at any time of day or night - a pastime that hadn't thus far proved compatible with holding down a permanent position of employment for any great length of time. His most successful career move to date had been that of amateur drug dealer, breaking up the little jiffy bags of hash bought from his supplier into similar, much smaller five or ten pound bags (in monetary value – he hadn't yet hit the big-leagues and had no intention of ever doing so), spreading his stash more thinly with tobacco and actual grass plucked from their flat's shared garden to forward on to other kids at the local college he still attended. His Social Studies programme was looking set to meet a similarly sticky end to his working life though, the course leaders taking to not receiving completed assignments about as kindly as his previous employers had taken to him repeatedly turning up at midday looking mildly the worse for wear - and so it looked likely that he'd soon be needing to find some motivation to go out and find a job, a requirement not made any easier by the cause of the problem in the first place.

An almost permanent stoned haze meant that he placed little significance on what he considered to be the unnecessary hassles of modern life, such as personal hygiene – his lackadaisical approach towards it possibly another reason for his nickname, although on the rare occasions when he made the effort to chat up girls, he told them it was a reference to the cartoon skunk Pepe le Pew, in light of his obvious assignation as something of a ladies' man.

Despite having lived with the two of them for several months, Glenn Chambers had had to resort to bringing in the post each day to try to discover their real names. The many red-letter warnings and unpaid bills that landed on the mat, though, were invariably addressed using initials in favour of full first names and it was only a chance answering of the land-line – which somehow still hadn't yet been disconnected – that yielded Chip's real name, his mother asking for him only by the very Christian nomenclature that she herself had chosen. Glenn had been working his first job as a shelf-filler – now surely Stock Replenishment Coordinator? - at the local supermarket, filling shelves with jars, tins and bottles, facing them up to look as neat as possible. Unfortunately, to his mind, as neat as possible meant time-consuming perfection, placing items in their allocated slots one by one as though customers weren't a consideration, weren't going to come along the aisle minutes later and mess up his artistically prepared composition and, setting a template to be followed again and again in later life, it was this same fastidious care and attention to detail that led to his leaving the role long before any gold watch was ever on the horizon. His slowness was perceived as laziness. What should've been a position in which he'd be able to work *autonomously* was actually located on the shop floor and so inevitably involved dealing with customers on a regular basis - a skill that Glenn had not yet mastered, and arguably never would. The writing was on the wall long before the pen-lid had even been removed. He was however, there just long enough to get chatting with Chip, based out in the warehouse at the time. Glenn would visit his co-worker's gloomy back-of-house domain, lists of products required written in biro on torn off empty cardboard box lids, the two of them working together to re-fill Glenn's metal cage-on-wheels. Chip and Skunk were in their first flat together at the time. They'd both had jobs when they'd taken it on but Skunk had lost his soon after moving in and they very soon realised that perhaps they'd underestimated the burden of responsibility that came with adult life. They'd been struggling to make ends meet and neither wanted to lose face and have to return home to the supercilious *told you so's* of their parents. They had a spare box-room that could be cleared of junk – it's not like either of them had used the weights bench even once since dragging it up there where it now sat, fortunately designed to withstand heavy weight, hidden beneath an ever-growing mountain of clothes. A young adult, no longer the responsibility of the state, Glenn had been looking for a place to live. He'd seemed reliable, conscientious, the steady plodder type who'd be good for his share of the rent. Chip had brought him home one day after work to show him the room, barely big enough to fit a bed, and he'd jumped at the chance, not just of a conveniently situated fixed roof over his head but one

228

sharing with two other lads around his own age. A package deal with ready-made friends thrown in – how could he possibly refuse? He'd turned up with his single bag of belongings and moved in the next day. They'd gone to the pub to celebrate but the cracks had already started to appear by the second round of beers, Skunk shooting his friend with a *where the hell did you find this guy again?* look. It wasn't even anything that either of them could necessarily put their finger on. He just wasn't like them. Just a little…off centre. On paper, at least, he was saying all the right things, fitting in perfectly – but that was just it. On paper. It's like he was reading from a script, playing a part, lines delivered that he'd heard others speak but weren't his to use. He was an understudy, someone who'd spent his whole life waiting in the wings, hoping for his big break, his chance to come out on stage, stand under the lights and show them all what he was made of. He'd now got that chance and the crowd hadn't liked what they'd seen. But he wasn't stupid either, could tell straight away that he was losing them. And he knew from experience that damage, once done, could rarely be undone. He needed to salvage things quickly and make a good first impression but, in his eagerness, bordering on desperation, to do so, he tried too hard, over-acted and lost them forever. The book had been finally snapped shut on Glenn Chambers when, after a couple of beers, he'd criticised his new 'friends' for speaking in a derogatory fashion about a group of girls in the pub. Skunk had made a joke about one of them, saying that he bet she liked it rough, that he'd happily slap her about a bit if she asked him nicely. Glenn's simulated laughter and attempts to ingratiate himself within the group

229

switched off suddenly like a light, the bulb fading instantly to black, leaving only a brittle red filament glowing still hot and red at its centre. *Steady on mate* Skunk had said, *I was only messing about. Oh, I know. Me too* Glenn had replied, bringing himself back, forcing a laugh, pretending to be just playing a joke on his new flat-mate, though none of them believed it. *I might get a lock put on my bedroom door* said Skunk when Glenn went up to the bar to get a final round of drinks in despite their protestations, the mood of the evening now ruined *don't want to get butchered in my sleep by the Supermarket Slasher. Don't be having a go at me* said Chip, *if you weren't so bloody useless and hadn't lost your job in the first place, we wouldn't be in the financial mess we're in and wouldn't have needed to get someone else in. At least I did something about it. He'll pay his way – and more than either of us too so just suck it up. We don't have to be best friends with him. He's a means to an end. When you get another job and we're back on our feet, we can kick him out. Well I guess there's my motivation right there then* said Skunk. And it was true – the only time Skunk ever seemed to have any get up and go was when Glenn Chambers entered the room. He didn't like how his flat-sharer (because *flat-mate* seemed dishonest) made him feel; uncomfortable, the disapproving glances as he skinned up, the windows unsubtly opened to allow fresh air in and drug-smoke out, the many cloying pine-scented air-fresheners popping up, dotted about the place, plugged in at the wall sockets, a forest, seeming to multiply each time he came home; the way he asked if he'd had a good day like it was an accusation, a slant on his labour non-intensive

230

lifestyle, like he had a parent in the room - only one his own age, somehow making it even worse. He had to go.

'You got any more fifty pees?' said Chip, keen to recoup his losses and throw more good money after bad.

'Me? I'm all out mate. Was gonna ask to borrow a couple of quid for another pint.'

'Sorry, I'm skint too. I'm not playing this bloody thing anymore. It's costing me a fortune. Not even got enough money for any food on the way home. I'm bloody starving too. Hardly eaten anything all day.'

'Don't worry' said Skunk, 'Barney'll have something in the fridge – always does. You know what an old woman he is.'

Completing the trio of nicknames, Glenn's had been assigned in his absence, the product of a mildly inebriated conversation between the other two about their increasing difficulty finding new and ever more innovative ways to shake him off. *He's like a limpet* Chip had offered, *you have to scrape him off your hull before you set sail. Yeah* laughed Skunk, *a barnacle. Barnacle Bill* suggested Chip. *Nah, Barney,* said Skunk, *he's definitely more of a Barney.* And so the latest in Glenn Chamber's long list of pseudonyms was born and, perceiving it to be linked to The Flintstones, perhaps the result of some cartoon-themed choice made by his flat-mates, to fit in with their Pepe le Pew and Chip 'n' Dale characters, he embraced it, though part of him knew that this was likely just fanciful thinking, that the real reason was probably something altogether less pleasant. Well, it was certainly better than Glenda the Bender anyway.

231

P.

I collect my things from my locker and leave the gym, not bothering to change and certainly not bothering to shower. That's it then, one of my few remaining external havens now turned to rubble, another social pressure valve plugged, yet another window removed from the Fortress of Solitude that my existence has become – and that's what it is, an existence, because this is no life – more closely resembling a tomb with each new day.

I feel like crying. I don't, unless you count inside, but still I take some small comfort in the appalling weather, the knowledge that if I were, the rain lashing my face would disguise it, possibly from myself even. It's truly grim, the scowling sky pregnant with Turner-esque strokes of light and dark grey, the sun barely struggling through to let us all know that it'll be back at some point, though not today. Definitely not today. No, it'll likely be taking the rest of the week off, possibly back on Sunday - as perhaps you might expect. I put my head down as I walk, like this will make the slightest bit of difference in keeping me dry, squinting my eyes half-shut to similarly pointless effect. As I near the small industrial park, rather than continuing on past as I usually would, I take a right, turning down the short road to Super Shed, the local DIY superstore, figuring that it'll give me a temporary shelter from the monsoon rains which have just been cranked up a notch, making that sound that tells you without even looking out the window to not even *think* about going outside. I rush inside, plumping my sports bag, reshaping it to drain it of the small pool of rainwater that has collected on its surface, water dripping from every inch of me, leaving me stood in a puddle of my own creation, enjoying the sound of heavy rain machine-gun fire way up on the corrugated roof of the air-craft hangar sized building. There's a café in here too. Maybe I can grab myself a nice hot cup of tea and a piece of cake, buy myself some time too until things calm down outside, although I'm under no illusion that things are likely to brighten up as such, the best I can hope to wish for that perhaps they might at least abate. I take a stroll up and down the aisles first though. I like it in here. It's big. Big enough to lose yourself, to not be noticed by other shoppers, by store staff asking you if you need any help when you haven't purchased anything within five minutes of entering when what they really mean is *if you don't intend to buy something then clear off.* Obviously there's the ubiquitous security guard, but even he seems rather nonchalant in his duties, leaning on the Customer Service desk, chatting up the attractive young – too young for him certainly – woman stationed there. And so I browse at my leisure. I amble. I think about getting something for the flat, a plant maybe, some small trinket, a treat to perk the place up a bit, make it feel a little less like the cell that it's become. What it needs is a woman's touch, but I guess that's not going to happen any time soon. It's just going to have to settle for a dab of Glenn Chambers' feminine side. I pick up picture frames, tea-light holders, stalks of fake

233

flowers, the same kind of nest-feathering ephemera that I remember seeing in the home-wares section of the supermarket. It all seems a bit pointless. If I buy the tea-light holders that I don't need then I'll have to then buy tea-lights that I don't need either, to put in them. If I buy the plastic flowers that I don't need then I'll have to buy a vase of some description that I also don't need to put *them* in. If I bought the picture frames, I'd need to put a nice picture in them and I'm not sure I have anything suitable – because what do people normally put in them? Happy family snaps. I look at the professionally shot black and white picture that's already set within their borders, there to give you an idea of what the finished article could end up looking like, and think that maybe I'd keep it, tell people, if anyone ever visited, that that was my brother and his wife and their two gorgeous kids, just look at their happy smiling faces and yes, that was such a great day we all had down at the beach - and they'd probably tell me, socially obligated, how they could see the fraternal resemblance, just as people always feel compelled to tell new parents that their newborn looks like at least one, if not both, of them – and I'd smile, forgetting for a moment, almost believing it myself.

Still holding the picture frame, though looking through it rather than at it, I think of my own family, what little I remember - a vague picture of my grandmother's face, the image puffy and swollen, hard to crystallise, like I'm looking through a misted window, my attempts to wipe it clean with a recollective cuff only smearing it, obscuring the image still further.

Putting it back on the shelf, I gravitate towards the DIY section, lengths of four by two, packets of variably graded

234

sandpaper, specialist tools for every conceivable practical task. I like carpentry, always have. Like the look and feel of wood-grain, the tale it tells, the story of how it all began, that a tiny acorn could become a mighty oak which in turn could then become a ceiling joist, the principal supporting beam in an old country farm house, a roof over the heads of respectable God-fearing country folk, their brood of politely-spoken public school children, socks pulled up to the knees, playing innocently beneath it with the family Springer spaniels frolicking eagerly at their feet, tongues lolling. It's not until I pick up a wooden handled chisel, turning it over in my hands like a long-forgotten toy just rediscovered during a loft clear-out, that I realise the real reason why I came in here. A nice cover-story, a perfectly timed excuse, but it wasn't protection from the rain that drove me in here. I look at the price. It's easily the most expensive one in the shop - but worth every penny, if only for how much better having it in my possession makes me feel.

And then, finally, something nice happens to me. I meet someone. A lady. A really lovely lady. Oh, nothing like that – she's eighty if she's a day – but lovely nonetheless. I see her struggling with her trolley, like a wayward toddler which won't cooperate, as she tries to push it where she wants it to go, the wheels with other ideas of their own. She draws up in the same aisle just along from me, steadying her cart like a cowboy on the reigns, looking up at the tins of wood-stain and varnish above her. She already has a couple of large tins of magnolia paint in her trolley. I wonder how they got there. She doesn't look like she could lift a brush, though even from here I can sense a

235

steely determination in her blue-grey eyes that tells me she's not afraid to give anything a go. She sees me looking and smiles. It's a warm, kind smile, but one that somehow only highlights her sadness. I know that smile, thought I'd perfected it but, looking at her, I can see I was wrong. She's clearly had years more practice with it than I have. I feel drawn to her, compelled to speak to her and go over to offer to help.

'Excuse me, young man, I couldn't borrow you for a moment, could I?' she asks before I reach her, leaving me slightly disappointed that I don't get the chance to offer my services voluntarily. *You can keep me* I think, strangely, the thought popping in there all on its own when I don't even know her.

'Of course. How can I help?' I ask. 'Need me to get something down for you?'

'Well yes, something, but I'm not sure what exactly. I have some new fence panels being delivered tomorrow. I went for the cheaper ones, my pension doesn't stretch far nowadays, I'm afraid, but they told me that they're untreated, that I'll need to do it myself. I'm not sure which one I need. There's so many. It's all very confusing. Well, for a silly old woman like me anyway.'

'No' I say 'You're right. It is pretty confusing. There's so much variety these days that sometimes it just makes things harder than it needs to be. Half of these all do the same thing anyway but they give them different names and call them different things to make you think you need to buy more than you need to when half the time just one will do the trick just fine.'

We chat and she starts out by explaining that she just wants them weather-proofed. When I delve a little deeper it turns out that she'd actually quite like them painted a different colour too, a dark green so that they blend into the background with her beloved trees and shrubs. By the end of the conversation, I've helped to choose the materials she needs and offered to do the whole job for her, including installing the panels myself. Turns out she lives not too far from me. She argues against it, of course, tells me not to worry, that she'll get someone in, that she wasn't trying to drop a subtle hint by mentioning her lack of funds but I insist, convincing her that I love to work with my hands, that it's a hobby of mine, that I need the practice, that she'll be doing *me* a favour. She tries to negotiate an hourly rate and we finally agree that tea and biscuits seems a fair price – or rather, she says *we'll see* in a way that means that she's still going to try to pay me but I'm resolute in my decision not to take anything. The tea and biscuits was my little joke, meant to make her feel better about my working for nothing. I didn't want to tell her the truth – that my real fee, one that I'll gladly work all day for, was her company. As we stand at the till, paying for our items, I experience a feeling of overwhelming guilt as I pay for my chisel, quickly, not wanting her to pay it any mind, as if she'll suspect evil intention if she gives it much thought. It seems to scream *weapon* at the top of its lungs for being the only item I purchase, sitting there all alone on the rubber conveyor belt as though a forensics team should already be drawing a chalk outline around it. I tell the assistant I don't need a bag and slip it into my gym bag, where I intend to let it stay, and help Mary – that's her name – to load up her

237

new supplies. She has one of those tartan shopping trolleys. I consider asking where she got it but don't want it to come out the wrong way, to seem that I'm being disrespectful, so I say nothing. Perhaps if and when we get to know each other a little better, I'll try to find out. For all my previous criticism though, I have to admit that it's going to come in pretty handy for the walk home, what with all the heavy tins and metal fence support brackets we've bought. I wouldn't fancy twisted carrier bag handles cutting into my purple ended fingers for the half mile journey back from here.

We walk and talk. She tells me that she was married to Joseph. I somehow manage to check my knee-jerk reaction before it escapes, aware that she'll no doubt have heard decades of similar comments, all thinking themselves the first to make the glaringly obvious connection. The marriage was brief but burned brightly during its short life, until being snuffed out by the war, perhaps ironically by gas more specifically. He was Jewish, her childhood sweetheart. People said they were too young, that it couldn't last, that she was a different creed, should marry into her own - but he was the only man for her, the only man there has ever been. For her, love was a once in a lifetime offer. I ask her if she ever had any children and she confirms that Joe was the only father she would ever have considered, that not carrying his child, continuing his name, was her only regret. I think of saying something comforting, that their biblical namesakes never had a child of their own, but firstly I'm not sure of the relevance – it was just something that occurred to me – and secondly I'm not so sure that it's even true, what their full history was,

238

before or after Christ. For all I know, Joseph had an affair and they got divorced. I'm not sure the Bible covers that bit – all the attention was on their son obviously, what with all the miracles and the revelations that God was his real dad and that.

So she's been alone for the best part of seventy years. There's been a number of potential suitors along the way, all of which she tells me were unsuitable for one reason or another – in her eyes at least. I get the distinct impression that suitability has nothing to do with it, that she'd rather live with a perfect memory than with a second-rate stand-in. Perhaps that's why we hit it off so well. We have something in common. We're both used to being alone. Funny that it should be that which draws us closer together. But it does. As I drop her off, seeing her to the front door, helping her inside with her trolley, promising to be back first thing in the morning to make a start, I already feel a bond forming, a closeness that I haven't felt in….well, that I haven't felt. Sure, I had some nice foster carers. Anne was absolutely lovely, still sends me cards on birthdays and at Christmas with little update letters inside, but I always felt that I was one in a procession of many; that it was a conditional arrangement, a forced, unnatural referral from the legislation-driven system that I was a part of; that another poor, needy case would soon be taking my place, stepping into my empty, outgrown shoes the moment I was gone. But this. This is how it should be. A chance meeting. A click. It's what I hate about the online dating thing. You just don't get that. A different click maybe – of a button. Too consumeristic for my liking. I'm surprised they don't have virtual security guards patrolling the site

239

while you browse. Probably why I haven't logged on for a while – that and the fact that the only women I've met on it so far have been judgemental body-critics and pregnant alcoholics.

I almost skip the rest of the way home, I'm so happy. What a rollercoaster of a day this has been; the downward plunge of the induction day, which already now seems such a very long time ago; the further plummet of the gym encounter, followed by the steady rise to the apex of my meeting Mary and the sense of purpose which this has now brought to the coming days ahead. I'm almost at my front door before I even notice that I'm soaked through, that I no longer still have Mary's umbrella which I'd been holding over her, listening in fascination to her story as I dragged her trolley along.

r.

As Glenn walked to the kitchen to fix himself some breakfast he knew from the smell what had happened before he even got there, what he saw on entering only confirming his suspicions. Empty disposable plastic cartons and yellow styro-foam containers sat on the side, just feet away from the waste-bin. Sweet and sour sauce congealed in a little white styro-foam pot, creating an opaque maroon jelly, the gloop-covered lid face-down, stuck to the sideboard, surrounded by an abstract arrangement of bean-sprouts, chicken chow-mein and egg-fried rice. Why he expected any different after all this time, God only knew. As he began to clear it away, a sound of sheepish, socked footfall behind told him that Chip had entered the room. It wasn't that he could tell their footsteps apart but it certainly wasn't going to be Skunk at this unearthly hour of the day – namely morning.

'Was this Skunk?' asked Glenn, used to having the absent third party pilfer his stocks in an insatiable fit of the munchies - his dissatisfaction tangible.

'It was both of us actually' confessed Chip, knowing that Skunk wouldn't have done the same for him, shouldering his share of the blame in the hope that maybe Glenn might look at him more favourably - not that he

241

really cared if he didn't; it just made for less fractious living conditions if they were all of them happy. 'Sorry'

'I thought you had dinner at your parents'?' said Glenn 'You can't have been hungry.'

'I shared a dooby' said Chip, by way of explanation, prepared to suffer the look of paternal disappointment – he rarely partook - rather than admit the truth; that they'd excluded Glenn from their plans once again.

'Look, I understand it probably seemed like a good idea at the time but that was meant to be my dinner for tonight too. I was planning on eating it cold. There was plenty there. You could've at least left me some. I don't mind paying my way but it's not fair that you two never contribute anything food-wise. If it wasn't for me we'd have had no sugar in our tea for the past month – in fact, we wouldn't have had any tea to put it in - or milk for that matter. I'm not sure where you both think it comes from. When it starts to resemble cottage cheese then it needs to be thrown away - and down the sink preferably, not in the bin with the lid off where it stinks the whole place out. I know that Skunk thinks I'm having a go at his cannabis habit but the place would smell like a squat if I didn't make an effort to freshen it up a bit. And that's another thing. The place doesn't clean itself. I know he's got no money at the moment but he could at least clear up a bit around here whilst he's sitting at home all day. It's not fair on you either, having to come home to this. I don't mind buying all the bleaches and detergents like I have been but it wouldn't hurt him to use them whilst we're both out at work, covering his share of the rent.'

242

He knew how it sounded, even as he was saying it. Like a lecture. A nag. But he just didn't care anymore. Everything he'd said was true. How was it that they shared their home with a B.O. and dope-addled, small time drug-dealing, soon-to-be college-drop-out bum and yet it was he, Glenn Chambers, that was the outcast in this arrangement.

'He pays his way' said Chip, half-heartedly, knowing it not to be strictly true, unless *your way* was based on the amount of ground you covered in the flat on any given day.

'Well, look, can you please ask him not to touch my stuff anymore? He's more likely to listen to you.'

'It was both of us' reiterated Chip.

'This time, maybe. I'm sorry, I've said it before but I don't want either of you touching my food anymore, at least not until I start to see a little bit of give and take' said Glenn, knowing that he was compounding their unity, alienating them both beyond reach, his efforts to be friendly having failed so miserably, time and time again. 'I mean it this time.'

'Ok' said Chip, like a scolded child, when what he was really thinking was *Yeah? And what exactly are you gonna do about it?*

Q.

This is the first morning in as long as I can remember that I've been looking forward to waking up. In fact, the feeling is so unfamiliar to me that I almost think I've dreamt the whole thing. As cliché as it sounds, I notice the birds singing outside my window like I've never done before – like I've landed in a Bambi movie, to be serenaded by a blue-feathered chorus-line perched on a nearby branch, there solely for the benefit of my own personal musical accompaniment. The bedside alarm, which I set last night, as if there was the faintest chance of my over-sleeping, isn't due to go off for another hour yet. Everything feels different this morning; the hot pulse of the shower on the nape of my neck, the sugary crunch of my cereal, the fine grittiness of the toothpaste, the satisfying bite of the comb's teeth through my tousled bed-hair. *I* feel different. I feel….human. It's been a while.

Mary's place is only a five minute walk from mine. When I leave the flat, I feel like a regular person, like I'm visiting family for the day, rather than going off to help a virtual stranger that I only met for half an hour yesterday afternoon with some manual work. I feel like everyone else can tell too, is looking at me differently, like I'm one of them; members of an exclusive contentment club with secret hand-shakes, maintaining eye contact and sharing a knowing *good morning, lovely day for it* smile, rather than looking down at the ground, pretending to fiddle with their mobile phones like usual. Perhaps they're no different at all – perhaps it's just me. But they're right - it *is* a lovely day for it. What looked to be set in for the rest of the week turned out to be a freak weather front sweeping across the continent. Looks like we've had our share and it's now moved on to spoil some Welsh farmer's day somewhere, leaving us with bright, clear blue skies - the calm after the storm. I pass groups of shrieking, chattering, play-fighting, uniformed kids on their way to school, suddenly no longer afraid of what they might say, tipping them a hearty *morning* as I pass, which they return amidst giggles and backward glances. They're just animals at the end of the day – show them fear and they'll be much more likely to attack. Today I am fearless. Gladiator Glenn.

I soon arrive at Mary's place. It looks exactly like what it is - the home of a single widow for the past seventy-odd years. She hasn't kept on top of the general upkeep and, quaint and charming as it, the chocolate box has been crumpled and squashed, the cellophane long since discarded. There are likely a thousand jobs that need doing - non-specialist stuff that I could easily help her out with. I can see missing slate roof tiles, some still up there, just become loose, sections of broken guttering, the remaining sections stuffed full with leaves from the surrounding trees and likely now non-functional anyway. The whole place could do with a lick of fresh paint, never-mind the new fence-panels which the reversing beeps of a large flat-bed tell me are just arriving. If I don't get a job any time soon, looks like I'll still have plenty to keep me occupied.

245

I don't even make it to the doorbell before Mary appears in the doorway to greet me. She seems as happy to see me as I am her, possibly relieved too that there's a friendly face arrived to deal with the delivery guys. She gives me permission to sign on her behalf, not knowing how symbolic that is, what it means to me. I supervise the unloading, getting the lads to deposit the new panels propped against the existing, damaged ones, on the lawn where I can paint and prep them without need of putting down dust sheets, making a mess. When they've gone, Mary asks me if I've had breakfast, do I want anything. I tell her that I had a bowl of muesli and she berates me, tells me that rabbit food is no breakfast for a man, particularly not when he's working, and orders me inside where she's already got some bacon going under the grill and a pot of tea stewing beneath a multi-coloured, hand-knitted cosy.

Cosy. That sums her place up inside. It's the polar opposite of mine, brim-full of knick-knacks filling glass-fronted display cabinets like museum exhibits, safe from the ever falling dust that has settled elsewhere around the room, atop the many other ornaments and picture frames lining the mantelpiece and side-tables. Unlike mine, there are many family photos on show around the place, pictures of young children, great-nieces and nephews, she explains to me wistfully, a combination of pride and sadness in her eyes. With the exception of some of the more recent photographs, slid into frames over the top of their out-of-date counterparts, everything in here is dated. But not in a bad way. A fancy, modern, minimalist fitted kitchen and flat-screen TV wouldn't look right, wouldn't suit her – no more than if she'd answered the door in a pair of neon-pink, bubble-soled Nikes. Practical and comfortable for somebody a bit unsteady on their feet, somebody with a bit of an ongoing hip and back complaint, certainly - but *right*? Most definitely not.

We sit at the table and eat bacon sandwiches together, brown sauce squelching out from the sides of the soft, doughy sliced white, washing it down with a steaming mug of strong, sweet tea and, licking the grease from my fingers, I think that rarely has anything ever tasted so good.

'Well, best be getting on, I suppose' I say finally 'I could sit here chatting all day' and I wonder if it's the same for her. She certainly doesn't seem in any great hurry for me to get started as she tops up my mug from the huge pot that she can barely lift for a second time, listing off the infinite selection of biscuits available, housed within a similarly cavernous tin. But, lovely though this all is, I don't want to take advantage of her hospitality. I'm here to do a job and I intend to do it – well. Asking her where the materials are that we purchased yesterday, I thank her for the tea and sandwich, take my plate and mug to the sink - much to her objections, that she'll do it - and excuse myself, collecting up what I need and taking it outside.

The sky overhead seems even bluer than when I went indoors. The sun has already started its steady ascent, the damp mist from yesterday's rain evaporating into the air, creating a gentle shimmering quality to the light that feels like being in an underwater world, even the sound quality softened by the all-pervading moisture. I'm a deep-sea diver, breathing pure oxygen rather than the polluted mixture above that I usually have to share with everyone else, taking in their outward breaths as they suck in mine,

247

leaving me scrabbling for a ventilator. I feel my lungs purifying with each inhalation and exhalation, replacing the life-tar of recent months that should've come with a Government health warning on the packet. Good, honest, outdoor manual work. *I could get used to this* I think as I make a start on the fence painting, deciding to do this first before installing them so that I don't have to worry about cutting in around the posts. A nice clean job. And there's something about working outside that endears you to people, particularly the much older passers-by who presumably have all but given up on the younger generation as a worthless bunch of bone-idlers. Perhaps it's just that you're more on show, more accessible, though it should then follow that this were the case too with retail customer service roles but, in my experience anyway, doesn't seem to be so. I like to think that it's something to do with nature, that I'm rooted on grass, surrounded by greenery and, consciously or otherwise, this has a calming effect on people, makes them more agreeable, reminds them that we're all just brothers and sisters from another mother at the end of the day. Barely a person walks by without at least smiling or bidding me good morning, making witty quips that *you can do mine next when you've finished!,* many even stopping for a full-on chat, the trip to the paper-shop just an excuse to share the day with others. I speak to more people in an hour than I probably have in a month.

The morning whizzes by in a flash. I wouldn't have noticed the time, would likely have carried on working until dark if it hadn't been for Mary announcing from behind me that it was lunchtime, insisting that I take a break, despite my protestations that I just needed to finish up the section I was doing. *It'll still be there when you get back. Eat first* she says. I don't argue.

So, for the second time today, we sit together, eating and talking. Sandwiches again. Roast lamb this time, with lashings of vinegary mint-sauce soaking into the squidgy bread, creating pale green fingerprints along the crusts. Suddenly traditional home-cooked English grub isn't so low down on my list. The Archers plays on Radio 4. She tells me that she's been listening to it for as long as she can remember and I wonder which is longer. I wonder if they're the family she never had. It seems there's nothing wrong with her memory though as I ask her all about her husband. She talks about him like they were together only yesterday, so much so that I keep apologising for things I say, thinking I may have put my foot in it, said the wrong thing, as you might when speaking to somebody who's only very recently been bereaved. It's hard to believe we're talking about somebody who died in the Holocaust. Well, it's hard to believe that *that* happened at all. As she talks, the twinkle of his memory still glowing brightly in her eye, I ask if he made her feel like she was the only girl in the world. *No* she replies, surprising me after sitting thinking about it for a few moments, *the only one in his.* I ask her what the thing she loved about him the most was. *That he didn't know how special he was* she tells me, and I think that it's one of the loveliest things I ever heard, how much I'd dearly love someone to remember me in that way, and I tell her so. *I'm sure someone will, one day* she says, and that's enough for me for now.

Fuelled up with three more mugs of sugary tea and an obscene number of custard creams, I get back to it, working solidly until some of the same people I saw on their way in to town start returning, bringing with them comments of *still at it?* and *I hope she's paying you well!* They have no idea just how well. I finish up for the day, cleaning out the brushes as best I can, wrapping them in carrier bags to keep them from drying out, and ringing at the doorbell to let Mary know that I'll be back again in the morning - but a little later than today as I have a meeting first thing. A meeting. It sounds important. I don't want her to know that I'm signing on. I'm not sure why. Maybe I don't want her to judge me or maybe I don't want her to feel obligated to pay me, don't want to give her the reason she's been looking for. Either way, I don't elaborate. She tries to invite me in for more refreshments and much as I want with every fibre of my being to accept, to spend the evening in her company, drinking tea and reminiscing about the good old days like they belong to us both, I force myself to decline, thanking her but explaining that I have things to do at home when I have absolutely *nothing* to do at home. I can't accept. I'm meant to be helping a damsel in distress, not eating her out of house and home. If I stay then she'll end up offering me supper too. At the rate she's going, she'd have been better off just paying me the going rate and letting me feed myself. So I stand firm and say no, barely feeling the cold pavement through my damp, muddied trainers on the journey home, walking on air as I am.

250

S.

'That's it, then' said Skunk, sipping his beer.

'That's what?' said Chip.

'How we get rid of him. I mean, apart from the obvious nutritional and economic benefits, we just keep on eating his stuff until he finally has enough and leaves of his own accord.'

'That's great Scarface, but what about the long-term economic implications? We need the money. It doesn't look like you're in any great hurry to get a proper job and we can't exactly rely on your piddly little cash-in-hand side-line to pay the bills.'

'I'll get one, don't worry. I'll have more time on my hands once my assignment deadline's been and gone and I haven't handed anything in. I think they're starting to seriously doubt whether I even own a dog, let alone one with a penchant for pulp.'

'But what if you don't?'

'Don't worry so much, mum. You need to relax a little - I've got something just right for that when we get home. Look, we'll put an ad in the paper - do what people usually do in these situations. We can vet them first - might even get some little hottie with a load of fit mates who keep coming round all the time.'

'Don't tell me – lezzers?'

'You never know. Jesus, they couldn't be any worse than old bundle of laughs Barney that you picked. Maybe you should just leave the recruitment strategy to me this time. We could set up a little interview panel, just us two, here in the pub. It'll be like X Factor.'

'Bagsy you're Louis then.'

'You realise that makes you Simon?'

'Good point. Think I'd rather be one of the birds. At least I could sort myself out. Wouldn't mind his money though.'

'We wouldn't be looking for a flat-mate if you had his money.'

'I wouldn't be sharing with *you* if I had his money' said Chip.

'You really mean that?' said Skunk, looking genuinely hurt, as if he'd seriously consider maintaining their existing living arrangement with over a hundred million in the bank, albeit perhaps a little more prompt with the rent each month. In truth, he probably *would've* stayed as he was too, if only because he couldn't be bothered to move.

'I wouldn't start panicking just yet' said Chip, sipping his beer, already there. 'Just imagine it though. We could be sitting here now, having a few beers whilst our live-in chef was at home cooking up a storm in the kitchen, preparing something nice for us, having it all ready on the table waiting for us to get home and polish it off.

'Pretty much exactly like now then' said Skunk, causing Chip to snort froth from the top of his beer through his nose, the two of them high-fiving across the table.

'Isn't there an easier way?' said Chip, wiping his face on his sleeve, becoming serious. 'Seems a bit harsh. Why don't we just sit him down and talk to him, put our cards on the table and be completely frank, that we just don't feel it's working out? Honesty's the best policy and all that.'

'You can have a cosy heart-to-heart if you want, Oprah, but that's your choice. I vote we stick with plan A – and I say we start implementing it tonight. Don't know about you but I'm bloody famished' he said finally, playing his Joker, knowing the way to Chip's heart.

'Ok' said Chip, his stomach grumbling in consent. 'Plan A.'

R.

Jenny still isn't back. With a day at Mary's planned for afterward, it doesn't bother me nearly as much as it otherwise might have, although obviously I'm worried for her. Three weeks. I hope it isn't anything serious. The same stand-in is still in her place. Now *there's* an automaton I think, and seeing her even makes me smile a little where only last week it gave me a sinking feeling. I take a seat when called and she looks at me like a doctor just come out to the waiting room to break the awful, earth-shattering news about to cause my world to collapse.

'How did you get on on Monday?' she asks me, when I'm pretty sure she probably already knows.

'Fine thank you' I say, playing along.

'I'm afraid they already filled the allocation of Civil Enforcement Officer roles currently available' she says, confirming my suspicions, and I half expect her to put her hand over mine in a gesture of sympathetic condolence. I pull it back, possibly a little too quickly, just in case.

'Oh. That's good' I say, adding quickly 'For them I mean.'

'How did the day go though?' she asks, more for something to say than anything else. She clearly doesn't really care. Why should she? 'Did you get much from it? What were the other people like? Did you get on with

254

everyone ok?' she says, when what she really means is *was there anyone you didn't upset?*

'I like to think that I made an impression' I say. It's the best I can come up with at such short notice, on the spot like that. It's true at least.

'Yes' she says, the lone syllable pregnant with inference.

She moves on to list various other low calibre, poorly paid vacancies and training courses and I nod and smile, agreeing to anything she suggests, my mind already at Mary's, thinking of the bristles slowly drying in their plastic bags, wondering if I tied them tightly enough, if they're the kind with little air holes in to stop kids from putting them over their heads and suffocating. I think that I'll grab some biscuits on the way, make my own contribution to the tin, something that I don't recall seeing in there already, forgetting that I'm already contributing - another full day's labour. It just doesn't feel like work to me.

And the day goes much as it did yesterday, except that today I enjoy a brunch of beans on toast with grated cheese and a late lunch of last night's left-over lasagne. She tells me that she made it specially, that she doesn't normally make big, filling meals for herself these days, doesn't really have the appetite she used to, but it's got pasta in it and I need the carbohydrates for energy - same for the beans. I worry that she feels guilty for not paying me. She keeps making reference to it but I threaten to stop helping if she won't accept it for free, tell her that she's offending me, and she seems satisfied. Every time I obey her commands to stop for a cuppa or a bite to eat, we get chatting and I

255

have to constantly remind myself why I'm there. I think she forgets too, a look of surprise crossing her face each time I say that I'd best carry on with what I was doing. It's a funny old scenario. I feel guilty accepting her food and she feels guilty accepting my help, but neither of us enough to want to terminate the arrangement. Maybe we don't really feel guilty at all. Maybe we only *think* we should when we both of us realise that it's entirely mutually beneficial and, more importantly, enjoyable. Perhaps this is how things should work. Payment in kind. Abolish money altogether.

By the end of day two, the fence panels are painted, treated and in situ. They look good. I was right to persuade her to go the whole hog. The green looks great, the newly coated wood unobtrusive, almost invisible, wrapped around her beautiful English country garden. I call her outside to come take a look and she steps out in her slippers, surveying her grounds. She looks delighted and disappointed all at once.

'It looks fantastic' she says, grabbing my forearm, her hands icy cold, a warm glow spreading up to my shoulder and across my chest nonetheless. 'You've really done a most wonderful job.'

'Looks pretty good eh?' I agree. 'We were right to go with the green.'

We.

'Definitely. You're a clever old stick, eh?' she says, and I think *at last, someone realises.*

'So…..' she begins, unsure where exactly this leaves us.

'So…..' I echo. 'I was thinking that maybe I could come back tomorrow. I hope you don't mind me saying but I've noticed a few other things that need doing about the place. Just silly things, nothing major, but you'll probably struggle up ladders on your own and....'

Ladders?' laughs Mary, 'I almost need a stair-lift just to get up to bed at night.'

'Exactly' I say, relieved, not wanting to have implied that she's useless without me, can't fend for herself, when quite clearly she has been, and for a significantly greater length of time than I've even been on this earth too. 'So I thought maybe I could come help you out a bit longer. God knows I need the exercise' I say, thinking that I'm unlikely to be using the stair-master at the gym again anytime soon.

'Well I'd like that' she admits, mildly troubled. 'But you simply *must* let me pay you.'

'Mary' I say, looking deep into her watery, platinum-blue eyes, feeling that I can tell her the truth now, now that we know each other a little better, though I'm sure she'll probably still think I'm joking. 'Your stories are payment enough.'

t.

Twenty four hours. That's all it took before Glenn realised that his words had fallen on deaf ears. Less than that even, since this had all clearly happened last night, presumably when they'd gotten in from the pub again, no doubt having bumped into each other on the way back from wherever else it was that they were independently supposed to have been. It wasn't the not being included - that he could take. He'd had a lifetime of preparation after all. No, it was the overt disrespect, the proactive lack of regard for his feelings when for once he'd spoken up and made them perfectly clear. He wasn't surprised at Skunk but, after all he'd said recently, you'd think that at least Chip might have had the decency to hide the empty packaging away in the bin, not leave such a statement of complete disregard lying around all over the kitchen. Or maybe that was *exactly* what he wanted. Well, message received and understood - extremely loud and perfectly clear.

Glenn emptied the ravaged bones of the Thai-style chicken pieces into the bin, wiped down the worktops, scooping bits of Super Noodle into his palm and dropping them in on top. The sound of the toilet flushing let him know that the rest of the flat was coming to life, Chip entering the room shortly afterwards, yawning widely, hair dishevelled, braced for another lecture. But the earlier riser said nothing, only:

'Cup of tea?'

'Please' said Chip, uneasy at the chipper greeting, almost preferring what ought to have been coming instead.

'How was your night?'

'Oh, it was ok. Usual, you know - everyone wanting me to hold my nephew in the vague hope that the whole parental thing might be contagious, that a bit of being a grown-up might rub off on me, make me broody, want to settle down with a nice young girl and stop wasting my time. Just did the opposite if I'm honest.'

It was the level of detail that never failed to surprise.

'Well you were back late enough' said Glenn. 'I must've been fast asleep by the time you two came in.' It was a lie. He'd heard them come in, of course he had. It's not like they ever showed any consideration for the fact that he was in bed as they crashed around the kitchen, shouting to each other at the same volume they had been all evening as though the pub-music were still blaring in the background, replacing it eventually with their own from the Hi-Fi stacking system in the lounge. He said nothing. What was the point? They'd only argue that it was the weekend and he should lighten up, as if the day of the week made a blind bit of difference to their routine.

'Yeah. Bumped into Skunk on the way home' said Chip, Glenn having to stop himself from laughing in his flat-mate's face

'Oh, well that's good. At least the evening wasn't a complete waste then. So where had Skunk been?' asked Glenn, just for the sheer hell of it.

259

'Skunk? Oh…he…erm…I'm not sure. Oh no, yeah, he'd been for a couple of drinks with some of his college buddies. Said it was all a bit dry. He was just leaving the pub as I was strolling past, so we went back inside. Got chatting to a couple of the girls on his course. Stayed 'til last orders in the end.'

It was mildly clever, considered - a hotch-potch of truth and lies. Yes, they'd been to the pub, yes, they'd stayed until the final bell and yes, unbelievably, they'd got chatting to a couple of young ladies - even exchanged numbers - but Skunk's fellow college students had played no part in the evening, just as surely as Chip's family hadn't.

Another flush of the toilet – well at least he flushed this time – informed them both that they were all now up. Skunk strolled in looking absolutely no different from normal - he always looked like he'd just got up.

'Morning chaps' he said. 'Don't suppose you could do me one of those could you?' he said to Glenn, gesturing at the mug being passed to Chip. 'Woo, what a night!' he said, sweeping the long hair back from his face with the thumb and fingers of one hand.

'Turned out alright in the end then?' said Glenn.

'Yeah' said Skunk, non-committal, unsure what Glenn meant by *in the end.*

'You know, after the shaky start' he pushed.

Skunk looked to Chip for rescue and his friend dived in immediately.

'I was just telling Glenn about your college crowd being a bit boring and my having to come and save the day on the way home from seeing my sister.'

It was a good summary, concise, covered all the key plot points that he needed to be aware of.

'Oh, yeah. Well I don't suppose I'll be spending time with them for much longer anyway, so not a problem.'

'Not even the girls?' said Glenn and Skunk looked to Chip to step in again.

'Told him about the two girls from your course that we got chatting to last night' said Chip.

'Oh. Yeah. Of course. Yeah, definitely staying in touch with *them*' said Skunk, looking mighty pleased with himself, taking a crumpled beer-mat from the back pocket of his jeans and showing it to Chip. 'How fit were they?'

'I wouldn't go booking the honeymoon just yet' said Chip 'That might not even be her real number.'

'How smooth was I though? You have to admit. I was on fire. Just steamed on over there. They were helpless to resist.'

'It's amazing what you can do when you're not high' admitted Chip.

'Yeah, but it's not like you didn't know them' said Glenn, drawing their attention to the small-print of their own fabrication, turning it against them. 'I mean, they're on your course, right?'

'What's that got to do with anything?' said Skunk, irritated, the level of his glory called into question.

'I'm just saying. It would've been more impressive if you'd just met them that night.'

'Yeah, well thanks for the input Casanova but when I want criticism from somebody who spent Friday night humping his pillow, I'll ask for it.'

261

u.

And when he went there, the cupboard was bare – and so was the fridge and the freezer too. His words went unheard at the best of times. After his upsetting Skunk, undermining his sexual prowess that morning, there was no way that the two of them were suddenly going to feel bad about taking advantage, go out on a shopping spree, making up for lost time, a smorgasbord of goodies just waiting to be unveiled by him when he came in. Particularly not now the two of them had already had some contact with the two girls they'd met, their minds on sating an altogether very different kind of appetite. Watching him speaking on the phone, he hardly recognised Skunk. It was the most animated he'd seen him since moving in.

So he went shopping himself. Again. It was a catch twenty-two situation. He didn't want to have to keep buying food for the flat that then got eaten by the others but this still worked out cheaper than eating out every night. He wasn't prepared to go on hunger strike, just to make his point – he knew he'd probably end up starving to death apart from anything else - but he did have some say over *what* he bought. They clearly weren't averse to food with a bit of a kick – the spicy, oriental-style chicken-wings had gone down a treat after all.

Slightly out of his way to the supermarket lay a parade of small ethnic outlets; wooden punnets of myriad fruit and veg displayed out on the pavement, enticing people in, often if only to enquire as to the identity of some of the less recognisable organic shapes. Glenn had passed them by many times but, in spite of a growing interest in foreign food, had never actually gone in, deterred largely by his own ignorance. But the street had always smelled wonderful and he often went that way, choosing the slight detour to take in the glorious scents and colours, feeling like he were abroad briefly, on a mini-break, perusing an exotic foreign market.

He stopped off at Q-Min, a Tardis of a place, its unassuming green and white striped awning shading a narrow frontage to rows of shelves that stretched far back into the dark recesses of the shop, each one lined with large, clear bags of spices, nuts, seeds, dried fruit, seasonings and all manner of other ingredients necessary for the creation of culinary specialities from anywhere around the world - even the most remote of local dishes. The variety was astonishing. He couldn't believe how much cheaper it was in here than the big superstores too. A one kilo bag of crushed chillies was about the same price as a tiny jar of the same at Mega-Market. Glenn walked up and down the aisles, reading the hand-written labels, wondering what half the words even meant, wishing he knew more, could experiment more boldly.

'Can I help you at all?' asked the Asian shop-keeper in thickest Essex, barrow-boy twang, the words not seeming to come from his mouth, as though he were lip-syncing to a recording, his appearance every bit as dark and mysterious as the exotic produce he sold.

'Actually, yes,' said Glenn. 'I'm looking to make a chilli. But I want to make it hot.'

'When you say hot, do you mean *hot?*' said the vendor, having heard similar machismo requests before but knowing Western palates to be rarely quite so accommodating as they liked to think they were. Fortunately for him, his customers purchased on the understanding of a strict no returns policy.

'Yes. I mean hot. I want to use fresh ingredients. What's the hottest chilli you have?'

The shop-keeper merely laughed.

'What's so funny?' asked Glenn.

'I don't think you really want *that*' he replied.

'Why not? What's wrong with it?' asked Glenn.

'Just a moment' he said, disappearing off out to the back of the shop, pushing through a door of rubber insect flaps. A minute later he reappeared with a jar. 'This' he said, with an almost parental pride, 'Is Bhut Jolokia. The Ghost Pepper. It's by far the hottest thing in the shop. Possibly the world. We keep it out back in case people touch it. We used to keep it out front with the rest of the stock. We put a warning sign on it, telling people that it was dangerous, not to touch, but a sign like that is like a red rag to a bull. We had a lot of problems. Had to keep it locked away separate in the end where it couldn't do any harm. It's the Hannibal Lecter of the spice world.'

The careful way that he held the jar, with just the tips of his fingers, Glenn was surprised he wasn't wearing rubber gloves.

264

'It's really *that* hot?'

'Forty times hotter than tabasco. I heard they were thinking of weaponising it – grenades, pepper-spray, that sort of thing. This bad boy should come with a disclaimer.'

'Why do they call it The Ghost Pepper?'

'I don't know. Maybe because it makes ghosts of people?'

'Sounds perfect' said Glenn 'I'll take the whole jar.'

S.

Friday. The weekend. For most people, reaching the end of a working week is a cause for celebration, a chance for them to get their lives back for a couple of days until the trudgery of work begins again on Monday morning. But not for me. I don't particularly want my old life back. For me it's going to be two more days that I need to find ways to use up. Two thousand two hundred and eighty minutes. If I'm optimistic and take off two eight hour night sleeps, then that still leaves one thousand nine hundred and twenty to kill. Assuming an average of ninety minutes a movie, that would be approximately twenty films I'd need to watch to fill the void, taking into account a little time for washing and dressing of course, and even I'll admit that there's only so much time you can spend immersed in an imaginary world before you start to lose a firm grip on your own. Sure, I could read a book instead, but same difference.

But I'm not going to worry about that right now. The sun is shining and I have that Friday feeling regardless. The kids from the local school are passing my flat again as I leave. I say good morning and they say it back. I don't know what I was so worried about all this time. I feel bad for tarring all school children with the same brush but then, with my track record with them to date, I guess nobody could really blame me. I turn to look at them as I cross the

266

street. They're looking back, smiling and waving and another little piece of my faith in humanity is restored. It's amazing what a difference a few days can make.

I panicked this morning when I realised I'd overslept a little. Not that there's a fixed start time that I have to be there and I hate to admit it but I rushed around the flat like a lunatic getting ready, worried that I might miss out on breakfast at Mary's. So much for feeling bad about eating her out of house and home. But it wasn't the food that was my primary motivation. It was sitting at the wobbly-legged kitchen table (another job on my ever growing list) with her, listening to stories about Yossef – the name on her husband's birth certificate – and the other adventures of her long and full life. She may not have ever remarried, had a family of her own but she certainly hasn't lived in the shadow of her late husband's death all these years. She's been quite a girl, in all the best ways possible. *He would have been proud* I tell her, every time she pauses, mid-account, as if she feels guilty for having enjoyed a life without him.

When I arrive, it's to the same open-hearted greeting as always. Hard to believe I only met this woman on Monday. She invites me in for something to eat and we go through the same, well-rehearsed routine; me pretending that I don't want to impose and her insisting that I'm doing so much for her, that it's the least she can do, that she won't be able to accept my help if she can't at least feed me, and so I end up faux-reluctantly giving in, the two of us competing for who can demonstrate the most gratitude to the other. I actually think she wins this morning. I let her. After a lifetime of criticism, of being taken for granted, I

267

have to confess it's nice to receive a little praise for once. With each passing day at her cottage, the jobs are getting smaller, which is perhaps just as well since the breakfasts and lunches are getting longer and longer. Even the tea-breaks are becoming more frequent, to the point that by Friday afternoon I actually have to make a second trip out to replenish the biscuit tin. But I always make sure I finish what I came for that day, crossing tasks off of a list in a pocket-sized notepad that I always keep with me anyway (I never did get around to making a start on that cool words list) although adding two new ones to the bottom for each one erased. If I was honest with myself, I'd admit that I'm trying to find things to do, looking for things that need fixing - some of them quite ridiculous really - I can't tell you how happy I was when Mary apologised for the wobbly table. Some of the jobs I've done didn't really *need* doing at all, were just improvements, but at least I'm not damaging things just to repair them, although I'm ashamed to say that the thought did cross my mind.

With all the practice, I think my manual skills are improving too. I've always had a bit of a natural flair for carpentry and though largely self-taught, notwithstanding childhood woodwork lessons, I think the jobs I've completed have been to a pretty high standard if I do say so myself. I make a mental note to speak to my personal adviser at the Job Centre about it next week. I realise employers will probably be looking for people with formal qualifications but maybe they can enrol me on a course – one I wouldn't mind going on. Now I *really* have that Friday feeling. For the first time, possibly in my whole life, I think I may have just worked it out, found something that I really want to do. And not something that I might just about manage to hold down and plod away at either – something at which I could excel. I'm good. I'm really good. I know it deep down. I'm not sure I'd see myself fitting in on a big site, dealing with lots of other bum-crack-sporting, wolf-whistling hard-hats but I could end up working for myself, a one man band – autonomous. I picture my self-written card in the newsagent's shop window, the one where I buy the biscuits, the shopkeeper already mentioning, before it's even up, that his mother has a few jobs that need doing about the place and how soon could I fit her in, as he blu-tacks it to the glass. I imagine the phone ringing off the hook, elderly ladies calling me up, my name recommended to them by one of their friends from bingo who spoke very highly of the work I carried out for them, but mostly of me as a person – a polite, obliging, extremely talented and intelligent young man. I picture the leatherette bound ledger with the gold ribbon page marker that I have to buy from the stationers to accommodate all my regulars when finally my dog-eared pocket-book can squeeze in no more, no matter how small I try to write along the tops and bottoms of the pages. And suddenly I'm back to reality. *Oh, you've fallen in* says Mary as I look down and realise that I've been holding the soggy digestive in my hot drink for longer than it could take and it's finally given in and committed suicide, turning my tea into a sweet crouton soup. *You were miles away* she says, and for once I don't wish I was, though I can't look her in the eye for the moment for all my thoughts of infidelity.

Outside is dry and bright again. I wonder how differently things might have turned out if the weather hadn't cleared, had remained like it was on Monday. I wouldn't have been able to start with the fence panels so likely wouldn't have made a start at all. I don't know whether to be glad of the time I've had as a result or sad that it's coming to an end that bit sooner. If the lashing storms had continued I'd have the whole experience still to come all over again. But as I move around the property with my pad, I manage to fill another page. Mostly minor jobs – I even put down to mow the front and back lawns – but things that will make her life that bit easier for the time being nonetheless. I list:

Rub down, repair and re-paint side window frames – completely replace any rotted sections if beyond repair

Replace section of missing guttering and secure drainpipe to wall

Replace / prep broken fence panel in back garden (+ paint all same as front?)

Repair shed – possibly re-felt roof (check cost first – cover myself if not too much)

Sweep and bag up leaves

Fix kitchen table

I'm delighted. There's easily another week's work here, possibly more - certainly enough to look forward to, to get me through the weekend. And I don't think I'll have so much difficulty persuading Mary to accept the help any more now either. I think she's gotten used to having me around already. It's quickly becoming the norm for her, part of her routine, just as unquestioningly as cooking lunch for two.

When I get home I run a bath, treat myself to a well-earned soak, even put in some bubbles that I picked up from the Seven Eleven on the way home. I almost see the point of those little candle things right now after all. Perhaps I'll pick up some tea-light holders – that's them, tea-lights – over the weekend when I'm at Super Shed, picking up materials for Mary's. I lay there, sinking into the rising clouds of suds, my body aching all over with a satisfying stiffness, the wonderfully rewarding tiredness of earned fatigue. I step out onto the mat, towel myself down and slip on my towelling bathrobe. I go into the kitchen, switch the kettle on then go to my DVD shelf to choose a movie. I don't want anything, mainstream TV, the news particularly, dampening my high spirits. I settle on Phenomenon. It's a greatly underrated movie. If you haven't already seen it, it stars John Travolta as everyman George Malley, a thirty-seven year old (it's actually his birthday at the start of the film, which is how I know), small town mechanic; just a regular guy who develops extraordinary intellectual and telekinetic powers after experiencing an encounter with a bright light that literally knocks him off his feet. He tries to use his new abilities for the good of his community, to improve peoples' lives, but instead they end up getting him into trouble with government authorities when his intentions are misconstrued. Anyway, I won't say any more in case you

271

want to watch it. I don't want to spoil the ending but trust me, it really is well worth a watch - and not only because it stars JT either, although he *is* just as brilliant as ever.

V.

'But what has he *actually* done wrong?' said Stephanie.

'Yeah, what's he done that's so bad?' reiterated Danielle. 'Give us an example.'

'It's not so much that he does anything wrong per se' said Skunk, 'It's more that he *never* does anything wrong. He always has to be right, do everything properly, for everything to be just so. He's like a robot.'

'Like how?' said Danielle, still in need of supporting evidence.

'Like, he's always washing up for a start. I can barely finish my tea and put it down on the coffee table without he's grabbing the mug and taking it off to the sink, moaning about people leaving their slops lying around.'

'Yeah' said Chip 'And then he's there like a gunslinger with his anti-bacterial spray, wiping the ring from the table.'

'So he washes up your dirty crockery? That's the best you can come up with? That's the reason you don't like him?' said Stephanie.

'He wears marigolds for God's sake!' added Skunk, as if this explained everything.

'Well, he sounds like an ideal flat-mate if you ask me' said Danielle.

'An ideal flat-mate maybe' conceded Chip 'But not an ideal mate.'

'Yeah' said Skunk. 'If we'd wanted a housemaid, we'd have got a woman.'

'A female lodger you mean?' said Stephanie bristling, a sharpness in her tone indicating that all of Skunk's chivalrous good work to date might just be about to come undone.

'No' laughed Chip, stepping into the fray immediately, covering his friend's faux pas quickly, before he could dig himself in any deeper. 'He meant a cleaner, didn't you mate? We've been talking about hiring one.'

'Yeah' agreed Skunk, a little too eagerly. 'A cleaner. I meant a cleaner.'

'But why are you thinking of hiring a cleaner if you have Mr OCD living with you?' asked Danielle, obviously still yet to discover her true vocation as police investigator.

'If he ends up leaving' explained Chip, as if there was any chance of them ever affording to hire in outside staff when they couldn't scrape the money together for a bottle of disinfectant between them now, even with Glenn's rent coming in.

'If you throw him out, you mean' said Stephanie.

'No, we wouldn't be that cruel' said Chip, praying that Skunk didn't drink too much and end up divulging their plan to indirectly oust their absent house-mate – thinking *or that brave*, still unsure of the whole idea himself.

'So he cleans up after you both. What else?' said Danielle. She wanted answers for her file.

274

'Yeah' said Stephanie. 'Pray tell us more about this hideous Charles Manson figure that lurks beneath your roof, cold-heartedly rinsing your mugs.'

'He's just generally like a middle-aged man' said Skunk. 'Worse in fact. I got away with more when I still lived at home. He looks down his nose at you every time you do something that he doesn't really like'

'Which is pretty much everything' chimed in Chip.

'Yeah. Exactly. Pretty much everything. Like, he doesn't like it if you have one too many beers. Says alcohol makes people aggressive. He actually poured a whole bottle of Scotch down the sink a couple of weeks back. He said he dropped it and it smashed but there wasn't the slightest hint of a stain, no splintered glass fragments or whisky smell anywhere to be found.'

'Well he probably cleaned it all up properly. You did say he was very thorough' said super-sleuth Danielle.

'Yeah, maybe' said Skunk, unconvinced, suddenly angry about the wastage all over again, now that he'd thought about it.

'And?' said Danielle, still building a case.

'Ok, so God forbid you should make the slightest comment about any female on TV' said Skunk.

'What do you mean?' said Stephanie?

Yeah, what do you mean? thought Chip, worrying that his wing-man was straying again into dangerous, shark-infested waters.

'So, for example, he won't watch Baywatch. Says it *objectifies* women' said Skunk, as if this ought be hammer down, case closed, jury dismissed.

'What's so wrong with that?' asked Stephanie.

'What's wrong with that?' repeated Skunk, unable to believe what he was hearing. 'I'll tell you what's wrong with that' said Skunk, causing Chip to shift nervously in his seat, ready to intercede at any moment. 'Firstly, who uses words like *objectify?* And secondly, who doesn't like Baywatch? I mean, it's the most popular show in the history of television' said Skunk, as if it was the significance of this cross-cultural phenomenon that was the reason people tuned in.

'I wonder why' said Stephanie, not wondering at all, the unspoken sub-text that it wasn't exactly her favourite programme either.

'You could be on that show' said Skunk, oblivious. 'You've certainly got the figure for it.'

Chip flinched at the comment but was amazed to witness the exact moment that the girl visibly softened before his eyes, the budding staunch feminist in her stepping momentarily to one side to let the compliment pass as she smiled and took a self-conscious sip of her Spritzer through a bendy straw. She was still young. She'd learn.

'So' said Danielle, recapping on what they'd learned about their serial joy killer so far. 'He respects women, doesn't drink and is good at housekeeping. He sounds perfect. Maybe we could get him to come live with us if you two don't want him'

'Ok, fair enough. I'll admit it doesn't look bad on paper but just wait until you meet him' said Skunk. 'Then you'll see what we mean.'

'Well we're not likely to if you never invite him out with you, now are we?' said Stephanie.

276

'Of course you are. You can meet him tonight if you like. Come back to ours after we finish up here, have a few more drinks, put some music on. What do you say?' said Skunk, thinking that perhaps Glenn Chambers had his uses after all.

T.

Sunday morning. I have another stab at watching TV, wilfully optimistic that I might find something I can settle into with my bowl of cereal- but it's all race and religion as usual. I have to admit that I just don't get any of it – and the more I watch and read about it, the less I understand. To my mind, it all seems so simple. If you're right and your God exists, well then, he (or she - or both, because surely God is all things to all people, even a hermaphrodite, no?) created everything, including the non-believers and those of other faiths. In fact, he/she created those other faiths, assuming that is that faith is something which can ever be created - but then God can do anything can't he/she? As for race, well, the subject is covered to death, perpetuating the 'issue' on channel after channel, forcing me to share the opinions of chat-show hosts, 'expert' panellists on group debate programmes and members of civil rights activist groups on a documentary claiming that a whole host of significant historical figures - not least among their esteemed number, that most celebrated of all wordsmiths William Shakespeare - were actually black. Personally I don't care *what* damn colour he was. All I know is that the black ink flowing from his quill onto the white page combined to create some of the most unsurpassed beauty in human history. And really, there is no black and white is there? 'Black' people aren't really black – a total absorption of light – and 'white' people aren't white – a total reflection. In fact they're not even colours – they're monochromes - if you want to get all technical about it. If we had to choose, had a gun to our head telling us to pick from the epidermal Dulux chart, then I guess you could argue that we're all brown – only different variations up and down the range, some more towards magnolia and some more mahogany. Place any two people of any ethnic origin side by side and I doubt you'd ever get a perfect match. Like fingerprints. It's only different quantities of the same ingredient, melanin, a protective pigment against the sun's harmful UV rays, that's stirred into the mix in different quantities that lets us know whether we'd look better in the bedroom or the bathroom. But we no longer live in a black and white world. Sure, there are still atrocities committed every day - that will never change – until of course we aren't entirely satisfied and wipe ourselves out completely. That's just what we are as a species. But we *have* moved on surely? We're coloured, glorious technicolour – each and every one of us – if you insist on assigning labels. We're green when inexperienced or with envy, green around the gills when we're sick; blue when we're sad or cold (or dead); red with anger, embarrassment, physical exhaustion or when sunburnt (pink when less so); white when we're shocked or afraid; black of mood when we're down or depressed; even orange when we're from Essex – occasionally - and yellow when we're cowardly. The most popular two-point-four-children nuclear family on the planet are yellow for God's sake; in fact, I believe it was Homer (he of The Simpsons, not The Odyssey) that perhaps summed religion up best with the immortal line 'thank you God, for saving us from the swarm of bees you sent'. But surely it's not only the colour setting that's important – surely it's contrast, brilliance, brightness, sometimes even volume, that count too. We all have white teeth, share eyes of infinite variants of blue, brown, green and grey, hair of equal numbers of colour and style. We don't place nearly so much emphasis on these things. Well, one guy did and look how that turned out. I just don't understand why so much focus is put on our outer waterproof membrane – which, let's face it, none of us asked for, had any say in; all brought here against our will, the birthday suit we arrived in chosen *for* us, just the same. We talk about race like it's one we can win, rather than the united fun-run for a single worthy cause that it should be.

And then there's a commercial break. An advert comes on for a bag of small, chewy sweets. *Taste the Rainbow* exclaims the tag-line, enforced in jiggling, brightly coloured words across the screen, and I think that there's more sense spoken in that thirty second advert than there has been from all the theologians, cosmologists, historians and ministers of the past two hours put together.

U.

Sunday afternoon. Here are some interesting animal facts that I learned during my internet surfing today. I've placed them in alphabetical order to avoid any preferential prioritisation, any mistaken assumption on your part that they're ranked according to some sliding scale of interestingness attributed to them by me. I think all animals are amazing, from the tiniest single-celled filamentous algae to the mighty blue whale - perhaps with one exception, although I'll concede that we are indeed truly amazing in our ability to colonise and harvest the earth - I'd be a fool to argue that one. I've also tried to avoid facts that you'll likely already know - for C, for example, I haven't told you how fast a Cheetah can run – but at the same time, I've selected species that you're likely to have heard of, even without a previous enthusiast's interest in natural history, in the hope that this will help to engage you, capture your imagination and perhaps promote an even greater appreciation of wildlife in the future. So here we go:

You probably already know that albatross have the largest wingspan of any bird but did you know that once the chicks fledge, they fly out to sea, spending most of their time on the wing, often not returning to land for up to five years?

281

Barnacle geese (don't worry, it won't be all birds but I wanted to give credit where it's due) in Greenland often build their nests extremely high up atop huge rock formations to avoid predators on the ground. Whilst this virtually guarantees the survival of their young in the first couple of days after hatching, they soon need to eat. As grazers, living on a diet only of grass, this means that they have to follow their mother, taking a leap of faith of many hundreds of feet onto the craggy escarpment below if they're not otherwise to starve to death. Whilst extremely resilient, many don't make the monolithic free-fall; those that do still prone to marauding hungry arctic foxes when they land, waiting for a fluffy mini-meal to land in their laps. And we worry about our kids walking to school on their own.

I promised not to repeat the usual speed claims but I will tell you one of the ways they get there. Unlike other cats, cheetahs have non-retractable claws which effectively act like running shoes when they're in hot pursuit of their prey. I'd tell you more about these highly specialist animals but they've had their trumpet blown enough in the past already.

Despite what the Lexus ad says about hummingbirds being the only creatures able to fly backwards, dragonflies can too. In fact, they're masters of flight, able to move in any direction in pursuit of their prey or whilst engaging in aerial combat with a rival. A more interesting claim to fame though might be that the damsel fly nymph breathes through its anus.

Whilst proof of their graveyards is unsupported, elephants are the only animals apart from man known to have death rituals. If a fellow family member dies they will try to revive it with food and water and then, once it is clear that it's dead, will often dig a shallow grave and attempt to cover it with dirt and branches. Their herds are believed to have similar levels of cooperation to troops of chimpanzees.

Though often aggressive, ferrets may be dispatched quite simply.

Giraffe have the highest blood pressure of any mammal, necessary to get the blood pumping from their heart, against gravity, up their famously long necks to their brain. Fortunately they're also equipped with an inbuilt valve which regulates this highly pressurised flow of blood when they bend down to drink or they'd blow their own brains out.

Phylogenetically (surely top slot in my *Glenn's Great Words* list if I'd been keeping a note) speaking, hyenas are actually more closely related to cats than to dogs, though their behaviour more closely resembles the latter.

Most young impala are born around midday, when their predators are more likely to be resting.

When killing their prey, most cats aim for the neck. With their incredibly strong jaws, Jaguars go for the head, their bite able to crush through skull. Their name comes from a Native American word meaning *he who kills with one leap.*

Killer whales – or orca as they're more accurately known - well, where to start? I could easily devote this whole list just to them and still not even scratch the surface. Well how about that technically they're not whales at all but the largest member of the dolphin family? Highly intelligent animals, they have the largest brain per body size of any species other than ourselves, with one particular area known to be responsible for emotion even more developed than our own (which personally I'm surprised isn't the case in more animals). Their social structures are so advanced and so unique from pod to pod that many zoologists have referred to them as cultures. One of the fastest animals in the ocean, they frequently cover a hundred miles per day on their travels - so clearly don't belong in swimming pools, made to jump through hoops.

In the wild, all lemurs are found only on the island of Madagascar.

Hard to believe if you see one but the manatee, or sea cow, is thought to be the creature responsible for the existence of the beautiful mythological mermaid. Sailors out to sea for months on end, their vision and judgement impaired by nutritional and vitamin deficiencies, would hallucinate when they saw them resting up on rocks. No doubt also deficient in other areas further south, it was perhaps an advanced case of wishful thinking too.

Nile crocodiles are estimated to be responsible for the death of around two hundred people per year and can eat up to half their own bodyweight in one sitting.

Osprey conservationists discovered that if they splattered them with white paint, previously unused man-made nest sites, built as migratory stop-offs en route between Africa and Scotland, were then settled upon much more successfully, the artificial appearance of guano presumably instilling greater trust in the birds where before they'd been only suspicious. When an Osprey catches a large fish, it will turn it around in its talons so that it faces forward, to reduce drag and make for easier carriage.

284

Polar bear fur isn't white - it's transparent. It's only the reflection of sunlight and snow that gives it its white appearance. The individual hairs are hollow to trap warm air, acting as insulation in the way that a micro-fibre quilt might. The skin beneath their fur is actually black.

The quoll, a carnivorous marsupial native to Australia, was at serious risk of being wiped out from eating the poisonous Cane Toad, a non-indigenous species introduced by man (of course). In a bid to correct our wrongdoing, a lone zoologist had the seemingly wacky idea to make Cane Toad sausages, laced with enough of a sickness inducing chemical to cause significant nausea though not quite enough to kill a potential diner. Once the quolls ate the sausages, the after-effects meant that they never went near them again and the scent and taste association meant that they never went near the toads again either. This was obviously deemed a huge success but even more amazing was the fact that the trial subjects then passed the information on to their young, teaching them not to go near the toads, ensuring the preservation of future generations and ultimately the entire species. And people say that sausages aren't good for you. Try telling that to a quoll.

I've stroked a rhinoceros's cheek and the skin there's not nearly as tough as you might expect. The difference between the black and white rhino has absolutely nothing to do with their colouring. The white comes from a misinterpretation of the Afrikaans word *wyd* meaning wide and refers to the shape of the larger animal's mouth, designed for grazing. The considerably more aggressive black rhino, with a more beak-like arrangement for picking off leaves, branches, shoots and fruit, was then so named by default.

There are a number of theories as to the naming of the secretary bird, a terrestrial bird of prey that does more walking than flying – often up to twenty miles per day. One is that it looks like it's typing whilst tackling its prey, venomous snakes included, as it hunts on foot. Another may be a crest of black-tipped quill like feathers. Another still may be from the Arabic *saqu ettair,* meaning hunter-bird. It also has a dense covering of feathers on its upper legs which act like leg-warmers, presumably providing additional protection from snake-bites.

Unlike their lion cousins, tigers live largely solitary existences, an occasional encounter with a potential mate one of their only liaisons with another of their species once leaving the maternal fold, other than perhaps the odd aggressive confrontation with another adult male. Even their mating attempts can result in serious injury, with females often as unpredictable as males. At nursery I started out as a Tiger…..

The uakari is a small species of South American monkey best known for its naked face which ranges from pink to deep red in colour. The reason for the baldness is not known but what is clear is that it's a good indicator of health, sick animals turning notably paler. The faces of those in captivity are notably lighter than in the wild too, perhaps suggesting an indication of mood.

Although historically the bald head of a vulture has been thought to keep it clean and enable greater ease of accessibility when feeding at a carcass, it is now believed that it may play a significant role in thermoregulation.

286

The reintroduction of a single pack of wolves has been almost single-handedly responsible for the regeneration of Yellowstone National Park. When the wolves were originally wiped out through hunting some decades back, elk and deer populations, now with few natural predators to regulate their numbers, grew exponentially, overgrazing on many plant species upon which other animals relied. The return of the wolves saw the herbivores sustainably managed, their herds become healthier as they were picked clean of the old and sick. Beavers returned to use the now readily available willow needed for their dams and the resultant new ponds and wet-land areas created habitats for aquatic life which came back too. Even grizzly bears have since been found to have benefitted from the increased abundance of fruit and berries, the energy rich natural sugars so essential to building their fat stores and see them through the harsh winters.

There isn't really an animal that begins with X – unless of course I risk losing you with reference to some pretentious Latin phylum or scientific genus. Oh there's a fish called the X-Ray Tetra – you might even have one yourself in a tank at home – they're one of the most popular freshwater fish kept in aquariums today. Well there you are, there's an interesting fact. But there isn't much. In fact, there isn't much that begins with X full-stop really, in the grand scheme of things, not even in the dictionary. Perhaps X is symbolic - an abbreviation for extinct – what every animal on this list will inevitably become if we continue as we are, blindly sticking our heads in the sand like the ostriches that aren't mentioned here, though quite easily could have been, certainly would have been deserving enough, as they all are. If I came back, did this again in ten, twenty, thirty years, I wonder how much harder – easier - it would be, how much less I'd have to choose from. Would I list battery hens under B or H? Would I even be able to fill the list? Perhaps I'd need to put them under both.

Anne used to have a Yorkshire Terrier. Not sure if I mentioned that before.

A zorse - I kid you not - is the result of cross-breeding between a male (stallion) zebra and a female (mare) horse. The final product looks more like a horse, only with stripes, and is often bred specifically as a trekking animal to transport people and goods up and down the mountains. A male zebra and a female donkey is called a zonkey, whereas a male donkey and a female zebra is called a zedonk. This got me to thinking about other possible combinations. Would a zebra and a hippo be a Zippo for example? I guess that's probably something we're unlikely ever to see, even with artificial insemination, although with genetic engineering advancing the way it is, who knows what aberrations our amateur Gods tinkering away with their test-tubes and petri dishes are going to come up with?

V.

I leave the weekend behind as a child discards a well-intended but ungratefully received birthday gift. Rising early, I collect my things together, emptying my gym bag (I still harbour no thoughts of returning just yet) of all but the still as yet unused chisel, adding a few other hand tools and my power drill, excited at the prospect of a rare excuse to use it. Mary's garage contained many of the basics for my needs so far but the roof and windows are going to need something a little less time-worn and rusted and anyway, I take a craftsman's pleasure in looking at my list, working out what I might need, laying them out on the bed then packing them away - hopefully a taste of things to come. I'll get myself one of those leather tool-belts. A gizmo for every job - like Batman.

When I leave the flat, my atypical Monday morning happiness is infectious. Sombre-faced children on their way to school, on default setting though possibly not even sure why, smile back at me as I pull my front-door closed, hoisting my bag over my shoulder in exaggerated fashion, as if this will let them all know that they're not alone, that I too am off to carry out a hard day's work. The sun not yet fully risen, the heavy weight slung across my back reminds me of my brief stint with the Postal Service and I feel grateful that they let me go when they did, think about how,

289

if they hadn't, I might very well still be there, quite possibly until retirement; would never have met Mary and so would likely never have discovered my true vocational calling. It's all starting to come together. Good things come to those who wait and all that. Well I've certainly been patient. Nobody can deny me that.

Arriving at the cottage, I press the door-bell and wait. The house seems dark and not because there are no lights on either – just…. *sadder* than usual. Well I'm here to fix that, cheer the place up a bit with a little TLC. When there's no answer, I become concerned, pressing the bell again, harder this time, as if this will somehow make it more effective, relieved to see a faint dark mass crystallising slowly into shape as it approaches the heavily frosted glass at the side of the door. Gnarled fingers fumble with the safety-latch and the door creaks gently open. Mary smiles but it's a grimace too. She apologises for keeping me waiting, tells me she's been in a bit of pain but I can tell that when she says a bit, she means a lot. I ask her what the problem is and she tells me it's just her arthritis playing her up again but I get the distinct impression that there's more that she's not telling me. As if to stop me speaking, asking more probing questions which she'll then have to fend off with untruths, she keeps talking, explaining that she's had a bit of a bad weekend with it but that she'll soon be ok, especially now that she's got me here to keep her mind off things, and it occurs to me that perhaps I needn't have taken the weekend off after all. Perhaps she wanted me to keep coming over but didn't like to ask, assuming that I had to meet the highly pressurised demands of my whirling social circle, whilst I was thinking

290

much the same thing about her - that I'd be encroaching, in the way of visiting family, that sort of thing. Perhaps great-nieces and nephews aren't always so great when it comes to checking in on their elderly relatives.

She apologises for not having breakfast on and I tell her not to be silly, lying that I had something before I left the house, but again she ridicules what she calls my rabbit food. She tells me that she did at least manage to venture out as far as the corner shop to get a few bits. She says she doesn't know about me but she's starving and would I mind making her a nice sausage sandwich and sharing one with her. I say that of course I wouldn't, suspecting that she's not really hungry at all, just wants to make sure that I eat something substantial myself.

I put the sausages under the grill, butter some bread with proper butter, thick how she likes it - it certainly hasn't done her any harm so far and besides, she has no margarine or low-fat spread in the house anyway, doesn't believe in it. I slice the cooked sausages in half, lay them out neatly across the sliced white and she laughs at my fussiness, tells me that I'll make somebody a wonderful husband some day, causing the knife to pause briefly, wondering if she's right. I smack ketchup onto both, figuring that even this looks too much for her to manage this morning, and serve the table, finishing up with two mugs of tea which I had to pour away first time around and re-start, forgetting that she still uses granules rather than bags.

We sit together there in the kitchen, the room breakfast-warmed but also by the two of us, feeling the glow of each other like we're in a Ready Brek commercial. Mary asks me about me and I try to change the subject, to turn it back

291

on her, telling her that her life is much more interesting, but she stands firm, says that we've talked about her enough already, that she wants to get to know a little more about this mysterious new man in her life. I tell her that there isn't really much to tell and she dismisses my words as nonsense, says that if that's true then it's a waste, that still waters run deep, that she could tell the moment she first met me that there was much more to me than meets the eye, says she's rarely wrong about these things. I ask her if it's a good thing and she asks me what I think. I tell her I'm not sure and she seems surprised, asks me what happened in my life to cause me to sell myself so short, doubt myself so badly. I tell her that I'm not sure, that I don't really know where to start, that it was such a long time ago, and realise that knowing when it was probably gives me my answer. The conversation is getting a bit too heavy for my liking. It's nice of her to ask but the fact that she was interested in the first place was enough. I don't want to discuss it any further. This certainly isn't cheering her up in her time of suffering, although I wonder if it's this that caused her to think about asking in the first place – that she was already in shadow anyway so related more to mine. I stuff in a huge mouthful of sandwich, the sticky dough-ball rendering me physically unable to speak for a moment and I think she takes the hint, stops with her previous line of enquiry to ask instead about the work I'm planning on doing today.

I work hard, almost frantically so, throughout the morning, trying to shake off the residue of breakfast, the grey picture of the past that I'd just started drawing out in my mind, like an etch-a-sketch. The only thing that causes

292

me to let up and slow down a little is the knowledge that the sooner I get everything finished, the sooner my time here may be over. It seems to work and by lunchtime, just like the day itself which is turning out to be another beauty, I'm much brighter. Any hint of darkness that might still have been tickling me gently with its ever fumbling tendrils was slapped away by Mary, calling up to me to come down for a tea-break. As I clamber down the ladder, wiping sweat from my brow - even though it's still almost cold enough to see my breath - I see her standing at the front door, carefully lowering a tray with a steaming mug and a small cupcake with a lit candle in onto a brick wall at the edge of the lawn.

'What's with the cake?' I say.

'Made a batch specially' she says.

'What have I done to deserve this? ' I ask, 'or have we just finally run out of biscuits?'

'No, got those too. It's a special occasion.'

'Really?' I say, wondering if somehow she's managed to find out that it's my birthday in a couple of day's time, then feel guilty for being so self-obsessed, realising that she couldn't possibly know, that she probably means for her – maybe something to do with Joseph.'

'Anniversary?' I take a guess.

'Yes' she says.

'How long?' I ask.

She twists a liver-spotted wrist to look at the tiny gold wrist-watch there. 'Exactly one week today' she says, smiling, though not nearly as widely as I am. 'I got you a present too' she says.

'You're not serious?' I say, overwhelmed to say the least, the cake already more than anybody has done for me in decades.

'Don't get too excited' she says. 'It was only a few pounds. But I thought it might come in handy. I hope it doesn't seem presumptuous but I'm a bit slow on my feet these days and I don't want you standing out on the doorstep in the rain if I can't get there quickly enough when you arrive in the mornings. Means you can come and go as you please when you need to use the bathroom or fix yourself a snack or a cuppa too.' She hands me a gold coloured Yale key and in placing it in my palm, it's like she's unlocking my heart. 'I'll make sure the latch is off first thing when I get up.'

'Mary, I can't take this. It's too much. You hardly know me' I say.

'I know enough' she says. 'Besides, it'll make it easier for you to make me something too whilst you're at it.'

294

W.

'See, this is what I mean' said Skunk, pulling his head back from around the box-room door. 'Half eleven on a Saturday night and he's in bed fast asleep.'

'Yeah, but if you don't ever include him then what do you expect?' said Danielle.

'I'd expect him to have some friends of his own' said Skunk. 'He's only been living with us for a few months. Although, having got to know him, I'm not surprised that he doesn't.'

'Ssshh' whispered Stephanie 'He'll hear you.'

'No he won't. I told you. He's soundo.'

'Ok, what sort of music do you ladies like?' said Chip, moving to the stereo in the lounge, casting his eye down the Argos CD tower. 'I hope it's grunge or looks like you're bang out of luck.'

'Ooh, I love a bit of Nirvana' said Danielle.

'Yeah but you can't play that with your friend asleep in the next room' said Stephanie.

'Course we can' said Chip, delighted at having received a request for one of the few artists he was able to provide. 'We won't play it loud. Kurt and the boys coming right up.'

He placed the disc on the tray, pressed a button and watched it slide back in, the novelty of the relatively recent acquisition still not yet worn off. The familiar opening guitar chords of *Smells Like Teen Spirit* strummed softly into life.

'Ooh, I love this one' said Danielle, shaking her head, her hair falling over her face as she accompanied on air-guitar.

'Fuck that' said Skunk, striding across the room. 'You can't play this quietly. Needs a bit of volume to be fully appreciated' and he twisted the volume control un-delicately round, the cheap speakers blaring, struggling to cope with the sound as it was intended to be heard.

'It's a bit loud!' shouted Stephanie, adding 'What about your neighbours?' realising that their slumbering flat-mate alone clearly wasn't going to provide sufficient motive for a little consideration.

'Fuck them too!' said Skunk. 'It's the bloody weekend for God's sake! It's not even midnight yet. They can sleep all day tomorrow if they don't like it.'

'It *is* a bit loud mate' agreed Chip.

'Look, if someone knocks at the door and complains then we'll turn it down, ok Granddad?'

'Ok' agreed Chip, not wanting to seem like an old fuddy-duddy in front of the girls, the music getting to the rock and roller within him already marinated in alcohol.

'You wouldn't hear it even if they did' suggested Stephanie.

'Oh, come on' said Danielle, 'Skunk's right, we're only young once. It *is* Saturday night. They can lie in tomorrow.'

'Exactly. Thank you, Dani. Glad somebody here isn't completely over the hill already just yet. Right. Do you ladies like a smoke?' asked Skunk.

'Sometimes when I'm a bit drunk I do' said Danielle, easily led, having received his stamp of approval once and liking how it felt.

'I think he means drugs' said Stephanie.

'Yes, Stephanie' said Skunk, sarcastically. 'I mean drugs' and sitting down at the sofa he took a small tin out of his pocket and laid it on the coffee table, popping it open. 'Here's one I prepared earlier' he said, taking out a smooth, expertly rolled joint.

'What is it?' said Danielle. 'What sort I mean?'

'This, my angel' said Skunk, taking a long drag as he lit the joint in the unnecessarily high flame of his lighter, 'is happiness in a heartbeat. A couple of puffs on this and all your cares and worries just melt away. Stephanie, perhaps you should have one all to yourself.'

'I don't need drugs to make me happy' said Stephanie.

'Yeah, I can see that' said Skunk, holding his breath to keep the smoke down, his voice already changing. 'Well you certainly need something love.'

Chip was still over at the music collection, oblivious to what was going on behind him, desperately scanning for some more Nirvana, a Pearl Jam album in his hand as a contingency plan.

'A drink would be nice' said Stephanie.

'That's more like it' said Skunk, happy that he hadn't lost her altogether. 'What can I get you? Beer? Beer? Or perhaps a beer?'

'I don't suppose you have any wine?'

297

'I'm not so sure we even have beer actually' said Skunk, passing the reefer to Danielle and heading to the kitchen to check the fridge.

He reappeared moments later, a white plastic tub in his hand.

'Now *this* is exactly the sort of thing I'm talking about' he said, waving it in front of him like he'd just found a smoking gun.

The semi-transparent container clearly contained some sort of mince-based foodstuff. On the lid was an adhesive label, the words *GLENN'S – PLEASE DO NOT TOUCH* written neatly in upper case letters with black marker pen.

'What's so wrong with that?' said Stephanie. 'He just doesn't want you nicking his stuff, that's all.'

'Yeah, mate. At least he said please' added Chip.

'What's so wrong with that? What's right with it you mean? Do I seriously have to explain? It's wrong on so many levels. Where did he get the container for a start - a Tupperware party? It's about the only party he'd ever get invited to. He prepares his own home-cooked meals and saves them for later. How old is he? And you realise he must've gone out and bought the blank stickers to make his little label with? Where does it all end? You realise we're probably going to start finding little warning signs all over the place now, telling us off for different things. Don't leave the lid off the toothpaste, please flush the toilet…'

'Keep off the grass' said Danielle, giggling herself into a coughing fit, smoke snorting out of her nose like a baby dragon.

'Yeah, well fuck him!' said Skunk, heading back out to the kitchen and returning shortly afterwards with four bottles of cold, out-of-date lager, handing them out. 'That's it, girl, get it down you' he said to Danielle, noticing that she was still smoking. 'Jesus! How long was I gone?' he said, taking the inch of joint remaining back from her as she slumped back into the sofa cushions. He took another healthy toke himself, the end flaming orange as it disappeared down to his index finger and thumb. He stubbed the roach out in the ashtray, stolen from the pub one time, then rose again to head back out to the kitchen. 'Dunno about any of you lot but I've got the munchies' he said.

As the bowls being taken down from the cupboard shelf clattered and the microwave pinged shortly after, Glenn Chambers lay in his bed and smiled.

W.

I have to admit that the key was a good idea. As long as she gets up and unlatches the door in the mornings, she can go straight back to bed if she's not feeling good or take her time getting washed and dressed without having to worry about being decent to let me in when I turn up. It also means that I don't have to worry about being late, keeping her waiting, if please God she manages to muster the strength to go out – like tomorrow for example when I sign on. She was looking very doddery yesterday, the rosy hue missing from her cheeks when I kissed them goodbye last night.

I follow my usual morning ritual and leave the flat, pulling the door closed behind me, almost stepping straight out into a group of passing school kids. It's clearly a much better school than the one where I worked briefly. The uniforms are all pristine and properly fitting, squirming heads combed tidy by doting mothers and socks pulled up to knees, for now at least, until gravity has its way. A row of three nattering schoolgirls hold colourful ring-binders scrawled with biro. I try to take a look at what's written there, the latest craze, and see only pairs of initials bound together in temporary declarations of love by the fickle number four. It's no doubt a small thing to those who've been implicated in these fleeting marriages but what I

300

wouldn't have given to see the initials GC inscribed on somebody's folder just once, however quickly it was then crossed out, no sooner replaced by the next flavour of the month. But those days are long gone; the only time anybody's going to be tenderly etching out my name anywhere now... One of the girls sees me looking and hugs her folder tight to her chest, protectively, like a shield. I try to explain that I was just being nosy, curious at her customisation, but the words tail off as they bounce off the back of her retreating pony-tailed head, which turns a couple of times to look back at me. This defensiveness is such a shame but I can't really blame her, suppose I should be glad that she's been raised properly by caring parents, warned to be wary of strangers. We talk about a lack of community spirit like it was some divine force handed to us in the good old days to share out like sweets, only to be cruelly taken away from us in later years by that same higher being - not something once but no longer created *by* us. *Well, I'm doing my bit* I think as I head on towards Mary's with a spring in my step.

I walk up the path but, despite having a key, don't really feel comfortable using it just yet so ring the doorbell like usual. There's no answer. I kind of knew there wouldn't be. I think that Mary already knew she wouldn't be here to greet me this morning when she gave me the key. I think that was the whole point. The house is silent when I walk in. Out of habit, I go straight to the kitchen. There's a note on the side, tucked beneath a box of eggs and half a loaf of sliced white, telling me that she's feeling very tired this morning so has gone back to bed for a bit. In a barely legible, spidery scrawl, it tells me to make myself an egg

301

sandwich and a cup of tea and help myself to anything else I can find. I don't look for anything else, finding only the tea bags, milk and sugar. I consider making Mary something and taking it up to her but don't want to invade her personal, private, upstairs space. She might not be respectable for a start. I call up to her, gently, not wishing to wake her if she's asleep. There's no answer. I think about it for a few seconds then call up again, just one more time, a little louder but still not a full-on shout. Still nothing. I think about it again, decide to let her lie in and get on with working through my list. I skip breakfast. I feel guilty cooking myself something in her house and it won't feel right, sitting there eating alone with her asleep upstairs - that and the fact that my stomach is already full with a fist-sized knot at her lack of response.

I head outside and decide to start with a low priority task, pulling out the lawnmower and connecting up and unravelling the extension lead. I tell myself that it will be a good idea to do it now whilst it's had a few days of sunshine, that there are dark clouds rolling in and it might rain this afternoon but, if it could speak, the single fluffy octave of white cotton wool wandering lonely across the clear sky overhead would tell me that I was doing it in a further attempt to rouse Mary from her slumber, from whatever that might mean.

As I walk up and down, creating neat, perfectly straight parallel lines in the grass, the sense of order calms me, brings a renewed sense that all is well with the world. I'm as thorough as ever, the front garden fit to rival any bowling-club green by the time I let the blades spin slowly to a whirring stop, unplugging the power and winding up

302

the cable. Elsie, the lady next door, leans over the fence, says something to me. I wonder how long she's been there, whether she's been trying to get my attention for some time, and I walk back out of the garage to apologise, tell her that I didn't quite catch what she said. Turns out it was only the standard joke, that I can do hers when I've finished if I like. I laugh and think that ok, I will. A bit more noise - get Mary back up on her feet. Much to her great surprise, I tell her to open her garage door then so that I can get to her sockets and start pushing the mower up the path, out the gate and along the pavement to hers. She's all profuse apology, that she was only joking, that she didn't mean for a second for me to take her seriously, but I tell her that it's really no hardship, that I like being outside, that her garden isn't even that big, that it won't take me five minutes. I joke, telling her not to mention it to the next house along though or I'll end up doing the whole street and she jokes back that maybe I should start charging, and she's not talking just tea and biscuits either. I think that if the carpentry work ever dries up then maybe I could add a small lawn-mowing round to my handy-man business. It's funny, you know - being there, I felt a bit like I was being unfaithful to Mary, taking advantage of her condition, straying next door for a little extra-curricular companionship the moment that she couldn't offer it. It's like it made the gesture I'd made, what I was doing for *her*, less special - like if you were all chuffed to bits on receiving a lovely compliment from someone, only to find out that they said the same thing to everyone, that it didn't mean anything, the significance diminished. I get the job done quickly, the lines deliberately not quite so straight as

303

Mary's to make up for my wandering ways, then rush back to hers, feeling better the moment I lift the latch and step through the gate, like I'm a deep sea diver, worried about the bends, just made it back in time to my decompression chamber. Chambers decompression. That's what Mary's place is – somewhere that the bubbles in my blood from the crushing ocean depths outside no longer fizz quite so painfully.

I crack on with the windows – a rather unfortunate turn of phrase but I assure you that I'm extremely careful - removing the old, crumbling putty with a chisel and putty knife (which miraculously I had in my bag, though God alone knows how it found its way there) and removing the wafer-thin glass in order that I can work more freely, repairing and preparing sections of frame to replace the panes more securely and draught-free later on. I break for an early lunch – not because I'm hungry from missing out on breakfast but because I want to check in on Mary, see if she's up. She hasn't made an appearance at the front door with a tray of tea and biscuits as she usually does but it's cold out and maybe she doesn't want to make the arthritis any worse than she has to. I let myself in and call upstairs, almost not wanting to in case it's met again with silence. It isn't. She calls my name and for once it's the greatest word ever spoken, immediately erasing my loss of appetite with a single syllable as my stomach lurches and grumbles, telling me that ok, enough is enough now, panic over, let's eat. I ask if I should come up and she says yes. I mount the staircase three steps at a time and find my way to her room, not difficult in such a small cottage, despite having never been up here before.

I stand in the doorway and she's sitting upright, a curled novel open face down on the bed beside her. The patchwork quilt looks heavy - so heavy that I wonder if that's why she hasn't made it downstairs, whether she's trapped there beneath it. She looks frail, a faint jaundice to her sallow skin, although it could just be the light. I ask her how she's feeling and she tells me all the better for seeing me. She asks if I saw the note, if I've managed to sort myself out and I tell her that I did, that the egg sandwich was delicious, that I called up to offer her one but she didn't answer and I didn't like to come up uninvited. She tells me that I'm a good boy and asks if I mind making her a cup of tea, sweet, three sugars please, when normally she doesn't take any. I tell her of course not, offering to make her some lunch too. She says she's not hungry but it's my turn to play mum, insisting that *she* eat something, keep her strength up, a couple of slices of toast at least, and she gives in.

I eat two egg sandwiches for lunch, my hunger back with a vengeance and knowing that if she checks, the number of missing eggs will now corroborate my story. I take her up tea and toast on a tray, one with Marmite, one with marmalade and one plain, just to maximise the chances of there being something that she fancies, can stomach - or a starter, main course and sweet if she finds once she gets started that she's hungrier than she thought.

I'm much happier now. I tell her that I'll check in on her later and get back to it, aware that time is of the essence today, that I can't leave her windows unsecured and letting the cold in, particularly in her present condition. I usually listen to a small portable radio that Mary has in the kitchen,

305

usually spend a good chunk of the day manoeuvring the pull-out aerial into different positions to find the tuned-in sweet spot but today I leave it off, working in silence in case Mary calls out to me, the only sound the frantic chirrups from the hedge-sparrow-filled bushes outside. Without the hourly news bulletins, I lose track of time and almost cry with relief when Mary appears downstairs to tell me that it's time to clock off for the day, though not before a cup of tea and another of her cakes to fuel my journey home. I tell her that it's only a five minute walk and she counters that they're only cupcakes. We sit at the kitchen table and she tells me that she's glad to be up, that she likely won't sleep well tonight now but she looks to me like that won't be a problem, still looks exhausted. We chat briefly. As I watch her nibbling around the edges of her cake, more for my benefit than anything, I'm worried she only got up to *stop* me from worrying and don't want to wear her out. As I take my plate over to the sideboard, brushing the crumbs and the little grease-proof paper cake liner into the pedal bin, I notice the three pieces of toast lying there, but say nothing. I can't force her but if she doesn't eat anything again tomorrow then I'm calling a doctor whether she likes it or not. At her request, I let her link my arm, walk her into the lounge and switch on the TV set. When she tells me that she's comfortable, has everything she needs, I tuck her tartan blanket over her legs, reminding her that I have my Wednesday morning meeting again tomorrow and won't be in until a bit later, then kiss her on the cheek and leave.

X.

'That wasn't very nice' said Chip without turning from making himself a cup of tea, for once up before Glenn as the latter walked into the kitchen.

'What wasn't?' said Glenn, a picture of naïve innocence.

'The little surprise you left in the fridge.'

'Surprise?'

'The tub of chilli or whatever it was' said Chip, impatient.

'You tried it? Not your cup of tea?' said Glenn.

'No' said Chip 'I didn't try it. Thank God. But Skunk did. I don't know what you put in it but he had some sort of anaphylactic shock - an asthma attack or something. Said it felt like his head was caving in. I've never seen him so animated. His eyes were bulging out of his head and he couldn't even speak properly to tell me what was wrong.'

'Oh dear. Allergic reaction, you think?' said Glenn. 'I *did* put a sign on it. Maybe I should have added *may contain nuts* or something.'

'Are you for real?' said Chip, finally. 'I'm talking about how hot it was.'

'Well that's microwaves for you' said Glenn. 'I'm always saying that they're dangerous.'

307

'I think you know full well that I'm not talking about the temperature. And how do you know that he heated it up in the microwave anyway?'

'I just assumed. I wouldn't have expected him to eat it cold and couldn't imagine him using the cooker. I'm not sure he even knows how.'

'Well, I hope you're pleased with yourself' said Chip. 'He made himself sick. Put his fingers down his throat to try to get rid of whatever it was. Said it was burning his insides. I think the combination of spice and acid on the way back up finally finished him off for good. Not sure he'll be up for a while. I just checked in on him. He's white as a sheet.'

'Oh dear' said Glenn, thinking *that'll be the Ghost Peppers then*. 'Well, like I say, I *did* put a message on it. I like my food with a bit of kick but I know it's not to everyone's taste. I hope it didn't mess things up with the girls.'

'No. Thankfully. My one wasn't exactly what you'd call impressed but she just thinks I'm really sweet and caring now because of the way I looked after him. His one was so stoned out of her mind that she had no idea *what* was going on. And that's another thing. He swears someone messed with his stash. Said he'd never have made one with that much gear in it. Said he couldn't afford it for a start.'

'He doesn't think I had anything to do with *that*?' said Glenn.

'No. He said he would've if they hadn't still been so neat. Said only somebody who'd had a hell of a lot of practice could've rolled something as perfectly as him and he knows you've never so much as tried a menthol.'

'Exactly. Is she ok?'

'Who?'

'The girl who smoked the joint. Do you know if she's ok now?'

'All I know is that they didn't leave until really late. By the time I'd finished with Skunk it was getting light. The first birds were singing and the sun was coming up. It would've been quite nice and romantic if it wasn't for that fact that I had to help Stephanie get her friend down the stairs and out to the cab. Luckily we eventually got one to take her. The two before that drove away as soon as they saw her. Said they didn't want her throwing up in the back right when they were at the end of their shift. What a nightmare.'

'Well, I hope she's ok' said Glenn, his continued concern arousing Chip's suspicion until he remembered how pro-women his flat-mate was.

y.

Chip read from the list whilst Skunk pushed the trolley.

'One large whole chicken, free-range, preferably organic if we can afford it.'

'Bloody hell! Have you seen the price of these things?' said Skunk. 'I'd expect a golden-egg-laying goose for that money!'

'Mum said it'd be much nicer if we bought the decent stuff' said Chip. 'Says you get what you pay for. Do you want to make up for Saturday or not? Think we need all the help we can get, don't you?'

'Fair enough' said Skunk, reluctantly, his remaining cannabis supply not stretching out nearly as far as he'd expected when he came to divide it up into smaller bags for redistribution. Funds were going to be even tighter than usual this month.

'Don't worry. I'll sub you the money. Again. Right, ready cooked, peeled prawns.'

'Prawns?'

'For the starter. Gotta have a starter. Prawn cocktail. All the best dinner parties have them. '

'Seems a bit poncey to me. I'd rather spend the money on booze for some *real* cocktails.'

'I'm sure you would mate but we're aiming for damage repair here, not more mayhem. I don't think getting them ratted is going to create quite the suave, sophisticated impression we're after.'

'That *you're* after you mean. My way would be much more likely to get us in their knickers.'

'Yeah, well, maybe in the short term but if we plan on seeing them again after the weekend then I think we just listen to me for once. It's alright for you, you were all tucked up in bed whilst I was carrying your one downstairs and trying to get her into a cab.'

'I was tucked up alright' said Skunk, still refusing to believe himself entirely to blame.

'Yeah, well let's just get this done shall we?' said Chip. 'Prawns.'

'Think they were in the last aisle' said Skunk.

'Blimey, you were actually paying attention?'

'Not exactly' said Skunk. 'But there was this woman with huge charlies bending down to pick some up as we went past. I could see right down her top, bra and everything. Possibly even a bit of nip. Thank you, Lord, for those glorious chiller cabinets.'

'I'm surprised you even noticed what she was holding.'

'I know what I'd have liked her to be holding.'

'Yeah, ok Benny Hill' said Chip as a middle-aged woman pushing a trolley with a child seated in one end looked across in disgust, placing a packet of Super Noodles back on the shelf, as if Skunk's words had managed to contaminate them somehow. 'Keep your voice down.'

'And I'd have liked it to end up smelling of prawns too' said Skunk, more for the benefit of the woman than his friend, at which point Chip grabbed their trolley, wheeling it quickly away in the hope that his flat-mate would follow.

'What about dessert?' said Skunk, as they headed towards the bakery section, the smell of fresh bread warm and reassuring in his nostrils.

'Oh, good point' said Chip, glad that his friend was finally getting into the spirit of things. 'What were you thinking? Any ideas?'

'I was thinking that maybe I could make some cakes.'

'No!' said Chip, nipping the idea in the bud immediately, hoping to God that it was given in jest. With a maverick wingman like this, he was always going to be Goose in the equation - crashing and burning in dramatic style. 'How about we just go with black forest gateaux? Can't go wrong with a bit of BFG.'

'Fine' said Skunk. 'And don't forget the cheese board.'

'I don't think we've got enough for cheeseboard too' said Chip, looking in his wallet and attempting a quick rudimentary tot-up of the contents of their trolley.

'I was joking' said Skunk. 'Jesus, how are we friends?'

'I ask myself that all the time' said Chip.

Back at the flat and the lads were loading the fridge when Glenn walked into the kitchen. He couldn't quite believe what he was seeing. So his words hadn't gone unheeded after all. The chilli had made a lasting impression, helped drive his point home. Perhaps from now on there might be a little more mutual appreciation and respect.

'You guys been shopping?' he said, stating the obvious.

312

'Yeah' said Skunk, his head obscured by the fridge door. 'Got any labels left?'

'Labels?'

'Yeah. For this lot.'

'He means that we've got the girls coming over for dinner on Saturday' said Chip, mediating. 'This is all for then so you can't eat any of it, I'm afraid.'

'You're throwing a dinner party?' said Glenn, incredulous.

'Yeah, well last Saturday didn't turn out quite as well as we'd hoped so we have a little making up to do' said Chip.

'Yeah and it's a foursome. We don't need anyone cramping our style so if you could make yourself scarce...' said Skunk.

'Make myself...But I don't have any plans to be out on Saturday night.'

'You don't say' said Skunk, still focusing on arranging items in the fridge to avoid having to look Glenn in the eye, which he found difficult enough at the best of times.

'Well, look mate' said Chip, not wishing to antagonise things. 'We'd really appreciate it if you could *find* something to do. Skunk does have a point. It would feel a bit weird having a romantic meal for four with you there in the other room.'

'Romance? Who said anything about romance?' said Skunk, thrusting his pelvis and making explosion sounds with his mouth whilst slapping an imaginary behind. Glenn just looked at him, expressionless, wondering what on earth had possessed himself to think that a little respect was ever possibly on the horizon.

313

Z.

Saturday morning came around. Chip managed to scrape some money together and sent Skunk out to pick up a copy of Nirvana's MTV Live Unplugged album, making him promise not to stop off and spend it at the pub which he knew he'd have to pass on his way to the shops. Perhaps he should've just gone himself but they'd both risen late and he wanted to get the food prepped so that they weren't having a last minute panic when the girls turned up. He didn't want to be all hot and bothered when he opened the door to greet them, wanted to make a good impression this time around. He liked Stephanie, and not just because she was pretty, although she was – very. No, she had integrity, didn't suffer fools. Given Skunk's performances to date, it was nothing short of miraculous that he'd gotten this far, that she'd agreed to come back for more. He sensed though that he couldn't blow it again, had jumped straight to his ninth life - that next time he'd be headed straight back to solitary, without passing go and without collecting two hundred-pounds. He congratulated himself on his excellent idea, the target album ticking the Nirvana box whilst still a more civilised, dinner-party-friendly acoustic collection than the heavier Bleach or In Utero, which could be melancholically chilled-out one minute and wailing like a branded banshee the next. Besides, sending Skunk out on a mission meant that he wasn't under his feet, stinking the place out with his smoking and getting stoned before their guests came. Damage limitation - that was the aim of today's game.

He opened the fridge door and knew immediately that something was wrong, although not consciously so, didn't realise that the light hadn't come on as it usually did. Even before the trapped smell of stagnant air wafted out, drifting into the room as tangibly as the ever permeating haze of Skunk's marijuana smoke. He took the chicken out and broke the seal of cling-film covering with his finger-nails, a little of the fetid scent of off-chicken escaping into the room. Next he took out the prawns and found a corner edge, peeling back the plastic lid. They were even worse, gag-inducing, almost giving himself whiplash as his head snapped back, recoiling from a testing sniff. They'd already had one bout of vomiting last time the girls had come to the flat. If he cooked and served up any of this lot, they'd all end up in bed alright - but with food poisoning – assuming of course that he didn't kill them off completely with the double hit of salmonella and rotten shellfish. He opened the windows to allow the smell to escape and some fresh air to enter, instantly welcoming in a good display team of flies too which had no doubt clocked their favourite aromas carried out on the breeze for miles around. He took a bin-liner from the cupboard beneath the sink where Glenn kept all his cleaning products. Glenn. It had to be him. He must've unplugged the fridge. It couldn't turn itself off, unless of course it was broken, had just stopped working. There was no telling how old it was, it had been there when they'd moved in, although it looked in considerably better

315

shape now than it had then since Glenn had moved in with them, immediately setting to work with his cloths and sprays, bringing it back to its former glory on his first day there. Pulling it out, Chip checked the plug which he found still in the wall-socket, the switch pressed down to the *on* setting. So maybe it wasn't Glenn. He felt bad briefly. He followed the lead along with his fingers to the back of the fridge, to make sure that he was looking at the right plug, not one that powered some other appliance. Halfway down, he located the cause of the problem. The white plastic-covered cable was severed in two. He pulled one end out from the gloom at the back of the fridge and into a shaft of daylight to get a proper look at it. It wasn't a neat cut, didn't look like it had been done with a blade - it looked like it had been....chewed. Rats? Mice? Glenn was always nagging them about leaving food lying around, for that very reason. He didn't dare say anything to him for fear of hearing *I told you so.* Whatever the reason, he needed to do something quickly or tonight was going to be another disastrous evening down the pan and, quite possibly with it, his chances with Stephanie. Perhaps he could catch Skunk before he spent the CD money, could use some of that to buy something else. It might not be as nice but it would be better than nothing. What were the chances of his pal doing as he was asked straight away anyway, without any deviation from the instructions? He'd probably be wandering up and down the high street right now, eyeing up women. If he could just get to him before he hit the record store.

Chip was still tying his shoe-laces when he heard the key in the lock. Oh no, Glenn was back. He needed to get into the kitchen and push the fridge back into place before he noticed and asked questions.

'Entertainment committee's back!' shouted Skunk, walking into the lounge looking as pleased as punch with himself, placing the pink and grey HMV bag down on the coffee table and walking back out of the room, kicking his shoes off in the hall.

'Unbelievable. The one time I don't want you to be and you're super-efficient' called out Chip.

'What do you mean? I thought you'd be pleased. I almost stopped for a quick pint first. Thought I could probably buy something different, cheaper - one of their back catalogue maybe.'

'For God's sake! That wouldn't have worked though Skunk. I specifically said that it had to be *that* album.'

'Don't get your knickers in a knot. I said I *thought* about it. I did as I was told though, didn't I? Don't want you blaming me when you fuck things up with your girlfriend. You're quite capable of doing that on your own. You've had enough practice - 'ere, what's happened here?'

'Eh?'

'The fridge is all hanging out.'

'Oh yeah. About that. That's what I was about to say. Houston, we have a problem.'

'Why? What's wrong? And Jesus, what's that stink? It smells like your mum's minge in here.'

'Trust me, it's nowhere near as bad as it was. And don't open that bin-bag, I'm throwing it out.'

'What happened?'

'The fridge is broken. The food's gone off. We can salvage some of it but the chicken and prawns are ruined.'

317

'But aren't they the two most important bits?'

'Yep. Pretty much. I was just leaving the flat to come find you. Was hoping to catch you before you spent what little money we had left on the CD.'

'You could always pretend we're vegetarians. Birds love that sort of shit. They lap it up. She'll think you're all deep and sensitive and all that bollocks.'

'Yeah. Or we could just take the CD back I suppose. Get the money back and buy something else to eat.'

'Yeah. Ok. Come on then, I'll go back with you. But you're going in to change it. I'll wait outside. Bloody embarrassing. I only just bought it. You can tell them I just gave it to you as a birthday present but you already had it or something. So what's wrong with the fridge anyway?'

'The power cable's been sheared through.'

'Cut, you mean.'

'No, I have to admit that that was my first thought but it looks like it's been gnawed. Mice probably.'

'Yeah, whatever. There's only one pest that needs to be exterminated in this flat and I think we both know who that is.'

'I really don't think it was him, Skunk. Take a look at the wire. If it was cut, it'd be neater. It definitely looks like it's been chewed through.'

'Yeah, but by what? Or should I say *who*?'

'Can you honestly see him sitting there chewing through it?'

'I wouldn't put anything past him.'

'He'd have electrocuted himself.'

'Not if he disconnected it first then plugged it back in after.'

'Nice idea, Columbo, but I don't think so somehow.'

'You don't think it's a bit of a coincidence that it's worked fine all this time and suddenly we fill it up for the first time ever with a whole load of nice stuff for a meal that he's not invited to and it mysteriously stops working? Have you already forgotten what he did last week? How malicious he is?'

'Hmm, I see what you mean' said Chip.

'I say we give him his marching orders. Today.'

Four hours later, music exchanged for meat, the heat from the fan oven warmed the kitchen, the aroma of home-cooking filling the flat as Glenn Chambers walked in. The place had even been tidied up. So they *could* do it if they tried, they just needed the right motivation – which turned out to be something that unfortunately he personally would never be able to provide. As he came into the kitchen, he noticed the askew fridge before he noticed the earnestly askew expressions on the faces of his flat-mates.

'Hey. What's up guys?' he said.

'We have something we need to talk to you about...' began Chip.

'We want you out' said Skunk, diving in, not prepared to wait, a rare moment of proactive dominance.

'I know' said Glenn, 'you already mentioned. Don't worry, I'm not sticking around. I'll be out of your hair before the girls get here. I'm meeting a couple of old friends for a few beers' he lied, still not yet sure exactly *what* he was going to do with himself for the evening.

'No, he means that we want you out permanently' said Chip, taking his friend's lead, thinking the damage now

319

done, no point beating around the bush. 'We're giving you notice, I'm afraid. You've got until this time next week to find somewhere else to live. I'm sorry.'

'Are you?' said Glenn, calmly, holding his gaze so that Chip was forced to look away.

'Am I what? Giving you notice?'

'No. Sorry.'

In his room shortly afterwards, Glenn Chambers packed his bag of his few personal belongings. Apart from the problem of having to actually find somewhere, moving for him was about as simple a process as it was possible to get, short of being a fully-fledged hobo - a knotted knapsack slung over his shoulder on the end of a knobbly, whittled staff. They could keep their week. He'd spent his whole life moving around from place to place, relative to relative, foster placement to placement, job to job. What was one more move? He'd had high hopes for this one, living with two lads his own age, but perhaps with hindsight he should've seen the warning signs, paid attention to them from the start. Badgers, Ferrets, Skunks. That was it. No more weasels. Perhaps if the heavens had been slightly kinder, things might've worked out a whole lot differently. Another time, with another third party, he and Chip might even have been friends. He had potential, wasn't so bad deep down, but he was weak, always took the easy option. Well, if this Stephanie was as amazing as she was meant to be then she deserved better. Much better.

The lads were sitting in the lounge, working together to dispatch a plague of advancing zombies, the sound of machine gun-fire, hand-grenades and death groans the soundtrack to Glenn's imminent departure. He walked into the kitchen for the final time, to get himself a glass of water. He saw the note still on the side, meant for if he'd come in when they hadn't been there or hadn't heard him, which was most of the time when the Playstation was on. *Slow-cooked lamb in the oven. Please leave on.*

Too slow for my liking said Glenn to himself, turning the knob round to its maximum heat-setting before slipping quietly out the front door to avoid any tearful goodbyes. And to think he'd once dared to believe that adulthood might be any different.

X.

Today is my birthday. As usual, I haven't told anyone, for a couple of reasons. Firstly, there's been hardly anyone to tell, except Mary of course, and I don't want her feeling obligated to get me a present, which I know she would. Besides, I've had a gift and a cake with candle from her already this week. There's Jenny at the Job Centre but it doesn't look like she's coming back and even if she did, she'd already know anyway, has all my personal details available at the tap of a key. Obviously I can't expect any preferential treatment from her or she'd have to make a fuss of all her clients, which of course is simply out of the question. Secondly, if I don't mention it to anybody, then I don't feel quite so bad when they fail to acknowledge it, when the phone remains silent, when no cards are waiting for me by the front door when I go to check. So this Wednesday is just like any other and if by *any other* I mean last week, then that's just fine with me.

I leave the flat slightly earlier than usual this morning to get to the Job Centre so I miss the river of school kids meandering past. Where previously this avoidance was one of the few advantages for me of sign-on day, today I have to admit that I miss them, miss the untapped potential of youth which I now feel I've caught a little of myself; have been to the careers adviser within myself and identified

322

what I want to do with the rest of my working life, albeit a little later than some.

As I board the bus into town, a minor miracle happens and rather than only rows of surly faces staring into space through condensation drenched windows, a lady smiles up at me and moves her bag from the seat next to her to allow me to sit down. Perhaps she can sense my special birthday aura which, despite my earlier comments, I still feel even if nobody else knows about it. She glances across at me to receive my thank you with a smile and I consider speaking but change my mind, deciding to contain the moment, not shatter the illusion with my fumbled attempts at small talk which will probably end up with her feeling trapped there, regretting her polite gesture. If she wants to talk she can.

She doesn't, except to say excuse me when she needs to get off and there's a slightly awkward moment where I then get up too and make my own way to the front of the bus, worried that she might think I'm only doing so because we shared a seat when clearly the town centre is a final destination for at least half the other passengers too. I'm being silly, overthinking things. Either way, I alight from the vehicle and beat a hasty retreat, wanting it to be quite apparent that I'm ahead of her, not following along behind, even though she very likely hasn't given the matter a second thought.

When I arrive at the Job Centre and walk in, making sure as usual that the security guard receives at least one warm smile today, I'm blessed with my second *big day* surprise. Jenny's back. I take a seat in the orange cushioned waiting area and give her a smile too, this one a little more familiar than the one I just gave at the front

323

door. She smiles back at me but it's not the one I usually get from her, doesn't quite fit properly. It's like she borrowed it. It doesn't…..*suit* her - in the way that someone might see an outfit in a glossy magazine, rush out to buy it then wonder why it doesn't look nearly as great on them as it did on the supermodel they'd first seen wearing it. Perhaps she's still not feeling well, not yet fully recovered. She probably came back too soon, worried about her targets and her clients. Maybe she realised it was my birthday today after all and didn't want to miss it. No, I'm just being silly again. She looks pained. I hope she's ok.

I wait for just a couple of minutes which seem like a couple of hours before she calls me over.

'Morning. How are we today?' she asks. Her words are friendly but her tone is not. Not unfriendly, just not friendly. Formal.

'I'm fine, thanks. Been keeping busy you know. More importantly, how are…'

'Yes. Well about that' she says, cutting me off. 'I have something I need to give you' she says, handing me a white envelope which her look of consternation tells me doesn't contain a birthday card.

I open it up and read:

Dear Mr Chambers,

It has been brought to our attention that you may have been carrying out paid work which you have failed to declare to either the Department for Work and Pensions or a member of staff at your local Job Centre Plus. In light of your current status as a claimant of Job Seeker's Allowance, this could amount to Benefit Fraud and as such, you are required to attend an interview under caution at the time and date of your next signing day. You are entitled, indeed encouraged, to seek appropriate representation and may be accompanied at the interview by a designated supporter of your choosing.

Please be aware that this letter is by no means an accusation of guilt and merely serves to investigate the matter further in order to ascertain whether or not there may be any truth to these allegations.

The interview is however compulsory. Your full cooperation in this matter is expected.

Yours sincerely,

Stephen Mallory,

Investigating Officer

I read it again, the paper trembling in my hands. I must've misread it, misunderstood its meaning. This can't really be happening. Never mind that I'm innocent, that I've been helping out an elderly pensioner out of the goodness of my heart. I'm a phantom. Nobody knows I exist, let alone enough to bare me malice, to want to *grass me up*. I imagine that usually in these situations, the fraudster is

325

flicking through their brain-files, picking out bulging profiles of likely accusers, people they've upset in the past, those with a possible axe to grind - but I can't even do that. I can barely think of anyone with whom I'm even on first name terms. How has it got to this? And so quickly. I've only been working at Mary's for just over a week. Unless maybe someone from the Job Centre was walking past when I've been out on the roof or something, put two and two together and come up with five. I'm dumbstruck, don't know what to say. When I do finally manage to utter something, I guess it's not exactly the best thing I could have said, not exactly a convincing declaration of my innocence.

'Who reported me?' I say. It's that which bothers me most, that and the fact that it had to be Jenny who gave me it. It somehow would've been a lot less painful receiving the letter from her stand-in. Why is it that the only time people want to barge in on my life is when I want to be left alone?

'Well, obviously I wouldn't be allowed to tell you that.' she says. 'But I don't know anyway. It was probably anonymous. It usually is.'

Anonymous. Well I know all about that. Could be written on my headstone.

It's frustrating, I know. When you watch a movie, it's agony when the innocent party won't speak up and explain fully - clearly and concisely - the simple misunderstanding of which they've just been a victim. But please understand that I was caught by surprise. My mind was racing, though not nearly so much as my emotions, heart ruling head, making intelligent, coherent communication nigh on

326

impossible. Even if I *had* managed to get my thoughts together, why should I? I'm tired of trying to explain myself. All I can think is that this just isn't fair. That it's my birthday. That there wasn't even a card with my usual letter from Anne on the mat this morning, that maybe it'll come with the second post, that I never got to do the afternoon round myself, wonder how different it is from the early morning slot.

'Mr Chambers? Are you ok?' says Jenny. So it's already Mr Chambers now is it? No more Glenn. No doubt she doesn't want to be my friend anymore, doesn't want to be associated with a criminal.

'How are *you*?' I say. Of course *I'm* not ok. I would've thought that was patently obvious. 'I'm glad to see you back. I was worried about you. I hope you're fully on the mend.'

'Yes I…'

'It's my birthday today' I say.

'Yes, I just noticed that on my screen. Hap….' She stops herself just in time, realising how ridiculous it would be under the circumstances. 'I'm sorry to have to do this to you today of all days.'

'Oh, don't worry. It's not a special one' I say, thinking that they never are. 'Will that be all? Do I have to do anything else?'

'No, not right now. Actually, I'm afraid I can't authorise your money today either' she says, twisting the knife, 'not while your case is pending investigation.'

'Ok. Thank you' I say, rising from my seat.

'Mr Ch…Glenn, are you sure you're ok?' she says.

327

'Never better' I say, because have I ever been? I mean, really and truthfully, what else did I expect?

I leave the building, forgetting to smile at the security guard on my way out. I just want to get home right now. I'm in no state to go round Mary's, don't want her seeing me unless I can be bright and breezy for her. She'll know something's up immediately and I haven't even told her that I sign on yet, although she must've wondered about my employment status, how I manage to have so much time on my hands to be helping her out. I just don't want to give her any reason to think any less of me. Perhaps she thinks I'm a lottery winner or something. Perhaps that's the real reason she wants me around. I'm joking of course – at least I can still do that I suppose. I wait in line at the stop, passive smoking the cigarettes of the queue in front of me chaining in panic at the thought of a whole twenty minute bus journey without one. I get on the first bus that comes along, don't even bother to look at the front to check that it's going my way - most of them do, although it'll be just my luck today that it's one of the rare ones that doesn't. That might not be such a problem if it just kept on going, forever, taking me ever further from my life. I sit at the back and look out the window, watching the grey world go by. It feels like I've been doing that my whole life. Just one time it'd be nice to have someone waiting for me at the other end.

It's the right bus. I've lived here long enough to know every detail of every building. Familiar landmarks pass by one after another. I see faces out on the pavement that I've been seeing around for years, decades even, and wonder

328

how it can be that I recognise them so well yet have had absolutely no impact on them myself. A community of individuals.

When I step off the bus, the mood in the air feels different. The natural conclusion would be that it's just me that's different, that I've just received some bad news so obviously won't be feeling as positive as I was on the way in. But no, it's more than that. I'm sure of it. Granted I'm not helping matters but I'm certain it isn't just me. The atmosphere is charged with a negative energy that hits me like the heat of an opened oven door. I need to get home, to my sanctuary, my Fortress of Solitude which suddenly I'd be glad of having no windows in. I don't want anyone seeing in and there's certainly nothing outside that I wish to look at right now.

I walk quickly, the distance somehow taking longer to cover for it. Perhaps it's just that my hurried steps are shorter than the longer, loping strides I take when I'm relaxed. I just don't seem to be covering ground nearly as speedily as I'd like, to the point that I almost consider hailing a cab, before realising how embarrassing it would be to have to get in and let the driver know the pitifully short fare they just stopped for.

The end is soon in sight but, as I near my flat, I can see from along the street that something's amiss. As I get closer, I see that my front door's been daubed with graffiti. Terrific. That's all I need right now. Letters sprayed in red, like I'm living in Black Death London, a victim of bubonic plague. And as the single word comes into view, I realise that I probably *am* the victim of rats. *PEDO.* That's what it says. And I thought that was a good school. They can't even be bothered to spell it properly, unless of course they genuinely believe that I'm some kind of foot specialist whose business could benefit from an increased public awareness campaign. I'm being flippant but that's not how I feel. I need to try to do something to trivialise it but it doesn't work. Truth is, I feel crushed. You might think it a gross overreaction to two tiny syllables but instantly I no longer want to live here – here in this flat, possibly this world - anymore. My retreat, the one place that I always felt safe, has been tarnished forever. Sure, I could go out and get some graffiti remover to clean it up, possibly even get rid of it completely – only, I will never be fully rid of it now. A little part of me will always dread coming home every time I go out, wondering what I'm coming back to; more graffiti, a broken window, maybe worse. I feel like Shrek when he comes out of his swamp-hut to be faced with pitch-fork wielding locals, wanting the monster among them out. Only, a loud roar isn't going to do the trick this time. I'm not nearly scary enough. Even kids don't fear me. For me there's not even a Donkey – and certainly no Fiona. Am I really such an ogre? I want to turn around and go back the way I came but I have nowhere else to go so I turn the key and go inside.

Usually when I close the front door behind me it's with a certain sense of satisfaction - relief that I'm blocking out the world outside. Now though, I feel like I'm blocking myself in, all I can think about the hurtful word written on the other side, like a neon sign, advertising to all and sundry that I'm some sort of sexual deviant when my exploits in that department have mostly been carried out alone, usually whilst I was asleep.

I sit in my front room, on the edge of the sofa, my fists on my knees as if posing for a school photo. I don't get comfortable. I'm not sure I will ever be comfortable here again. Birds chirrup outside but even that doesn't seem to me the beautiful, warbling, sunny song of usual; now much more are they staking claims, angry declarations of territorial rights, no better than football hooligans challenging others to come and have a go if they think they're hard enough. I notice that the mirror above the fireplace is smeared, could use a clean. From my position seated down below, looking up, low winter sunlight streams in through the blinds, washing across the glass, highlighting the layer of fine dust specks that aren't usually so apparent. Without thinking, I go to the cupboard under the sink that contains my cleaning products and take out a bottle of glass-spray and a cotton anti-static cloth that I bought specially for just such a job. I go over to the mirror and wipe it down, like a window-cleaner, starting at the top and working down to the bottom right-hand-corner. I unsettle the frame so that it isn't sitting straight and as I hold my arms out to adjust it, it's like I'm holding myself out at arm's length, getting a good look at myself for the first time. Who am I? *What* am I? If I don't recognise the person looking back at me then how can I possibly expect others to? All I know for sure is that whoever that is, he's let me down. Again and again, he's let me down - at every possible turn. And he'll let me down again. No more. I punch him in the face, shattering the mirror into pieces. Clean pieces at least. I look at them there on the floor, dozens of tiny Glenns – mini General Zods trapped in a constellation of two-dimensional eternities - looking back up at me, questioning, asking what the hell I'm playing at. Seven years bad luck. Seven? What's seven more? I'll do that standing on my head. My knuckles are badly cut, blood running down from them onto the cord carpet. I look down and watch the droplets falling in a steady drip, drip, drip. Usually I'm fanatical about this sort of thing, would be rushing to the sink to get a wet cloth and some Scotch Guard foam-spray to clean it up before the first spot landed but what's the point? I look at the worn, threadbare carpet and wonder why I go to so much effort to keep it spotlessly hoovered when it's so tatty and tired anyway, will never look nice - a metaphor for my life. And who's ever going to see it if I don't? The flow of blood starts to slow as the coagulation process begins to kick in and I consider getting it going again, only this time much faster. How easy it would be to fix everything. I wouldn't need to move from this spot, could just bend down, pick up one of those jagged shards and....

I'm being selfish. I can't let Mary down. She's expecting me later than usual but I said I'd be there and I'm a man of my word – a good word, not the kind of word that others who don't know the first thing about me want to label me, in foot-high letters for all the world to see. And that thought makes me feel a little better; that the word on my front door is based on nothing more than a friendly morning smile; that *they're* the ones with deviant thoughts, not me. I go to the bathroom and run my hand under the tap, watching the claret marbling the white basin like tie-dye as the blood spreads out in the water, another bit of my life force swirling down the plug-hole, lost forever. I take a length of lint bandage and wrap it around my knuckles,

332

tucking the end inside and securing it with a safety pin. For a lifelong bachelor, I'm very well equipped when it comes to stuff like this. I hold my hand down by my side to encourage the blood-flow to the extremities, to see if it holds out or the blood starts to seep through, and I'm satisfied that I've done an adequate enough repair job. I just hope the cumbersome white covering doesn't impede my ability to do Mary's repair jobs. I look like a boxer, back in the locker room, getting ready for a fight, which in a way I feel like I am, every time I leave the flat. She's going to cause such a fuss when I get there and she sees this. If that's the case then perhaps it wasn't such a stupid thing to do after all. I could use a little fuss today. She'll want to know how I did it of course. Hopefully she won't think I've been fighting because, like I said, that's what it looks like. I can't lie to her. I'll just say I cut it on some broken glass. I only hope she doesn't think I mean the glass in her windows or she'll blame herself.

I leave the flat without ever looking back, oblivious to the cold despite not wearing a coat, already numb. Much as I don't want to leave it there, don't want to draw unnecessary unwanted attention to myself and my abode, I simply can't face expending any energy on it right now. What little I have left I need for the short walk to Mary's where hopefully she'll recharge my levels, and I hers.

As I turn into her cul-de-sac, I already feel better, then a little better again when I see her cottage, a little more when I lift the latch on her gate and even better still as I press the doorbell. I think that by the time we share a cuppa together, I'm going to be feeling almost human again.

333

Disappointingly, there's no answer, no sign of life. My first reaction again is worry, but then I look at my watch and realise that this is the latest I've got here since I started coming. Suddenly my worry turns to hope as I realise that perhaps she's feeling much better, has managed to get up and about, out of the house even. I press the bell a second time, harder like before, and then when there's no answer again, take the key from my pocket, put it in the lock and turn. The door opens a few inches then catches on the chain. My stomach lurches.

'Mary!' I call. 'Mary! It's me, Glenn! Are you ok?' I shout through the narrow gap.

When there's no answer, I call again, trying not to give away the panic rising steadily in my voice. Again there's no sound and I push my face into the gap, trying to listen for any hint of movement. She might be in the shower, the bath, on the loo. But she'd have come down first and taken the latch off like she said she would. Perhaps she hasn't woken yet. I remember thinking how exhausted she looked yesterday. It's only just after midday. Morning's barely over.

I consider breaking the door in. I've never told her of course but the latch isn't really much more than a psychological aide. It wouldn't take any great effort on my part to shoulder barge the door, break that pathetic little chain that wouldn't look out of place hanging round a teenager's scrawny neck. I could fix it easily afterwards, probably just need to re-fill a couple of splintered holes, add it to my list of jobs. But knowing the way that my day's going so far, I'd probably end up getting reported by someone from neighbourhood watch, have the police turn

334

up and arrest me for breaking and entering, criminal damage or something. Yeah, probably best not to disturb her. I know how it feels to have the entrance to your home violated. Probably best just to leave her to sleep. Yep. Definitely. That's what I'll do. I'll leave her alone. Let her rest in peace.

I back away from the house, a loyal subject not wishing to turn my back on my queen, a mark of respect. Suddenly I'm aware of the cold, feel naked, like a baby bird fallen from the nest; no, not fallen, pushed - by a cuckoo chick. Through the side gate, I see a pair of jays flash stone pink and iridescent blue across the back of the house and I wonder what currency they carry. They're just magpies in party frocks after all. No doubt a party I'm not invited to as usual. Extra joy perhaps? I should be so lucky.

And the next thing I know, I'm standing at a bar, a note in my outstretched hand, waiting for the bar-man to notice. I don't recognise the place, have never been in here before. I don't remember how I got here, couldn't honestly tell you if I got a bus, a taxi or walked the whole way. I don't even know how far I am from home – could be a few minutes, could be a few hours. I could easily look at my watch, the clock on the back-bar to get a rough idea but I don't think of that, am not sure that I really care either way. I'm here now and that's all that matters. I don't normally go in for drowning my sorrows. If I did that every time I was having a bad day then I'd pretty much be a full-on alcoholic by now – or long since dead from liver failure. Perhaps I should've - perhaps it might've made things easier, but I always felt that it was just brushing the problem under the carpet, pushing it deeper under the skin, embedding it ever further into the rich, dark, inner soil of my soul until it grew into a mighty oak, impossible to chop down. I thought, naively perhaps, that riding the storm, hitch-hiking my way along the rocky road, suffering the misery and pain like some sort of emotional flagellation would see me come out the other side a stronger, more well rounded individual, able to take on anything that life then threw at me. I just never expected to still be playing dodge-ball all these years later – didn't expect the public stoning to take quite so long, be quite so vicious. But I'm no longer so idealistic. My eyes are finally open. I'm exactly where I need to be. I just want to block everything out, booze myself into oblivion, a state of consciousness – or unconsciousness, same difference – where nothing matters, nothing can hurt me anymore. There's still a lot of the day remaining and if my stomach needs pumping at the end of it, well….please - don't. I don't fear death; what I fear is life – another day in mine. I'm not being morbid, not wallowing. I'm merely stating facts - telling it like it is. I have no self-pity and don't expect any from anyone else. I just think that I've given it enough of a go now to know all I need to. Anyone else would've given up long ago. So I order a large scotch and coke. The first of many. Bottoms up.

The first thing I notice are her arms. The faint leopard-print pattern of smudged bruising there looks like somebody went for finger-print testing at the police station then grabbed her on the way out - which quite possibly they did at some stage. I've seen marks left like that before and know it wasn't from over-zealous affection. She's clearly been gripped, but not in the throes of passion and certainly not in the loving way that she held my arm that night. None of my business. Stay out of it, Glenn. Have yourself another drink – it's your birthday after all – treat yourself. But the second double kicks in quickly, marring my judgement. I turn my head in her direction, more overtly than before; let's face it, I was never not going to. I get a better look this time and move up to her face which I recognise immediately, taking me aback. I'm so transfixed by this realisation that I haven't noticed her 'friend' noticing me; at least not until I hear the singing – if you can call it that - from across the bar behind her:

'The moment he walked in the joint, I could see he was a man of distinction, a real big spender....' a mumbling instrumental break where he either didn't know the words or didn't want to be calling me good looking or refined and then 'hey, big spender.....!' followed by a heavy smoker's laugh. It's her PR man or whatever he calls himself.

I ignore him, turn away, down my drink and order another. He's bored with me already, had his fun, gone back to his goons. I make short work of the third then order a fourth double, this time without the mixer. The sugar is too sickly sweet on my teeth and I want to feel the heat at the back of my throat as it goes down.

'In a hurry?' says the barman.

'It's my birthday' I say. 'I'm celebrating.'

'Oh. Happy Birthday' he says, in a way that tells me he can see it's not really – happy, I mean. He takes my glass from the bar and pushes it up against the optic, no regard for the fact that it's not clean, telling me that this one's on him. It's the first time I've been bought a birthday drink since I turned eighteen, although I'm not naïve enough to

337

think that he actually intends to put any money in the till from his own pocket and pay for it himself. Too little – and certainly much too late.

Without allowing myself time to think about it, to change my mind, I down what's now effectively a treble and head straight on over.

'I want my money' I say, tapping him on the shoulder to turn him around. It's only when I'm standing there in front of him that I realise he's with the whole of the large group of people behind him, each blessed with that same degenerate gene that could see them all related.

He looks deliberately down at his shoulder, brushes it ever so slowly with his hand as if removing an irritating bit of fluff. The rest of the group have stopped talking with each other now, turned to see what this is all about. 'What money?' he says.

'The fifty pounds you owe me.'

'Well actually, technically speaking, it's *you* that owes *me*. But I'm prepared to overlook it so why don't you just know what's good for you and do the same?'

'Me owe you? How do you manage to work that out?' I ask, though why I'm expecting to enter into a reasonable negotiation with this brute I don't know. Must be the Scotch.

'Well I already explained about Skye' he says 'So, as far as I'm concerned, that matter was already settled. But now you're here in my members-only club without ever having signed up, as far as I can recall...'

'Members only...?' I begin, looking at the bartender for corroboration. He just looks back at me, offering me a *sorry but I'm not getting involved, you're on your own here, I'm afraid* shrug, before busying himself wiping the inside of a clean pint glass with a filthy tea-towel.

'Yep. That's right. Very exclusive too. State of the art facilities; pool table, dart-board, fruity, quiz machine. And you'll never guess how much it all costs?'

I just look at him. He says I'll never guess so I don't try.

'Bullseye. A nifty. Half a ton. Fifty Great British pounds to you, sir. Sterling. Amazing coincidence don't you think? Seems everything's fifty these days eh? Now, I was prepared to overlook it, allow you a free trial visit, but if you want to start getting all pedantic about who owes who what….'

'It's his birthday Will' interjects the teen barman suddenly, perhaps hoping that the regular might go easy on me, knowing what might otherwise come next and not wanting any trouble whilst he's temporarily managing the bar alone.

'Oh, really? Many Happy Returns of the day' says Will. 'Well in that case, get this man a complimentary free shot – on my tab. Got to keep the public happy, eh Paul?' he says to the young barman, already down the bar, pouring out a black Sambuca from a heavy, square-sided bottle. 'D'you know, I once heard that a happy customer tells one person about their experience but an unsatisfied one tells nine. Can you believe it? Nine! Where's the sense of justice in that? Can't have you slagging this place off to all your friends now can we? Don't want the joint closing down or poor old Paul here will be out of a job. Actually, where *are* your friends? Not here yet? Meeting you later?'

339

He looks at me, cruelly, waiting for an answer which again doesn't come, which he knew wouldn't.

'You do *have* friends? I mean, you wouldn't be drinking alone on your birthday would you? Nobody's *that* sad, surely.'

He looks at me again, leans in as if the answer to his question will lie deep in my eyes, close enough that he can surely see the tears welling in them – tears of frustration, not upset, I'm used to that – which, sparing me, haven't yet broken free. The rest of the group are looking too, laughing and making comments which I don't hear, have learned to block out.

I turn around and walk away, leaving the dark aniseed shot stuck to the bar, untouched. As I approach the main door, the draught-fed air cools even before I reach it, wafting ice cold as I open it, causing me to gasp a sharp intake of breath, bracing myself for my exit. I look to my left and lying on the bench-seat there see a pile of coats which must belong to Will and co since there's nobody else here in the tiny working man's club. Among them I see the familiar denim jacket with the sheepskin collar, turn around to see if they're still watching me leave. They aren't. The whole episode was that insignificant to him that he's already back deep in the throes of his previous conversation, picked up where he left off, my interruption no more than a set of parentheses, an inconvenient commercial break. I've probably already left his thoughts completely whereas he'll haunt mine for months, years even. Out of spite – and because it's absolutely freezing out – I pick up his jacket and close the door behind me.

Stepping out into the air doesn't make me feel more drunk like I've often heard it can. Perhaps it's the adrenaline still coursing through my veins but I feel more sober now than I did when I arrived – when apparently I was on automatic pilot, since I still have no idea where I am, don't recognise the buildings around me at all. I can still hear the sound of raucous laughter and frivolity inside, though not clearly, can't make out if they're still laughing at me. Why should I care? Would I want them as friends even if they'd have me? Am I really *that* desperate? No - I'm not. With friends like that.... But I doubt he's really *anybody's* friend. Not really.

I walk for several minutes before managing to hail a cab. Even with the sheepskin collar up, this short jacket isn't really ideal for a mid-winter afternoon - one of those where it's so bitingly bitter that even the very air itself appears tinted a stonewashed denim blue, a watercolour of its summer oil.

'Where you headed, guv?' the cabbie says to me and I'm just about to give him my address when I remember the first thing I'll see when I get there.

'Nowhere' I say to the pair of hazel-brown eyes watching me in the rear-view mirror. 'Absolutely nowhere.'

341

Y.

I missed a bit.

Stood there unmoving in the damp, foggy air, I can still hear them in the pub behind me, the warm yellow glow of the windows reaching out like the lure of an angler fish, belying the cold-hearted, fang-lined bowels inside. I'm about to start walking away when a voice speaks from my periphery.

'I'd put that back if I were you.'

I turn around, startled. It's Skye. She's leaning against the wall of the building I've just left, smoking a cheap Dunhill, the foot of one calf-length-booted bare leg beneath her fake fur coat crooked up against it, as if she'd topple forward if she tried to rely on only her own balance for support.

'I'm sorry?' I say.

'The jacket. I'd put it back before he notices. He won't be happy. It doesn't suit you anyway.'

I take it as a compliment, like to think she means it in a good way.

'His happiness is of little concern to me, I'm afraid.'

'You *should* be afraid. It'll be your concern if he ever sees you again.'

'I'll take my chances' I say. *He'd be doing me a favour anyway, put me out of my misery.*

She drags the last inch of life out of her cigarette, flicking it out into the road in a tiny firework of glowing ember flakes. I watch her take out another.

'Shit' she says, 'should've saved that' as she fumbles about herself for a lighter, realising that she could've used the end of the last one.

Still watching her, I put my hands in my – his – pockets. There's a book of matches there. I take it out and ask her if she needs a light. She seems surprised – perhaps she remembers that I didn't smoke when she first met me before she realises that the matches probably aren't mine – but thanks me and steps forward as I make a hash of striking first one and then a second of the flimsy card matches, blaming them for being damp before I manage to fire one up at third attempt. As she leans in to position the cigarette into the flame with her lips, she turns towards it and it illuminates the right side of her face which until now I've failed to notice. There's some heavy bruising around her eye and cheekbone and her lip is split near one corner. I have to grip my forearm with its opposite hand to stop the match from shaking visibly in front of her suddenly.

'What happened to your face?' I say.

'Accident in the workplace' she says, unconvincingly blaze.

'You can claim for that, you know? I saw an advert' I say.

'You're funny, you know that?' she says. I don't know why I'm funny but I like the way she says it – like I'm funny amusing, not funny weird.

'No, I'm serious' I say.

343

'Look, honey' she says, 'I appreciate what you're trying to do, but it's fine - really. Just an occupational hazard in my line of work. Don't worry yourself about it. I don't. I'm used to it. Happens all the time.'

'In customer service?'

'There are always dissatisfied customers and the customer is always right, haven't you heard? Should've just paid my broker his commission on time like I was supposed to.'

'Your broker? You mean your agent in there?' I say, subconsciously holding the open edge of the jacket I'm wearing.

'Thanks for playing along, honey, but we're all adults here. I think we both know he's my pimp.'

'Your p….. ? Yeah, of course' I say.

She smiles - a smile you might expect to see on the face of an actor who just found out they didn't win the Academy Award for Best Actor, despite their best efforts to reveal their self-perceived worthiness as the camera pans onto them to witness their spirited, sporting applause – and takes a long draw on her cigarette, whittling it to almost halfway with a single drag, the growing length of grey ash hanging on for dear life.

'But…' I say, slowly putting the pieces together. 'Isn't that what *he's* there for? To protect you from fist-happy woman beaters? Isn't that what you pay him for?'

'Yeah, that business arrangement generally works out pretty fine except for the odd occasion when there are mitigating circumstances.'

Her terminology. She's either seen as many legal shows as me or has more than likely spent a fair bit of time performing a starring role in her own courtroom dramas.

'Like what?'

'Like, when I'm in breach of contract.'

'I'm not with you?' I say, perhaps not wanting to be, because not knowing would certainly be easier.

'Like, when the fist-happy thug is *him*. He isn't contracted to protect me from himself unfortunately. It's a sub-clause.'

'*He* did this to you?' I say. She smiles another of those non-smiles. 'And you still stand in a bar and drink with him like nothing's happened?'

'You don't understand, honey.'

'No' I say. 'I don't.'

'I don't expect you to.'

'I don't want to.'

'Well, perhaps that's just as well. Don't try. Go home, honey' she says, tossing her cigarette to the ground and stamping it out with a twist of her boot. 'It's cold. You don't belong here.'

She turns around and goes back inside, the sound of fake, alcohol-exaggerated laughter increasing momentarily as the door opens, leaving it feeling stiller and quieter out here when it closes. And she's right of course. I don't belong here. I don't belong anywhere. What is the point to me then? Surely I was put here for a reason? I walk up and down the street, working myself up, a boxer again, not looking my opponent in the eye, pacing back and forth in the corner of the ring like a captive panther. I can't get the image of her face out of my mind. The feeling of déjà vu,

345

that I've come full circle – that everything else has been merely a build-up to this moment, that it's time to act, to finally do something, let the world know that it can't just go around doing whatever the Hell it likes without any fear of repercussion. It doesn't happen like that in the movies, in my comics, in the many, many books I've read – and nobody questions it then; they expect it even. Perhaps that's what's wrong with the world. That we don't practice what we preach. We're good at the theory but fail the practical every time. Even the police can't do what they need to nowadays, their hands bound with red tape, common sense and judgement replaced with human rights and equal opportunities for all, even – especially sometimes - the criminals, those that deserve it least. Well he can't get away with it. It isn't right. I'll go back inside, grab a bottle from the bar, I've thought about it before, played it out in my mind, only this time...

And then, suddenly, the door swings open again and he steps outside, shielding his lighter flame from a non-existent breeze before it's even closed behind him. Has she told him, betrayed me, seriously chosen him over me? Has he come for his jacket?

'You still here, birthday boy?' he says, letting me know that she can't have said anything after all. And then he spots it. 'Hey, I've got a jac......' and realises that his isn't just like mine at all. Mine *is* his. I'm shivering uncontrollably now, my legs trembling to the point that I hope they won't betray me. I try to tell myself it's the cold – I've been out here some time now – but I know deep down that that isn't it. But it isn't fear, it's something else entirely. Something altogether different.

Excitement.

I pull the jacket closed tight across my chest - and that's when I feel it. Security.

The knife is still there.

'What the fuck do you think you're doing with my jacket?' he says. Do these people all attend the same elocution lessons, I wonder? For last words, they're pretty ignoble.

He steps forward but stops in his tracks as I pull out the knife, releasing the lock, letting the blade shoot forth, glinting in the light from the pub window. Suddenly he's not so confident, isn't facing an unarmed woman anymore. And the weird thing is, I realise with perfect clarity that I'm not bluffing, not holding it there as a deterrent. I *want* him to keep coming, to attack me, give me an excuse. Any excuse. And then I realise something else. He's already given me one. His life is all the excuse I need. So it's with that which he must pay. It just seems so obvious. Like I don't really have a choice. That this is the only option. A fleeting moment of sanity amidst all the madness.

I don't wait for him to say anything else and don't say anything myself. When I've thought about this moment, lying alone in bed at night, I always had the idea that I'd espouse something really profound, quote some really cool passage from the bible like Samuel Jackson in Pulp Fiction – but a different one, I don't want to plagiarise - maybe one of those that Mr Savage taught us. But now I'm here, I don't want to spoil the moment. Talk is cheap. He'll certainly have nothing worth saying and my carefully chosen words would be wasted on him anyway.

347

I stick the knife in his stomach, watch his eyes go wide in disbelief as I push it all the way in, bury it up to the handle. He falls to his knees before me – where he belongs – holding his hands clasped together, as if in supplication, over the blood-soaked hole in his t-shirt in a futile attempt to hold his life in, stop it escaping down his jeans (Seriously? Double denim? Even I know better than that) onto the pavement and down the kerb, snaking into the drain. He looks up at me, small suddenly, like one of those broken mirror-shard reflections. Now it's my turn to look down my nose at him. His eyes remind me of those rescue dogs, appealing beseechingly to my better nature, the Ying to the Yang that just stabbed him – but that side of me already flew the coop, got in that cab over half an hour ago. He needs putting down. Bleep bleep. I've started so I'll finish. I stab him again in the side of the neck, pushing through sinew and tendon, in behind the laryngeal prominence, the protrusion formed by the angle of the thyroid cartilage surrounding the larynx – I learned about this stuff during one of my many Sunday afternoons on the internet, even fancied myself as a doctor once upon a time, when I still dared to dream. The Adam's Apple. Ignoring the pathetic gargling of his own blood in his throat, I twist the knife so that the blade is facing forward then slice through it, dissecting it in half. Sliced apple. Source of man's original sin. There's something quite poetic about it, don't you agree?

Well, I think so. I know I should run, get out of there while I still can, but I don't. I can't. I'm transfixed. I've never watched somebody die in front of me before. Well, not that I can really remember, and certainly not so quickly like this. I want to savour the moment - the action crescendo to a life of empty talk diminuendo. And besides, what's the worst that can happen? That I end up spending the rest of my days in a cell? All those guards, other inmates, the meetings with counsellors, parole officers? Possibly even *sharing* a cell? A captive companion. Or perhaps gunned down by police marksmen in the climactic finale to a nationally televised manhunt, the thrum of helicopters hovering overhead like vultures sensing an imminent kill? Neither sounds so bad to me. I watch fascinated as blood ribbons obscenely like something out of a horror spoof, gradually slowing to a pulsing waterfall down his neck and chest, collecting in a pool in his groin, mixing with the urine there until he slumps forward, his face smashing against the curb, shattering his front teeth - by which point that's the least of his worries. I can't even say that a red mist befell me, that I lost my mind in a fit of rage. I'm perfectly calm. In fact, I don't think I've ever been *quite* so calm before.

I wipe the blood crudely from the blade of the knife under the arm-pit of the denim jacket, not bothering about finger prints on the handle as I place it back in the inside pocket. I then take the jacket off and drape it gently over the motionless body lying face down on the ground in front of me. Whatever happens, I want it to be me that killed him. I don't want him getting off on a technicality, dying of hypothermia. Besides, I'm not a thief, unless you count the life I've just taken and I'd argue that he'd no more earned the right to it himself than I had to take it.

And that's not the only thing I'm innocent of. I need to get home and clean that door.

349

Z.

There's much made of what happens to you just before you die - the traditionally accepted version of events of course being that your life flashes before your eyes – but, as far as I can make out, what happens just before you kill gets pretty short shrift. Well, I can tell you now that it's pretty much the same – that is to say that, for me at least, that's how it was. Much of my murderous show-reel was actually rather pleasurable; a fantasy life of escapism, a life in film, a TV trailer of excerpts for a season of upcoming movies all set to the score of Nirvana's Negative Creep which I remember being played so regularly in one of my many former rental accommodations; John Travolta as Vincent Vega in Pulp Fiction saying that it would've been worth a vandal keying his car just for him to have caught them doing it; the same character stabbing down with a syringe, piercing the breastplate of an overdosing junkie, the hit of adrenaline causing her to spring up gasping for life like a Jack-in-a-Box; John Rambo camouflaged with mud and twigs, emerging from a tree trunk like a phantom, his knife at the local bully-boy sheriff's throat telling him with gravelly menace to *let it go, let it go or I'll give you a war you won't believe!* But it wasn't all movies. Individual cells from comics I'd long-forgotten made an appearance; Batman taking on the dark streets of Gotham alone; Judge Dredd blowing post-apocalyptic mutants to smithereens with a ridiculously oversized gun. And there was a pinch of real-life in there too, words and pictures; devil pokes, a brindle-coated dog with a woman's face – a face I don't recognise but know I know – whimpering sobs through the bars of a cage, the mutation's back mottled with black burns; and as he fell, my victim (so unfamiliar to have one rather than be one for once – I'm not sure I'll ever get used to it), a tower of red wooden building blocks toppling in slow-motion to the ground, liquefying on contact into a single viscous puddle, flowing towards me like molten lava as I jump back to avoid getting any of the hissing bloody fluid on my bare feet, melting me into it like the Wicked Witch of the West, only a puff of steam and pointy hat remaining, floating on its surface like a toy yacht on a boating pond. It was actually really rather beautiful in a gothically surreal kind of way.

Epilogue.

To Whom it May Concern,

Firstly, apologies if this note is long. I was never really given the chance to speak uninterrupted before so hope you won't begrudge me this one small indulgence. Even now, at this late hour, I care what you think, want you to understand that, despite a lack of accredited certification to the contrary, I was an intelligent, decent man with something to say, something to offer all along, if only somebody would just pause for a moment and take note. I realise of course that I may now have become one of those very sensationalist news headlines that I always found so abhorrent but hope that this will go some small way to helping you understand. I'm not sure you ever will. I'm not sure I ever would in your shoes. I'm not sure I do in mine.

When I set out, right from the start, for as far back as I can remember, my intentions were only ever honourable. But, just as water smoothes the hardest stone, the constantly crashing waves make sand of the toughest boulder, so too did I allow life to chip away at me. I was eroded. I'm not proud of what I did but feel that if you look deep into your heart, you'll admit that you too must shoulder some of the responsibility for your own not inconsiderable part. We are all of us human beings – whatever that means – but we are organisms too; living, breathing collections of flesh, blood, bone and nerve, responding to external stimuli just as surely as a plant responds to sunlight. Even the most radiant of sunflowers kept in prolonged darkness will eventually wither and perish, as those houseplants here in my flat have, deciding that even they couldn't bare to spend a moment longer under this roof, no matter how carefully I tried to place them by the windows.

An automaton. A robot. If my parents were the mad scientists that created me, produced the circuit board of my DNA, then it was life that programmed me. Frankenstein may have had his input when he input his love (when it was there, if indeed it was ever really there at all) into my mother but I like to think that the monster wasn't inside me all along – a tapeworm gorging from within until it finally outgrew my outer struggle and I could contain it no longer.

By the time you read this, I will be long gone – hopefully to a better place. Where is that place? Heaven? I never considered myself a religious man but if I had to choose a belief system, then I guess I'd have gone with Buddhism. I believe in karma, that the life you live determines that which you move on to. Am I in credit? Was all the happiness that I was yet to collect after a lifetime of hurdles erased with a single brief act during the final sprint to the finish?   Who knows?   I'm not sure how the pricing structure works.   Perhaps I'll be a dung beetle by this time tomorrow.   Perhaps that wouldn't be such a step down after all.   Perhaps I'm completely off the mark.   Perhaps it's all just random.   Arbitrary.   A drop off at a bus stop, abandoned in the middle of nowhere with nothing in your pockets, left to get on with it and build a life the moment the dust settles.   If that's the case then I could be anything next time around - even the Queen of England.   For now though, I've reigned only over the kingdom of my own life and feel that I've outstayed my welcome.   It's time to abdicate.   So I leave as I arrived – naked, my eyes wet with tears, albeit alone, no gathering of naive, hope-filled eyes watching proudly over me.   Farewell my future subjects. Hopefully next time you'll listen.

The King is dead, long live the Queen!

Bye for now.

Glenn.

Printed in Great Britain
by Amazon